NO RETURN

NO RETURN

ZACHARY JERNIGAN

NIGHT SHADE BOOKS
SAN FRANCISCO

First Edition

ISBN: 978-1-59780-456-1

Night Shade Books
www.nightshadebooks.com

For Amy Martin

Continent of Knoori

Dareth Hlum

Onsa

Dalan-fele

Dalan-fele

Casta

Golna

Baseç

Tansot

Stol

Steps of Stol

THE MONTHS OF THE YEAR

Month of Ascetics
Month of Alchemists
Month of Mages
Month of Sectarians
Month of Fishers
Month of Surgeons
Month of Sawyers
Month of Smiths
Month of Drowsers
Month of Financiers
Month of Bakers
Month of Finnakers
Month of Soldiers
Month of Clergymen
Month of Pilots
Month of Royalty

PROLOGUE

The people were small, quiet, and simple. They had no name for themselves.

They lived at the top of the world of Jeroun, in a windless and barren valley with no accessible entrance, on the shore of a nameless salt lake—perhaps the most beautiful lake in the world. A deep and flawlessly clear cerulean blue under the cloudless sky, its shallow waters never froze and rarely rippled. Almost perfectly circular, it measured twelve miles across, yet the people neither fished nor set craft upon its surface. Now and then, they drank and collapsed on the shore, subject to visions induced by the ensorcelled liquid.

Their valley had once been home to a great civilization, the site of a city inhabited by the continent's extinct native people, who were called elders by common men. Mummified corpses measuring over three yards in length lay everywhere, naked to the ever-present sun. A great many lay buried in the rubble of their buildings, which had been worn nearly unrecognizable by time and sun. With few eroding forces, this process had surely taken thousands upon thousands of years. A stone could not chip the building materials.

The corpses were beautiful, black-skinned and thin-limbed like insects. Their faces were broad-nosed, mouthless and severe. Downy translucent hair covered their bodies, lengthening and darkening into bristly fur on their scalps. Many were tattooed in bright colors. Though as dry inside as the valley soil, impossibly their skin had the texture of calf's leather and tasted like sugar-preserved meat. Ground to a fine powder, their bones tasted metallic and bitter, but caused the mouth to salivate, curing thirst.

The nameless people had consumed a very small percentage of the corpses, as neither skin nor bonedust needed to be ingested in great quantities. The meat and organs were inedible and lay about in piles that would not rot. Had the larger world known what magical resource existed in the valley, empires would have waged wars, sacrificed thousands, in order to possess it. For the men and women who lived along the shores of the nameless lake, this was immaterial. To them, the elders were merely food.

While the diet provided scant nourishment for the brain, a body could survive well on nothing but elder skin and bone, guaranteeing that it need never sleep, need never worry about clothing itself. In groups of two or three the people of the valley walked the shore of the lake, all night and all day, single-mindedly stripping small pieces of skin and grinding bone ends. They walked naked even in the depths of winter and never felt the cold.

From time to time, they met others of their kind and shared a meal. They did not talk. Usually they stared at the placid surface of the lake together. On rare occasions, those who faintly recalled a friendship or long-dead romance held hands and watched the stars, but never for long.

There were good reasons not to stare too deeply into the sky.

‡

Eating elder skin and bone, a human of hardy stock could live a long time indeed. The average age of the inhabitants in the valley was over five hundred years, and the oldest individual had lived for seventeen centuries. She had in fact not been born in the valley, though her reason for coming—as well as the means of her arrival—were long since forgotten. The nameless people were her children, but this knowledge too had been lost. Time had bleached her mind of any urges other than to eat and to watch the sky.

In the valley, she alone remembered the reason men should fear the sky. She had cemented this fear in her children but was now too old or too simple to feel it herself.

Fear had become fascination.

And indeed, she could not have picked a better location from which to view the sky. The valley experienced four hundred cloudless days out of four hundred and thirty-two calendar days. The thin, cold air did not distort the constant burn of the stars or the fractured face of the world's immense, bone-pale moon.

Nor what preceded moonrise.

Every evening, the woman sat and watched as the objects rose above the horizon. The largest of the steel-colored, circular masses was nearly a third the size of the moon. The smallest could only be seen during the early morning, when sunlight reflected on its edges. Twenty-seven in all, she counted. Elsewhere, beyond the reach or understanding of the people of the valley, men called the arrow-straight arrangement the Needle, or sometimes the Spine. Unbeknownst to the woman, on the world she alone had counted all of the objects with the naked eye.

She knew on some level that they were weapons.

She had also discovered their construction. They were not flat structures, but slowly rotating spheres. They were not solid, either, but spindly, like gigantic cages.

It was as if their maker had taken thin-rimmed carriage wheels and welded them along a centerline so that the rims fanned around a vertical axis. The woman had stared long enough to note their slow rotation, the slight shift as one rim caught the light and another gave it up. This effect was most easy to see on the odd days the moon remained in the sky well into morning. The speed of the spheres changed from time to time, and sometimes even seemed to stop. Such alterations depended on factors the woman could not begin to guess.

Well into her hundredth year in the valley, the night sky had been just stars and moon. Later, one object appeared. Then two. Eventually they extended like a bead necklace nearly a fifth of the length of the sky, smallest to largest leading to the moon, twenty-nine in all. They seemed to pull the moon across the sky, led by some invisibly massive draft animal.

Over the next five hundred years they had moved slowly to form a diamond pattern, then a cross. For a while they had floated around the moon, sometimes nearer, sometimes farther from its surface, and then they trailed it across the length of the sky. For a long time, the woman thought they had disappeared completely, until she saw the edge of one peeking out from behind the moon.

In her seven hundredth year in the valley, the two smallest spheres had fallen to the earth. The woman recalled it dimly, the fiery streaks as the objects hit the atmosphere. They arrowed in opposite directions, and so she had tracked one as it sped westward over the horizon. She waited for something to happen, and when it did not she turned to the east and witnessed a great flash of light. Hours later, the ground shook. The following day a blanket of rainless clouds rolled in, almost touching the spires of the jagged summits ringing the valley.

It grew much colder for several years, which affected the people of the valley not at all. The woman felt some sadness that she could no longer watch the sky, but she had still been young enough then to take comfort in the closeness of her children. When the clouds lifted, the objects were scattered across the night sky so that not all could be viewed at once. Over the course of a decade, they moved back toward the moon, finally taking on their original, straight arrangement.

As the brains shrunk in their skulls, the people of the valley drifted apart. The woman circled the edge of the lake alone, drinking its hallucinogenic waters regularly until the greater part of her consciousness lifted free of her body. In time her children forgot that she was their mother, and she pushed them away when they approached her. A low growl lodged deep in her chest.

Now and then even the taste of skin and bone grew sour in her mouth.

She did not put a name to it, but she thought often of dying. She watched the sky and hoped to see the objects falling, their beautiful trails of fire dissecting the sky into a giant wheel. She had no religion, no memory of Adrash, the god the other men of the world worshipped, but still it was a form of prayer—a silent, inarticulate longing for change.

‡

Jeroun spun slowly at Adrash's back, thousands upon thousands of leagues distant. The moon, its gaze locked on the darkened world, loomed to his left, closer though by no means near.

Adrash floated before a motionless iron sphere, dwarfed by the wall of one immense rim. Its smooth surface extended in all directions. This close, its curvature could not be discerned. The eye tried and failed to see a furthest edge.

Welded onto its surface was a handle small enough for a large man to grasp with two hands.

Adrash gripped it tightly. He spread his legs, appeared to plant his feet on the nothingness of the void, and pulled. The heavy muscles of his chest and shoulders bunched with the effort, his sinewy torso turned, and slowly the handle moved forward. At the fullest extension of his arms he stepped to the left and repeated the process. In this way, he spun the sphere faster and faster. His body became a blur of frenzied movement.

Eventually, he stopped and drifted back from the wall, the rapidly approaching edge of which had still not come into view. A comfortable ache suffused his body. Though unnecessary, the exertion had felt good. In the past he had chosen to move the spheres with his mind, but those days were over. It was unsatisfying, somehow. Now he preferred to feel the texture of the metal, the elongation and contraction of muscle tissue.

His body was that of a man, well over two yards tall and coldly beautiful, a marble statue brought to life. But for his eyes—which glowed a harsh yellow-white, lacking iris and pupil—the seamless white material of his armor sheathed him smoothly from crown to sole, hugging the curves of his powerful frame. Broad-shouldered and narrow-waisted, he held himself like a professional soldier, spine straight, hands in loose fists. The features of his face were mere suggestions above the strong line of his jaw.

From a greater distance, he regarded the sphere. It had become recognizable as such despite its vast scope. Still farther out, the structure appeared delicate and airy due to the great distance between rims. A decorative bauble, a fragile ornament through which the stars burned. To the sphere's left, a great distance away, spun its larger brother. To the right, a slightly smaller brother. The others were not yet in sight, and the pale hulking weight of the moon suddenly seemed to loom far too near, as if it were pulling the three spheres into it.

Adrash increased the speed of his retreat. Before long the entire chain of twenty-seven spheres became visible. Positioned halfway down the line, he tried to admire the precision of their placement, their carefully calculated speeds. His last adjustment had guaranteed that once every month the sun's light would hit the spheres in a particular way, turning the Needle into a line of pale fire in Jeroun's night sky.

Of course, he would not witness it from orbit.

He considered how few of the world's inhabitants would notice the effect. Those who did would react by pressing their fists to their heads and praying, or by blotting out the Needle with one hand and cursing.

Both prospects depressed Adrash. Still, he resisted the urge to begin another series of adjustments.

For many hundreds of years, much of his time had been spent altering the positions and speeds of the spheres, an obsessive drive to find the perfect expression of his dissatisfaction. Finding this abstract expression, he believed, would calm him, heal the wounds in his soul. Ultimately, he had grown weary of the monumental effort and returned the spheres to their original alignment, stringing them in a line equidistant to each other, aligned to the moon's orbit perfectly, and thus narrowing his focus.

The only adjustment he allowed himself now was rotational speed. Once, he had spun the spheres so that each revolution matched exactly for a full year. Four hundred and thirty-two revolutions per hour. One hundred and twenty million times the rims passed before his eyes without any revelation. Then he had slowed down and sped up every other sphere in increasing increments so that the fastest two were at either end and the middle one remained still.

He felt compelled to explore every permutation. Ultimately, he wasted time, distracting himself from the decision he would soon have to make.

Return to Jeroun as mankind's redeemer, or cleanse the world of mankind forever.

‡

Unfortunately, time had only made the world's destruction more of an inevitability. Though Adrash had successfully put off the decision for seven thousand years—first by exiling himself above Jeroun, and then by creating the Needle itself—his relationship to the people of the world had not changed.

He could not love mankind, because he saw their brilliance for the thing it was: an exquisitely frail quality that could never make up for the effects of their fear. In fact, more often than not intelligence compounded mankind's negative tendencies. The aggressive wielded their intellects like weapons to subjugate the humble and the less gifted. Given free reign—and there was little reason to think they would not eventually achieve complete dominion—such men would bury what little virtue remained in the world.

No, he could not forgive men their pettiness, their squabbling, their ridiculous and violent worship. Of course, as a young god he had spent several eons encouraging this behavior, but in truth men had never needed encouraging. How could one change the nature of men? Twenty thousand years of Adrash's urging—two-thirds of his life, bent to this endeavor—had not made them more peaceful, any likelier to see reason.

Nor, obviously, did the threat of annihilation.

They could not pretend ignorance. Adrash had made his feelings known for millennia. When his words and actions had failed to inspire permanent change, he abandoned mankind for the void. As their empires had grown ever more contentious, he dredged material from the blind side of the moon and constructed the Needle. At the height of their power and hubris, he had hurled the two smallest spheres down, killing hundreds of thousands and blanketing the earth in dust for a decade. The Cataclysm, as men now called it.

These efforts to communicate his desperation had been folly, Adrash now understood. Mankind's ingenuity in the face of trial was short-lived, and Adrash did not possess the energy to continue reminding them of their priorities. He felt the constant temptation to simply complete what he had begun with the Cataclysm, and send all of his weapons to their task.

You have been too patient, he told himself. *You have waited on them long enough.*

And yet—inexplicably, in the face of all reason—hope remained. When he could stand to hear them, he listened to the thoughts rising from the world below, hoping to hear a call rise above the others and proclaim change. He wondered if his constant adjustments to the Needle of late were an attempt to signal this person, to create a sigil in the sky for a prophet to recognize.

For there had been prophets once, he felt sure: Men and women who had spoken with fearful, exquisite voices—voices that resounded into the bowels of the earth, filled the void with light, and nearly shook Adrash's heart to a halt.

They had existed, had they not?

Sometimes, Adrash wondered if he had only invented these avatars to keep from going mad.

Sometimes, he wondered if he had prevented madness at all.

Perhaps his obsession revealed the rot that had already spread throughout his soul.

‡

He turned somber eyes away from the Needle and looked upon Jeroun, a bluegreen marble rolling on a sheet of stars. A shallow ocean covered the world but for two small continents straddling opposite sides of the equator: Knoori, the home of man, and Iswee, the perpetually cloud-covered home of the slumbering elders. Everywhere else, uninhabited islands lay scattered like windblown seed.

From experience, Adrash knew the difficulties of navigating between those islands, of traveling from Knoori to Iswee. Mortal men rarely dipped foot in or sailed upon the ocean for fear of its predatory fish and reptiles, but Adrash knew those beasts numbered fairly far down on the list of dangers. Nonetheless, for eons he had preferred to live upon the ocean, where he could be alone, a man instead of a god. But for his armor, which he usually caused to retreat until it was a white helm clinging to his hairless scalp, the sun had shone on his bare black skin.

As the world turned, Knoori rose on its side, a confused mass of sharp-toothed mountains, high plains and parched barrens. Cities spotted the continent, a hundred magefire lamps revealing their shapes. Here, Tansot, a five-pointed star of purple radiance. Here, Seous, a blue snake lying along-side River Anets. The sun edged out from behind the world's swollen belly, unhurriedly extinguishing these fires. For a few seconds Lake Ten turned into a reflecting pool. The pine hills of Nos Ulom became a blanket of jadestones, the deserts of Toma molten gold.

The world was blindingly beautiful.

Adrash could not bear to look any longer. He closed his eyes against the radiance, let the tumblers fall in his mind, and unlocked his soul, allowing the world's prayers to flood in.

The first to announce itself: *A wordless cry from an imbecilic mind.*

The nameless woman called from the unmapped valley in the Aspa Mountains—a place shielded by such deep magic that even Adrash had to concentrate in order to see it from orbit.

He heard the woman's appeal with such clarity because it was old and familiar to him, but he had little sympathy for the people living along the shore of the ensorcelled lake. The majority of mankind lived in far worse conditions, though most had more variety. The old woman had stumbled onto one of the world's great secrets and used it to sire a race of idiots. While highly nourishing to bone and muscle tissue, once ingested elder skin acted on the human body like a slow poison, causing prenatal damage and retardation of the brain.

The people of the valley were useless. Adrash ignored their clumsy, aimless prayers, though they were loud. Due to the proximity of so many elders and their ancient buried magics, the valley acted as a focusing lens.

In a lukewarm way, it bothered Adrash to see so much power put to so little. There were times when he wished someone would discover the valley's secret. The resource would be hoarded and abused, of course, but it would be an interesting development. If it fell into the hands of the Stoli govern-ment, Adrash could expect a great deal more traffic in orbit. Dozens—and in time, hundreds, even thousands—of outbound mages would rise from the surface of Jeroun, high on reconstituted elder blood, eager to make names for themselves.

They would come with gifts and weapons, open hands and fingers tipped with magefire. Arcing lightning from one to another as they flew toward the moon, ready to challenge their god or simply beseech him to show compassion.

They would all die, burned to cinders by the light of Adrash's eyes, crushed to dust in his arms. His palms itched thinking about it. He tightened his fists, remembering the way a man's blood burst from his body in the void. For a brief moment he even felt the rekindled flame of his youth, a time when he had impulsively aligned himself with this or that leader, capriciously giving vent to his lust for warfare.

No, he had never been a charitable god—not a father or an easer of pain. It would be enjoyable, punishing those who came calling at his door.

Nonetheless, he shook the vision of violence from his eyes. Useless conjecture, and ultimately an undesirable development. Best if he never had to look a man in the face again. He let his thoughts drift away from the nameless valley, searching for more encouraging, or at least interesting, voices.

Men prayed to him for rain atop the broad, slightly tilted tops of the Aroonan mesas, clasped hands permanently dyed red with the blood of sacrificed bandi roosters. They cried openly for rain, which had not come in strength for three years. Their women, who neither prayed nor begged after years of burying their children, spat at this display of weakness.

In a seedy flat above a basket shop in Jompa, a prostitute prayed for fifty cril, otherwise he would be dead by morning. He had gambling debts. Adrash knew also that the man had jaleri eggs lining his urethra and would be dead by month's end.

On the southeastern shore of Nens Abasin, a young acolyte of The Unending Luck cast her line and prayed for an old, sick fish. She had no desire to incur the soul debt for taking a new life. The order forbade her from throwing back a catch, yet her luck had been so abysmal lately that she would not hesitate to do so. Breaking the rule would undoubtedly mean more bad luck in the long run, thus reinforcing the cycle, but the girl did not care. She could not see how it mattered. Luck touched some and shunned others altogether.

Adrash felt the briefest moment of communion. He wished he could answer the girl's prayer. If he were closer to the world's surface, perhaps he would asphyxiate an old fish and let it lap upon the shore at her feet. He had once, if rarely, enjoyed this kind of intervention.

In the cold mines under the Old City of Ghys, nearly a mile below the searing sand of the Tomen Desert, a Demni mage prayed her alchemy had been correct. She could not remember if the spell was heart before liver, and what effect the wrong order would produce.

It was not heart before liver, Adrash knew. The smell of the infusion would attract diamond spiders. The mage would soon have a great deal to worry about, and for a moment Adrash was tempted to watch the ensuing battle.

Instead, he focused elsewhere. His mind touched here and there, lingering on the personal entreaties, passing over the formulaic prayers and liturgies. Prayers to other gods—those shadowy figures Adrash had once caused to live and then destroyed, and whose memory somehow managed to linger in the souls of men—he ignored. They were of the same quality as those directed to him.

Words damning him he saved for last. They were the most amusing.

He had no expectation that this time he would find what he was looking for. A singular voice might never be found. The world might be destroyed tomorrow, should he find his patience at an end. Or the world might go on forever while he spiraled into new realms of madness.

The spheres spun at his back, waiting.

PART ONE

VEDAS TEZUL

Vedas watched the square through a crack in the stockroom door.

The pulse pounded in his throat and temples, causing his vision to shudder slightly. He felt calm despite this, assured by the familiar sensation. As the street scene grew lighter, its weathered doorways and stonework angles more defined before him, he settled into the comfortable hum of readiness.

The black fabric of his suit hugged his powerful frame like a second skin. He stood in the traditional waiting stance of the lo fighter, feet shoulder-width apart, hands resting lightly atop his staff, which came to just below his chin. Back straight, knees slightly bent. A man could stand in this posture for many hours, minutely shifting his weight from foot to foot, meditating on the subtle tense and release of muscle.

Behind him, sixteen children were trying and failing to contain their nervousness. They were a quiet group. Nonetheless, Vedas heard and recognized every movement behind him. After eight hours cramped together, he had come to identify each youth's breathing and nervous habits. They scratched themselves, sniffled, sighed. They fingered the black sashes tied around their upper arms, needlessly adjusting the material that marked them as official recruits to the Thirteenth Order of Black Suits.

The acrid smell of vomit was everywhere. Someone always threw up, first time out.

At least, Vedas reasoned, he had not been forced to knock the weak-stomached girl, Julit Umeda, unconscious. She had covered her mouth and leaned back, causing the sick to run down her red shirtfront. The only sound had been a few drops of fluid hitting the floor. Vedas reminded himself to reward her afterwards. New recruits did not typically think that quickly, especially after standing for so long.

He watched the square. The abbey master, Abse, had assured him the meeting would occur within an hour of dawn. Vedas closed his eyes for a moment and projected wellbeing to his superior, to his brothers and sisters. He imagined them walking straight-backed and proud, staff ends clicking on the paving stones, muscles shifting under smooth black fabric of their elder-cloth suits.

It will be a good day, he told himself.

He turned from the doorway and regarded the recruits. Those who could shuffled back against their neighbors. Vedas had memorized their faces and names the night before, noting which he thought would hold up well. He was heartened to see he had been wrong about a few of them, and right about those he had appraised highly. As usual, the youngest proved the most resilient, though not always the most patient.

In the dim light of the stockroom, their faces were washed out and grim, smudged with dirt, painted to look like fierce animals or demons. Not a real whisker among them. Surely, they had spent time in front of mirrors, pumping themselves up. A few had purchased—or more likely stolen—black woolen shirts and trousers for the occasion. One boy even wore a homemade mask to complete the look.

A brief vision of Vedas's own first battle as a recruit flashed before him. He had been a little more experienced, though not much.

He reached into the fold of his hood for the sound-isolation spell, held up the vial so that the recruits knew what to expect, and broke the seal. One boy cursed softly as the pressure in the room suddenly changed. They pinched their noses and popped their eardrums.

When Vedas spoke, his voice sounded as if it came from a great distance away.

"The moment is almost upon us. You've done a good job of waiting." A brief flash of white as he smiled. His skin was only a shade lighter than the suit he wore. "I'm proud of you. It seems I've chosen well.

"Remember the signal." He held up two fingers, one finger, and then his fist alone. "At that instant I will open the door and we will charge. Follow me closely. I will lead you to the enemy's back. Locate unsuited enemies. Double up on them if you can and don't play by the rules. Aim for the genitals and the eyes. In close quarters, remember to use your elbows and the weight of your feet. Most importantly, remember to keep focused on your target. Don't get distracted by anything else. Make me proud."

Vedas dropped the spell just before it abated. The pressure lifted. He met the eye of each recruit before stretching the hood over his shaved head. The children regarded the tall, wide-shouldered shadow before them, gazes lingering on the two small horns on his temples. Slowly, he caused the hood to crawl over his face until only his eyes were visible.

He saw momentary fear in the recruits' stares. They shuffled against one another. Most likely, few of them had seen a fully shrouded Black Suit up close, and only half-believed the claims that a man could wear cloth made from the skin of an elder and let it become a part of him, an extension of his will.

Now you know, Vedas thought. He nodded and turned back to the door. He disliked the drama the moment had required, but had grown accustomed to it. Perhaps it was even necessary, as Abse claimed, a brief spell of near-religious awe to steel the mind for what was to come. *You become a symbol*, the abbey master had once said. *More than a man—a figure worth following into battle.*

And indeed, the children had become jittery behind Vedas. The fear had not abated, but nerves would see them through.

He watched the square. Before long, from the east he heard the sound of staffs clicking on paving stones: His brothers and sisters—the Followers of Man. Softer but growing in intensity, from the west he heard the answering rat-a-tat of dueling sticks clacked together: Rivals—the Followers of Adrash, the One True God.

The recruits would not have to wait much longer.

‡

In 12472, just before Vedas's seventh birthday, his parents had relocated from Knos Min in order to assume a diplomatic post in Golna, almost two thousand miles from the only place he had ever known. At first frightened by the city, Vedas soon came to think of it as home. Knosi were well regarded in the east, and he was treated with respect. A natural athleticism endeared him to his peers.

His parents discouraged sectarianism, in fact had never subscribed to a faith, but they could not prevent their son from allying himself with the other children of Smithtown, the vast majority of whom had been raised Anadrashi. In his tenth year, Vedas was recruited by the Black Suits of the Eighth Order and began taking part in legally sanctioned street battles. His parents disapproved, but traditional Knosi culture considered a ten-year-old boy an adult, free to make his own decisions.

In Vedas's twelfth year, Knos Min raised the tariffs on Hlumi tobacco products. Relations between the countries took a sudden downturn, and the eastern nation began expelling Knosi nobles and political figures from its borders. Vedas's parents, on a brief sabbatical on the northern coast, were forced to leave without their adolescent son. For a brief time, Vedas lived in the homes of various friends, and then he lived on the street.

Word reached him of his parents' death in the Month of Royalty, 12478, almost a year after their departure. By this time, he had become messenger and errand boy to Saatreth, the abbey master of the Seventh Order of Black Suits.

Messenger, errand boy, and plaything.

The Seventh had successfully kept their history of pederasty a secret from the city's other twenty orders for over three centuries. Upon discovery of their transgression in the spring of the following year, Abse volunteered the Thirteenth to right the wrong. They removed the recruits, killed the men who had once been their faith-kin, and left the abbey a charred pile of rubble.

"I can send you back to Knos Min," Abse told Vedas. "There are a few other boys orphaned by the debacle between our two countries. But that trouble has long since abated, and the recent succession of the dictator in Nos Ulom has resulted in an oddly peaceable country. Your passage across the continent would most likely be safe."

Vedas parsed the master's language. "My parents are dead."

"Yes. I have heard." Abse offered the somber, black-skinned boy a stiff smile. "Surely you have relatives?"

"Yes," Vedas answered. Of course he did, two uncles and an aunt, but he had no interest in leaving Dareth Hlum. He only half understood why the abbey of the Seventh had been destroyed. True, Saatreth had not been a father or a friend. He had hurt Vedas badly enough to leave scars for years to come. Nonetheless, it was the abbey that had provided shelter and given Vedas an identity.

"Relatives are often a great comfort in times of change," Abse continued. "On the other hand, I have heard that you are a talented young man." He held up a finger. "I am not obfuscating my meaning. No one in this order desires the services Saatreth desired. By talented, I mean only that word has reached me of your martial prowess."

Vedas interpreted again. *Fighting*. Here was an area in which he excelled.

"I want to keep fighting," he told Abse. An awful thought occurred to him. "I killed a boy during practice. Is this why you're making me go home? I didn't mean to do it."

Abse pursed his lips. "I am not making you go home, boy. If you choose to stay in the order, you will undoubtedly kill someone again. Sectarian battle is dangerous. That is why it is so tightly regulated in Knos Min." He paused, pale eyes fixed on Vedas, before speaking again. "If you want to continue fighting, you must stay here. You will be an acolyte for two years. If you pass martial training and your doctrine classes—no easy feat, I assure you—at that point you will be offered a suit. Understand, it is no small matter to be given such an opportunity. Suits are prohibitively costly to produce—more so every year. Most are acquired through the deaths of our brothers and sisters."

Vedas stared at the man whom he would come to know as master. The odd, fine-boned face that appeared only a few years older than Vedas's own. The small frame sheathed in black. The light in the room changed as clouds moved outside, revealing the barely noticeable designs on the man's suit. Vedas regarded the abbey master's face again, and for a moment it seemed that fractures formed upon it. A mapwork of fine lines. Paper crumpled and ironed out.

"Is this what you want?" Abse asked. "To stay here?"

Vedas agreed without a moment's hesitation.

‡

The Black Suits entered the square first. Twenty men and women, clothed head to foot in seamless black. Some had formed relief designs on the surface of their skin-tight suits. Others had thickened the malleable elder-cloth in strategic areas, creating body armor and helmets. A few had formed bone-hard striking surfaces along the forearm or shin, spikes at knee and elbow. A lone brother had grown his suit's horns into vicious prongs.

Few chose, like Vedas, to retain the smooth, unadorned texture of the cloth, and fewer still masked their features completely.

All skin tones were represented, for Vedas's order culled recruits from each of Golna's major ethnic neighborhoods. *Diversity is a strength*, Abse claimed, and so allowed the brothers and sisters a great deal of freedom. Plaited and matted hair grew from faces and sprouted from helmets. Tattoos curled around eyes. Plugs of bone pierced lips and brows.

The men and women of the Thirteenth Order of Black Suits had little in common beyond the color of their suits, the hardness of their bodies, and the horns on their hooded heads. They had become brothers and sisters through physical pain. They prayed and fought for the downfall of Adrash together, proudly displaying the color of opposition.

More than half their number preferred weapons other than the lo. These dropped their staffs upon entering the square and lifted hammers from their shoulders, unsheathed swords, twirled flails, and readied razored shields. The four who had formed weapons out of their suit material eschewed handheld weapons altogether.

The Black Suits stopped in the center of the square, eyes locked on something Vedas could not yet see. Abse, a thin, diminutive figure holding two broadswords half as long as his body, took a step forward from the group and stamped his foot, as if anchoring himself to the spot.

A howl sounded, a ragged-edged bellow that offended Vedas's ears and caused the recruits to mill uneasily at his back. He recognized the sound and cursed inwardly.

A second after announcing itself, the hellhound catapulted into the square, skidding a mere body length from Abse's feet. A crest of purple fur bristled along its broad back. Smoke rose from its drooling mouth. It stood at the shoulder taller than the abbey master.

Abse neither flinched nor gave ground. Bringing a hellhound was a serious and dangerous breach of etiquette, only technically allowed because Vedas's order had been allowed to choose the location. The abbey master would not allow this as a distraction. His eyes never left the advancing line of White Suits that followed the dog.

The Thirteenth had never fought this order, the so-called Soldiers of the Appropriate Desire, but Vedas had done his research. He had briefed every brother and sister of the Thirteenth, assuring their preparedness as best he could. Superficially, the Soldiers were a similarly outfitted, non-mage order, legally registered within the city. They had not gone south of the law for three years. Abse and Vedas had predicted a clean battle.

The hellhound said otherwise—as did the two white-suited women at point, the tops of whose staffs glowed with green magefire.

Their numbers, at least, were correct. Including the hellhound, Vedas counted twenty Soldiers, accoutered in a similar if more conservative manner than his own brothers and sisters. They had only gathered eleven new recruits, he noted in relief, and had not encouraged the children to wait in hiding before the attack. They followed at the order's back, peering through the mass of white-suited figures, trying to locate their rivals and failing.

Small blessings were never discouraged.

Best not to waste it, Vedas reasoned. A small risk might be taken to assure his recruits.

He spoke softly to them without turning his head.

"You heard it. They've brought a hellhound. Doubtless some of you've seen them at the carnival. They are dangerous, yes, but this one can't touch you. The White Suits don't have the authority to allow that."

This was technically true, of course, but it was not the whole truth. Though intelligent enough to understand instructions, hybrid dogs did not always follow the rules of the battle. Sometimes the primal urge to hunt could not be denied. The chances of an attack were slight, but it was a chance nonetheless.

There is always risk, Abse was fond of saying.

"You needn't be afraid," Vedas continued. "No one can touch you but other recruits. Keep your eyes on your enemy. Close out everything else."

No one answered. Vedas frowned within his mask. Any minute now. He focused on a White Suit, a heavily built man standing well over seven feet. A warhammer with a head that must have weighed thirty pounds rested on his shoulder. A thick chain at the end of its handle led to a viciously pronged grapple, which hung from the giant's right hand.

Vedas noted the giant's sinuous midsection, calculating how much speed it could generate. He guessed the man would create a vacuum around himself. No one would want to get in close and risk having their head torn off. Nonetheless, the man would have weaknesses. He would be slow to recover from swinging those huge weapons.

You're mine, Vedas thought. He held up his hand, two fingers raised.

Outside, Abse whistled, and as one the two groups leapt forward. Vedas caught a brief glimpse of the abbey master's small frame ducking under the hellhound's body, broadswords thrust toward its belly, and then lost sight of him amid the press of bodies. He wished Abse luck. A smart move, taking out the beast early.

Black and white mixed. The White Suits' new recruits backed away from the roiling crowd.

Vedas lowered one finger.

Magefire arced over the brawling bodies, found its target. A scream went up. Vedas recognized the voice of a sister and shut it out. He set his knuckles against the stockroom door.

The White Suits' new recruits clustered together, casting confused looks about.

Vedas made a fist, pushed the door open, and shouldered the frame aside.

Two hundred and fifty pounds of tempered muscle charged up the stairs, followed at the heels by sixteen scared children. They screamed as they flowed forth, as if the sound would drown out their fear.

‡

Three months after Vedas's twenty-second birthday, an opponent's clumsy sword stroke had disemboweled a pair of his recruits. A sister and brother, perhaps eleven and thirteen years old. Their wounds, so unexpected and gruesome, stopped the battle in its tracks.

Vedas knelt by the children. The boy was already dead, the stroke having severed his spinal cord. His sister did not so much as twitch. She lay in the street as if she had decided to take a rest. Only her eyes moved, searching the sky.

Suddenly, she shuddered and tried to lift her head.

He clamped a hand around her jaw, holding her in place.

"Hurts," she said. "What—?"

Vedas looked up, instinctually searching the crowd for Abse.

"Shh," he said without looking down. The smell struck him, and he winced. "You'll be fine."

"I want—" The girl swatted weakly at the arm holding her head immobile. "Mommy. My legs hurt. Zeb."

At once, Vedas remembered her name. Sara Jol. Zeb was her brother. Had been her brother.

He still could not meet the girl's stare. Abse was nowhere to be seen.

"Don't worry," Vedas said. "It'll just be a second."

The girl spoke no more. She inhaled three quick, shallow breaths and died.

After dinner, Abse and Vedas conferred in the library to discuss the incident. A waxpaper packet lay on the table between them. The death wage, an ounce of bonedust for the children's parents: nearly half a year's standard pay.

"They came to Golna from the badlands of southern Casta a year ago,"

Abse said. "They knew their children had been recruited and approved. We have no reason to expect recriminations. The man who killed them has reason to worry, of course. Perhaps his order does, as well. It was reckless, allowing the man to fight."

"We should have recognized the danger he posed."

"Ridiculous. We were at war, Vedas."

Vedas's hand closed around the waxpaper packet. "I will take it to the parents."

Abse frowned. "Very well, though it is not your responsibility."

"Whose responsibility is it?"

The abbey master opened his hands, palms up. "What are you looking for, Vedas? Let us be honest with one another. You want someone to blame other than yourself. You want someone to suffer as you suffer, and so you try to shame the order by implying that we have not taken responsibility. In your guilt you cannot see that it is not your fault when a recruit dies—not your fault, or mine. The children are warriors, just as you and I are warriors. The children are weapons for the greater glory of man, just as you and I are weapons for the same cause. You need not seek someone to blame, for there is no one to blame."

Vedas closed his eyes and breathed deep into his stomach, struggling to contain the rage the abbey master's words roused within him. Since taking over as Head of Recruits at the age of seventeen, he had heard a variation on the speech three times. He could see the reason in it, but reason did not erase guilt—a fact the abbey master did not seem to understand.

"I could have done more."

Abse rose, and still stood only a little taller than the sitting Vedas.

"How? By standing behind them, by moving their arms and legs?" A rare expression of annoyance crossed the abbey master's face. "You will not begin to think that way. A good leader readies as best he can, knowing that no amount of preparedness can assure the life of every man in his command. In time you will embrace this fact. In time, you will not cling so tightly to your pain. For now, however, you must simply move forward."

‡

The giant's grapple caught the end of Vedas's staff and ripped it from his hands. The rounded edge of one prong grazed his temple, spinning him to the ground. He shook the stars from his eyes and rolled to the left to avoid the swiftly descending warhammer, which landed, shattering pavement less than an inch from his leg. He rose into a crouch and immediately leaned back, planting a hand on the ground to steady himself as the man swung his grapple at Vedas's face a second time. He felt the compacted air of its wake as a soft slap.

The giant grunted, obviously surprised that he had not connected. Off-balance, he twisted to bring his weapons back around. Before he could do so, Vedas shifted his weight forward, sweeping his right foot into the man's left ankle. Though it felt like striking a concrete pillar, the joint broke with a loud snap. The man did not cry out, and managed to twist so that he fell on his back. The ground shuddered.

Vedas saw the counterattack coming. Admiring the White Suit's persistence, he rolled to the right just as the warhammer fell, slamming into the street where he had just been. Momentum carried him onto his feet as the grapple arced over the man's prone body. From the ground it was a clumsy throw, and Vedas caught it easily.

The man reacted quickly, however, jerking the chain back, but Vedas was already moving in this direction. He stamped his left heel into the man's left inner elbow, deadening the arm holding the hammer and simultaneously using it as a springboard.

He calculated in the second before his right foot landed on the giant's face. He noted the thick fabric armor covering the bridge of the man's nose and reconsidered his attack, angling his foot for the neck rather than the head.

Cartilage crunched satisfyingly under his sole. The giant's roar became a gurgle and then a wheeze as Vedas landed in a crouch beside his head.

Vedas dropped the grapple and rolled clear before the giant could attack again—but he knew even before completing his turn that the man was finished, dead or in great need of medical assistance. Vaguely, Vedas hoped the battle would end soon so the man could get the help he needed. Death was an unfortunate fact of sectarian battling, best for the orders if kept to a minimum.

One must always remember, Abse often reminded the brothers and sisters, *we are tolerated only as long as we do not draw too much attention to ourselves.*

Besides, Vedas was not without compassion. He hoped the giant's faith in Adrash lessened his pain. The sentiment conflicted with the views of his order, but this troubled Vedas not at all. He had risen above such trivialities. His faith was unassailable.

Vedas stood at the center of a battle still going strong. Everyone had either paired off against an opponent or moved to assist a weaker brother or sister.

Several Black Suits had fallen, but so had a handful of White Suits. Through the thick of fighters, Vedas saw Abse at the gathering's edge, engaging one of the mages. The other lay at his feet, face disfigured by burns. The staff he had taken from her spun in his hands and struck, spitting magefire.

On the opposite side of the square, Vedas spotted the recruits. He could hardly tell his own from the opponents', and started to jog in their direction.

Howling, the blurred form of the hellhound came at him as he rounded a fierce melee. Vedas had only half turned when its shoulder slammed into his right hip and lifted him into the air. He spun three times before hitting the ground face first. His limbs whipped into the ground and his suit stiffened to minimize the impacts, but he felt them all the same.

Apparently, Abse had not been successful in taking the hellhound down. The beast had not uttered a sound since the beginning of the battle, and Vedas foolishly assumed it had been incapacitated. Banishing the embarrassment from his mind, he rose.

The dog was headed straight for the recruits.

Vedas ran, knowing he would never get there in time to stop the animal if it intended violence.

What else could it be intending? he asked himself.

He was still twenty paces from the recruits when the hellhound closed its jaws around the girl's head. She disappeared under the creature's body, but not before Vedas saw the black sash tied around her left arm.

‡

Abse called Vedas to his chambers after the post-fight toilet. The two sat, separated by a small lacquered table. They ate cold dumplings and mutton and drank hot fahl tea, the reason for the meeting hanging unspoken between them as they chewed and sipped. The abbey master had never been one to rush matters, even when both parties knew the outcome.

Vedas's hood was gathered at his neck and he had made his generous, well-formed features blank. The smell of vomit and blood had not left his nose. The sequence of Julit Umeda's death replayed itself before his eyes. From experience, he knew that in time the memory would fade. It would never disappear completely.

The abbey master finally set his cup aside. "I have been mulling over a decision. Oddly, this morning's event has made it easier to make." He reached forward and gripped Vedas's shoulder. "It is not impossible that someone will hold you responsible for the girl's death. We have been lucky in the past, but we have never lost a Tomen recruit before. I do not want to see you get hurt. Therefore, you must leave the city."

Vedas nodded, unsurprised. Two months previously, Abse had been given the task of choosing Golna's representative to Danoor, the decennial tournament between the world's Black Suit and White Suit orders. For two months, he had pretended to weigh his options. All the while, Vedas had known he would be the one leaving.

Typically, the prospect filled him with anxiety. He had not left Dareth Hlum since passing its borders as a child. He did not relish the prospect of travel with others, spending nights in close quarters. The fighting itself did not worry him—he knew his own strength—but he could not imagine the moments afterward. The congratulations. The tearful thanks. Most of all, he dreaded the speech the winner would be required to give.

The fact of Julit Umeda's death had temporarily rendered these concerns meaningless.

The master's smile did not reach his eyes. "I thought I might even go to the tournament, but this works out just as well. Congratulations. You will represent the city of Golna at Danoor on the eve of the half-millennium. It is a great honor, of course."

Vedas nodded again. The honor was lost on him.

"Vedas." Abse spoke the word as if it exhausted him. "You could show some appreciation. I take the task of choosing very seriously. There are many worthwhile candidates, and my choice need not come from this abbey. In fact, I would be wise to choose from another order. For political reasons, you see."

Vedas waited. The man's chiding tone bothered him, but only slightly. Certainly, Vedas did not let it show. At thirty-four years old, having spent twenty-two years in the abbey, he had long since learned to control his emotions around the abbey master. Their interactions were routine, transparent. They were like father and son. The same waters of love and resentment flowed between them. The same fictions bound them.

"To be exactly truthful," the master said, as if his thoughts had lingered on the same ground, "I had not seriously considered going myself. Nor had I considered another. It is a hard journey from here to Knos Min, and that is only the beginning of the trial. Golna's champion must be strong, body and soul." He gestured with his hands to encompass the whole city. Another shallow smile. "Who else would I choose?"

Vedas met the older man's eyes. "And the girl's death is a good excuse. Convenient."

Abse shook his head. "Its occurrence today makes it easier to rationalize sending you, but I would still prefer it had not happened. It is no minor thing, losing a recruit. A small fortune in bonedust will exchange hands as a consequence—a wage to the child's parents, a fee for the funeral, and more than likely, a bribe to our local magistrate. We have an excellent record, but no one is above examination.

"Making matters worse, of course, is the child's lineage. Tomorrow, someone will have to visit her family and assist with the funerary rites according to custom. Of course, there is no guarantee that this will mollify the Tomen community, but to do otherwise is to invite a riot."

Vedas raised his eyebrows. "Someone?"

"It will not be you. I will assign another person to the task—maybe two or three."

"I will go."

Abse sighed. "Do you know, I used to wish you would learn to see the world as your brothers and sisters see it. But I have stopped trying to understand your guilt. I have stopped hoping that you will be anything but what you are. Nonetheless, my acceptance extends only so far. You cannot have everything you desire."

Vedas regarded Abse, wondering how far he could push the man. He noted the fine lines at the corner of the abbey master's mouth and eyes, appearing like cracks in porcelain. At times Vedas imagined he could see the sutures of the man's skull, as if his skin was merely thin veneer over a death mask. The abbey master was an enchanted creature, it was generally agreed, but no one in the order knew just what sort.

For all the mystery, Vedas understood one thing: Abse possessed an odd mind. Even at his warmest, his emotions were never quite believable. Now and then it seemed that a construct stared out from behind his dull eyes, measuring the world in weights and figures instead of souls and personalities. Sectarian battles were mere arguments, a number of triumphs. Deaths were inconveniences, a number of setbacks.

"I represent your best chance for victory at Danoor," Vedas said. "I demand a wage."

The memory of Julit Umeda's death asserted itself again. The hellhound's jaws closed around her head. The weight of its body carried her to the ground. Vedas banished the vision from his mind, only for it to be replaced by the memory of breaking the hellhound's neck, knowing that he was too late. Picking the girl's limp body up, surprised at how heavy she was in his arms. The smell of vomit rising from her shirt.

"Please," he said.

For a moment the room was silent. Then Abse nodded.

Fate sealed, the tension in Vedas's shoulders eased fractionally. He would leave the nation of Dareth Hlum. He would travel the length of Knoori to compete in Danoor, representing Golna's Black Suits in the near-eternal dispute between the Followers of Adrash and the Followers of Man. In the land of his ancestors he would win glory for the orders and converts to the faith, or he would die.

Before leaving, he would visit the parents of Julit Umeda, offering what comfort he could.

BERUN

The city of Golna, capitol of Dareth Hlum, was an arid splinter in the easternmost flank of the continent of Knoori. Roughly arrowhead-shaped, its southern and northern shores were bordered by the split end of the river Riolsam, which the residents simply called the Sam. On both shores the privileged had built their private estates, beautiful and airy buildings of imported oilwood and glass, outfitted with private docks below broad balconies on stilts.

The clear waters of the sea some men called Jeru and others called Deathshallow lapped perpetually at the broad eastern beachfront, which the poorest residents called home. Though the shore was undeniably beautiful, beasts had a habit of hauling themselves from the water and terrorizing the citizens along the beach. As a result, the slums' makeshift defensive wall was forever being repaired.

The majority of Golna's million souls did not live near the water, however. They had spread over the rocky, dry-shrubbed hill that dominated the island, segregating themselves into ethnic communities of various sizes and economic stature. Eventually, each came to embrace and jealously guard a principal industry.

This is how Butchertown became Butchertown. Everyone trusted a Vunni with a knife, as long as it was poised over a sheep or cow carcass. Theirs was not a prosperous community, but it was safe and clean, and it comprised the northeast tip of the city. Built into the steep side of the hill, its houses leaned at crazy angles toward the sea. Blood ran in channels into the sea.

Butchertown was famous for its butchers, of course. Its pastush bakeries—the only ones of their kind outside Vunn itself—were also quite renowned. The city's most attractive prostitutes lived on the Avenue of Broken Pottery. And the Anadrashi temple in the Square of Nights, O'men As, was generally considered to be Golna's most austere.

For close to a decade, however, the community had been known for one thing above all else: the constructed man known as Berun. He had fought in and won many of the fighting tournaments the city had held in the previous eight years. Though strong men had on occasion incapacitated him with the blow of a heavy weapon, only mages and those highly skilled fighters possessing elder-cloth suits stood a likely chance against him.

He lived on the roof of a Black Suit abbey, home of the Seventeenth Order, though he himself abstained from sectarian violence. Every day from sunrise to mid-afternoon he rested, absorbing the sun's rays for nourishment. In order to get the most sunlight, he allowed his manlike body to relax completely, spreading into a large circular carpet of dull bronze spheres of varying sizes.

The two glowing blue coals of his eyes perched on the roof's edge, connected to the main mass of his body by a thin tendril of spheres no larger than green peas. He took pleasure in watching the early morning routines—the corral of cows and sheep, the haggling over wares in the ruins of the Shoen Adrashi temple, and the extinguishing of the red magefire lamps lining the Avenue of Broken Pottery.

The ordinary activities of men fascinated him, though it was a rare occasion when he engaged them on a social level. Too often, such streetside conversations turned into discussions of religion or money, and Berun had little use for either. This afternoon, like most afternoons, would find him in the abbey courtyard, observing the brothers and sisters at practice. Perhaps the abbey master would ask him to help with the training. It amused him to slowly choreograph an attack for the novices, and let them pummel him with their staffs.

Only large gatherings and other interesting events drew him out of the building. Fights and festivals were his favorites, but he also enjoyed taking part in the charitable works the Seventeenth organized on occasion. There were always buildings to be rebuilt, families to be comforted. The west end of Butchertown bordered Querus, a small Tomen neighborhood. Though both communities professed forms of Anadrashism, neither could agree on the particulars. Bombings, alchemical and chemical, were not uncommon.

Humans were odd, in Berun's estimation. Odd in their preoccupations. Surrounded by others of their kind, knowing their concerns were mirrored a hundred thousand times over the course of generations, they still did harm to their neighbors.

As the sole member of his species, Berun considered this odd, indeed.

‡

In the Month of Bakers he had turned twelve years old. He did not tell anyone, for the age meant nothing. In truth, he was little different from the being he had been upon waking for the first time. Experience left its mark, but his fundamental nature could not be altered.

He had not been created in Golna. The dialect in which he spoke, full of rolled R's and elongated vowels, was not common in the city. Its speakers, the people of Nos Ulom, had long been banned from Dareth Hlum. The nations were old enemies. Whereas Dareth Hlum took great pride in its religious neutrality, allowing any sect to proselytize and even battle in the street if properly registered, Nos Ulom took equal pride in its conservative Adrashism, the expression of which the government closely monitored.

Dareth Hlum considered Nos Ulom a nation of dangerous extremists.

Oddly, if this had not been the case, Berun would never have been allowed into Dareth Hlum.

Before achieving fame for fighting in the city, he had achieved notoriety in Nos Ulom for assassinating Patr Macassel, High Pontiff of Dolin. The man, arguably the most powerful religious figure on the continent, was killed in his sleep, skull crushed beyond recognition by hands twice as large as a normal man's.

Berun had not bothered to destroy the elder eyes that had been set into the rafters above Macassel's bedroom. As dictated by custom, court mages blinded a slave and implanted the elder eyes so that they could be read, after which the manhunt officially began. For twelve days, the royal mount followed the constructed man through the pinefields of southern Nos Ulom. On the morning of the thirteenth, Berun slipped across the border to Casta, leaving forty-two men dead and many more injured behind him.

The government of Nos Ulom tried its best to cover up the story, claiming Macassel had died of natural causes. They never offered an ounce of bone or skin in bounty for Berun's body.

Their clumsy efforts of obfuscation failed, and Berun became a hero to the various Anadrashi factions of the continent. Adding insult to injury, Nos Ulom's Royal Redcoats failed to stop locals from burning the home of Ortur Omali, Berun's creator and the nation's most powerful mage. Nothing of value was found in the rubble, and few believed the official story that Omali had died in the conflagration.

Of course, these events overjoyed the governors of Dareth Hlum. When word reached them that Berun was living in Casta's capitol, they sent him an invitation to a tournament in Golna, hoping the constructed man would choose to stay. The fact that Berun himself symbolized a sort of religious extremism was inconsequential. The governors wanted him for the sole purpose of aggravating Nos Ulom.

Their efforts at seduction failed. Berun proved uninterested in creature comforts and money. Fortunately for the governors, Golna had one thing that interested the construct: fighting. He had fought in Casta, where nearly everything was legal, but had not approved of the gambling houses, establishments run by men who thought nothing of pitting a man against a lion if there was a profit to be made. If a man wanted to risk his life, Berun reasoned, he should at least be given a chance.

Violence and camaraderie compelled Berun, not money. He found himself allying with the Black Suits of the Seventeenth, though he had never found reason to hate God as they did. His affection for his new brothers and sisters grew. Their passion inspired his respect. He refused to engage in their violent arguments of faith, but he would defend their abbey and fight alongside them in tournament.

The transaction was simple. He lived on the roof of a Black Suit abbey, home of the Seventeenth Order, and protected his adopted family. He gave his tournament winnings to the abbey master, Nhamed, who then filtered the funds through to the community. In return, Butchertown loved Berun.

Gradually, the White Suits moved out entirely. During the eight years Berun had called the Vunni neighborhood home, the majority of Adrashi had defected to the Black Suits due to his association with them—this, and the White Suits had never gained much of a foothold among the violently Anadrashi Vunni population anyway.

If holding a position of influence bothered Berun, he gave no outward sign, but at rare times he wondered if his convictions were not in fact his own. He wondered if he had been programmed by his creator to act this way or that, tipping the balance in the Anadrashi's favor, just as he had been forced to kill Patr Macassel. At his most paranoid, Berun worried he had been created as a weapon to strike at Adrash, precipitating the great cataclysm all Adrashi men claimed would come about if the Anadrashi triumphed.

From time to time he became lost in visions. He who did not sleep relived the murder of Patr Macassel as though it were a dream, brass fingers tight around a throat that turned to white stone, crumbling in his hands.

The episodes had become more frequent of late, repeating a message he could not comprehend.

‡

The street wavered before his eyes, signaling the beginning of yet another vision. Possessing no means to stop it, he relaxed and let the sensations overtake him.

Immediately, it was not as he had come to expect. He did not wake in the hallway before Macassel's bedroom door.

He possessed control over his limbs.

He was not alone.

A mage with hands of burnished steel walked with him through the forest named Menard, a vast pine slope north of the Aspa Mountains. He knew the location well, though the trees in his vision had grown into elder-figures: Tall, impossibly thin men of purple, lustrous wood instead of flesh—demi-gods cursed with a thousand arms, elongated skulls, and eyes growing like berries on their fingers. Branch-tips brushed against him like insect antennae, trying to insert themselves into the crevices between the spheres that made up his immense body.

He lumbered clumsily, as if he had not drank from the sun in weeks.

The mage talked at his side, meaning lost in riddles and bad jokes, gesturing with his hands. When he rubbed his fingers together, they sounded like singing bowls. When he clapped his hands, they tolled like bells. Though Berun recognized the mage, he could not place or name him.

It seemed they walked with a purpose, but the reason for this too escaped his grasp. He spent a great deal of time avoiding branches. He found himself grateful for the mage's constant talk. If silence descended upon them, other voices took up the slack. Quiet at first, they became louder and louder until the components of Berun's body vibrated together uncomfortably.

"Pay attention," the mage said at some point. "You are about to receive instructions." The message came with clarity in the middle of an otherwise unintelligible rant, as if the man had woken from a dream to deliver it.

Berun resolved to remember the words.

In time they came to a great manor house of blackwood and stone. They arrived without warning, without a break in the forest. He recalled entering no glade, yet the building stood in the center of a treeless expanse. Though its angular facades were dark, the structure seemed to glow under the moon.

Turning to the mage, his thousands joints creaked like a carriage's rusty leaf spring.

"Has it always been night?" he asked. His deep brass voice sounded as if it came from the other side of a wall.

His stare was met with eyes the color of wet soil.

"It will be," the mage said, and began walking toward the house.

Berun had seen the structure before. Something about it set the spheres deep inside him spinning, jerking like animals in a packed cage. He did not want to follow the mage, but a look back revealed that the elder trees had closed ranks, denying him any path of return.

‡

The manor house's immense blackwood door leaned forward in its frame, stretching above Berun's head. The stoop felt slick under his feet, as if the stone were coated in ice. He fought to keep his balance.

The mage looked up at him expectantly.

Berun struggled for a time, falling and rising and falling again. When his knees hit the stone, they rang like iron nails struck with a hammer. He tried scoring the stone itself for purchase, but the landing proved as hard as diamond. Finally, he braced himself as best he could and punched the door. His right fist and part of his forearm exploded into their composite metal spheres, showering him, falling on the stoop like marbles from a child's bag.

The door creaked open.

"It is polite to knock," the mage said, stepping into the dark foyer.

Berun concentrated, but the spheres would not return. Strangely, this did not bother him overmuch. He examined his shattered right arm in wonder, attempting to move phantom fingers. He watched the simulated lines of sinew in his forearm, marveling at the way the broken rows of tiny spheres still moved in a detailed imitation of muscular contraction.

The mage turned to the open doorway and mumbled something. His steel hands glowed softly in the darkness, beckoning. He stepped backward, and for a brief moment light flared in his face: two pinpoints of amber fire in each eye socket.

"I'm coming," Berun said. He stepped into the house, and the light failed completely. He turned to find the door closed. Or perhaps it was still open and someone had stolen the moon and stars. Gradually, he discovered that not every source of illumination had been extinguished. Not quite. A bluish glow ringed his vision. He considered this, confused.

Just as the realization struck, the mage spoke: "We see by the light of our eyes."

The double pinpoints of the mage's eyes returned, positioned before Berun, though he could not tell how close. Cautiously, he stepped forward. Solid, flat ground beneath his feet. The amber lights neither receded nor grew closer, and so he kept moving toward them. Much as he had experienced in the forest of elder trees, time lost all meaning.

Eventually radiance began to seep back into the world. He now walked down a hallway. The mage advanced several paces before him, the hem of his dark cloak brushing the purple, thickly carpeted floor. Stylized elder trees stretched from the floor, arching above them on the ceiling. As they walked, Berun thought the images became even more like elders. They took on definition until they appeared ready to step out of the walls.

The hallway was long. It did not slope upward, yet Berun found he needed to lean forward slightly in order to reach the nondescript doorway at its end.

The mage looked up at him expectantly. Berun knocked.

The door opened easily and the hallway disappeared. The sun hung in a cloudless sky. Berun and the mage stood on a vast field of short yellow grass sparsely blanketed with blooming azure flowers. Before them, the horizon was flat and somewhat close. Berun swiveled his head to look behind and found the same view. To either side, however, the horizon seemed to draw to a point a great distance away. It seemed they stood on the top of an immense wall.

He looked down. At his feet a fat man slept, dressed all in white. As with the mage, Berun recognized but could not place him.

"Kill him," the mage said. His eyes had become large, liquid pools of amber in which two doubled irises swam. Two figure eights lying on their sides.

"Why?" Berun asked. Without consciously deciding to do so, he knelt before the sleeping man and reached for his neck. He had not thought of his shattered right arm in some time, and the sight of it surprised him.

"One hand should be enough, Berun," the mage said.

Hearing his name spoken broke the spell. The artifice of the vision sloughed off like a layer of dust, and Berun became aware of his body on the rooftop in Butchertown. He knew the heat of the sun there, a very real sensation that split his worlds in two. All at once, the link between waking life and vision felt very tenuous. Berun regarded the body of Patr Macassel, then stood and turned to the mage.

"Father," he said. "Where am I?"

The mage Ortur Omali smiled. Deep within Berun's chest a sphere knocked against its neighbors.

"Wrong question," Omali said. "You should ask, 'Where am I to go?'"

Berun stared at his creator. The man had aged.

Realization struck. "You're really you," Berun said.

Omali's smile broadened. "Inconsequential. Ask me where you're supposed to go, Berun."

Confused, full of questions, Berun nonetheless obliged.

"Danoor," Omali said.

"Why?"

Omali inclined his head to the man at Berun's feet. Macassel had disappeared, replaced by a tall, strongly built man. He wore a black elder-skin suit, but its surface shifted on him like oil, revealing patches of skin that varied from light to dark. One moment, the pink paleness of an Ulomi miner. Next, the rich oilwood brown of a Knosi fisherman. He grew. He shrunk. Twice, his suit took on the hue of milk and his skin turned black.

Berun looked up. The great mage's form blinked on and off. For a moment, his entire body appeared out of focus. An intense frown of concentration scored deep lines in his face. He caught Berun's questioning look.

"I cannot quite find the focus now, but he is here somewhere. He does not invite others in. Perhaps—" His steel hand shook as it rose to his mouth and pried his lips apart. He yawned as if the muscles of his jaw were sore. "Ah. I have found him again. For all his resistance, he is nearly as open as you are, Berun. His alignment is unclear, however. I cannot yet make a decision about him. Soon, though. Soon. But that does not concern you. Your mission is simple: You will watch him, and await my command."

"Who?" Berun asked.

Omali blinked out of existence again, and reappeared after a handful of seconds. The man at Berun's feet did the same. Suddenly, the view Berun had of the street in Butchertown superimposed itself over everything. It blinked on and off. The vision started to fade around Berun.

"Who?" he asked again. "Tell me, Father."

Omali shook his head, frowned. He started to speak, stopped. For a brief moment, he had no mouth, just a smooth layer of skin below his nose. After several false starts, he finally spoke in a voice that grated like a whetstone against a rusty steel blade.

"A man who will upset the balance. He is—"

Before any more could be said, the vision ended.

‡

"My father has summoned me on an errand," Berun told the abbey master. "I must go to Danoor."

Nhamed looked up from his meal. He dipped his chopsticks in the steel cleansing cup and positioned them precisely on his napkin. The dinner items were arranged before him carefully, aligned so that each complemented its neighbor. He ran hands over thighs and stomach, as though seeking to brush invisible crumbs from him. He sighed, eyes roving around the nearly empty room, landing everywhere but on Berun.

Berun did not mind the wait. The master was an interesting man to observe. He projected an air of tense, even awkward fastidiousness inside the walls of the abbey, which clashed oddly with the wild zeal he displayed in battle.

"Explain," Nhamed eventually said.

Berun described the vision, the details of which had not faded, but cemented themselves in his mind. When he looked inward, he could recall the events as if they had occurred in the abbey the day previously.

Nhamed's eyes stared fixedly above Berun's head. "To my knowledge, your creator is dead. You think a dream enough to leave the city? There are men who will remember your name along the road." He furrowed his brow. "Men who... Men who will not be friendly."

"I know this," Berun said. "And yes, it's enough."

Strangely, it was. Despite his youth, Berun was not naïve. Omali had never appeared to him before, but it explained why Berun had recently experienced visions with such regularity. Surely, Omali had caused them for a reason. Perhaps this trust itself proved that his creator had programmed him for certain behavior, but Berun was not generally given to flights of speculation.

Besides, he surmised, there would be fighting in Danoor. To celebrate the new year, the city had scheduled a secular tournament to follow the contest between the Black and White orders. That alone was reason to go. For a moment, he questioned why the trip had not occurred to him before.

Nhamed's eyes finally found Berun's. "Then we will miss you. Will you..." The master cleared his throat delicately. "Will you return? We have grown fond of you, and the White Suits..."

Berun caught his meaning. "I will return," he said. "And I will bring money."

Nhamed raised his eyebrows and made a noncommittal sound. Berun assumed the man would not try to stop him, but he had misjudged people before. Men, he knew, often hid their intentions from themselves. They made decisions without knowing why.

"Well," Nhamed finally said. "If you insist upon leaving, I have just received word of another man's journey to Danoor. Golna's champion has been chosen." A sour expression crossed his face. He moved his lips, apparently searching for words. "He is, I know, a man of honor. I have never trusted his master, but I do not doubt his charge. It will be safer to travel with him. He may even protect you."

Berun refrained from laughing. "Who is he?"

‡

The abbey masters had arranged for Berun and his traveling companion to meet the following morning at the Tam Docks in Heblast, the westernmost neighborhood in Golna. Impatient to get moving, Berun arrived early and attempted to distract himself by watching the fishermen unload the night's catch from their flat-bottomed riverboats. In quick time, butcher stalls were erected. Chum buckets overflowed. Restaurant and foodstall owners filled the boardwalk, straining past their neighbors to offer money for the best cuts.

Nhamed had given Berun a description of Vedas Tezul, but he disregarded it. He would not search the crowd for a particular face. Like Ulomi men, Knosi all looked the same to him. Most likely, it would be some time before he was able to differentiate Vedas from his countrymen. It made far more sense for the man to find Berun.

Of course, resentment spurred this decision, as well. The presumption of Nhamed, thinking Berun needed protection! He wondered why he had allowed himself to be corralled to the docks, why he did not even now walk away. He always knew the direction in which he traveled, could always place himself on the map of Knoori his creator had placed inside his head. Surely, he could walk from Dareth Hlum to Danoor in three and a half months. One and a half months would have been enough time. Nhamed worried too much.

Nonetheless, Berun waited, curious despite himself. A Black Suit—perhaps the man Omali had commanded him to watch. Certainly, Berun had received no message not to accompany the man, even though his presence slowed travel considerably.

Despite having spent a day and night meditating on Omali's mystifying words, Berun had not been able to achieve peace. Indeed, his indignation only grew. He chafed at being controlled, but did not know enough to call his mission a fool's errand. What if Vedas truly did pose a threat? Berun would not revolt against his creator without a compelling reason.

Conceivably, he did not possess the means to revolt. He shifted from foot to foot, suddenly restless. Winning tournaments in Golna had bolstered his confidence, assured him of his strength. The possibility that he had underestimated his own weakness discomforted him.

The sun rose above the horizon, and the crowd began to clear from the boardwalk.

"You are Berun?"

"Yes," Berun rumbled. He turned from his view of the river and regarded the man.

As he had expected, Vedas Tezul was to most appearances a typical Knosi, broad nosed and black skinned. Unlike many of his countrymen, however, he did not wear his hair in long matted cords or as a halo around his head. Instead, he chose to shave his scalp and face bald. He had not adorned his elder-cloth suit with artistic designs or caused it to form thick armor. Overall, Berun considered the effect somewhat unimpressive, as if the man were only half-finished. Even his posture was unnaturally stiff. He looked like a man who had never become comfortable in his skin.

"Ten days." Vedas said. "Nbena is only two hundred miles. You can manage twenty miles a day?"

Berun bit back his first reply. "Yes," he said simply. Was the man an idiot? Of course he could walk twenty miles a day. He could walk miles around Vedas Tezul.

"Do you need to purchase any supplies?" the man asked.

Berun stared.

Father, he thought. *This can't be the man you want me to watch.*

CHVRLI CASTA JONS

The old men of Basec thrust their staff-ends into the unfinished wooden stands of their small theater. They did not smile or stand in respect, and the weak sound of their applause drifted away with the dry breeze. Several of the torches had gone out during the fight, but no one had moved to relight them. Money changed hands quietly as the crowd of old men climbed the stands—white-robed figures disappearing over the hillock like undead returning to graves.

Churls lowered her tattooed arms and looked down. The boy's body lay broken on the blood-spattered dirt at her feet, a vertical dent running the length of his pulped face.

"Peace," she said, expressionless.

She patted herself down and rubbed her bare skin, checking for unnoticed injury and letting several grams of dirt float free from her leathers. Her eyes felt scratchy in their sockets. She pulled a torch from the perimeter of the fighting floor and searched the ground for thrown coins.

"Coins," she muttered. "Fucking savages."

A quick search found seven, barely worth the effort. One beer's worth, probably. She dropped the torch and retrieved her sword from the ground. Its pitted surface came clean with a little gritty dirt. Lastly, she clipped the coin belts free from her and the boy's waists, and cut each bag open. Sixty-four bona, as she had been promised. At the expected exchange rate, it

26

would get her two grams of heavily contaminated bonedust. Hardly worth the effort of conversion.

She was tired, disappointed with the fight's outcome. The boy had been trained well, and killing him had not been her intention. He never stopped attacking, though, even after she broke his left femur and kicked the flail out of his hand. Grunting through a mouthful of blood, he crawled after her. No one in the crowd called it done. Resigned, she had finally flipped him over and crushed his skull.

Fucking savages.

Still, one had to live somehow. In her own estimation, Churls possessed no other skills to speak of. Gambling had gotten her in quite a bit of trouble a year previously, so it would be some time before she could return to Onsa, where the real money was. Shame the men of the badlands had so little money. Shame they had so little talent. They took what entertainment they could from watching their boys fight, watching them die.

There were good reasons so few fighters made it out here, Churls knew. One had to be in dire straits to scrounge in the dirt for coins.

Leaving the body where it lay, she climbed the shallow steps of the theater. An odd feeling, as if she were being watched, made her pause at the top. Her heart pounded against her ribs.

"What do you want?" she asked. She tried to make her body move forward, and failed.

She turned. A pale figure stood next to the boy's corpse: A white-skinned child, dressed in a white school tunic. Her hair, her slippers, her socks—all white. Her face could not be seen from the top of the theater, but Churls did not need to see it. She would have recognized the girl's posture anywhere. Few children had ever communicated world-weariness so well, or at such a young age.

Churls had not seen her daughter for at least three months. A decade had passed since she had seen the girl alive.

"Hello, Fyra," Churls said.

The girl nodded, gaze never leaving the body at her feet.

You killed him, she said.

"Yes." Churls sighed. "I killed him."

Fyra disappeared and reappeared next to her mother. Involuntarily, Churls flinched, just as she had done when the girl surprised her by popping out from behind a corner when she was alive. Fyra had lived with her grandmother, and as a result Churls never became accustomed to children. Not even her own daughter. The fact that the girl had become a ghost did not change matters overly much.

Fyra looked up at Churls with eyes far older than a ten-year-old's. They alone were not a shade of white, but clear and blue like her mother's.

Did you like it? Fyra asked.

Churls took a step backwards just as Fyra reached for her hand. It was a coincidence, Churls reasoned to herself, yet she stared at the little hand the way one might stare at a live scorpion.

"No," she answered. "I didn't like killing him at all."

Are you sure? Fyra said. *You liked killing the last man. You told me you did.*

Churls frowned. She knew the man her daughter referred to. The last time Fyra appeared, Churls had just killed an infantryman of the Castan Third in a fair fight. He had nearly bested her, and she had enjoyed every moment.

"That's true." Churls smiled awkwardly, like a person trying on an expression for the first time. "But that was a very different situation. You do see the difference, don't you, Fyra?"

The girl looked down at her hand, and slowly let it fall back to her side.

She said, *There's no difference, Mama. This one's just as dead as the other one.*

Churls shook her head. "You're not seeing what I mean. The man I killed in Donda was a trained warrior. He and I both knew what we were getting into. The difference is clear. I know you're old enough to see it. And you can, can't you, now that I've explained it?"

Fyra disappeared and reappeared next to the boy's corpse. For a long while, she simply stared at him. Churls grew uncomfortable and tried to think of something to say. Surely, the child could tell the difference. She was not, after all, a child.

Fyra cocked her head like a dog, then cocked it the other way.

No, she finally said. *I don't see the difference at all.*

Their eyes met from across the theater. Churls formed the old words in her mind, working up the nerve to speak. *I wish you wouldn't watch me when I fight. I wish I'd been there when you died. I'm happy I wasn't. I love you. I hate you. Why don't you leave me alone? Don't leave, sweetie. Stay.* Though the words were true, none of them sounded right, and her lips would not move no matter how hard she tried. Nonetheless, a raw lump formed in her throat, as though she had been speaking for a long time indeed.

"I..." The word was a croak. "Fyra, you..."

I don't want to talk about this boy anymore, the child said. *And someone is waiting for you in your hostel.*

She disappeared, back to the land of the dead.

‡

Churls finished her fifth beer, worried that the evening might result in a bad decision. Frankly, the situation felt out of her hands. The young men in the bar, none of whom had been present at the fight but had heard of her victory—young men who were nothing like their fathers, who knew the price of killing—would not let her pay for her drinks. And as the fight and Fyra's appearance had not stopped troubling her, she decided to keep drinking.

Last but by no means least, she had no intention of returning to her hostel.

Someone is waiting for you.

Fuck that, Churls thought. Probably trying to collect on her debt. She owed nearly sixty ounces in gambling losses. Onsa was only eight hundred miles away, and she had not been overly attentive while covering her tracks.

As if on cue, a hand fell on her shoulder. She did not tense up, but let her right fist drop into her lap like it had fallen. Closer to her sword, better position for an elbow to the groin.

"Thought I'd find you here," a familiar voice said. There was garlic on his breath. "Another drink?"

Churls closed her eyes and smiled into her empty glass. "This is a bad dream, then, isn't it? Of all the people I wanted to see, in all the world, you're the last." She turned to the speaker and winced theatrically. "You look like shit, Gorum. You know you look like shit? You woke up and told yourself, I'm going to look like shit today?"

The man grinned. "I'm one of the only friends you got left in the world. Better be nice to me."

They laughed and embraced. She held the contact longer than usual.

Over his shoulder, Churls saw scowls on a few faces. *We bought you a beer*, the expressions said. *And now you're running off with him?*

She had experienced their kind of attention many times before. In the badlands, miles from anything resembling civilization, she became something of an exotic treat. Her freckled skin and short-cropped brown hair, her muscles and tattoos and scars, marked her as a different species from the long-haired, slate-skinned local women. Their thin hands and feet barely peeked out from folds of draped cloth while Churls walked about in leather halter and brass-pleated skirt.

The men of the badlands thought her small breasts were cute. They thought the gap between her two front teeth was cute.

They could get possessive very quickly.

"Boys!" she yelled, disengaging from Gorum. "The round's on my friend here!"

Still no smiles, but they took their drinks while Gorum scowled and paid. He understood such things, though Churls knew his preference was to push his luck as far as it would extend, and then break some bones. He had been a fighter once, before discovering how much money could be made representing other fighters. He arranged matches for them and took a percentage of the cut.

She had been a disappointment to him of late. She had lost too much money gambling, started drinking too much, and started losing fights. As things got worse, she took to fighting easier opponents. Less money, less respect. Soon the strongarms were knocking on her door, leaving threatening messages at her haunts. She left Onsa the autumn of '98 and kept a low profile, avoiding city centers as much as possible. Gorum had not contacted her, presumably because she was no longer bringing in any real money.

They had been lovers once, what felt like a long time ago.

"How did you get here?" she asked as soon as the beer was distributed, the bill paid. They sat together at a corner table, close but not touching. His fingernails were dirtier than she had ever seen them. The tops of his forearms were sunburned. He did not like horses or camping, and never strayed far from cities. Something extraordinary had brought him to her.

"Construct horse, if you can believe it." He rubbed his thighs and grunted. She imagined the cost of such a thing and whistled. He continued. "I was actually finishing a tour of the Five Sisters, looking for talent. Not much luck. In Dunn, I received a message and knew I had to get to you. Fortunately, you were easy to find."

"Well then, that's that. What's this message all about?"

He wiped foam from his mustache. "An opportunity, Churli. Have you heard about the tournament in Danoor?"

"You can't be serious." Of course she knew about it. What else occurred at the end of every decade and attracted every madman in the world? Of course, this year's would be even madder, falling as it did halfway through the millennium. "It's a thousand miles away, through places I'd rather not go. Besides, I try not to mix religion and killing. Liable to get you killed."

"I know, but hear me out. I hadn't considered Danoor a possibility, either, but everything just fell into place." He paused to take a drink. "I looked at the bracket structure, and the odds are good—better than good, Churli. After that I concentrated on finding suitable travel companions. Of course, I can't guarantee anything."

"You never could. No one can call a fight that large. And shit, Gorum, you know I don't like being set up. No, shut up. I don't want to hear about them yet. Before I consider anything, and I'm not saying I'm going to, I need to know what's at stake. How much will this tournament win me?"

"There's two hundred and fifty pounds of pure-grade bonedust in it for you if you make it to the winners' bracket, not to mention your cuts from the preceding fights."

Churls shook her head. "Holy hell. What's the winner get?"

Gorum smiled. "One thousand—drawn on the royal reserve bank of whichever government you choose. And this is separate from the Adrashi and Anadrashi bullshit. They compete against each other for only two days, white against black. I don't even think they're fighting for dust. The real fun starts on the first day of the new year." He held up a finger. "But because the sects are hosting the whole thing, it's their rules."

"What does that mean?"

The smile broadened. "The eight fighters who make it to the winners' circle may opt out with their cuts."

Churls felt mildly insulted. "Are you saying I can't win?"

"Yes." His hand fell over hers. "The gambling houses are going mad with the news. Berun registered before leaving Golna. Even at your peak, you couldn't have taken him."

She felt more insulted, but knew he spoke the truth. "How, then," she asked, "do you know I won't be matched against him in the lower rounds?"

Gorum shrugged. "I don't, obviously. The odds, though, are in your favor. One in eight isn't bad, and they're trying to organize the groups geographically."

That kind of bracketing would not work out well, Churls reasoned, because more than a few fighters from Dareth Hlum would have dropped out when they heard Berun was fighting. Still, she could count on many people using Gorum's rationale, hoping to avoid Berun and drop out once they made it to the winners' circle. Adrashi fighters with backers, especially—men who could afford to travel across the continent in luxurious wagon trains, assured of their safe passage through Nos Ulom—would still find a way to attend.

"Still," she said. "How do I get there? Nos Ulom's not the friendliest place in the world, and I sure as shit won't go through any part of Toma."

"The people I want you to travel with aren't taking that route."

Churls looked at him, hand raised to signal another round. "What other route is there?" It dawned on her. "Lake Ten? I suppose that solves a problem, but it'll cost going through Tansot. And Bitsan isn't the friendliest city in the world, either. You stopped that fight with Hoetz just because his people had scheduled it there, remember—even though I had arranged for a..." She curled her upper lip. "Chaperon."

"Regardless, that's where you'll sail from. Oh, and one other thing. Neither of your companions are trackers. Somehow, you must convince or fool them into going over the Steps."

This was too much. Churls slapped the table. "That's five hundred miles out of the fucking way! What kind of fool would travel over the Steps when they could walk in a straight line through Stol?"

Gorum looked torn between wanting to grin and wanting to duck his head under the table.

"Your kind," he said. "Now let me explain."

‡

Even with all the money at stake, it took some time to convince her. The young men of the badlands waited as long as they could, eventually shuffling out with wistful glances in her direction. The bartender upended the rickety chairs and stools, and then poured himself a drink, seemingly content to sit and listen to Gorum and Churls talk.

It was after midnight when they stumbled into her hostel bedroom. They unclothed each other clumsily and made love on blankets she would not have touched sober.

For Churls, it was like walking into her apartment in West Onsa, smelling the faint mildew rot everything took on near the ocean, stretching out in her favorite chair. She missed the city, of course. She had spent most of her life away from it, fighting in some form, but she had always known in which direction home lay.

Sleep would not come. She sat in the room's only chair, flipping a throwing knife in her hand and watching Gorum sleeping. Finally, she retrieved her sword and polished the blade with spit and a pinch of bonedust.

He shook her shoulder. "I gotta go."

Her blade lay naked across her thighs. She did not remember falling asleep, yet the details of their conversation the night before had crystallized in her mind. She blinked away a map of Knoori marked with the planned route he had told her they would use.

Ridiculous. Sailing across Lake Ten. Craziness, traveling so far with strangers. She reminded herself that returning home without the money to pay off her debts was not an option. Neither, if she valued her sanity, was the prospect of remaining in the badlands. She could only kill so many untried boys before her soul withered inside her, or left of its own accord.

"Okay," she said. "You gotta go. Ten percent?"

"Yes." He pulled her out of the chair and embraced her, crushing her arms against her sides. "Ten percent. I've tried my damnedest to give you a chance at success. I wouldn't travel this far for anybody else. You know that, right?"

She pressed her cheek against his. Brief contact, a last reminder of home. He still smelled of garlic. His wife was from northern Nos Ulom, where they put garlic in everything. *To keep the dead away*, he had once told Churls.

He let go. "How much dust do you have? Do you have enough for your sword?"

She raised an eyebrow. "I always have enough for my sword."

"Good. And for money?"

"That depends. What's the interest?"

"Fuck you," he said, reaching into his pocket. He counted out waxpaper packets of dust, and handed her five of the larger ones. "There. That should be enough for travel."

She weighed them. An ounce of high grade. *Should be enough.*

"Thanks, Gorum. Any other advice?"

He stopped at the door, turned back. "As always, it's best to reign in that murderous instinct of yours. You never know when the tables will turn and you'll find yourself on the other end of the blade. A little compassion could save your life. Don't roll your eyes at me—it's true. Mostly, though, my advice is just to watch out for Berun. You've seen him fight, I take it? Back when he lived in Onsa?"

She nodded. "You took me. The fight lasted all of half a minute."

"Then you know not to expect any pity from him."

She smirked. "Contradictions, contradictions. And the Black Suit, Vedas?

How reliable is this source of yours? How do you know he can be trusted?"

"I already told you: I don't. I've given you all the information I have. You'll be their guide—it's up to you to create trust."

"I'll be lying to them, Gorum, delaying them by weeks."

"You'll be saving their lives by changing their course. Listen, you can't afford not to do this. The gambling houses will send someone after you eventually. Probably several someones. Not strongarms. Dangerous people. This is the only way to dig yourself out." He opened the door. "And I went to a lot of trouble to get here."

Churls considered her response. Possibly, she would never see him again. If she died, he would eventually find out—mostly to discover the fate of his dust, maybe a little because together they had once been something.

"Thanks," she said.

‡

Churls did not leave that day. The old men of Basec had agreed to pay for two fights, and as much as she loathed the idea of killing another inexperienced boy she could not turn down the money.

Gorum had arranged a live horse for her, an extravagance he had condoned only because time was pressing. On horseback, she could expect to arrive at the designated gate into Dareth Hlum two days before her traveling companions. There, she would need lodging. She would need to bribe entry officials to inform her the moment Berun came through. With any luck, she need not touch Gorum's money until they were well underway to Danoor.

She spent the afternoon practicing in a roofless abandoned building. For the first time in days, the sun cleared above her. She thrust and parried, swinging her dull, heavy sword in tight arcs, footwork kicking up a fine cloud of dust around her. A light sheen of sweat highlighted the flow of hard muscles under the freckled skin of her shoulders and arms.

Finished, she stood, breathing easily. She retrieved the pail of water she had brought from the hostel, disrobed, and washed the grime from her body as best she could. The air and water were cold, but the sun warmed her.

She enjoyed dinner—not so much the taste but the weight in her stomach—and tried not to think of the commitment she had made. Relying on others had never been her strong suit, but facts were facts. A lone traveler was a target.

Night had already fallen when she left the hostel. She walked the treeless path to the theater alone. The boy's body had been removed. The ground had been raked and the torches lit.

Soon, the old men began to arrive. As they topped the hillock and descended into the stands, not one paused to stare at the Needle extending across the sky above their heads. Neither did they gaze at the moon, which sat massively on the razor-backed hills directly before them. The men of the badlands were not dreamers, Churls knew. They woke before sunrise to graze their goats on paperweed and thorny sage, and died defending the animals. No mystery, no mysticism in that. If Adrash chose to destroy the world, they could do nothing to stop it.

Likewise, life would go on just the same if Adrash chose to redeem it.

Though Churls did not like the people of the badlands, she felt an odd communion with them. They understood that fate could not be bargained with. It held a person like a mother holds her child, lovingly or with revulsion. One did not get to choose.

The boy Churls was meant to kill stepped into the circle of firelight. He sneered at her disdainfully, but failed to hide the underlying fear. She saw it in the set of his shoulders, the hesitation in his steps.

Looking away, she caught movement before her in the stands. It did not surprise her. She had almost expected it.

A small white figure stood on the hillock, staring into the sky.

EBN BON MARI

They commenced a light breakfast on Ebn's balcony when the sun was a finger's breadth above the horizon. Light fare, Ebn had told Pol. Nothing fancy.

A lie. In truth, she had woken two hours before dawn to oversee the preparations.

Blood warm orange and kiwi juices. Rashl eggs and sheep tripe, scrambled with dandelion greens, scallions, and bitter basil. Earling potato and pigskin fritters with hot mustard aioli for dipping. Pomegranate juice cooled with carbonated rosewater ice cubes. Rapeseed oil and mint-filled pastries. Unleavened anisebread topped with crumbled goat cheese, smoked tigerfish, and shaved horseradish. Black wine from the A'Cas Valley. Finally, lefas bean and lemon zest sorbet she herself had made the night before.

Neither spoke while eating. Pol picked at the fritters and pastries, which saddened Ebn, but his obvious enjoyment of the pomegranate juice and anisebread nearly made up for it. Being so easily swayed by his moods annoyed her, but after seven years together there were reactions she had learned to accept.

She tried not to stare at him as they sipped the wine. This, too, she had expected.

He is not so beautiful, she had tried to tell herself many times. He was not the ideal elderman, certainly: too thickly built, too coarsely featured, and all that white hair. On a darkened street, an observer might mistake him for

pure human, not a halfbreed at all. In close quarters, of course, one could
not fail to notice that his skin was not a shade of brown, but purple. One
would not miss his double-irised eyes, which shined as though they had been
plucked straight from an elder corpse—a rare trait even among hybrids.

Such distinctions meant little to him. Even on the coldest of days, he wore
little clothing, clearly unembarrassed by the two closed fists raised in relief
on his pectoral muscles, a mutation which made it appear as if a man were
trying to push his fists through Pol's body. Of course, mutations were not
rare among eldermen, but few chose to display them. Most, like Ebn, had
been encouraged since childhood not to broadcast their unnatural heritage.
Amongst their own, they till sought to hide who they were.

Pol had been sixteen when she first saw him. Her hearts had leapt against
her sternum to see those fists on display. His pride had bewitched her.

This morning, she kept herself from staring by forcing her gaze outward,
over the terracotta roofs of lesser structures. Positioned three-quarters of the
way up the purple-bricked Esoteric Arts building, her apartment announced
her status to the city. From the balcony one could count the brightly stained
sails of His Majesty's Inland Navy, as well as measure the depths of Lake Ten
by the varying hues of its bluegreen water.

The view bored and somewhat frightened her, but she pretended interest in
order to busy her eyes. Eighty-seven years old, acting like a love-starved youth.

Pol sipped his wine unhurriedly, and Ebn's eyes drifted to the moon. Bone-
pale, it sat in the lower quadrant of the quickly brightening sky, unwilling to
set for another several hours. Nearly half of the Needle had descended below
the horizon. The second largest sphere seemed to rest atop her companion's
head. She squinted, trying for the fifth or sixth time that morning to determine if it spun faster than it had the day before.

It did not appear so, at least not to the naked eye. A relief. She hated the
days when a change was obvious. She hated the flutter of fear in her veins as
she greeted the sky every morning.

Pol set his empty wine glass on the table. "Thank you for that," he said.

She smiled. "There is one more thing." She raised her hand, summoning
a servant for the sorbet.

Pol frowned after his first spoonful. "Is this lemon?"

"Yes," Ebn said, cursing mentally. The man could be so finicky.

He pushed the brass goblet forward with his index clawtip, as if it contained something poisonous.

She shrugged. "No matter." She waved the servant forward again.

Pol reclined in his chair, legs stretched out under the table. The side of his foot brushed Ebn's ankle briefly. Like a fool, she inched her calf over until their skins touched lightly. He would not notice, she knew. He was the most preoccupied person she had ever met. Also the most private. His life outside the confines of the Royal Sciences Academy was a complete mystery. Had he friends in the city? He did not seem the type. A lover? Despite their years together, he had never discussed intimacies with her.

He yawned. "I was somewhat disappointed to receive your note yesterday. I was slated for an ascension this morning. Measurements, nothing exciting, but nonetheless... You know the feeling, Ebn. A week without looking down upon the world feels like a week wasted."

"Yes, I know the feeling," she said. Outbound mages were loath to miss even one orbital ascension. There were only so many years in their lives, after all. "My apologies for the interruption of your schedule, but I desire your counsel on something. Recently, the changes in the Needle have caused the telescopists some consternation. We have not—"

"What is recently?" he interrupted.

"Several weeks," she lied automatically. It had in fact been over a year of increasingly erratic changes, but he need not know that. "We have not seen variations of this frequency before, both in the speed and direction of the spheres."

"Yes," he said. "I have heard rumors."

She suspected he had. In fact, he probably knew a great deal more than he let on.

"The fact will be announced to the general academy later today," she said.

He smirked and gestured to encompass the campus. "You think they will have an answer to the riddle?"

She smiled wanly but did not rise to the jibe. "We cannot keep this to ourselves."

"Of course we can. We own the telescopes. All information about the Needle is filtered through us. Everything else is myth and foreign hearsay, so easily discounted by the academy. There is no advantage in opening the discussion up. Clearly, the changes reflect a shift in Adrash himself, and finding someone who can explain the god's mind is not possible. We will have as much luck listening to seers proclaim doom in Vaces Square as we will have listening to the responses of the general academy."

She fought the temptation to concede the point. Perhaps unavoidably, he had absorbed a great deal of her cynicism. At the same time, he had not yet come to grasp the reality of academy politics: Concessions had to be made in order to achieve one's goals.

"We need funding for further research," she said. "And the best way to acquire funds is to reveal a problem that must be solved."

"If you have already decided, why am I here?"

She touched his hand lightly. "I agree with you that Adrash's will cannot be known unless he himself announces it. I also do not want to assume the changes reflect hostility, but we must assume they do. Thus, the only thing we can change is our approach to Adrash. Before the noise of the academy's panic fills my head, I want to discuss this fact. Speak freely."

A smile just touched the corners of Pol's mouth. He had always spoken freely.

"We must be more aggressive in our supplication."

She waited, but he had said all he intended to say.

"I disagree," she said.

They nodded to one another, expressions blank. It had been a year since they had last discussed their positions. She had hoped his would change over time, but it was only hope. In truth, her intention in talking with him had not been to exchange views, but to inform him of the decision she had already made. That she, Captain of the Royal Outbound Mages, needed to talk around the issue instead of dealing with it directly angered her.

Fortunately, he could read her quite well.

He sighed. "Tell me what plan you have concocted."

‡

After Pol left, Ebn squirted a solution of reconstituted elder semen and menstrual fluid into her womb. Five hours later, she had nearly reached the end of her spell-casting.

Naked, knees spread to the noon sun, she reclined on a chaise a servant had carried onto the balcony. At the juncture of her long, slender thighs, the fingers of her right hand caressed a blood-red flower. She moaned softly, in time to the waves of pleasure spreading through her body. The muscles of her stomach bunched and released. Her buttocks lifted from the cushion, fell back.

No one could see her from the apartments above, for she had erected a visibility barrier.

Her skin was the exact color and texture of eggplant, and far hotter to the touch than a human's. Veins slightly darker than her skin, nearly black, spiderwebbed and branched over the sinuous lines of her body, which was hard and angular. Like most eldermen, her mouth was small, her teeth sharp. Unlike most eldermen, her eyes were emerald rather than amber, her hair just a shade lighter than black. Her variation was not as extreme as Pol's, but it did cause the occasional second glance.

Many thought her quite beautiful.

She closed her eyes. The sunlight caught and refracted in the fine transparent down that covered her body, causing her skin to shimmer as though it were wet. She did not in fact sweat, and like a desert cat avoided touching water to her skin.

Her moans became louder as she neared orgasm, and her hand descended so that it lay flat against her clitoris. The tongue in the center of her palm lapped hungrily, and she began to gasp. Her left hand, encased as it nearly always was in a black glove, rose from the cushion. She bit a clawtip, pulled the glove off, and spat it to the floor. The tongue in this palm emerged and began licking her left nipple. The small, toothless mouth it had emerged from suckled but made no noise. The tendons of her neck stood out. A sliver of emerald flashed from behind her eyelids and disappeared. As the pleasure increased, her hips rose from the chaise completely.

A line of clear fluid dripped from underneath her right hand and fell on the cushion, where it hardened almost immediately, puckering into a clear pebble. It rolled off and onto the balcony, where a great many more were scattered.

She screamed. The sound fell somewhere between a dog's bark and a seagull's cry. No one heard it, for she had erected a sound barrier.

"Pol," she moaned as she wound down.

The arch of her body collapsed. She panted, ribs standing out on her whip-thin frame. Her breasts bobbed high and tight on her chest. Now that her hands' work was done, she balled them into fists, forcing the tongues back into their mouths and fighting a vague sense of nausea. Absently, she reached to the floor, hand still clenched, using the claws of index finger and thumb to retrieve the glove.

She pulled it on and rested a moment. Then she began to cast her spell again.

✝

She could replay the fantasy in great detail, for much of it had actually occurred. Sixty years previously, during a routine solo ascension to the moon,
she had tried to seduce Adrash. Time had not made the fact of her transgression any easier to confront, yet the memory had its use. Desire of that
magnitude—hunger that compelled one forward, even to the point of destruction—created a uniquely efficacious mental state for casting a spell of
compulsion. Of course, she had altered the memory so that it veered from
history at the right moment, ending in satisfaction rather than violence.

As she relaxed, the sounds of the city below gradually faded away, replaced
by the nothingness of the void. It flooded her mind, cold beyond reason. The
world of her fantasy rippled into focus, materialized into existence.

The moon's fractured surface rushed by underneath her, less than a stone's
throw distant. It seemed to reach for her, drag her down. Adrash floated
above her, the plain, graceful geometry of his body half in shadow. With his
eyes closed, the divine armor covered him completely.

They were alone.

She shivered with fear. Though the outboud mages and their telescopists
had observed the god immobile many times, Ebn did not know how she
had managed to approach him unaware. Perhaps, she reasoned, he had lost
himself in meditation or entered into a state of hibernation to conserve
energy. Many academics believed that even someone as powerful as Adrash
could not survive easily in the void.

Or perhaps, Ebn said to herself, *he has led me here on purpose.*

No, a more prudent part of her whispered. *You are here to observe, nothing
more. Flee before you bring destruction upon yourself!*

She ignored the voice of reason. Knowing the act to be pure madness,
she cast a spell of protection around Adrash's body, a bubble of breathable
atmosphere, and joined hers to it, shuddering as the temperature dropped
precipitously. Such spells never joined perfectly, always allowing a bit of the
void in.

She raised the heat immediately, and cautiously floated closer to the god,
drawn toward perfection beyond mortal comprehension. Here was an attraction beyond any she had felt before, beyond what she would later experience
with Pol. The intensity of her compulsion felt dangerous, as though she were
standing on the edge of a cliff. The tongues in her palms stirred, pushing at

the fabric of her gloves.

She reached forward and stopped. She had no desire to touch Adrash with a barrier between them. The skin of her thighs and throat tingled.

Undressing was a laborious process, as the suit she wore had been designed for traveling the void, protecting its wearer in the event of a brief spell failure. All of one piece and black, sectioned like armor and tattooed with brown sigils, it came off her body like an insect's shed skin. Her eyes stayed fixed on Adrash as she pulled slowly free.

Her body was chalked in a unique bonedust blend—ground elder bone, sinew and skin, an extra precaution against the void: she had not become an expert mage due to genius, but thoroughness. Opening her fists, she allowed the mouths in her palms to open, her tongues to taste the trapped air.

Adrash had not stirred. He might as well have been a statue of white stone. He glowed in the light of the sun, brighter than the moon in the sky. She traced the outline of one heavy pectoral muscle with her left index claw before finding the nerve to lay the back of her hand against it. The surface of the divine armor was cool, only slightly colder than a man's skin but infinitely smoother. Flawless. The muscle underneath gave to pressure just as it should.

In every way he was her opposite. Thickly muscled rather than wiry, pale rather than dark, unlined rather than mapped in vein. They shared height, and that was all, she being somewhat short for an elderwoman, he somewhat tall for a man.

Her right hand went to her womanhood.

He failed to react to her tentative caress, so she moved closer, running her palm and its tongue over his smooth scalp, the contours of his body. He tasted clean, like water or snow. She avoided the prominent bulge of his genitals for a time, but eventually temptation overcame her. She ran her hand down the ridges of his belly and cupped his testicles, allowing the tongue to lick along his confined length. She closed her eyes and moaned.

Here, if she had been truly remembering rather than fantasizing, Adrash would wake. The light of his eyes would blind her and his voice would roar in her mind, flooding her, pressing against the inside of her skull until the blood ran from her ears. Then, moving faster than sight could follow, his fingers would be around her neck...

She turned from such thoughts with practiced ease and continued. He became hard under her caresses, but could not break free from the skin of his armor. His length stayed pressed against his testicles under the smooth barrier.

Like anyone, as a child Ebn had been educated about Adrash. *Nothing is impossible for him*, the tutors had told her. *He can split the ocean and walk around the world. He can stop the moon in the sky.* He could do all of these things, but in her fantasy he could not break free of embrace of the divine armor.

His entrapment excited her. He still had not opened his eyes, had not moved his arms or legs. Touching herself, she wrapped her legs around his, heels tight below his firm buttocks. She placed both hands on his chest and ground herself into his erection. She kissed the faint outline of his mouth, and slowly it responded—so slowly that at first she believed herself to be imagining it. His lips warmed, became hot. They parted and her tongue met his. He tasted of cinnamon and anise. His arms encircled her waist.

She opened her eyes.

Adrash had become Pol. He stared at her with two sets of pupils, and the corners of his mouth twitched. His hands fell to grip her hips. Her hearts beat off rhythm as she guided his length into her.

She screamed.

‡

For sixty years, two decades longer than most eldermen lived, Ebn had rented a closet-sized room in the southern wing of the Academy of Applied Magics library. Its single window looked out on three academy rooftops liberally covered in pigeon droppings. Beyond these, humble, single-story buildings carpeted the broad eastern valley floor. Not a river or lake in sight.

She preferred the office to her sumptuous apartment, just as she preferred oil lamps to alchemical candelabras. Here she had built shelves that covered the walls, filling them with every important book she owned. Cracked-spined novels and pornographic picture books mingled with esoteric texts on religion and the magics. Two shelves buckled under the weight of her most prized possession: the twenty-seven volume *Historig Jerung*, Ponmargel's survey of mankind's recorded and fabled antiquity. Twenty-four millennia of history, nearly two hundred pounds of text. She had read it through only once.

From the ceiling hung her favorite models. An airship she had built as a child, struts showing through a thin sheepskin gasbag. An elephant-drawn carriage. The twelve known planets, spinning lazily around an orange sun.

Knickknacks collected during a long career lined the windowsill. Presents from associates and mementoes from travel, mostly.

Papers littered her desk and gathered dust in piles. A half circle of clear area remained, though it too was busy with ink blotches and compass scratches.

She had built a hinged bed that secured against the wall under her desk. Seven days out of nine she slept here, even though it was a mere five-minute walk to her apartment. Certainly, she loved close spaces and the smell of books, but her preference was based more upon the position of the office than its interior. The Needle crossed the upper portion of the window for a mere nine days in the Month of Sawyers. The rest of the year it sailed clear over.

Experience proved that if she saw it too often her optimism failed her. It became impossible to deny the obvious any longer: A string of steel cages large enough to affect the tides was not an ornament. It was a threat of annihilation.

Of course, the inhabitants of the world knew this as well, but they had the luxury of ignorance, of self-deception. They prayed to Adrash for redemption and fought wars of faith, believing their efforts had an effect, all the while succored into a false sense of security by the Needle's apparent immutability. Despite its fluctuations—and time had turned even the Cataclysm into a minor fluctuation, a myth—it had extended across the sky for fifty generations. It had become fact, passed down mankind's generations. For all their words of doom, few believed in the threat of actual destruction.

Ebn knew better. She had experienced Adrash's wrath firsthand, and only escaped it by a miracle. Allowed to approach him while he slept—a miracle in and of itself—she had been spared to do the work of proving the world's worth.

This responsibility weighed upon her. She considered her weaknesses, and wondered if she might not be overcome by temptation a second time. Surely, she had lived life fearful that someone would repeat her mistake. For fear of bringing ruin upon them all, she had assured that no outbound mage ventured too close to Adrash.

For decades, this cautiousness had seemed a virtue, but age had brought with it doubt. Perhaps, she reasoned, she had hobbled her mages to keep them away from the god. Perhaps she had merely been biding her time, waiting for another opportunity.

At night, she dreamt of surviving the death of the world with Adrash at her side.

‡

Ebn allowed only one person to meet her regularly in the office. Qon et Gal, her second-in-command, had been her friend since the age of six. For forty years Ebn had shared her age-nullifying treatment, a unique alteration to the standard alchemical solution developed by her predecessor, with Qon alone.

Growing old, Ebn joked, would be awful without someone to share the indignity.

Qon rolled one of the clear pebbles Ebn's spell had produced between her clawtips. She held it close to her nose and sniffed. Her eyes narrowed.

"No," she said. "I have never seen one, but I have heard of it. Apparently, sex spells require a fine touch to produce the desired effect." She eyed the full clay jar. "How long have you been working on these?"

Ebn shrugged, cheeks darkening almost imperceptibly as she blushed. "A year, approximately. I can only do it every couple of weeks, it tires me so much. Before beginning, I studied and practiced for several months."

Qon's eyebrows rose ever so slightly. "Poor you."

"Shut up," Ebn said good-naturedly. "I talked with Pol over breakfast."

"Ah." Qon's expression did not change, though she knew of her friend's attraction. She had voiced her low opinion of Pol many times, speaking honestly as a true friend should. "It was as you expected?"

"Yes."

"And these?" Qon nodded at the jar. "You intend to seduce him, then sway him to your viewpoint?"

Ebn sighed. "You think that little of me? No. I have already talked with him. He does not see our perspective, but he understands my command: Adrash must not be approached by any one mage. Making our intention clear is dependent on everyone acting in concert." A brief memory of her hands on the god's flanks flashed through her mind. "Even then we do not know what may offend him."

Qon nodded, silent. Ebn knew her lieutenant did not take the explanation at face value. She would not come out and ask if Ebn intended to seduce Pol, but undoubtedly she wondered. If Ebn did manage to seduce Pol—an act she had dreamt many times but could hardly conceive of doing—all speculation would cease. In fact, Qon would probably congratulate her.

Ebn picked up a spell, rolled it between her palms. "I have been producing these with no clear intention in mind. Talking with Pol this morning gave me an idea, however. I think we can use them to show our goodwill to Adrash."

"Are you sure this is wise?"

Spent, Ebn smiled without feeling. "No. I am not sure it is wise. But if you will sit with me I will try to explain. Maybe we can work the kinks out together."

POL TANZ ET SOM

T he taste of lemon lingered, cloying in his mouth. He prepared a heavily spiced lunch on his own and ate it over a collection of stamped forms, struggling not to let anger overtake him. Fourteen separate requisitions for alchemicals, denied in the last month.

Clipped to the final form was a note from the department bursar:

Pol Tanz et Som, M.O.: Due to the ever-rising prices of the elder corpse market, we must reject the additional alchemicals you have herein requested. Perhaps in the future, your research will warrant an expenditure of this magnitude.

You are invited, as always, to make use of recycled materials in the faculty labs.

Recycled materials! Drained, lusterless ampoules of spent magic, barely suitable for the most basic of spells! Apparently, the administration expected him to do advanced research with fingernail clippings and candle wax. Maybe they thought prayer alone could sustain him.

Pol wondered if he could bring himself to ask a senior mage for assistance.

No. He possessed little stomach for begging favors from his peers, and such eldermen were likely to report his more esoteric undertakings to Ebn. At times, he felt as if she had persuaded the entire corps to watch him. Even the most conservative of his recent proposals had been met with suspicion. Some of the junior mages expressed interest in his theories, of course, but the junior mages were powerless and thus easily manipulated. They would spy on him to advance their careers.

46

You are too young to be so ambitious. Wait your turn.

He brushed the forms into the trash with the gnawed ostrich anklebones. He absently popped a gingersalt candy in his mouth and considered the problem. By its very nature, the academy did not cater to new thinking, and in the ranks of outbound mages the effect was even worse. He would need to take an unconventional tack if he had any chance of acquiring what he needed to resume his research and weaken Ebn's position.

A more diplomatic approach, she had said. Ridiculous.

He left the apartment, not yet sure where he was going. The hallways were nearly empty. A quick spell, no more than a brief automatic query, gave him the time: thirty-three minutes past two. That explained it. Lunch and catnaps in the slanting sun. Eldermen were adept at many things, but afternoons were not one of them.

Pol himself felt the pull of a full stomach and sunbath, but the energy of youth sustained him. At twenty-three, his constitution was at its most agreeable. As a boy, it had seemed forever would come and go before his body would respond to his wishes. Then again, without the age-nullifying treatments that came with high rank in the academy, in ten years he would be an old man.

His thoughts, ever in movement, veered from one possibility to the next. Did he know anyone in requisitions? No. Archaeology? Geology? No. No one in the churches would help him, he felt sure—and their security was tighter than all other departments combined, their oaths the most binding. One could never underestimate their magics, either.

If Pol needed further proof of his desperation, the fact that he considered thievery sufficed.

Suddenly, a possibility presented itself to him. He did know someone in the medicines department, a young man whom he had bedded for a brief time several years previously. A human, beautiful in a thick way, not all that precocious but eager to please. A dark-haired Castan. He worked in the morgue. They had rutted on an examination table, once.

Jorrin? No. Jarres. That was the name. He had confessed to Pol that some of his mates filtered alchemical juices from the human and elderman corpses in their custody. They had made quite a bit of money this way.

Pol left the Esoteric Arts building and angled toward the White Ministry Hospital.

‡

The Avenue of Saints honored those who had died defending the name and nature of Adrash. Statues of men and women, eldermen and human, lined the avenue as it wound through the academy grounds. It was the end of summer, and the vala trees had bloomed copper and purple. Arching over the roadway, they created a perpetual twilight in which the saints took on a sinister bearing.

Evertin The Belligerent appeared ready to jump from his marble base and start hacking away with his greatsword, which scholars claimed he had called Harrowing. Domas Alastetl rested wearily on her throne, a great wound in her side, face so cunningly carved it seemed to move as one passed. And Oilo The Ghost hovered above his plinth of skulls and weapons, a fluid, ferocious form barely recognizable as human.

At the intersection of the Avenue of Saints and Villus Street, the exact center of the academy grounds, stood a statue of Adrash. Pol made a point to visit it every day, for it represented the god during wartime, in his most awful aspect—this, and it reminded Pol of home, where the iconography displayed a harsher edge than in the capitol.

Carved from a block of unveined black granite, the sublimely proportioned god stood prepared to meet an enemy. At first glance his posture seemed to convey an odd calm, but close examination revealed the tension in his neck and shoulders, the flexion of his forearms. His feet rested upon a base designed to look like a sphere of the Needle. Its rims disappeared into the ground and roadway.

The sculptor had dripped molten red gold onto Adrash's heavily muscled torso and arms: the blood of men and beasts. The god's left arm and portions of his chest and back had been carved from white marble, and the join between black and white was a sinuous line, showing that the divine armor had begun to sheath his body. Yellow gold covered his eyes. But for the armored section he was naked. The sculptor had endowed him with assets befitting a god.

Pol's eyes lingered on this detail for a few seconds. Pressing his left fist to his forehead, he bowed deeply before moving on.

He had not always believed in Adrash's benevolence. What he mirrored as a child could hardly be called faith, and what he rejected as a youth could not be called informed. He had felt as if his mother were forcing him to believe. For many years he had transferred his frustration onto Adrash, who became in his mind a bully of monumental proportions.

When he left his mother's conservative Adrashism for the academy, he carried some of these sentiments with him. A sixteen-year-old boy, elderman or human, could not be expected to recognize his own arrogance for what it was—especially when that boy had recently arrived from Pusta, the Kingdom of Stol's exclave on the coast of Knos Min, a virtual world away from the capitol. The boy's blind arrogance could be a shield against the prejudice of his peers, who thought him a backwater fool.

Quickly adapting to their fighting style, Pol learned showing mercy came back to bite more often than not. So he stopped showing mercy. By the age of eighteen, he had killed seven men in self-defense and fought eleven duels. He became known for his temper and skill, as well as his genius in the magics.

He did not defend the reactionary beliefs of his youth or the people of Pusta, both of which he had long since come to view with amused disdain. Instead, he railed against the rote pronouncements of his teachers and peers, the mindless repetition of dogma. His own faith became a thing of fire and muscle. Adrash would not look kindly upon a weak people, sitting in contemplation, asking for his favor. The god, Pol came to believe, responded to strength. He did not want followers, but leaders.

The Avenue of Saints ended. At Skintree Road, Pol waited for a gilded carriage to pass before crossing the street, though he did not bow to the nobleman or woman inside as strict decorum dictated. An outbound mage, in whose veins elder blood flowed, bowing to an earthbound human? Ludicrous.

Once out of the manicured academy grounds, one could not help notice the change in atmosphere. It stank of human and animal waste, cooking fires, and cheap alchemy. Putrid, human smells, but they bothered Pol not at all. He had become used to the fragrances during his frequent trips out.

You take too many risks, Ebn had told him on more than one occasion. Typical of the outbound mages, she rarely traveled into the city, and never alone. Attacks on eldermen, even in the clear light of day, were not uncommon. But for ascensions into orbit, several of the senior mages had not left the academy in decades.

Pol refused to restrict himself so. Urban Tansot offered a range of products and services unavailable within the confines of institutionalized academia. Inevitably, many experiences had ceased to compel him—drugs, in particular, became superfluous as he grew into his magical talent—but sex had not. Partners were for the taking if an elderman knew where to look.

He reached the hospital, a clean, austere building that contrasted sharply with its dilapidated neighbors—a common sight in Apetia, the most culturally and economically diverse neighborhood in Tansot. Technically part of the academy, White Ministry benefited from its patronage as well as the city's. Its grounds were immaculately maintained, to Pol's eyes somewhat overdone. A stereotypical Stoli statue of Adrash, farcically epic and devoid of personality, stood in the front entrance courtyard.

Pol walked past it without a glance.

‡

Jarres had grown a thick beard that did not flatter him and acquired several pounds of muscle that did. His chest strained against the white medicines tunic, and despite his serious intentions Pol found himself mildly aroused. Nothing like an old lover to tempt a man from his course, he knew.

In his estimation of himself, Pol had one major weakness.

"Tanz?" Jarres asked, eyes moving down Pol's body. "How long's it been, mate? God, what, two years? You look good."

Pol smiled. He had forgotten how raggedly the man spoke. Medicine, more than most magics, did not require a surplus of intelligence. The body was relatively simple, after all. During their affair, Pol had picked up more than a passing knowledge of medicines from Jarres—a fact that probably accounted for the relationship's dissolution. Medical mages guarded their trade secrets every bit as jealously as other disciples of magic.

Pol clasped Jarres's forearms and kissed his cheeks. "Almost three years, Eamon." Thank Adrash the other man had spoken his name first. Pol had forgotten that in public Jarres preferred to use second names: the convention in Weas, the city of Jarres's upbringing. "You look well yourself. You have certainly filled out."

Jarres laughed, squeezing Pol's forearms in return. His teeth flashed, straight and white, contrasting with the heavy darkness of his beard. Laugh lines had deepened alongside his nose, around his light blue eyes. Pol remembered why he had been so attracted to the man, and reconsidered his stance on the beard.

They disengaged somewhat awkwardly, and Jarres looked Pol up and down again, one eyebrow quirked.

"Why are you here?" he asked.

Blunt as well as ragged, Pol recalled. Yet it was oddly refreshing after his meeting with Ebn.

"I am here to ask a favor. Have you a place where we can talk? Somewhere private?"

A smile fought to reach Jarres's mouth, and won. He closed his eyes for a moment and then said, "My shift is over in eighteen minutes."

‡

Exhausted, they lay together on Jarres's bed. Pol had thrown a leg over the man's thigh, but felt otherwise content to dry alone. Unlike most eldermen, Pol enjoyed the feeling of fluid on his skin. Large bodies of water made him uncomfortable and he did not enjoy swimming, but the occasional bath was nice. Sweat was nicer. A uniquely human smell, sweat. He had come to appreciate it in the same way he had come to appreciate the smell of lake water.

Jarres blew a stream of pipe smoke at the ceiling. "Now that we're relaxed, let's have the truth. You've got a great many men to choose from in this city, which means you're here for something other than a simple fuck."

"True," Pol conceded. "I am. Do you remember when you talked about the black market with me? You had a friend."

Jarres turned his head away from Pol. "Yeah, I remember all right. They let Kolin go, Espe nearly went to jail, and I had to talk before the head surgeons—was forced to defend myself when I'd done nothing wrong. If you're looking for that sort of thing, I think you better look someplace else. Thanks for the lay, but I can't help."

"I'm not asking you to start up a business, Eamon." Pol laid a hand on Jarres's lean stomach. "I need a few things only. Me. I need them. No one else will know what we are doing and no one knows how much alchemy the corpses have in their veins until you mark it down. You could do it. You said it yourself." He inched his hand downward slowly. "Or were you just bragging?"

Jarres groaned—not in pleasure, but frustration. A bit more pushing and he would relent, Pol thought. He felt confident in his ability to reduce simple men to formulae, spells to be cast and then molded. His clawtips moved lightly through Jarres's thatch of pubic hair. The man's cock shifted, began to swell.

"I will be honest with you," Pol said. "My research is at a standstill, and

I have no friends at the academy. I cannot afford to pay you much, but you will have my gratitude."

Jarres chuckled, and pushed Pol's hands the final inch.

"Just your gratitude, huh?" he asked.

Pol smiled. "This is how I show my gratitude. But you need to do this per my instructions, Jarres. I need specific things."

Jarres flexed his hips and sighed, this time with pleasure. "Yah, I can do that, I suppose. You have a list?"

"I will write it out for you afterwards. I know you must be careful not to arouse suspicion, but the faster you do this for me the more grateful I will be."

"Understood," Jarres said. He yawned and stretched out under Pol's ministrations, clearly enjoying himself. "When you're finished there, how about celebrating our new arrangement? Visit the docks, see a fight like old times?"

Pol considered. It had been some time since he had seen a fight, and even longer since he had seen a good one. The docksides attracted the best. Still, there was work to be done. Planning.

Before he could answer, Jarres spoke. "You've heard of Shav? No. He's a quarterstock they've got fighting tonight. A close cousin of yours, maybe."

Pol stopped considering instantly. He would go. He had never seen an elderman's offspring, and knew no one who had. Though elder sperm fertilized any species' egg, the product of the coupling was seldom fertile. On the rare occasion that it was, its offspring suffered extreme birth defects. This quarterstock Jarres spoke of was possibly such a one. Most likely, the whole thing was a hoax, but it could not be ignored on that basis alone.

Pol wondered why he had heard nothing of it. Academy biologists estimated the world population of eldermen to be less than one hundred thousand. They were expensive and risky to gestate, but highly valued for their magical facility. Surely the living child of one would be of interest.

Or perhaps even some use.

‡

The walk from Jarres's apartment took them through two of the roughest neighborhoods in the eastern quarter of the city.

Composed of southern Ulomi and western Castan immigrants respectively, the populations of Donsiter and Torn would not brook the other's existence. Tansot's governors had on several occasions begun campaigns to turn the tide of sectarian violence, but to no avail. With the support of the city's conservative Adrashi churches, the Ulomi of Donsiter were slowly gaining the advantage over their atypically militant Castan neighbors.

This did not make Donsiter any safer. Though its denizens strutted outwardly, inwardly they feared Torn's increasingly desperate acts. More than this, perhaps, they feared being in the churches' debt. The churches would remember and extract two grams of bonedust for every gram spent in assistance. In fact, they had already begun. The church soldiers stationed in Donsiter took what they pleased.

Torn, on the other hand, had peopled itself with criminals, men and women the seniors of the community hired to help wage their war. Murderers and thieves, out-of-work and disgraced soldiers of the Tomen border, Anadrashi reformists and scrabbling gladiators, all of whom took the money offered to them and caused trouble. The streets became a place to air one's grievances with one's fist or weapon.

After dark, a man took his life in his hands if he walked the streets of either neighborhood with less than two men at his side.

Pol and Jarres armed themselves accordingly. Pol carried his hand-carved liisau, a seven-foot tall ironwood staff tipped with a foot-long dagger blade and butted with steel. He had designed the weapon to suit his unique fighting style, which blended the staff arts common to eastern Knoori and the many bladed styles of Pusta.

Jarres carried nothing so exotic. Holstered over his left shoulder was a compound crossbow, an ugly little quickdraw that had probably cost him a week's salary. Castans were famously skeptical of magic and the reliance on magic, often arming themselves with muscle-powered arms rather than the more common alchemical varieties. At his right hip swung a vazhe, a short, heavy broadsword held in contempt by nearly all Stoli swordsmen. *Better for chopping wood,* they claimed, glossing over the fact that vazhe-wielding Castans had kept Stol out of their border for nearly seven hundred years.

Pol's staff-end rang hollowly on the hard-packed earth. He refused to slink in the shadows like an animal, and had not asked the other man's opinion. Jarres did not appear overly discomfited by this.

Though he would not admit so, Pol found himself wishing for a confrontation. He had restrained his anger with Ebn. He had been patient with Jarres. He could not be otherwise, for his plans depended on Ebn's ignorance and Jarres's assistance, but the acts would never be enjoyable. Now, he wanted release.

Unfortunately, no one presented him with an opportunity. The night was quiet but for the rustling of scrawny sycamore trees lining the roadway. Before very long they arrived at Docksides Boxing, a large, low-roofed building on a floating platform at the end of two stationary docks. They stopped at the entrance to one, where a doorman waited under a single torchlight.

Pol became impatient as the sunken-eyed man held their entrance fee, a half-gram bag of dust, open under his nose. *As if the man could discern anything with such dull senses*, Pol thought. Academy studies revealed that most of the bonedust used as payment in the city tested below forty percent pure. Ground sheep bone was the most common filler. If properly trained, an elderman could smell the difference. A human? Never.

Jarres became impatient as well. "Satisfied?" he asked the doorman, whose skin looked like wrinkled parchment in the flickering light.

The doorman shrugged. "Suppose so. Smells okay. But this ain't enough."

"Not enough?" Jarres shook his head. "Put it on the scale."

Pol grinned at the doorman's expression. It was a serious insult, asking a money handler to weigh dust. The doorman spat at Jarres's feet and then dropped the waxpaper bag on the scale on the stool beside him.

"I told you," he said. "Half a gram. Not enough."

Jarres laughed, but there was a definite edge to it. "The entry has always been half a gram. What are you trying to pull?"

"Not tonight, it ain't half a gram." The doorman folded the bag and held it out so that Jarres could either take it or add to it. "Tonight's one whole, on account of the quarterstock we rustled up. Idiot's fighting that bitch Stasessun everybody loves. She's gonna kill him for sure. Biggest fight in a long time. So, one gram. Pay or leave."

Pol took out a thin leather wallet. "Here," he said, handing the doorman another bag. "Half a gram of pure, and if you insult me by smelling it I will probably murder you where you stand."

The doorman looked unimpressed and started to open the bag. Pol stepped into the cone of torchlight and leaned forward, forcing the man to look into his eyes.

"Shit," the doorman said, backing against the light pole. "Okay. Okay. I don't need to smell it. Don't touch me, please."

Pol straightened, pretending shock. "Surely, you do not think I want to?"

Jarres clapped him on the back and they entered Docksides Boxing. The tension in Pol's shoulders began to ebb away as the smells reached him.

Sawdust. Blood.

Sweat.

‡

The quarterstock Shav was not a hoax. Pol had caught glimpses of him through the crowd before the main fight began. Rolling his immense scarred shoulders, loosening his bullish neck.

In most ways, he seemed the perfect compromise between human and elderman. His skin was lustrous, a rich lavender hue, and Pol could see a fine sheen of sweat on his brow. Well over six feet tall, he must have weighed close to four hundred pounds. Thick slabs of muscle hid the slight skeletal and ligamentary anomalies of his build, but he stood with a slight forward tilt like an elderman, as if he were always on the balls of his feet. Any half-competent anatomist would be able to identify the subtle differences at first glance.

His copper hair was trimmed to stubble and his features were thicker, softer than an elderman's. No sign of physical retardation marred his face.

One detail alone surprised Pol: two stubby horns sprouted high on either side of Shav's forehead.

The victor of the last fight, still swaying unsteadily, announced the main event.

"Stasessun!" many in the crowd chanted. It grew as more picked up the call.

A tall, coffee-skinned woman of ambiguous ethnicity, heavily tattooed and clad in simple gauze wrappings, stepped from the crowd. Pol could tell from her walk alone that she would be a formidable opponent. Her limbs were thin blades of muscle and bone.

The whistle sounded. She came out fast and strong, swarming around the lumbering Shav, who ducked his head into two meaty fists and took the onslaught of jabs and knee thrusts. He did not attempt to fight back, and the crowd laughed. They clearly thought the fight a washout, the quarterstock a moron. At the end of round one, he looked flushed but unhurt. Stasessun rolled her eyes, and sat facing away from him in her corner.

She started taunting him in the second round. She spat, cursed, and laughed, all the while taking carefully placed potshots at his ears and shins. Most of the crowd laughed with her, but a few held back. Late in the round, having taken her abuse without fighting back for almost three minutes, Shav launched a slow but well-timed cross that glanced off Stasessun's temple and sent her staggering. She snarled and came forward, landing a few rapid blows before the whistle sounded.

"I'm impressed," Jarres told Pol. "I've seen only a few men go past the second round with her."

Shav smiled as he walked to his corner. He bled from multiple cuts around his ears. Bruises pocked his forearms and shins. A few in the crowd crossed to his corner to offer words of encouragement. Stasessun's fans looked on in annoyance. The mood had taken a turn.

The third round began. Stasessun came forward, unsmiling. She hopped from side to side as the quarterstock watched from between his fists, the unmistakable glint of calculation in his eyes. Her first punch got through, landed square on his chin. He shook it off but did not recover in time to block the two kicks that followed, landing on either thigh. He grunted and watched her, taking hits.

By this point the crowd was subdued. They watched Shav, and waited.

The moment came. Stasessun moved in close, following a right jab with a left shovel hook to Shav's temple. He caught her fist halfway to its target and, quicker than Pol would have thought possible, caught her under the chin with an uppercut—a gracefully fluid move that lifted her off her feet.

The sound of bone breaking was clear and distinct in the silence.

She landed on the floor, neck clearly broken. Her life bubbled from her lips.

Shav tipped his head to either side, vertebrae popping loudly.

After a short pause, the crowd erupted. Pol yelled with them, cares for the moment forgotten. Men jostled against him, unconcerned that he was elderman and they human. Someone slapped his backside and he did not turn to see who had done it. He pictured Ebn there with him, back to back with the rabble, and laughed out loud. She would never understand the allure of violence, the intoxicating feeling of forcing another to submit.

"Hey!" Jarres yelled in his ear. "You want something to drink?"

"Yes," Pol answered immediately. The response surprised him. When had he last been intoxicated in public? A year? Two? No matter. Surely Adrash would approve a sacrament in his honor. In return, he would bless Pol with wine and song and violence—perhaps even a new friend in the struggle to come.

"Yes," he repeated, peering over the crowd to locate Shav. He had no intention of letting the quarterstock disappear without introducing himself. "I will definitely have a drink."

PART TWO

VEDAS TEZUL

The Castan Badlands lay beyond Nbena, the fifteenth gate in Dareth Hlum's five-hundred-mile-long defensive wall of Dalan Fele. Since very few had business in the badlands and no one traveled to the region for pleasure, most of the routes leading from the capitol to Nbena were ill maintained. Many could be dangerous to the unprepared traveler.

Roads that had long ago become footpaths climbed over the Turilen Mountains and crumbled into the Puzzle Sinklands. Cannibal tribes, descendants of Castan infantrymen who fought in the Third Autumnal War, preyed upon the unwary traveler in the Unes Forest. Though a few villages survived off the minimal trade closer to the gate, their people lived in fear of raiders who came from out of the scrubland. Child slaves moved through Nbena like water through loosely stacked rocks, and none of Dareth Hlum's governments had been able to put a stop to it.

Vedas and Berun took a winding, eleven-day route to the badlands gate, averaging just short of twenty miles a day. Though the pace did not tax Vedas overmuch, it took several nights to become accustomed to sleeping under open sky, and even longer to accept the reality of travel rations. His stomach grumbled constantly. He measured the fullness of his biceps and thighs, trying to gauge the extent of muscle loss day by day. Perhaps the twenty pounds he had gained in anticipation of Danoor would be insufficient.

Largely out of a feeling of obligation, for several days he attempted to engage Berun in conversation. The constructed man had little to say on the subject of fighting and war, however—little to say, period. When he did speak, he seemed sullen, as though resentful of Vedas's presence. In an odd way, Vedas sympathized. He had not wanted a traveling companion either, but Abse had insisted.

Thus it was a relief to shrug off the burden of communication, and Vedas wondered if walking in silence would soon come to feel like walking alone.

Five days out from Golna, having seen no trace of raiders or cannibals, he began thinking Abse had exaggerated the perilousness of their route across the nation. He began to hope a peaceful journey would ease the memory of Julit Umeda's death.

This proved not to be the case. Far from the centers of law, violence found them.

Two men ambushed them as they rose on the sixth morning near the lakeside town of Adres. Vedas met the first, slapping the clumsy sword-thrust aside with his palm and jamming suit-stiffened fingers into the man's temple, knocking him unconscious. Berun ignored the axe thrown by the second. It clanged harmlessly off his brass shoulder as he threw one of the stones he carried into the bandit's face, lifting the man off his feet and killing him instantly.

"That was unnecessary," Vedas said.

Berun shrugged. "They intended to kill us. They would have killed others."

The bandits wore identical silver necklaces, from which hung a golden pendant in the shape of a fist. Though valuable and by rights the victors', Vedas refused to remove them.

"They're Adrashi symbols," he explained to Berun.

"What harm would it do to take them?" the constructed man countered.

"None. But I won't dirty my hands with the task."

On the seventh day, a woman appeared on a narrow pass between the Sawback Mesas and broke a spell before them, rooting their feet in the mountain itself. Quicker than Vedas could have imagined, Berun decoupled the spheres below his ankles and jumped free. By the time he landed, his feet had fully formed. He swept the woman into the rock wall. She rebounded, and then crumpled to the ground. To free Vedas, Berun pulverized the rock around his feet. Vedas's suit stiffened under the blows, shielding him from injury but for a broken toe.

The woman bled liberally from a shallow wound above her ear, but appeared otherwise uninjured. Vedas tore a strip of cloth from her voluminous robes and wrapped it tightly around her head.

Berun lifted the leather pack from her shoulder and searched it. In addition to a pouch of dried meat and a solid ball of catgut, she had carried with her twelve spells, ranging from colorless liquids in ampoules to waterproofed firestarters. The largest was a tiny porcelain jar sealed with wax.

"I won't touch them," Vedas said. The sight of the unknown magic chilled him to the core. "We don't know what they are. Besides, I've heard stories about what happens to men who steal witches' potions."

"I'm not a man," Berun answered. "They must be useful or valuable to someone." He pressed the collection of spells to his thigh. When he took the hand away, they were gone.

Vedas did not want to kill the fourth attacker, an emaciated young man who rushed at him from a barley field deep in the heart of the Wruna Valley. Vedas disarmed him of sickle and rake easily enough, and aimed a knockout blow to his temple. But regardless of what he tried, the boy would not go under. Eventually Vedas noticed the symptoms: dilated pupils, puffy hands, and a white crust at the corners of his mouth.

Dropma Fever, spread through sweat and saliva. Given the appropriate medicines, a full recovery might have been possible, but the closest village was nearly ten miles back along the road, and the young man was in no condition to lead Vedas to a nearby homestead. Possibly, the whole region had become infected.

Fearful of contracting the disease, Vedas would have asked Berun to kill the boy, but the constructed man had run ahead to scout the hilly path before them. Not for the first time, Vedas regretted leaving his staff in Golna. Abse had forbid him to take Order property. A good ironwood staff cost almost as much as a month's provender.

No help for it, Vedas thought. He allowed his suit to mask his face and broke the boy's neck with one blow.

He still stood, fully sheathed in his suit, when Berun came pounding down the road several minutes later.

The constructed man looked from Vedas to the boy and back again. "Why did you do this? And why have you covered your face?"

"The boy was sick. Dropma Fever. I fear I might have contracted it." Vedas held his hands out from his hips, afraid to touch the rest of his body. He possessed little practical knowledge of disease. "I think my suit will protect me, but I won't be sure for a few days."

Berun shrugged, apparently unconcerned.

"I'd like to wash myself," Vedas said. "Did you see any water ahead?"

"A creek runs across the road a few miles from here."

Vedas washed himself as best he could. They began walking again.

Two day later, they crested a rise and saw the three-hundred-foot slopes of Dalan Fele.

Berun appeared unimpressed. He had seen it several times.

Vedas remembered it only dimly from childhood. He breathed shallowly from lungs that felt stuffed with cotton, tried to take in the scope of the wall rising over the tallest trees and disappearing to view on either side, and collapsed.

‡

The memory of being carried, swaying from side to side, cradled in rock-solid arms. The sun in his eyes, then shadow overtaking. A wall stretching above him. The wall falling, rising, falling again, a gigantic door. Two glowing blue orbs, hovering in the air. A cold, brassy voice repeating his name. More voices, yelling, echoing on stone. The whisper of canvas. Warm light suffusing, the world organizing itself. Tent poles. Being laid on a soft surface. Blackness. A new voice.

Focusing on the voice, rising up through layers of pain.

Vedas woke, and found that he could not scream.

"The suit should have protected him," a man told Berun. "That is, if he wore the mask the entire time." He adjusted his spectacles and stared up at the immense man of brass standing silently before him. "Did he wear the mask the entire time?"

"I wasn't there and he didn't tell me," Berun answered. "Can he see us right now?"

The man leaned over Vedas. He filled a tiny plunger on the bedside table and moistened Vedas's eyes. Once opened, they seemed unwilling to close.

"I don't know," the man—a doctor, Vedas belatedly surmised—said.

"Will he die?"

The doctor swallowed and looked down at Vedas again. "I don't know that either. He's still in the intermediate phase of the disease, which is good. Receiving the spell before the fever breaks increases his chances of recovery considerably. If the spell doesn't cure him, though, and his fever breaks, he'll only have a few days before the disease destroys his mind, turning him into an animal. Death will follow soon after."

"Is that why you've bound him?"

The doctor lifted his hand from the leather wrist strap it rested upon. "Yes. I can't predict when the fever will break, it happens so suddenly. He could be dangerous."

Struggling to focus on the conversation, Vedas's mind swam through a fog of heated torment. Every breath was agony, as if someone were holding a live coal against his ribs. The pulse throbbed in his head, a rhythmic pressure that compressed his eyeballs and sinuses. Every muscle in his head and neck ached with tension, and he could not unclench his jaw. His limbs did not pain him, but their numb unresponsiveness was troubling.

He saw the world through thick, milky glass. He could neither move nor close his eyes. When the doctor moistened them, his vision cleared only a little.

"Why haven't you unclothed him?" Berun asked. "Won't he be too hot?"

Vedas's heart threw itself against his sore ribs. He tried to move, to open his mouth or at least moan. He had not removed his suit in two decades. Only his head, anus, and the tip of his penis touched open air. He had heard of others removing their suits from time to time, but the Thirteenth taught that true connection with one's suit could only be achieved through constant contact. The thought of a stranger removing it, touching its inner surface, filled him with rage so strong it sang in his bones.

The doctor sighed. "No. Even though I live in Nbena, I'm not a fool. I used to live in Ulias, where I worked on a number of suited men. I know how elder-cloth works. Look." He laid a hand on Vedas's chest. "Do you feel that? How cold it is?"

Berun scowled. "Hot and cold mean nothing to me."

The doctor cleared his throat. "Ah. Then you'll have to trust me. Your friend has a deep connection with his suit. In a way, it knows what he needs and is trying to provide it to him. Without the suit, I suspect his fever would already have broken. Either that, or he would be dead."

Berun shifted from foot to foot, the spheres of his body whispering against each other. "You won't let him die."

"I have very little say in the matter," the doctor said. "And you haven't paid me."

An odd sound, like marbles being rubbed together in a child's hand, came from within Berun's body. A moment later, a box composed of small spheres emerged from his stomach. He plucked it free and it collapsed in his hand, revealing a collection of multicolored bags. He selected one and passed it over Vedas's body to the doctor.

The man held the bag up to the skylight. "This is good for half."

Berun selected another. "I thought I was being generous with the first."

The doctor met the constructed man's stare. "That was generous last year."

"You won't let him die," Berun said again.

The doctor shook his head wearily, slipped both bags of bonedust into his vest pocket, and turned to the bedside table. He returned with an ampoule of amber liquid, and broke it open. Vedas distantly felt the doctor's fingers as they peeled his lips back from his clenched teeth and poured the liquid down. He did not taste the spell or feel it trickling into his throat.

The smell of iron did reach his nose, and quickly overcame his senses. A shutter closed over his eyes, leaving him in complete darkness. The pain shut off suddenly. Vedas found himself alone in his mind, unable to sense his body. He drifted, untethered. No eyes, no ears, no nose—nothing. For a timeless moment, he was not a man. Maybe the spell had banished him to a far ashen corner of his mind so that it might work on the disease. Maybe the spell was not in fact working, and now he simply waited for his body to stop functioning.

Berun's last words came to him without a voice: *You won't let him die.* The phrase repeated over and over again, confounding in his current state, neither dead nor alive. *You won't let him die. You won't let him die.*

Suddenly, light burst through cracks in the shutter before his eyes and he found himself back in his body. A scorching needle bit into his mind and set his skin aflame. Every joint in his body cracked at once. He screamed, arching up from the mattress, straining at the straps that bound him. Hard, cold hands the size of shields pressed him down. Someone else pressed a wet rag to his forehead. As the sedative spell contained therein seeped into his skin, he felt the overwhelming urge to shut his eyes. His eyelids dragged closed, burning like sore muscles being stretched.

His screams became words.

"Take me home!" he yelled.

"Take me home!" he rasped.

"Take me home," he whispered before falling into unconsciousness.

‡

In the warm interior of the doctor's tent, Vedas drifted in and out of sleep. Dreams weaved around him, meshing fluidly with waking moments. A large man of gold rubble stood beside his bed, fell to the ground, rose in the body of the fever-mad young man he had killed on the road to Nbena, and then shrank to become a young girl with a black sash tied around her left arm. A candle wavered before his eyes. The flame dropped upon him, engulfing him without heat or pain. Someone spoke his name, and Vedas recognized his own voice, his father's or mother's voice, Abse's voice—droning, becoming music.

Time stretched and contracted as it does for the drugged. The passage of the moon above the ventilation hole in the tent's ceiling took hours, and the changing of the sheets under him happened in a handful of seconds. His body reacted unpredictably to touch. He neither grimaced nor groaned when someone palpated his ribs and chest, underarms and neck. He laughed instead. Tears flowed from his eyes when someone put a warm rag on his forehead.

Finally, darkness descended on his mind, complete and total immersion. He slept soundly.

"Do you hear me, Vedas?" someone said.

Vedas opened his eyes. A slow, luxurious process, letting light into his skull. It spread from there, suffusing his whole body, centering in his stomach and genitals. A warm tingling, similar to but infinitely better than blood rushing into a numb limb. Though he had experienced the effect of a spell wearing off before, this proved to be a different sensation entirely.

He smiled. The muscles of his face were sore, but it felt good nonetheless. He lifted a hand to his chest and exhaled with relief. They had not removed his suit. As reality crept back, he enjoyed the texture of smooth fabric and muscle underneath his fingers. His hand drifted over the ridges of his stomach and paused.

An erection pushed almost painfully against the fabric of his suit.

A polite cough. "Can you hear me, citizen Tezul?"

Vedas's head swiveled to regard the doctor. His hand fell to his side. "Yes, I can."

"Good." The doctor pressed fingertips against Vedas's chest, ribs, and stomach. "I think you can stand now, but not too quickly. You're still weak."

Berun walked into view. "Here," the constructed man said, offering Vedas two fingers to hold onto. Vedas gripped them and rose on rubbery legs. His bowels felt loose. Everything hurt. Running fingers over the wiry stubble on his head, he found that even his scalp was tender. Now that the novelty of the world had begun to leach away, the light in the room was too intense, the noise from outside a painful racket.

"We're still in Nbena, I assume," he said. "How long have we been here?"

"Just one night," Berun responded. He looked over Vedas's head at the doctor. "Do you have instructions? Medicines to give him?"

The doctor shrugged. "He's not dead, so the spell worked. He's cured. I'd recommend at least one night's rest before continuing your journey, plenty of water, and food. The pain is mostly muscular tension, which will fade in time. If you want to buy more sedative spells, I'll gladly sell them, but they aren't good for him."

Berun shook his head. "No. He'll deal with the pain."

‡

The town simply called itself Nbena. Its citizens on both sides of Dalan Fele wore metal badges, which allowed their free movement from one nation to the other. Apart from the Autumnal Wars, the last of which had occurred three centuries previously, Dareth Hlum and Casta enjoyed a congenial relationship. Dareth Hlum looked upon Casta as a younger, less civilized version of itself, while Casta considered Dareth Hlum amusingly tidy and idealistic.

The different personalities were reflected in Nbena's layout. On Dareth Hlum's side, the streets formed a grid. They were wide and clean, and the evenly spaced clay buildings that lined them were unpainted. Quietness and sobriety ruled. Even the stunted oaks appeared at regular intervals. On the Castan side, roads existed where foot and barrow wheel needed them to be. They were uniformly dirty. Once-brightly painted buildings leaned over alleyways and crumbled cheap bricks onto the street. Loudness and gaiety ruled.

The doctor had recommended an Anadrashi tavern on the Castan side named Brickchurch. Unlike its neighbors, it had been carved into the sheer stone facade of Dalan Fele itself. To Vedas, raised believing in the wall's impregnability, this seemed almost sacrilegious.

Standing before the tavern's doorway, he swayed as a brief spell of dizziness nearly overtook him. Black motes swam at the corners of his eyes and an odd pressure built in his ears.

Berun's fist closed around his bicep. "Steady. You have to eat. Come on." He led Vedas into the tavern's dim interior, where the air was cool and still and smelled of stone. Eyes followed the pair as they navigated the furniture and sat at a rear corner table.

Vedas leaned forward on his forearms, fighting the urge to drop his throbbing head onto them. "This isn't pleasant."

Berun grunted. "What do you want?"

"To go back to sleep," Vedas answered immediately. "I'm hungry but I don't feel like eating, which is a first." He licked chapped lips and reconsidered. "I suppose I could eat, but before that I need a pitcher of water. Plain, no lemon or mintgrass, and I'll pay the extra for ice. Then I'll eat whatever they have in the kitchen. I'm not picky."

Berun walked to the bar and ordered. Vedas watched him through half-closed lids, feeling a vague sense of unease. *You won't let him die*, the constructed man had said—but why had he said it? They were nothing more than traveling companions. Such concern made Vedas uncomfortable. He liked uncomplicated relationships, and disliked owing favors.

"Excuse me."

Vedas's eyes snapped open. Only a handful of seconds had passed, yet a woman now stood before him, short sword naked on her left hip. By the look of her corded arms and shoulders, she knew how to use it. Vedas shifted his hips slightly and inched his right hand over the table's edge for leverage. It would not be a graceful move if he were forced to defend himself. The slightest tensing of muscle in his legs and back stung sharply.

The woman's pale eyes held his. "Your name is Tezul, right? Vedas?" She spoke with a slight Onsi accent. Her voice was deep but not unfeminine.

"Yes," he said.

"And your companion? He's the construct Berun, right?"

"Yes. Who are you?"

She shifted her weight in an odd fashion, as if she had suddenly become uncomfortable. She gestured to the chair across from him. He nodded and she sat, crossing her legs to the side. For a moment he fought the temptation, and then glanced quickly down. Her calves and thighs were well formed, muscular, freckled and hatched with scars. The tattoo of a sea serpent wound around her right ankle. She brushed short brown hair from her forehead and yawned, revealing a gap between her two front teeth.

Berun arrived, index finger hooked around the handle of a pitcher. The woman turned to stare up at him.

"Who are you?" he said.

"What is that?" she asked, nodding at the pitcher.

"Water. With ice."

She made a sour face. "My name is Churls. Churls Casta Jons. I have a proposition for you."

BERVN

The air grew sharper as they ascended into the badlands. Berun noticed it as a minute change in the sound of his spheres rubbing together, while Vedas experienced nosebleeds.

"You'll get used to it," Churls told him.

"Nosebleeds?" Vedas asked without a trace of humor.

She started to laugh and caught herself. "No. No, I meant the air. You'll get used to the air." She stared at her feet, opening and closing her mouth as though considering her next words carefully. None followed, however.

Eventually: "It's even drier than I thought it would be," Vedas said.

"They do call it the badlands," she answered.

He frowned. "I didn't make the connection."

She shrugged. "That's... understandable."

Berun watched his companions carefully. He could see the thing between them, but not as if either yet recognized it. Their conversations were infrequent and stilted, though both kept at it. Churls and Vedas reminded Berun of certain individuals in the Seventeenth—men and women who, despite forming attachments, could not succeed in forming lasting bonds. The pressures of living and fighting together overwhelmed them.

Berun had never understood human sexuality. Then again, he had not given it much thought. He watched his companions because it interested

68

him, but he himself had no intention of assisting. If Vedas and Churls desired awkwardness, they had it. If they desired more, they would need to
broach the subject themselves.

The first day wore on with Dalan Fele straddling the horizon at their
backs. The nearly treeless ground, red like pitting iron, stretched before
them. Some geological process had tipped the floor of the world ever so
slightly, and before long Berun ceased to notice they trod an upward slope.
To either side barren, saw-edged hills rose, flanking them in straight lines.

"We walk on the bed of the river Zaos," Churls explained. "It stopped
flowing long before the birth of man, in the age of the elder."

She walked easily, eyes watchful. She squinted ahead and shadowed her
brow to stare into the sky. Berun wondered what she was looking for. He
had not spotted a ground animal since they started, and the only birds rode
the air so far above them they looked like specks. Golna had scavenger birds,
too. They were not dangerous as far as Berun knew.

His curiosity finally got the best of him, and he pointed these things out
to Churls.

"Those aren't birds," she answered. "It's a trick of perspective. A wyrm
could carry a man away in one claw, and probably tear even you apart.
Fortunately, they come down only every once in a while. Adrash willing, it
won't be today." She spat twice, an automatic warding gesture Berun recognized. "I'm being so watchful because there are animals that live below our
feet. Earthmovers. They crest about as often as wyrms touch ground. If one
does, it's best to recognize the signs early."

"They're dangerous?" Berun asked.

Churls shook her head. "Not at all. But wyrms are, and they love earthmover meat. They don't like men much, either, so I plan on being far away
from one if it lands."

Berun turned to Vedas. "Have you heard of this?"

Vedas grunted. Though he had started the day in good form, hours of
exertion had taken their toll. His face was flushed and his breath wheezed
from him. Still, he pushed himself, maintaining a quick pace on stiff legs,
only stopping to eat or drink. Even when coughing fits doubled him over,
he kept moving.

Again, Berun offered to carry his pack.

"Quit asking," Vedas said. "I'll get better by walking, not resting."

Berun shrugged, by now inured to the man's stubborn pride. Vedas would walk himself to death rather than admit weakness.

Churls, on the other hand, had gladly accepted Berun's help. Instead of dividing the ungainly packs between the travelers, she let him carry the huge bundle of firewood and the eight two-gallon bladders of water. She had watched in fascination as he drew the cords of the luggage into his back, so that they appeared to grow out of his metal flesh. The extra two hundred pounds bothered him not at all.

When darkness fell, shutting off the light as though someone had blown out a candle, they simply stopped walking and set up camp. Churls dropped her pack with an audible sigh and unrolled her wool-and-down sleeping bag. Vedas lifted the firewood and water from Berun's back and then watched as Berun punched a fire pit in the ground.

"Will that attract earthmovers?" Vedas asked Churls.

She shook her head. "Back when their magics were good, the badlanders used to try and raise the animals to the surface in order to hunt wyrms, but nothing they did worked. I doubt they never tried pounding on the ground."

Berun could only sense texture and vibration, not temperature. He surmised that it must be quite cold, however, for Churls sat as close to the fire as she safely could. The muscles of her jaw jumped as she chewed her gammon. Vedas, forearms crossed loosely on his knees, stared into the fire and occasionally allowed a glance in her direction.

Berun regarded one, then the other, wondering who would break the silence.

"You aren't cold?" Churls asked Vedas. She kept her eyes on the ground and spoke quietly, obviously more ill at ease now that night had fallen—now that she and Vedas were so close. It fascinated Berun.

"No," Vedas said. "My suit keeps me warm."

"Cool, too?"

He nodded. "It keeps me comfortable. Within limits."

"It makes you stronger and faster, right?"

"A bit."

"I've seen suited men before, of course, but never up close. The White and Black orders are less common in Casta and Stol than in Dareth Hlum, and those you see are almost always fully covered." She looked up. "You can make it move, can't you?"

Though he nearly always wore the skin-tight hood, Vedas had not yet covered his face in her presence. He smiled and the edges of the hood drew in around his features. In the shifting firelight, it looked like an illusion.

Churls's eyes widened. "When I was a child, vendors sometimes displayed elder-cloth at the fabric markets in Onsa. They don't let you touch."

She leaned toward him, hand out. "Can I?"

Berun saw Vedas's right hand tighten around his left forearm. The man nodded. Churls ran her fingertips over his shoulder, and then pressed her palm flat. In the firelight his suit took on the sheen of volcanic glass, and her hand stopped moving. It lay there, rooted to him, a part of him. The moment stuck, and Berun felt a faint vibration inside himself: the nearly imperceptible shudder of a spinning sphere deep within his chest. For an instant, it seemed that a hooded figure stood behind Vedas, hand raised in the air. Poised to strike. The gleam of silver metal.

The moment broke, and Churls's hand dropped. She stood to ready her bedroll, and Vedas met Berun's gaze across the fire.

"What are you looking at?" Vedas asked.

‡

Gradually, the earth became brittle. It cracked in tiny wavelets around their feet. The slope of the ground leveled out and the wind picked up. These subtle changes trickled into Berun's mind, as did the fact that another traveler had not come upon them since leaving Nbena.

Churls took out her compass more and more often. Berun let her, though he knew they had been traveling south in a straight line for two days. According to his internal map, they were currently some twenty-five miles from Dalan Fele, roughly the same distance from the southern coast of Casta. Staying the course, they would reach the ocean in another day. The ruins of the stone bridge that had once linked Was Anul to the mainland were visible from this shore, men claimed. On a clear day, the smoldering crown of the island itself could be viewed.

While the possibility of seeing these sights enticed Berun, he could not understand why Churls had chosen this route. Even the deserts of Toma held life, but the coast between Dalan Fele and the Steps of Stol was rumored to be barren, waterless. Already, the foliage had petered out to the occasional thorny jess tree. The clouds, too high to form rain, formed an impenetrable grey roof over their heads.

Vedas gave no sign he recognized anything out of the ordinary.

Not surprising, Berun thought. The man was a city creature, and even a competent tracker could lose his sense of direction with the sun buried in the clouds.

Berun considered the situation. He would let Churls lead without comment for another day. Surely, she did not intend to continue southward toward the Steps. Undoubtedly, she had a reason for diverting them. Perhaps she meant to avoid bandits or some other danger. He trusted her, in fact enjoyed her company. Aside from her awkwardness with Vedas, she projected a confident and easygoing nature.

The same could not be said of Vedas, a man who continually aroused Berun's ire. It was not the Black Suit's arrogance, taciturn manner, or sullen moods—Berun had encountered such things before, even in the best of men. No, the source of the antipathy lay deep within, as though it had been stamped upon every sphere of Berun's being. He found himself looking for new reasons to dislike the man. He fought the urge constantly, but achieved little headway.

It was not difficult to imagine the source of this manipulation. The illusion of the hooded figure the night before had proved it. Berun regretted the fact that Omali chose coercion over communication. He could not help wondering if his father had judged Vedas inaccurately.

He feared what he might be forced to do to the man.

Father, Berun broadcast. *What danger can Vedas possibly be to you? Speak to me.*

Less than twenty miles from the coast, they set up camp as they had the previous night. The ground crackled under them as they settled around the fire. Vedas—tired but visibly healthier than the day before—watched Churls prepare a soup of dried potatoes, vegetable stock, and salted mutton. She used a travel pot with a locking lid, so as to not waste water.

"May I hold your sword?" he asked.

"Sure." She turned on the balls of her feet, drew her short, dull blade and flipped it, offering it to him hilt first.

Vedas ran his fingers over the pitted steel but did not bother testing its edge. He stood and walked a few paces away, rolling his shoulders.

Stepping through several forms, his strokes were fluid and economical. Berun knew from conversation that barehanded and staff technique comprised the majority of the man's training, but it clearly had not ignored bladed weapons altogether. While he was not a master of the short sword, Vedas was by no measure incompetent.

"Not bad," Churls said after several minutes. "But you're treating it like a sword."

Vedas looked from the blade to her face, and back again. "I won't deny that."

She stood. "You miss my meaning. Any fool can see my blade has no bite." She held her hand out. "I stole my first sword from a dead infantrymen. My brother wouldn't let me run in his gang with people who knew how to hold or care for it properly, so I had to teach myself. I imagined every tree and fence post was an enemy, and hacked away."

The weapon came to life in her hands. Each attack was a steel blur punctuated by a moment of complete stillness, the end product of her viciously quick parries and thrusts. A crushing blow to the temple. A sideswipe aimed to crack ribs. A vicious upswing into the groin. With the weight of the blade behind it, her blows would likely pulverize even the thickest bones.

She stopped as suddenly as she started, and sheathed her sword. "I called my technique The Dull Sword. Quite creative, don't you think? Not surprisingly, I'm the sole practitioner of the art. It's not the beautiful thing fencing is."

Vedas shook his head. "I've never seen anyone use a sword that way," he said, voice soft with admiration. He turned away, coughing into his fist.

Churls dropped her head. Seeing further into the spectrums of light than a man, Berun saw the flush of her cheeks and drew his own features into a smile, a demon mask above the fire.

Vedas had finally done something charming.

‡

Berun scooped handfuls of dry dirt and snuffed out the fire. He brushed the char away from the larger pieces of wood, revealing the unburnt flesh underneath, and set them near the bundle to cool. This task finished, he soon became restless. Just as he had done the first night out, he cautiously began constructing sculptures out of the firewood. He moved slowly, as quietly as a snake whispering through grass.

Vedas and Churls did not stir, and so he proceeded to the next step, mirroring each sculpture by rearranging the spheres of his body—a slow, painstaking process. The arrangements became more complex as the night wore on, until finally he achieved his goal: a break in the link, so that one group of spheres no longer touched the other. As he broke the magnetic bonds of his being, an intense feeling of pleasure passed through him. His mind blinked rapidly on and off, each instant of existence mounting upon the other until he felt on the verge of decohering completely, scattering on the ground like droplets of mercury.

Creating sculptures and mirroring their shape had been his habit from the moment he woke in his father's foundry. Quite possibly, his father had instilled the urge in him out of compassion. Berun could not sleep or obtain sexual release, and so the sculpting occupied his mind and kept his vital energies from stagnation. He was, despite his mechanical composition, a being who had inherited a man's spirit, a man's needs.

On rare occasions, instead of sensual release he experienced a hallucination, the details of which never varied. His mind drifted of its own accord and rose above the world as it shrunk slowly below him, ripping open along a seam on its far side and spreading like a blanket under his feet. He counted the multitude of islands speckling the surface of the ocean. He lost himself in contemplation of the permanently spinning storm that lay on the other side of the world, sure that if he stared long enough the clouds would part, revealing what lay beneath.

Sustaining this vision for long was an immense effort. Something always drew him away. His father, no doubt, confounding his creation for arcane reasons once more.

Berun's curiosity burned intensely, yet there was little cure for it. The world was a known quantity, and had been for millennia. Several large land-masses lay just off the coast of Knoori, many of which bore the signs of ancient inhabitation by the elders. The remains of bridges, avenues that had once linked to the mainland, lay crumbled underwater. Beyond the islands stretched the ocean, breached here and there by tiny spurs of rock never meant to support life. The outbound mages of Stol had captured this image of Jeroun from orbit—a hundred times, a thousand. Reproductions had made their way across the continent long ago.

An unending storm across the ocean? Madness.

Tonight, Berun began to feel the call of the vision early on. It lay just under the surface of his consciousness, almost frightening in its potency. He felt as if he might fall forward, crack through the thin crust of earth at his feet and never stop falling. For the first time in his life, he fought to stay grounded in waking reality. He struggled to reconnect the two halves of his being, and failed. The towering buildings he had erected to mimic the sculpture trembled as wave after wave of dizziness crashed upon him. A voice spoke from the heart of the wooden city. The ground shook with its volume, drowning out the words.

Atop a tower of bronze spheres, Berun swiveled one searing blue eye, searching for his companions.

They were gone, as were their supplies. No indentation in the ground where Churls or Vedas had lain, no sign of the fire. Instead, before him spread the complete map of Jeroun, intricately drawn in the loose dirt. Danoor glowed like a molten glass bead, and a line of fire extended from it to Berun. On the other side of the world, the perpetual storm glowed as if an island of magma were being born under its cover. The Needle blazed in the sky above, stretching from horizon to horizon, closer and more radiant than the moon itself.

Berun looked down again to see an invisible finger tracing a figure in the dirt: a man with no features except for eyes and two small horns sprouting from his forehead.

"Father!" he bellowed. "Father, what is this?"

The unintelligible rumbling voice cut off abruptly, and the wooden city drew itself off the ground. Rustling, splitting and cracking, it formed the cloaked shape of Ortur Omali.

Affection swelled inside Berun so rapidly that he immediately questioned its authenticity. Without knowingly intending to do so, he rose and took on his familiar shape. He held Churls's sword, a ridiculously small weapon in his outsized right fist. A toothpick.

The mouth under the cloak smiled, a wicked arrangement of wood slivers. "What is this! What is this!" his father echoed. "A possibility. A potentiality. The Black Suit could be a snake, could be an eagle. Could be a worm, could be a leech. One thing is sure: he is the man to watch."

"Vedas," Berun said. "He's only a fighter."

"Appearances only. Is God a man?" Ortur Omali stretched elaborately, creaking like a dead tree in the wind. His fingertips were splinters, long and stiletto thin. Two pinpoints of light flared in each eye. "There is something odd about him, child. Something troubling, or possibly even encouraging. It is tough to tell the difference, sometimes. I may need him destroyed. You must avoid attachment."

"Why? How will you decide?" Berun had so many questions, yet his mind struggled through the confused logic of dream. His brows knitted in frustration. He brought his fist up and discovered that he could not open his hand to drop the sword.

"I don't need this to kill a man," he said. They were not the words he had intended to say.

The great mage laughed: the rustle of fallen leaves. "It is not a weapon, Berun. It is a demonstration."

The air wavered before Berun. It became a curtain of shifting darkness behind which the figure of his father shuddered and fell apart. The sound of twigs snapping came to Berun distantly, and the earth shuddered beneath him. A crack formed in the map drawn on the ground. A rent opened, its crumbling edge racing toward Berun. He tried to pick up his feet, but found them rooted in place.

He tipped sideways into the black chasm.

Abruptly, the vision ended.

Berun stood over Vedas's sleeping form. Churls curled in her sleeping bag a few feet to his left. Her sword belt lay on the ground next to her, empty.

The weapon was weightless in Berun's hand.

‡

They continued south in a straight line. The air grew colder, the wind stronger. Powerful gusts kicked up fine salt crystals embedded in the thin soil and flung them against exposed skin. Vedas covered his face. During the heaviest gusts he walked half blind, the suit material grown to cover his eyes. Churls pulled leather chaps and jacket from her pack and wrapped her head with the scarf she used as a pillow. Berun barely felt the wind or the abrading sand, but the going was slow for the other two.

They stopped just before the sun set. Instead of pounding down a fire pit, Berun concentrated to form a pick at the end of his arms and then tore a shallow depression in the hard-packed earth. He lined the windward side with excavated rocks to shield Churls and Vedas from the wind, which became even more ferocious after dark, ushered in from the ocean that lay only a handful of miles away.

It was time to broach the subject of Churls's route.

"Why aren't we headed west?" he asked after his companions had finished dinner.

Vedas looked up from the fire, turned his head to regard Churls.

She shifted, obviously uncomfortable. "I hoped I wouldn't have to talk about it." She sighed in response to Berun and Vedas's silence. "Really, I thought it was obvious. I thought maybe you'd seen the error in your plan."

"What error?" Vedas asked. "Why would we travel south?"

"Because of you," she said. Her eyebrows rose suggestively. "Don't you get it?"

"Me?" He frowned. "Are you mad?"

She sighed again. "Would you consent to travel with a cloak? Wear it at all times?"

Berun had discerned her meaning, but remained unconvinced. Before Vedas could answer, he spoke. "Casta is neutral and Stol is moderate Adrashi. There's no reason for Vedas to cover his suit."

Churls laughed. "Oh, yeah? Then I must be misinformed. I've waylaid us unnecessarily and I apologize." Her smile disappeared. "There are three tribes living in southern Casta. The Aumarveda, the Quinum, and the Lor, all three of which are devoutly Adrashi. They wouldn't hesitate to attack a heathen like Vedas. Fortunately for us, they do not venture near the ocean. Who would if they could avoid it?

"As for the moderate Adrashi of Stol, in general I've found them far less accepting to foreigners—Anadrashi foreigners in particular—than eastern lore has it. Even if Vedas is not attacked outright, he'll be a target for thieves and men eager for a fight in every hamlet. Added to this, Ulomi immigrants are common to the central valleys of Stol. Someone would undoubtedly recognize you, Berun. And unlike Casta, Stol is a land of magic users. Even you could get hurt. In all cases, a confrontation would hold us back. Our best option is to travel the Steps, where by all accounts the populous is sparse and peaceable, more concerned with living than fighting about religion."

Berun considered. The idea possessed a certain appeal. He had always wanted to see the Steps. "How far out of the way is your route?" he asked.

She licked her lips. "About five hundred miles."

"Out of the question," Vedas said. He appeared to calculate quickly. "That will put us in Danoor with less than a week to spare. It's possible we'd miss the entire tournament. We need time to settle in. There are training sessions, events in preparation for the tournament that I've promised to attend. My order must be properly represented." He looked at Berun. "Why didn't you tell me we were going the wrong way?"

Berun shrugged. "She's our guide. I trust her."

Vedas's expression did not change. "You trust her? Your master and mine gave us the route. Instead of heeding them, you're going to simply trust her?" He turned away. "I agreed to her company. I'll listen to her advice. I won't agree to this."

"Is that how you operate then, Vedas?" Churls asked, eyes fixed on the fire. "They tell you to jump and you jump? Well, their route is fucked. Neither

of you have been in this area before. Nor, I doubt, have your masters, otherwise they wouldn't have told you to travel through the middle of Stol. The
ground is fertile, and there are people everywhere. We couldn't avoid them.
You're lucky I'm here to set you off course."

She kicked at the fire. Sparks flew and streaked away with the wind.
"Listen, I want to get to Danoor as badly as you do. I have money riding
there—money I need. My route is your—our—best chance to get there in
one piece. So you'll miss the events leading up to the tournament. At least
you'll be alive to fight!"

She shook her head. "I admit that I need you. The journey would be too
dangerous for me alone. All I need you to do is trust that I know best."

The wind howled over them. Vedas grimaced and stretched out on his
bedroll.

How easy it would be to leave him, Berun reasoned.

The thought lingered in his mind. As one recalls a forgotten dream, he
realized he had been playing with the idea of abandoning Vedas for quite
some time. With less than a gallon of water and no navigation skills, being
caught in this corner of the world would have been the man's death.

In lockstep, a series of other memories came to Berun.

Yes, he had pictured Vedas Tezul's death, on many occasions. He had enjoyed it. The recognition of this fact horrified him. To have one's body bent
to the task of murder was a horrible crime—to have one's mind bent to hate,
yet another.

He waited for Vedas's breathing to change, signaling sleep.

"We'll do what he says," Berun rumbled softly. "He'll see that this route is
best. Still, I was wrong to keep this from him."

Churls closed her eyes. "Fine."

The fire died down to coals. "Why?" she finally asked.

"I'm not sure," Berun answered. "There's something about him. I think
you see it, too."

Churls scooped dirt and doused the coals. "No. I don't see anything."

CHVRLI CASTA JONS

The Steps began in the fertile southern plains of Stol, extending some seventy miles to the coast and more than four hundred along it. From a hundred miles away in southern Casta, the Steps had looked to Churls like nothing more than a smooth mountain slope. Closer, the scale was even harder to conceive. Ascending to a height of twelve thousand feet in seventeen evenly spaced, gently sloping rises, the Steps stopped abruptly at the ocean, shorn clean by a giant knife blade.

The elders had carved the Steps from the continent's longest mountain chain, it was said. For what purpose, no one knew. Along with the Dras Alas Citadel in northern Casta, the crystal dome over the island of Osa, The Inverted Bowl in the central valley of the Aspa Mountains, and the Glass Plain in northeastern Knos Min, the Steps of Stol displayed the enigmatic power of the elders. Many believed spirits and enchanted men inhabited such places. Immortal black magic practitioners and corpse miners.

As a result, the Steps were largely uninhabited. One of Gorum's friends, a scholar, had traveled southern Stol extensively. He claimed small, long-lived men lived upon the highest and most fertile steps, where unusually warm winds brought moisture in from the ocean. According to him, these men lived in a state of peace and primitive prosperity, knowing neither marriage nor jealousy. They shared their men and women, and Adrash smiled upon them. Even the rare Anadrashi who came through their lands was treated with respect.

Churls took the story with a grain of salt, for many of the tales she had heard differed markedly from the scholar's account. Nonetheless, she had been to the central valleys of Stol. Gorum was right: better to take her chances with tall tales and wishful thinking than violent reality. At the very least, fewer men lived on the Steps. Churls believed in odds above all else.

It was said a man could stand at the edge of the highest step and stare down at the glass-smooth face of the cliff, counting the geological layers of the world. It was also said a man must be careful at the edge, for sudden gusts could take hold of him and carry him far out over the ocean. Capricious, the demon winds sometimes returned him unharmed, but most often spun him in the sky, toying with him as a child does a rag doll. Bored, eventually the wind dropped him into the ocean or dashed his body against the wall.

Churls considered such tales bullshit. Wind was wind, and only an idiot stood up on a precipice when the gusts were strong.

Many years ago, she had shared bread with an acolyte of the Placci, a small elder-worshipping cult in Anlala. She claimed the elders had created the walls as permanent testament to their power. "They will stand immutable until the elders return to claim their kingdoms," she had told Churls.

Calves and thighs warm from walking uphill, she listened to Vedas tell a similar tale, and tried not to roll her eyes. Living in the city had filled his mind with so many ridiculous things. They walked a mere hundred feet from the edge. He could see for himself that the cliff face was not evenly cut. Shrubs took root in its crevices and huge sections had crumbled completely. Twice, they had to veer around immense rockslides. Though she never doubted some magical process had carved the Steps, she rejected the idea of their ensorcelment.

She had seen the Citadel at Dras Alas, and it too was crumbling away, eroded by wind and time.

So much for permanency, Churls thought.

‡

Each step consisted of a three-mile slope ascending seven hundred feet, topped by a two-mile stretch of grassy plain. Halfway through the first day, the clouds broke above them and warm winds blew in from the ocean, buoying their spirits and feet. By the time they stopped for the night, they had reached the base of the fifth step. Vedas, almost fully recovered from his illness, glowed with health and high spirits. For the first time in two weeks, he appeared to forget his anger over their course change.

His course change, Churls reminded herself. Berun had given Vedas the choice, after all. Thankfully, the man had seen the sense of her position. Not that being right had endeared her to him. Clearly, he was not the kind of man who forgave easily.

Churls observed him as they prepared dinner, and worried his good mood would dissolve when he woke to sore calves and thighs. Up until the Steps, they had traveled on relatively flat land. Climbing for so many miles, even at such a shallow grade, could take its toll on the fittest man.

The following morning, this proved true. Though he did not complain, Vedas looked like someone who had been run through a gauntlet. Exertion revived a slight cough, which he worked hard to conceal. The weather improved over the course of the day, blowing dry and warm, yet they still fell a mile short of the ninth step. After dinner, Churls read weariness and frustration on Vedas's features. She noted how he grunted as he stood to relieve himself.

He was a beautiful man, she admitted—but this alone did not explain her attraction. He had stubborn pride, but none of the ingrained arrogance that made so many men insufferable around women. He had little experience beyond that of fighting, but he learned quickly. Her short bow had become a formidable weapon in his hands, and he was patient enough to hunt with it. His navigation skills grew every day. On several occasions, he had noticed the signs of dangerous beasts before she did.

Certainly, she grew tired of his superstitions and his prejudices, though they did not surprise her. She had never considered Anadrashi any less prone to the irrational than their devout opponents.

What was the difference between a man who believed in God's love and a man who did not?

Nothing, as far as she could tell.

Why, then, did it feel as if there was something more to him? Why did he loom so large in her mind? She had seen beautiful men before. She had met talented, even genius men. It rankled her, being drawn as if by physical force to Vedas Tezul.

Who was he to warrant so much attention?

Berun believed in Vedas's uniqueness, surely. He had not tried to convince her that this was the case—had only mentioned it the once—but his feelings were increasingly obvious. He watched Vedas whenever the man was not looking, and Churls wondered what the constructed man saw beyond the graceful flow of muscle under the slick skin of Vedas's suit—the way the material clung to him, revealing more than it hid, emphasizing the rise and fall of his buttocks, the tensing of his broad shoulders.

She wondered what Berun saw in Vedas's restrained smile. Thick, sensuous lips framing straight white teeth made whiter against the darkness of his skin? Or merely a smile?

She had to shake off her arousal several times a day. It was pathetic and moreover worthless, feeling that way. Beyond the occasional glance at her backside or chest—a meaningless gesture, yet another male's inability to control his eyes—Vedas had never given any sign of returning her desire. Besides, she could not keep her big mouth shut. Each night, though she tried to keep the conversation neutral, she managed to offend him. He was so easily affronted, and she so easily discouraged.

If Berun were not there to interject now and then, the two would have parted ways out of frustration long ago.

Vedas returned to the fire.

"No Dull Sword tonight?" she asked. She had been teaching him the technique intermittently as they traveled. Though humorless, he was a good student. Of course he was.

He met her eyes briefly as he sat. "No."

"You'll feel better tomorrow," she said. "You're still breaking in your travel muscles."

He smiled tightly, little more than a grimace. "I had no idea there were so many muscles in the leg. I thought the hills of Golna were enough to prepare any man for simply walking uphill. And then there's my training. In the abbey, we use weighted gloves and staffs. We lift barrels of sand over our heads." He stretched his legs out and grabbed his ankles. He groaned. "I think I'd rather do that for twelve hours than repeat today."

The wind picked up. Berun shifted to the right and slowly made his torso flatter to shield the fire. "I wonder what it feels like to get tired," he said. "I notice when a task becomes more difficult, but I don't understand pain or tiredness. They're just words."

Vedas grunted and released his ankles. "You're not missing much." He angled his head to the sky. The Needle had not fully risen, and so he did not curse Adrash by touching the horns of his suit. Instead, he breathed in deeply, his taut belly inflating like a drum. "I smell pine trees."

"Me, too," Churls said. She frowned, deepening the lines around her mouth. "Wait a minute. There are no pine trees east of Anlala that I know of, certainly none in Dareth Hlum—it's too far east. How would you recognize the smell? You don't look like the kind of man who frequents perfumeries."

He grimaced. Once again, she had said the wrong thing.

"I may not look it," he said, "but I have on occasion. There are plenty of Knosi in Golna, but I wasn't born there. My parents came to the city when I was just a boy. I barely remember Grass, the city of my birth, but I do remember the smell of sagoli pines. The stunted trees lined our street like little old women in frocks. On the way across the continent, I smelled other types of pine. Slightly different smells, but mostly the same. Sometimes, I buy pine oil. I don't care what kind. Having the smell in my room reminds me of something... Something I might forget if I don't remind myself."

Berun shifted, but had nothing to add. He spun two rocks in his hands like Churls had seen monks do in Fali. They were nearly perfect spheres, diminishing in size every day. In a month, he had ground four pairs into marbles.

Churls simply nodded, and then retrieved her sword from beside her pack. With bonedust and spit, she started polishing, in truth to keep from confronting the silence. She could not name the emotion Vedas's words aroused in her. Sadness, certainly, but this was too general. Longing?

Yes. Longing.

Did longing make Vedas different from any other person she had known? Or was it that he chose to voice it when so many others would rather keep it buried? He did not have to say such things. He could just as easily lie, keep his secrets.

‡

Maybe he can't keep a secret, a voice said. *Maybe he's an honest man.*

Churls opened her eyes and growled softly.

She had not been sleeping soundly. Sometimes it felt as if she could predict when her daughter's ghost would appear, as though she had been drifting toward the meeting all day long. It felt disconcertingly similar to when she wandered in search of water, knowing in the back of her mind that it was close. She had always been a good tracker, a good hunter, and wondered if close communion with spirits was responsible.

Not one to indulge in such speculation by nature, Churls was forced by circumstances to consider the possibility. Five years ago, the ghost of her daughter had appeared, changing the structure of her world. The dead lingered in doorways and sat around campfires, just out of sight. The dead were real.

It was this, Churls knew, or admit she had gone insane.

She rose from her sleeping bag and walked away from camp. The moon was an iron shaving, the world shrouded. Daybreak was two or three hours away. She thought she saw the burning blue coals of Berun's eyes in the middle distance, but when she looked again they were gone, perhaps a figment of her imagination. Cool, humid wind flowed over the cliff's edge, instantly chilling her skin. Gooseflesh rose on her exposed arms and legs.

The ocean spread below her, a sky devoid of stars.

"Hello, Fyra," she said.

The girl appeared beside her. Churls fought the urge to step away.

I like him, Fyra said.

"Who?" Churls asked, though she knew full well whom her daughter meant.

Vedas. I like Vedas. You like him, too.

"I do," Churls said. "But I shouldn't. I have no reason to like him."

You think he's pretty.

Churls nodded. "He is. That's not enough, though."

Fyra walked two steps forward, to the edge. Her fine white hair lifted, became a halo around her head. Churls's fingernail bit into a scab on her forearm, puncturing it. Blood welled, and she smeared it with her fingertip until it became tacky.

"Why do you like him?" she asked.

A small shrug. *I just do. He's not like the other men you like. They say things they don't mean. They steal, they fight.*

"Vedas fights. That's all he does."

Fyra faced her mother. Churls met the stare, and it reminded her too much of looking in the mirror. Fyra had inherited so little from her father. Had someone in the afterlife told her about her half-sisters, who were curly-headed and olive skinned? Had she visited them, seen her father and stepmother?

What Vedas does is different, Fyra said. *He doesn't fight for money. He doesn't kill.*

"There's no difference, sweetie." Churls straightened her arms against her sides. "And Vedas has killed before. He's killed a lot of people."

By accident, Fyra insisted. *And the girl wasn't his fault, Mama.*

Churls wondered how her daughter knew these things. Had she been watching Vedas for long, or could she simply see into his soul? Churls did not like thinking that Fyra could read minds, but somehow this paled in comparison to the thought that her child had been observing Vedas since before they met.

And then it hit her. The obvious answer: Fyra simply believed Vedas. *Maybe he's an honest man*, she had said. Vedas had been forthcoming about his recruit's death, and Churls had only half believed him. She thought it equally likely that he had accidentally killed the child in the skirmish, and fled Golna to avoid the law. She considered this. Even while doubting his character, she had been attracted to him. Perhaps she had always believed him.

Foolishness, believing someone she did not know.

He doesn't understand you, Fyra said. *He doesn't understand people at all.*

"How do you know that? Maybe he just doesn't like people."

No, I'm right. I can see some of his memories—the strong ones, the ones that hurt. He tried to help the dead girl's parents, but he didn't know what to do. He wanted to say something, but instead he just stood there, looking uncomfortable while they cried. If you could see it, maybe then you'd understand.

Churls closed her eyes and took a step forward. The wind tousled her short hair. "He didn't say anything about that." She pictured Vedas ascending rickety stairs, knocking on a door, steeling himself to deliver the horrible news. Taking responsibility for the death of a child.

You should ask him about it, Fyra said.

Churls opened her eyes and found that her daughter had placed her tiny hand in Churls's own. She resisted the knee-jerk urge to snatch it away. But concentrating on the contact, she realized it felt like nothing. The breeze caressed Churls's hand, chilling the sweat on her palm. Holding her daughter's hand felt like air passing through her lungs.

You will, won't you, Mama, Fyra said. *You'll ask him?*

"I will," Churls said, and stood alone on the edge of the cliff.

‡

As she expected, Berun had not yet returned. Churls often woke in the hours before dawn, always to find the constructed man absent. He returned just before the sun rose. She never asked him where he had been. It was his business—productive business, sometimes. On four separate occasions, he had brought breakfast back with him. Two rodents with crushed skulls. Once, he had bagged a rodent and an owl, which Vedas refused to eat.

Each time, Berun had also returned with a new pair of rocks in his hands, ready to be ground down into marbles. Churls wanted to ask him about his nighttime activities, but could not find a way to broach the subject. Fairly certain he liked her, she did not want to run the risk of making him uncomfortable. He reminded her of Abi, the precocious child her sister had adopted. He even stood the same way, like he was waiting for instructions. Ever watchful. Sensitive.

Churls sat down, not tired in the least. Her eyes had fully adjusted to the night.

Vedas lay face down only a body-length from her, half on, half off his bedroll, posture unnaturally tense for a sleeping man. His left palm lay flat on the ground, but his fingers curled into the soil. He had pulled his right knee up until it was level with his waist, and the toes of his left foot pointed into the ground. Both calf muscles bulged with tension. He looked almost as if he were crawling, or climbing a wall.

Churls admired the twin curves of his buttocks, and wondered what would happen if she ran a fingertip between them. She indulged this fantasy while stroking her inner thigh. Her eyelids grew heavy as her fingers found their mark.

A sound behind her. A pebble shifting against another pebble.

Before she could move, Vedas pushed off the ground and leapt forward, aimed at a point just behind her. He twisted in the air as he flew, back grazing her left shoulder. She had barely begun to turn when his body, struck by something in midair, bowled over her. Pitching forward, she was unable to raise her hands before her face struck earth. Her lower lip peeled back and dirt ground against her teeth. A glancing blow, either Vedas or the thing he had caught, scraped along the right side of her head, nearly taking her ear with it. She roared into the ground.

A growl answered it.

Churls lifted her head in time to see Vedas and the cat disengage. He was a mere beat slower getting to his feet, and took a vicious swipe to the head. The blow should have taken his head off, yet he simply twisted his neck with the impact and kept moving. He circled the cat, a darkly furred, compactly muscular beast that must have weighed nearly as much as Vedas. It spat, hind legs twitching, front paw extended, swiping with dizzying speed whenever the black-suited man tried to close in.

Vedas took another hit to the head. Churls saw the white of the cat's claws, no less than two inches long. Again, Vedas took the impact as though it were a boxer's weak cross.

Churls rose to a crouch, the taste of blood and dirt in her mouth.

"Stay back!" Vedas yelled.

She had not noticed before, but he had masked his face completely. Unbelievable, that it alone had shielded him from the cat's claws. Unmindful of his warning, she snapped her head around to locate her sword, and crab-walked backwards to it. Its worn hilt felt good in her hands, but she doubted it would be of much use against the man-sized feline if it turned its attention back to her.

Snarling, the cat sprung toward Vedas. Falling under its weight, he caught its head in his hands before its canines found his throat. Slowly, he closed his fingers around its neck. Its back paws skittered along his legs, unable to hook claws into flesh. As Vedas's grip tightened, the cat thrashed ever more wildly atop his body. Its front paws slapped at his head, claws failing to sink in there as well.

Churls became aware of the sound coming from the animal's constricted throat. A low, almost human gurgle. She had heard the sound before. She had strangled men before.

She ran forward. Her blade passed through the cat's heart with expert precision, but the animal's seizures opened the gash wider, and then tore the sword from Churls's hands. Blood fountained from the wound, hitting her chest squarely, drenching her instantly.

Its heat shocked her, and she fell to her knees.

‡

The blood had created a tight film across her chest. It itched horribly, but she did not scratch at it. Her lower lip was swollen to twice its normal size, and the entire right side of her head burned as though it had been scoured with grit paper.

The sun had barely risen, and the world was beautiful. Almost six thousand feet below her and peppered with tiny islands, an expanse of bluegreen sea extended to the horizon. Sunlight passed through the shallow water as if it were glass, revealing the wrack-spotted sand below. Huge, paddle-finned reptiles drifted between the islands, their scale impossible for Churls to comprehend. Legend said the ocean was no deeper than a man could throw a stone, but this too was difficult to understand.

Men could not sail the ocean, so how could they know how deep it was?

The cat lay at Churls's feet. One leg had fallen over the edge of the cliff. Its fur was matted with blood and dirt. It had indeed been as heavy as a man. Berun had offered to carry it, but Churls preferred to do it herself. She had told the constructed man to stop apologizing. How could he have known a cat would attack?

Vedas lay recuperating. His suit had protected him from most of the damage, the fact of which still amazed Churls. She had examined his jaw and asked him to rotate his joints. Though these tests proved his injuries were not debilitating, his neck and right knee stiffened enough to worry her. Clearly, she reasoned, travel would have to wait until tomorrow. He complained, but Churls insisted he rest. She sprinkled suffun root over his breakfast, and he had fallen to sleep soon after.

It was an unexpected comfort, knowing that he lay in a deep sleep. The stress of hiding her attraction, of maintaining the fragile balance of moods between them, was so easily shrugged away. She did not have to think about answering his next question, proving to him again and again that she knew best how to lead them from one place to the next. She stood unclothed, relaxed as she always was after a fight.

She heard Berun's steps long before he reached her.

"I don't want another apology," she said without turning. "Save it for Vedas if you like, but I doubt he wants it, either."

"No apology," he rumbled. "There's a pond not far. I brought you water."

She turned. "I have…"

She shook her head. The constructed man dripped water from the bottom of his oddly distended belly. He had carried the water with him, but could not create a perfectly sealed container.

The spheres rolled away from the bathtub he had formed, and Churls peeked inside. She laughed.

"What?" Berun said.

"You brought a traveler with you. Look."

Berun's eyes rolled free from his face and tumbled slowly down his chest. Perched above the water, they observed the orange-scaled fish that swam in tight circles inside his makeshift stomach. He reached inside and cupped it against a wall.

"Keep it?" he asked.

"Too small," Churls said. "Feed it to the sea."

Berun nodded his great, eyeless head. "Yours, too."

Churls pushed the cat over the edge, and Berun threw the fish after it. The wind pushed both out from the cliff wall as they fell, arcing down to the distant waterline. Churls turned away when she could no longer see the cat's tumbling body, and climbed into Berun. The water was warmer than she had expected. A month's worth of grime floated free and mixed with the blood. Berun rearranged the floor of the tub, molding it under Churls's body.

She slept, and for the first time since leaving Nbena did not dream of Vedas.

EBN BON MARI

Every few years, she painted a new sigil on her voidsuit. The paint, a mixture of pigment, ground elder offal, bonedust, and reconstituted blood, soaked into the black leather, tattooing it near-instantaneously. The bond was permanent, and thus one had to be careful painting a sigil. A single misstroke and it was ruined, precious space and paint wasted. The elder skin needed to construct one voidsuit cost the academy nearly as much as a new building. Alchemical paint alone sold for forty times its weight in bonedust.

Ebn had never erred in her painting. For seven decades she had possessed one suit, the very same suit she had worn on her first jubilant ascension into orbit—a remarkable feat of preservation even among her peers, all of whom cared for their suits as if they were offspring.

Others constructed studios for their suits, directing sunlight through mirrored channels into mirrored rooms. Some kept theirs in cold storage closets, forcing a kind of stasis on the material. A few even doused their suits in alchemical light far more intense than nature provided. They hoarded their recipes, striving to reproduce the sun's spectrum of light exactly.

Ebn disapproved of these artificial means. She considered natural light more than sufficient for the nourishment of elder skin artifacts, and so kept her suit on a swiveling table enchanted to track the sun across the sky.

The demonstrable success of this technique, which seemed so crude compared to others, confounded many of her peers. Some attempted to replicate her setup, but ultimately could not rationalize leaving such a valuable possession out in the open.

It had not occurred to Ebn to worry about thievery for some fifty years. She had stitched spells of defense and detailed automation into the seams of her suit and sealed them with elder synovial fluid. The suit could defend itself physically and cast preprogrammed spells to ward off sophisticated attacks.

Like all articles of clothing composed of elder skin, the voidsuit developed a strong telepathic bond with its wearer. Ebn knew its condition at all times. With enough concentration, she could make it come to her. It lumbered like an ill-made construct, but it would power through enemies and walls in order to reach her. On an autumn afternoon in 12457, she had collapsed on the floor of the gymnasium, muscles unresponsive, the victim of a usurper's poisoning. Before the solution dragged her under completely, she summoned her suit.

It had carried her to safety, saved her life.

Though she knew it was not technically sentient, Ebn had never been able to stop herself from cooing to hers as she worked. Painting a sigil was an act of intimacy, a rare occasion to remove her gloves and let her tongues taste the air. They strained out of her palms, an oddly pleasurable sensation akin to stretching the tightness out of one's wrist, trying to lap at the paint as if they possessed minds of their own. By the time she finished painting, her hands were pleasurably sore from gripping the brush and keeping her tongues in check.

Her self-control all but spent, before capping the paint jar Ebn usually allowed her tongues to taste a tiny bit of paint. She dipped the straining tip of each organ into the thick brown fluid. The vague taste of iron and loam seemed to linger in her nose as her quivering tongues retracted into her palms. Bright motes, daylight stars, swam before her eyes. Her wrists twitched and she clenched her fists against the faint stirrings of nausea that preceded the euphoria.

She waited.

Though prepared for it, the wave always caught her by surprise. It lifted her off her feet and swept her away. Adrift in blackness, the sun nonetheless seemed to shine upon her. The same heat bathed her skin, invigorating her. She moved her arms as if she were swimming, though she had never before swum and never desired to. She opened her mouth and the heat entered her body, tasting of lemon and rose and marrow. Time stopped and she swam.

She would wake hours later, encased in her voidsuit, arms and legs sore from the unaccustomed exercise.

Today, she painted a sigil of influence—a simple, almost elementary character designed to increase its wearer's persuasive faculty. Her tongues remained oddly quiescent during the process, only venturing forth from her palms briefly to taste the air.

Sigil completed, she sewed twelve spells of compulsion into the joints where the suit's armored plates met at underarm and groin. Hopefully, for all of their jealous watching, not one of her lieutenants would notice the slight alteration. Certainly, they would wonder why she had painted what seemed such a simple sigil on her suit, and conjecture among themselves.

Only Qon knew the full extent of her plan. The spells would increase the sigil of influence's power, allowing Ebn to draw the god's attention and amplify the mages' message of goodwill—to seduce him into looking kindly upon them, in effect. A risky maneuver, surely, yet she believed it would work. She had diagrammed and re-diagrammed the spell's thaumatic output, proving its grace and subtlety.

She wondered what Pol's reaction to the plan would have been. Approval, possibly. Certainly, it was a more aggressive approach than she had ever espoused before.

She and Pol were not yet lovers as she had planned. In truth, her mind balked at the thought of using the spells of compulsion—the sex spells, as Qon had crassly labeled them—on him. But for the twelve she had incorporated into her suit, she kept them in the jar in her office, away from view. Maybe she had overthought the whole process of seduction, which should be quite simple in theory. Always in theory.

Slip them under his door, a voice urged. *Act!*

She imagined calling him with her mind, followed by his arrival at her doorstep. Undressing each other. His body under hers. Afterwards, the feeling of his long torso against her back, his lips brushing her shoulders.

The spells she had created were flawless. She examined them daily. They would bend him to her will entirely.

Banishing these thoughts, she returned her suit to its table. Before capping the jar of alchemical paint, she held her right hand over it. The tongue refused to emerge from her palm. She tried the left hand, to the same result. A good thing, perhaps. The aftereffects of tasting the paint were mildly disorienting, and she needed to keep her mind sharp for the evening's ascension. Possibly, the tongues had picked up on her restive mood and responded with a rare show of empathy. Their lasciviousness had limits, she knew. They were a part of her. They understood fear easily enough.

Ebn had good reason for fear. She had failed to seduce the god once already.

‡

Of course, history proved that many before her had been equally incautious. Even those whose statues now lined the Avenue of Saints had been fools in their own right—murderers, rapists, manipulators, acting in the name of Adrash. The world celebrated men and women of violent conviction, but ultimately the actions of such individuals had driven the god from the earth. Read with a discerning eye, the story of the world was one of brutishness, impetuosity, and spite.

The creation of the Royal Outbound Mages of Stol had been no exception. A common assumption was that the corps had been created in order to commune with Adrash, to coax him back to earth, but the truth was far less noble.

Three thousand years prior to Ebn's era, the king of Stol received word that the Republic of Knos Min had begun sending eldermen into orbit. A massive espionage effort produced no evidence to support this claim, yet the king could not very well risk being shown up by Knos Min, his nation's primary rival in the elder corpse market.

In 9209 MD, several hundred years after catching wind of the original rumor, the Academy of Applied Magics sent its first elderman into orbit. This mage promptly died of exposure to the void. The academy, urged on by the queen herself, did not stop at this one death, but persisted and eventually developed magics sufficient to the task of lifting an elderman into low orbit and landing her safely thereafter.

Stol did not attempt to keep its advanced program a secret. The newly titled Royal Outbound Mages became a symbol of the kingdom's magical development, and the mages themselves became figureheads of a new class. Eldermen, hardier and more prone to magical talent, soon came from all regions of Knoori seeking employment.

At its height, the corps numbered over eight hundred individuals.

Inevitably, not all who applied were accepted into the ranks, yet Stol never failed to exploit an asset No one knew how many eldermen perished as a result of experimental procedures tangential to the program.

Despite the kingdom's vast expenditure of resources, as time wore on the program failed to produce anything of actual or perceived value. A small but growing minority viewed the outbound mages' efforts—which at that time consisted largely of monitoring Adrash's movements—as blasphemous, asserting that no man had the right to enter the god's abode. By the opening of the ninety-fourth century, public support of the mages had eroded almost completely. Eldermen, so recently a beloved symbol of Stol, had become a suspect race, a source of anger and targets of violent reprisal.

By imperial order, the bloated program was cut to a fraction of its former size in 9365.

Oddly, this act proved foundational in energizing the corps. Reduced to a lean nucleus of fifty highly skilled eldermen, the mages reinvented themselves, purging their lore of any unnecessary ritual or tradition. With fewer resources, no longer under the eye of public scrutiny, they developed their own odd society. They restricted themselves to the academy grounds almost exclusively, fearful of a public who feared their race.

With their combined genius and magical talent, they developed and refined the voidsuit, a tool that increased each mage's magical capability fivefold. Reaching orbit in record times, they flew farther and farther away from Jeroun, even to the point of entering the moon's insubstantial atmosphere. They became fast and strong, and ultimately forced their way—through murder, deception, and magical coercion—back into ruling positions in the academy.

The majority of the mages had long since ceased to believe rumors of a competing outbound army in Knos Min, and redefined the program's mission. Convincing Adrash of the world's worth became the only goal. Over time, this became the academy's encompassing objective as well. Entire branches of magical inquiry were abandoned, faculty dismissed or executed for heterodox views.

In the span of a few generations, one question came to dominate all academic discussion: *Does Adrash love the peaceful, or does he love the strong?* Undoubtedly, the question had been asked many times, in churches and on street corners for millennia, but the development of advanced magics that allowed an outbound mage to travel to the moon—into Adrash's territory—made the issue less a matter of metaphysics than concrete reality.

How, the mages submitted, *can we approach Adrash without offending him?*

The debate went on for many years, but by the time Ebn bon Mari rose to the rank of Captain of the Royal Outbound Mages her predecessors had generally come to the same verdict: Adrash did not look kindly upon acts of aggression.

Of course, they possessed damning evidence to support this conclusion. The creation of the Needle itself seemed to have been spurred by a particularly violent display of the corps' strength in 10991. Seven hundred years later, the mage Dor wa Dol—driven mad by the sigils he had tattooed on his body with alchemical ink—had attacked Adrash, causing the god to send his two smallest weapons to earth, resulting in a decades-long winter. The Cataclysm.

These tragedies, Ebn's forebears determined, *are the result of our arrogance. We must not treat Adrash as if he were an equal met on the battlefield. Instead, we will beg his forgiveness. We will prostrate ourselves, offering gifts and tribute.*

Ebn had inherited this outlook: despite her own monstrous gaffe, she believed in it wholeheartedly.

‡

After breakfast, a knock on her door. Ebn hurried to the balcony curtains and drew them shut. The weighted hems whispered across the polished flag-stones, shutting out the sun completely.

Four of the sculptor's apprentices brought the statue into her apartment. Though each strapping human lad wore a worksuit of high-grade elder-cloth, they struggled under the weight of marble. Two strained at its head while the other two swiveled its torso, angling its massive shoulders through the doorframe.

"Could we get some light?" one asked.

"Shut up," Ebn said. "You measured everything yesterday. Your eyes will adjust."

The apprentices maneuvered the statue to the exact center of her living room and set it upright. Even in the near dark it was beautiful, but it was not yet the effect she desired. Without taking her eyes from the figure, she pointed to the curtains.

"Open them," she told no one in particular. "And when you do it, do it quickly. I want the sun to burst into the room, not crawl."

One of the apprentices shrugged and hauled on the golden rope. Light filled the room instantly, blinding Ebn for a heartbeat. The blackness fled from her eyes and the statue came into swift focus, as though the figure had materialized into her room out of nothingness.

The breath caught in her throat.

Adrash stood before her, head nearly touching the eighteen-foot ceiling. He stood relaxed, back straight and feet slightly apart. Carved from a single immense block of unveined white marble, the swells and depressions of his musculature appeared as smooth as polished glass, buffed to a high shine with several hundred grams of bonedust.

The armor had retreated from his head and neck, revealing his stylized masculine features and smooth scalp. Traditionally, sculptors used a black stone to show the true color of the god's naked skin, but Ebn preferred the purity of white alone.

His eyes were closed, his lips slightly puckered to kiss the globe cradled in his powerful hands. Though she could not see the detail from where she stood, Ebn knew the god's lips landed on Stol. She had designed it to symbolize Adrash's love for the world, but also to suggest the kingdom's centrality. For the last month she had spent far too much of her time quibbling over sketches and miniatures with the sculptor.

The chest must be just so. The genitals, just so. His thighs are too small, his head too large. She obsessed over the globe, even. The islands were too numerous or too uniformly shaped, the perpetual storm on the other side of the world spun the wrong direction. The sculptor, not to mention the entire arts faculty, must have thought her batty.

No matter. The statue was completed, and it was beautiful. Her time and the academy's funds had been well spent.

"Ebn?" Qon called from the open doorway. She stepped in. "I have been knocking for some time. I..." She stared up at the statue. "Good Lord Adrash. Ebn, I had no idea how beautiful it would be."

Ebn tore her gaze away. "I think I am insulted. What did you think I was doing with my time—carving a mantle-piece? Adrash needs nothing of any practical value, true, but he does deserve to be venerated properly." She could not contain her smile as she turned back to her creation. "Only now I cannot bear the thought of letting it go."

‡

Dustglass helmets cradled in the crooks of their elbows, forty-two outbound mages stood on the roof of the Esoteric Arts building. They were accoutered for a long orbital excursion, bandoliers filled with spells. Ebn noticed more than a few fresh sigils—blue and grey and red—painted on voidsuits, and approved.

A strong breeze had carried the smell of the docks, wet and rotting. Qon pulled a kerchief from her suit collar and covered her mouth, unconcerned if the younger outbound mages interpreted this as a sign of weakness. Though the smell made Ebn nauseous too, she stood stone-faced among her officers as the statue was hauled and deposited upright in their midst.

They were ready.

The moon had not yet risen, but the Needle already stretched nearly half-way across the sky. Positioned in the exact center of the roof, the marble god seemed to glow with its own inner light. Several of the older mages faced it and pressed left fist to forehead out of reverence. The younger lot stole glances at the statue, affecting airs of disdain. They could not ignore the existence of Adrash, but deference did not fit in well with the affected cynicism in vogue among the academy's young elite.

Pol stepped forward for a closer look. She could not read his expression, and refrained from asking his opinion. She admired the graceful curve of his neck above the collar of his suit. Once, not long after his arrival from Pusta, he had fallen asleep in a chair during a private tutorial. She had watched him for close to an hour, counting the doubled pulses of his jugular. Then, as now, she wanted to cradle his jaw in her hand.

She admonished herself for her preoccupation, which had only ever produced frustration.

"You know your role?" she asked him.

"Yes," he said, and patted the pack attached to his stomach. "I keep the spells at ready."

A whistle blew—a long, trilling blast that rose in pitch sharply before cutting off.

"Two minutes!" the huge tamer yelled.

Ebn and Pol retreated to the edges of the circular roof. Most of the mages had already assumed the waiting position. Helmets on, they lay on their backs, hands gripping the newly installed handles inset into the floor above their heads, feet hooked under the bar running the inner perimeter of the low roof wall. Minor magic would have secured them equally well, but Ebn thought it best not to tire anyone before the evening's major spell.

She watched the remaining officers ready themselves and then turned to the tamer, who gripped the thick shaft of the twelve-foot-tall sky-hook. A solid piece of steel, it resembled an immense shepherd's crook welded to a small, heavy platform on which the tamer stood.

"Your pet is in an agreeable mood?" she asked the heavily scarred man.

He shrugged heavy shoulders chalked with bonedust. "Seems to be. Tough to tell with Sapes, sometimes. She's temperamental, and this sort of thing's never been done before." He blew into the whistle again and bellowed the one-minute warning.

Their eyes met. The tamer smiled, and suddenly the stubby horns on his forehead seemed quite vulgar to her.

She flinched as a ragged scream tore through the night, far louder a sound than elderman or human lungs could produce.

"Better get settled, miss," the tamer said, positioning the grimy black-rimmed goggles over his eyes. "Dragon coming down."

‡

A long shape blotted out a section of stars above them. Wings the size of galleon sails forced waves of compacted air downward, pushing the voidsuited bodies into the floor. The wyrm roared again. Muffled through the outbound mages' glass helmets, the sound was nearly indistinguishable from the wind.

The beast descended and the pressure increased. Ebn craned her neck to see the tamer. He had wrapped his arms and legs around the sky-hook's shaft, but his goggled eyes were directed upward. He yelled, and whether they were incantations or encouragements, Ebn did not know. Wyrms were violently temperamental, and the elder hybrids the Tamer's Guild raised from hatchlings could only roughly be called tame.

Ebn assumed the tamer's lore would be sufficient to control the beast, for its task was simple enough. Still, she found herself mouthing a silent entreaty to Adrash for his blessing.

Apparently, he heard. The building shook as it took the wyrm's weight, and the air stilled.

Ebn opened eyes she had not realized were closed.

For a moment, the scope of the animal could not be fathomed. When she turned her head, the large black object a few feet from her head resolved itself into one of the beast's talons. She gazed up at its heaving stomach, a full thirty feet above her, and shuddered. It was so immense! She had never seen a wyrm up close. Craning her neck painfully, she located its head, which hung far out over the roof's edge. The animal seemed to be watching the city.

The tamer whooped, and Ebn shuddered again to see that vicious, wedge-shaped head swinging toward the roof. It came sailing in, and she lost scope once more: a giant black fist, a meteor tumbling out of the night sky. The visions fused, became a tooth-lined grin as long as two men, a gigantic double-pupiled eye glowing soft blue. The head lay against the stone floor, and above it floated the horned head of the tamer.

No, not floated. He stood behind the wyrm's head, and spoke in its ear.

The talons near Ebn twitched, scraping across the flagstones. The wyrm gripped the statue easily with one foot and Ebn winced, though she had strengthened the marble with reliable spells only hours ago.

The great head rose, dragging the length of its neck in an arcing line behind it. Flexing its haunches, the wyrm's stomach lowered until it seemed it would be impaled by the sky-hook. The tamer huddled under the beast, a huge man compressed into insignificance.

A cry rose in Ebn's throat as the wyrm leapt upward, sky-hook firmly gripped in its other foot. The gust of its passage pressed her flat into the roof, knocking the cry from her lips. She counted to thirty as the beast rose into the air, unhooked her feet, and slammed her gauntleted fist into the first spell on her bandolier. To her right, she saw Qon do the same.

Ebn whispered the gathering words, her own secret incantation to bind the mages' energy together and keep them safe during flight.

Immediately, she felt as if she were being pushed from either side—like a giant pair of hands squeezing her flat. Lines of red fire shot from the mages' bodies and wound together above the roof, forming a rope that shot heavenward, converging on the statue clutched in the wyrm's foot.

Any moment now, Ebn thought.

They shot into the sky.

‡

Rising swiftly under the wyrm's power, they spun slowly, a circle of suited figures at the end of a fire tether. Ebn's complex spell caused the mages' suits to repel each other, so that no one crashed into their neighbor. For all of her planning, however, she had not prepared herself for the nausea. Rising straight into orbit was one thing, spinning and being jounced around another thing entirely. She looked to the right and caught Qon's eye.

The woman was grinning.

"An odd way to enter the void," she had said when Ebn outlined the plan originally. "I see the need for the wyrm, I suppose, though I think in time we could develop a spell powerful enough to lift something as large as the statue into orbit."

"We do not have the time," Ebn said. "And I want us to be as fresh as possible when we reach orbit."'

Qon's eyes roved over the thaumatic diagrams again. "Two questions. Will the tamer be able to handle heights of this magnitude? Thirty miles is no joke, Ebn. And will this spell"—she pointed to the projections Ebn had drawn out—"be enough to lift the statue in the event several of the less experienced mages are disoriented from the ride? Or simply afraid?"

Ebn nodded. "The tamer assures me that he can make it, and I see no reason to disbelieve him. It is his life on the line, too. From the point where he turns back to earth, it is but a short push. I have done the maths over and over. You and Pol and I could lift it into orbit by ourselves if need be."

"Would we be able to affect any spells afterwards?"

"Probably not." Ebn traced the line of trajectory she had drawn, met her friend's eyes, and shrugged. "But I think it highly unlikely that thirty-nine well-trained mages will suffer fits of uselessness at the exact same time."

Qon quirked an eyebrow. "I think we crossed the line separating likely and unlikely some time ago."

POL TANZ ET SOM

From twenty miles up, Tansot was only a speck of light on the ebon blanket of earth. The stars above burned brighter every second. A vague but definite shadow above the spinning mages, the wyrm beat immense wings against air too thin for any natural creature to fly upon.

Pol pictured Shav, wrapped tight around the sky-hook, trusting in his pet's grip, shouting words of tamer lore and encouragement. As the air grew thinner, the spell the quarterstock had imbibed before calling the beast down supplied more and more oxygen to his body. He did not breathe in at all. Drawing in the cold would freeze his lungs instantly.

With greater height, sound itself began to fail. In his mind's eye, Pol saw Shav climbing the wyrm's legs and flank, shimmying up its long neck, straddling its giant head so that he might whisper directions into its ear. When his voice could no longer be heard, the violently shivering tamer crushed another spell against the wyrm's skull and pressed his ear to the wet scales, freezing the two beings together, forming a seal.

Tamer and wyrm's thoughts meshed and became one.

If the animal allowed, that is.

Even then it was a tenuous link, Pol knew, though he did not understand the process exactly. In the half-month since he had taken Shav as a lover, he had picked up more tamer lore than the guild normally allowed to outsiders.

Still, he was far from conversant. Strictly speaking, he had no desire to be. He knew without question that Ebn had made no study of their lore. If she had done so, her plan might not rely upon a madman and his unpredictable charge.

Pol considered the odd coincidence of Shav's appearance. Though not by nature a paranoid man, he could not avoid wondering how it was that Ebn had started looking for a tamer at nearly the exact moment of Pol's meeting one. Shav himself had expressed a similar sentiment. An odd confluence, surely, yet in Pol's experience such things often occurred without anyone's arrangement.

But coincidence or no, he could not ignore the potential in such a meeting of fates. He would turn it to his advantage by remaining vigilant, open to possibilities as they arose. The more connected he became to the world—the less like his timid peers, cloistered behind the walls of the academy—the better he would be able to mold events to suit his needs.

Fear is not an attribute of Adrash, Pol reminded himself. *It will not be one of mine.*

Ebn's spell pushed the mages farther and farther apart as gravity lost its hold, until their bodies spun nearly horizontal to the distant ground. The fiery tether binding them to the wyrm had faded to nothing in the rarified atmosphere, as Ebn had told them it would, making it difficult to see one another. The mages signed excitedly over their helmets nonetheless.

Pol did not partake in the simple conversation. Yes, he knew the plan. Yes, he knew his role. In the last month, Ebn had conducted thirteen briefings. If her officers did not yet know what must be done, they never would.

A quick and effortless spell, and Pol knew they had reached an altitude of almost twenty-three miles. Another hour, very likely.

Soon thereafter, Ebn would see the error of her conviction. Adrash had no interest in receiving supplicants, and even less interest in gifts. What need did a god have for baubles when he could cause steel monuments to rise from the moon itself? If the stories of Adrash were true—if seclusion had not turned the god into a shadow of himself—he would see their groveling as the insult it was, and react accordingly.

In Pol's estimation, the chances of the outbound mages returning to Jeroun were slim.

He sighed. Having made preparations for the worst, there was nothing left to do but wait.

He closed his eyes and considered the riddle of Shav again.

‡

The way his bulk occupied the small apartment near the docks, filling it so that it seemed he could not move without breaking something. Yet move he did. In private, Shav possessed an awareness of his outsized body that shocked Pol. Such poise could rarely be learned. Clearly, he affected clumsiness while fighting to trick his opponents.

Uncharacteristically and in opposition to the obvious hierarchy of species, Pol found himself intimidated by the quarterstock.

But it was not merely Shav's physical prowess that put Pol off balance. That the quarterstock was mad could not be denied. The sickness revealed itself primarily through his eyes, which stared through Pol more often than not, focused on images in his own mind. Sometimes his hands shook and his lips moved as though he were having a silent conversation. Slight tremors moved through him, often causing his whole body to vibrate like a tuning fork.

At times his madness bloomed into something else—something far beyond the bounds of mental imbalance, bordering on the mystical. While he slept, he spoke in different tongues.

Pol heard their cadence and rhythm and knew them to be true languages, though he recognized none of the words. His curiosity had compelled him to capture several of the monologues in acoustic jars and show them to a colleague in ancient languages. The man, obviously excited by what he heard, practically demanded to know where Pol had procured the recordings. Pol, unwilling to reveal his source, had walked away, little the wiser.

This was not all. On several trancelike occasions Shav had seemed to shift into another persona, changing tone, pitch, and vocabulary so completely that Pol wondered if the quarterstock were not in fact inhabited by other personalities. He had heard such things were possible.

Of course, he knew not to probe Shav too obviously. As their relationship developed, the quarterstock had revealed a deep, incisive intelligence, voiced in ever more sophisticated speech. Recently, he had begun to reveal troublingly precise insights into Pol's mind. He seemed to possess an instinctive clairvoyance, and as a result Pol no longer knew what to hide and what to reveal. The quarterstock seemed possessed of faculties reason could not explain.

These traits both repelled and attracted Pol. Shav was important, somehow—even if only because Pol willed it so. He had pursued Shav intuitively, unsure of his own motives, and the quarterstock seemed to be responding in kind. Like opponents in a game of yhor, they danced half-blind around one another, trying to peer at the other's pieces.

"You have a plan for me," Shav had told him the last time they met—undoubtedly, their most troubling conversation yet.

Pol finished his honey and saffron flatbread slowly, considering. A direct response seemed best. "Obviously I do, Shav. Beyond physical pleasure, I want to understand your hybrid nature. We have talked about it many times. My intentions are no mystery."

"No, Pol." The hybrid's thick fingers folded the bread around the spiced dates expertly. "That's not what I mean. I'm good at reading faces, and yours says you're hiding things from me. Things beyond pleasure and breeding. It's fine for now if you want to hide. I'll eventually figure it out, with or without your help."

Pol felt an all-too-familiar moment of paranoia, and quickly reviewed their conversation to make sure he had not revealed anything he had not meant to. He opened his mouth, sure of words to come.

"Don't," Shav said. "Denying it won't do any good. I've contacted a linealogist at your academy, and he confirmed my suspicions. A drop of blood or semen will answer all of your questions about my heritage. You have access to both. Of course, you would still need a linealogist to perform the spells, and then your study would be public. Somehow, I gather that isn't part of your plan. The linealogist was quite eager to know your name."

Pol's hearts beat harder. To be caught pursuing another guild's lore could land him in some trouble. The fact that he had no intention of casting linealogical spells would make no difference. If the administration searched deep enough, they might even discover that he had been pursuing his own unregistered research with illegally acquired alchemicals. The academy, which inherited any documents of magical innovation upon a mage's death, considered such illicit practices acts of sedition against Stol, punishable by death.

The chair creaked under Shav as he sat back. He did not need to smile to show his satisfaction. Not for the first time, Pol wondered what it would be like to fight the quarterstock—what it would be like to straddle his back and wrap fingers around his throat.

"No," Shav answered the unspoken question. "I didn't give him your name. Your secret is safe."

"Scholars and mages are jealous of their lore," Pol said, shrugging the matter away. "The linealogists are no exception. Nor am I. The tamers themselves, for that matter."

Shav shook his head. "There's more to it than that. Sometimes I think you're simply stalling, waiting for something to announce itself. I'm not... I'm..." Mouth working, he stared through Pol's chest.

The back of Pol's neck tingled as the shift occurred.

"The dragon and I," Shav finally said, voice lower than normal, words slightly slurred with the touch of an accent Pol could not name. "A halfbreed and a quarterbreed at this moment in time. The conjunction of the two is interesting, Pol. Interesting. I've seen a dragon crash into the sea, sure the animal had killed itself. Instead it surfaced, twisting its long neck and beating its wings upon the water, a great sea serpent clamped in its jaws—a sea serpent so large that it could've swallowed our tiny boat in one bite. Its skin shone like silver in the moonlight, and its thrashing frothed the sea like a child's hand slapping bathwater."

Pol did not interrupt, though he knew no mortal man had ever sailed upon the ocean.

Shav leaned forward, eyes liquid and unfocused. "The Needle had only risen halfway, and the moon showed a quarter of her face. I stared at the destruction coming swiftly: a wall of black water that blotted out the stars along the horizon. I waited and told my men to prepare themselves. Some of them prayed to Adrash, some to Orrus, and some to the devil." He dipped his head and touched his horns almost reverently. "Me, I just waited for the inevitable, almost wanting it. Most likely, I would die along with my men. An odd feeling, being that powerless."

He blinked. His amber eyes refocused. The corners of his mouth twitched, and he spoke in the voice Pol had become accustomed to.

"Someday soon, I think you'll know what that feels like."

‡

To Pol's astonishment, the statement had haunted him for days. Finally, chagrined that it should take him so long to see the light of reason, he dismissed the possibility that Shav had performed an extraordinary feat of magic. No, the quarterstock had merely read the signs of Pol's anxiety.

Though he had seen Adrash through the cloudy lens of magnification spells many times, Pol had never ventured within a thousand miles of the god. He had always run from the divine presence as he had been taught—yet if all went according to Ebn's plan, in less than two weeks he would encounter

Adrash in the flesh. The thought made his hearts thunder.

Pol examined his fear, and it disgusted him.

Is this the man Adrash will see? he asked himself. *A coward?*

Shame drove him forward. A mere day after talking with Shav, he began tattooing himself with alchemical ink of his own design—a foolhardy enterprise, surely. There were precedents, but only a few, and by accounts those men had gone mad.

Gone mad? An understatement, surely. The mage Dor wa Dol, driven to such insanity by his sigils, had single-handedly caused the Cataclysm. He had been captain of the outbound mages at the time, an elderman in the prime of his ability.

Clearly, even the hardiest elderman could not handle that much alchemy coursing through his body for long.

Pol knew the risks, having researched the possibility for years. Aside from the likelihood of overloading one's body with magic, the execution of each sigil had to be exact. One misstroke, and the consequences would be dire.

Nonetheless, he proceeded.

First, his left shoulder: a rudimentary warding sigil. His hand shook so severely that the character—four simple lines—took nearly an hour to complete. When nothing untoward happened—indeed, when his voice failed to rouse the symbol to life—he painted a second, slightly more complex character on his bicep: a flight sigil. This too remained dormant despite his attempts to activate it. Emboldened and not a little frustrated, he drew a sigil on his right wrist, his left shin, his stomach.

Once started, he could not stop. In numb horror he watched his body become a canvas of inert magical symbols.

The morning sun slanted through his windows. The day progressed, and then the evening. A week passed, during which he added several new sigils. He took to wearing long-sleeved, close-fitting garments. Whatever he had imagined might happen in time, did not. The black characters lay dormant despite his every incantation. He did not grow ill or suffer visions. Disappointed that years of expectation had apparently presaged nothing, he stopped tattooing himself.

It was only on the morning of Ebn's mission, as he contemplated the prospect of his own death, that he found the exercise had produced something of value.

The act of tattooing—of risking his body for the sake of power—had silenced his fear.

‡

The world flared against Pol's eyelids. He opened them in time to see the great fireball the wyrm had belched disperse into nothingness: A lightning flash, stamping the afterimage in Pol's mind—a fluorescing cloud, amorphous and vast, dwarfing the giant serpent that had birthed it. Its long, razor-toothed jaws opening and closing.

The other mages were already moving, fingering their spell-laden bandoliers. Pol would not mirror their anxiousness. He would not fidget. When the occasion called for action, his movements would be fluid and precise.

To his right, Ebn signed with fingers that glowed blue with magefire.

One minute. On my signal.

Forty-one mages signed their understanding, and waited. For sixty seconds, Pol thought of Shav, arms and thighs tightly gripping the wyrm's skull, bonedusted skin hoary with ice crystals. Were his eyes closed behind the heavy goggles? Or was he staring down at the mages even now, thinking his inexplicable thoughts? Perhaps he watched the stars, which seemed close enough now to touch. One last look before returning to earth.

Ebn's hands screamed actinic sapphire.

Now!

Pol smashed his gauntleted fist into the second spell in his bandolier. His tether reignited as the wyrm dropped the statue. Though he did not count to be sure, it looked like all of the mages had reacted in concert. Any who had not were now untethered, and would have to rely upon their own lore to return to earth or ascend to orbit. Whether their actions resulted in death or the simple shame of failure, Pol had little sympathy.

The statue fell through the circle of mages and Pol smashed the third spell in his bandolier. His body surged upwards. He felt a powerful tug as his tether took the weight, but kept ascending. He checked his speed to make sure he did not rise too fast. Others adjusted similarly, Ebn, Qon and the senior mages among them, yet it soon became clear the action was unnecessary. Gravity pulled weakly thirty miles above Jeroun, and even the youngest mages seemed to be handling their share of the weight.

The circle drew in. Pol read excitement on most of the faces. Qon smiled and signed with quick hands, unembarrassed of her enthusiasm. The others responded in kind.

Fools, Pol thought. It would be at least another day and a half before they reached Adrash, assuming he could be located. More than enough time to poke holes in any plan—enough time to get tired and cranky and edgy. Perhaps, Pol reasoned, they needed this momentary upswell of emotion to prepare for the long haul to the moon.

Once again, he had little sympathy. The path was clear. What benefit could be garnered from deceiving oneself?

Ebn met Pol's sober look and nodded with equal sobriety.

Now the hard part, she signed.

‡

On average, an outbound mage could reach the moon in thirty-six hours. Qon could reach it in twenty-seven, Ebn in just under a day. Pol had once traveled the distance in twenty-two hours, forty minutes, a full fifty-three minutes faster than Ebn's stated record. Of course, he had publicly recorded a less impressive time. Undoubtedly, she had done the same. A smart mage would not reveal his true power unless threatened.

Of course, such threats were common at the academy and came in all varieties, as did violence. The administration did not approve of murder as a means to advancement, but they made no move to stop it. Death kept the ranks slim and mean. The mages who survived planned ahead and bided their time. Eventually, they became leaders. If they remained vigilant, they stayed in their positions for a very long time, indeed.

As he flew, Pol wondered if it might be possible to unseat Ebn without killing her. When her plan ended unsuccessfully—assuming she survived the encounter with Adrash—perhaps she could be persuaded to step down. With great care Pol might then find a way to draw her to his side. She loved him, clearly, and that could be used to his advantage.

Still, her death would be the most convenient outcome.

And if Adrash took the lives of a few of the seniormost mages as well...

Pol thought of the opportunities their absences would create. He fantasized, a thing he did not often allow himself to do.

Thirty-six hours passed slowly in the void. The mages had little to distract themselves. Shy two youths who had failed to activate their spells in time, each was forced to pull a bit harder at his or her tether. The alignment needed constant watching lest someone wander, and so they slept in shifts, two hours off, four hours on. They signaled constantly to one another, reminding themselves to stay alert.

The blazing stars called seductively. If one listened closely enough, the emptiness echoed with their stately, hypnotic song. Drawing energy from one's flight spells was both taxing and monotonous. Bonedust-and-honey lozenges provided nutrients, but did not fill the emptiness in one's stomach.

For the less skilled, these factors often resulted in what Ebn had termed hypnogogic drift, a state wherein the body and mind uncoupled without the mage's awareness. A drifting mage thought he was operating at full attention, when in fact he had entered a dream almost identical to reality.

When the sun came out from behind the swollen belly of Jeroun below their feet, its light created yet another problem. Though nourishing to both suit and mage, the radiation proved too severe for sensitive elderman eyes. In response, the dustglass helmets polarized, locking each mage in a dim chamber where hallucinations arose easily. Suddenly, the emptiness seemed to echo with familiar voices, strobe with color. In such conditions it was easy to become disoriented and veer off course. A single mistake could send the statue tumbling, resulting in a massive waste of energy and time as the mages scrambled to right it.

In addition, many of the younger mages had yet to develop their remote manipulation sigils. They did not fully comprehend the way a massive object moved in the void—how deadly even a spinning body could be.

But the most common danger of navigating the void was simple forgetfulness. Drawing power and keeping a steady course became routine, so easily done even experienced mages could neglect spells that preserved life on its most basic level. Heat. Air. During the outbound mages' long history, many had been lost to the void, slowly having frozen or asphyxiated to death unawares.

Thus the mages looked to each other, orienting themselves back to reality over and over again. They traveled swiftly into the never-ending night, wrapped in thin bubbles of atmosphere that distorted and magnified the stars around them. They gestured to one another, carrying on trite conversations to keep their minds busy.

Traveling slower than he otherwise would, soon even Pol forgot his pride and talked of the food in Kengsort, the weather atop Miselo Hill, the wine of the Aspa foothills.

Thirty-six hours passed slowly. Tensely.

‡

They were still eight hours from the moon when Adrash showed himself. He appeared in an instant, matching the mages' speed at the center of their spread circle. His eyes flashed like the sun itself, yellow-white and harsh, washing out the figure behind.

The light pushed against Pol. It broke upon him in wave after glacial wave, stiffening his limbs. He squinted against the glare and fought the torpor that had been imposed upon him. Slowly—agonizingly—he bent frozen fingers, formed a fist and held it before his chest, ready to shatter a spell in defense.

Shaking like palsied old men, his neighbors to the right and left began assuming similar postures. Of course, their lore would be of no use against Adrash. Holding forty skilled mages in a thrall, even one that did not bind completely, spoke of power beyond reason.

Slightly above and to Pol's right, Ebn's hands erupted in blue flame.

Sever! she signed.

The distraction proved enough to break free of Adrash's ensorcelment. Pol's mind snapped back into focus, and he dissolved his tether. In ragged order, the others did likewise. Ebn waited for the last of her lieutenants to complete the task, and then allowed the statue to float free.

For what seemed to Pol an eternity, the tableau remained static. Orbiting the radiant god, the mages appeared small and insectile in their black, segmented suits.

The intense light shut off abruptly, scoring the image on Pol's retinas.

He blinked the scene clear to find it changed.

Adrash floated before the immense statue. His sinuous forearms were crossed beneath his broad chest, his head canted forward on his thick neck. Flatfooted, he stood as if upon solid ground. He had positioned himself face to face with the marble figure, and looked down upon the world cradled in its hands. But for the cold luminosity of his eyes, he himself resembled a sculpted object, an artist's anatomical model flawlessly cast in white stone.

Nonetheless, it struck Pol that Adrash was vastly more beautiful than the statue. He committed to memory every line of the god's powerful physique. His cock stirred against the tight base layer of his suit, and a tingling radiated into his thighs.

Ebn's hands flashed again. Pol tore his eyes away from Adrash, but found that he could not read the senior mage's gestures. Arms pointed at the god, she formed circles before her chest, an arc of crimson flashing briefly between her gauntleted fingers. A spell. Pol watched in shocked fascination as the seams of her suit began to glow at underarm and groin.

Adrash did not so much as twitch in response, but Pol felt the draw of her magic. He fought a compulsion to cross the space to Ebn, to take her in his arms.

She collapsed the spell between her palms.

Adrash's head now swiveled in her direction. She beckoned to him with signs.

Come here. Come closer.

The mages watched, unmoving, as Adrash turned. He took one step in her direction, two, and started walking toward her slowly, as though he were ascending an invisible staircase. Ebn smiled and spread her hands again. The spell twisted between her fingers, now as black and viscous as clotting blood.

What madness has possessed her? Pol asked himself. The plan had been simple: *Find Adrash, present the gift, and retreat. Do not deviate from the plan.* Pol had been tasked with moving the statue forward, stabilizing it in orbit above the moon. Though he thought it foolish to approach the god in this manner, he respected the consistency of Ebn's plan. One did not prostrate with a sword in one's hand.

This is the death of us all, Pol thought.

Halfway to Ebn, Adrash stopped and shook his head, for all the world like a man trying to shake an ugly thought from his mind. He turned from her and stretched forth his left arm, pointing his closed fist at the statue. No expression could be read on his masked features.

A tremor passed through Pol's limbs. Of their own accord, the sigils tattooed on his skin came to life, blooming into twenty-two points of searing agony. The air solidified in his lungs, stopping the scream in his throat. His hearts hiccoughed in his chest and died. For a timeless instant, his bones reverberated an endless note, on the verge of shattering...

As quickly as it had begun, the pain ceased.

The space between his heartbeats dilated: One... Two... Three...

The universe rang as if struck. Pol focused on the sound, sure that if he listened long enough he would hear the words that had originally set the stars in motion, the father of all incantations, the font of all magic. Opening his mouth, he let the sound inside. A warm draught tasting of cinnamon and anise, it rushed dizzyingly to his head, his hands, the twenty-two sigils upon his body. It tingled on his lips, pulsed at the tips of his fingers, begging to be liberated. He held himself at the threshold of release, every nerve singing in ecstasy.

Four... Five... Six.

Too late, he remembered where he was, his duty to the other mages.

Too late, he started to cast the spell.

Adrash opened his hand. The statue shattered, and the light of the god's wrath eclipsed the stars.

PART THREE

VEDAS TEZUL

They traveled in relative comfort across the highest Step, averaging nearly twenty-five miles a day. The sparse pine forest suited walking, providing shade and sunlight in equal measures. Even without a trodden path, the ground remained dry and stable. No boulders rose from the earth to trip feet. Numerous small rivers provided fresh water and trout, and lakes allowed them to bathe.

Weather during the Months of Clergymen and Pilots could be unpredictable throughout Stol, yet at the top of the world it was idyllic—neither hot enough to raise a sweat, nor cold enough to chill. In the early afternoon it rained lightly and never for long, leaving the world filled with clean smells. They passed through clouds of black flies, but after a few exploratory bites the insects proved uninterested in human blood.

The tranquility of the land defied the nervousness roiling in Vedas's gut. They were making good time, but he had not forgotten the day they lost following the mountain cat's attack. Danoor would not wait for them to be waylaid again.

He was not the only one troubled. The ease of travel ill suited Churls. It made her cranky, suspicious. She held herself ready at all times. Vedas saw it in the tensing of her shoulders, the way her fingers grazed the pommel of her sword.

"Do you think the forest is enchanted?" he asked.

"Possible, I suppose." She shrugged. "This is nothing like I expected, I'll grant that. Guess one or two of the tall tales had it right. Whether it's enchanted makes no difference, though—we have no defense against sorcery, so we'd better just hope it isn't. Right now I'm less concerned about spells than I am about poison-tipped arrows and axe-wielding mountain men. I know it doesn't look like that kind of place, but I believe in being prepared."

She advised Berun and Vedas not to veer too closely to the roughshod villages they glimpsed through the trees. Vedas, having contracted her cautiousness, agreed. Undoubtedly, they were spotted and heard—Berun practically sparkled in sunlight, and he made no attempt to silence his footfalls—but the locals wisely kept their distance.

Only once did someone present himself. On the third day a young boy, short, slightly built, and nearly naked, walked across their path and froze upon sight of the travelers. He looked just as surprised as they were and, without a sound, turned and ran like a rabbit.

Vedas put a hand to Berun's arm before the constructed man could launch one of his stones. "What are you doing?" he asked. Without consciously urging it to, the edges of his hood closed in around his features.

Berun stared at Vedas's hand. "The boy may bring others."

"And so you thought to kill him?"

The constructed man took a step backward. "No." He looked at Churls and shook his head. "No. I only wanted to incapacitate the boy."

Churls's eyes darted to Vedas, and then back to Berun. "Good instinct, but we'd attract more attention knocking the boy out than we would just leaving him be. After all, his people may already know we're here. If they don't, nobody's going to believe his story. A man with black skin and horns, and another man made of metal? Preposterous."

On the following afternoon, she stopped Vedas from shooting a lone sheep. "I know we're tired of brook trout," she said, "but look at how this animal moves. It's not wild. It's probably drifted off from the flock, and I'd rather not be caught poaching or get accused of it. Herders treat poachers worse than they treat murderers."

Impressed by Churls's quick thinking and watchful air, Vedas began following the path of her gaze. He stilled his steps when she did, tipped his head to the same angle. Gradually, he started to see what she saw, hear what she heard. He learned to identify the region's ubiquitous signs of inhabitation, both recent and lost to time. A snaking stretch of bare ground became a footpath. Rounded, moss-covered shapes—once indistinguishable to him from natural rock formations—rearranged themselves into extensive ruins that stretched for miles.

Even their route ceased to appear random. Churls nodded when he brought it up, pointing to the paving stones embedded in the roots of the largest trees. Suddenly, as though ordering itself from chaos, the dimensions of the ancient highway became obvious.

It humbled him to realize how blind he had been to this fact.

Heightened awareness came with a price, however. The suspicion that they were being watched grew as the days wore on. His skin itched under the gaze of so many unseen eyes. He flinched at birdcalls, ducked under rays of sunlight. He peered over his shoulder and invented figures between the trees. He recognized similar symptoms in Churls, and knew she saw his in turn. Neither spoke of it.

They reached the end of the highest Step without incident. Eager to put distance between themselves and the ghosts inhabiting the top of the world, they continued traveling by the light of the full moon for another two hours. Churls's arms swung freely at her side. She smiled at Vedas as they set up camp at the edge of the sixteenth Step.

He looked away, struggling to understand why the expected release had not occurred. Certainly, he continued to obsess over their schedule. He worried about chartering a ship across Lake Ten. And in only a few days' time, they would be traveling in the Apusht Vales. The people of the valleys, traditionally the stronghold of Stoli Adrashism, defended their border from the Anadrashi people of Toma. They would not look kindly upon Vedas or Berun.

For the first time since the night the cat attacked, Vedas gave these concerns a voice, holding forth like a man confessing his sins. He regretted the decision instantly, yet felt powerless to stop himself.

"We must catch a ship on the day we arrive...

"If we're not on Knosi soil by this date...

"We can't expect to travel as fast at night...

"I can't imagine what Abse would say to me if he knew..."

They had been over it all before, on many occasions. He had kept the debate going long after deferring to her better judgment.

Shut your mouth, he told himself—and finally, he did.

The millstone around his neck was no lighter. In the silence that followed, he considered what might be done to negate the words he had just spoken, and arrived at no solution.

Berun grunted. "I've heard these things before."

Churls sighed, obviously displeased to have her good mood sullied. "I thought we were through with this argument, too, but I guess you need one more go-round. We're making the best time we can, Vedas. We'll deal with Lake Ten when Lake Ten is in front of us. As for the Apusht, you're right. It's home to some of the most dangerous men in Stol. But it's a short walk compared to what we've traveled so far. We'll move at night. The border guard are warriors, not mages. While it won't be a stroll to the butcher's, at least we know what to expect."

Vedas closed his eyes, shamed by her self-control. She had not lashed out, as was her right. Rather, she had explained matters to him as if to a child.

She would not have to do it again, he vowed. Experience had confirmed the soundness of her judgment, had it not? She had proved herself more knowledgeable than Vedas and Berun combined. If she believed they would make it through unscathed, they would.

Reason failed to alleviate the weight pressing down upon Vedas's shoulders. He massaged the tight muscles over his ribs, trying to ease the tension constricting each breath. Filled with the awareness that he had not spoken his true concern—that he could not in fact identify the source of his disquiet—he stared beyond the fire, unable to shake the conviction that something had followed him down from the highest Step.

‡

Long after Churls had fallen asleep, he lay awake, exhausted yet unable to still his thoughts. A familiar condition. As he had done every night since the cat attacked Churls, he replayed the event in his mind, imagining all the ways it could have ended badly.

All the ways he could have failed.

When sleep finally came, it offered no release. Churls perished again and again, her throat in the cat's teeth or her chest opened by its claws. Held back by invisible hands, he could do nothing to help. He watched her fall beneath the beast's weight and tumble over the edge of the world, only to rise again and succumb to another violent death.

He jolted out of the nightmare every time she turned in her slumber. Stilling his galloping heart, he listened for a sound, anything out of the ordinary.

This is pointless, he thought. *She doesn't need me worrying over her.*

Knowing this to be true—indeed, that she would consider his concern an insult—for two weeks he had hidden the signs of his distress. He remained still throughout the night so as not to alert Berun, and pushed beyond his fatigue from sunrise to sunset. He never mentioned the pain that lingered in his jaw where the cat had struck him. The joint clicked softly when he chewed his food, ached like a rotten tooth before every rain, and throbbed when he worried.

He wondered if the beast had been born of magic, if it had cursed him for taking its life.

Of course, he reminded himself, he had not been the one to deliver the killing wound. Churls's strike had been a thing of beauty, an act of stunning strength and precision.

In retrospect, he should not have expected anything less from the woman, who routinely got the best of him during their nightly Dull Sword sessions. Though unable to match his suit-assisted strength, she made up for her relative weakness with speed that outstripped his own. More than once, she disarmed him before he registered her movement—a first for an unsuited opponent, in his experience.

Unlike most combatants, she possessed only two giveaways: She pursed her lips before pressing forward, and her right shoulder twitched prior to switching her weapon to the left hand. At times she did neither, causing him to wonder if she were trying to keep him off-balance.

Their bouts were silent, humorless affairs. She breathed evenly through her nose and never showed her teeth. Afterward, she smiled tightly, as though disappointed with the outcome. He concentrated on stilling his shaking limbs.

Now and then, he caught her staring at him, as if she did not recognize his face.

Could she see through his pretense? He doubted the simple fact of his exhaustion would arouse her sympathy. But for a few brief moments of communion, following their course change he had given his resentment free reign. The gap between them continued to grow with each passing day, and he did nothing to bridge it. They could not be called friends, not by a stone's throw.

By the end of their journey they would be strangers once more.

This outcome had not always seemed inevitable. He remembered the way she had looked at him when they set out from Nbena. After two decades of celibacy, the recognition of a woman's attraction—and his own desire in response—had shocked him. For a brief while he had actually fantasized about a sexual encounter.

Now, when he caught himself staring at the curve of her clavicle, the inside of her thigh, he recoiled from his arousal.

Abse, Vedas reflected, would be proud. Though the abbey master did not stop brothers and sisters from forming physical bonds, he had made his own position clear on many occasions: *Lust clouds judgment. Remember, Vedas, we exist for one purpose above all else—to achieve victory over the enemies of man. Others have heard this calling, and felt it their duty to raise children who believe as they do, but this strikes us as too delicate a solution. Ours is the direct path. Any act that does not further us along that path is suspect.*

Vedas recognized the truth in these words, and vowed to achieve an alignment of heart and mind. Accomplishing this, reason dictated, would allow him to see his path clearly again.

And yet... Again? The word rang false.

Had his heart and mind been in complete agreement when Sara and Zeb Jol were slaughtered before him, or when the hellhound took Julit Umeda's life? They had certainly seemed to be, but now he found room for doubt. It seemed unreasonable that a man, knowing his cause to be just, having acted in accordance with his principles—bending his every thought toward one unselfish goal—should bear the weight of so much guilt.

Vedas considered the possibility that his heart and mind had never been in accord.

‡

Another restless night and fourteen hours of stiff-legged walking brought two facts into focus: He could not continue on his path without confronting his doubts, and one more day of traveling in strained silence would drive him mad.

The solution to both was simple, if not easy: he would have to seek counsel with Churls and Berun. The sooner he reestablished a sense of fellowship with them, no matter how fragile or slight, the better able he would be to name the problem that had so far eluded his waking mind.

Nonetheless, their arrival at the edge of the tenth Step came too soon. He prepared dinner slowly, trying to order his thoughts into a coherent pattern. An apology, a justification, or simply an explanation for himself. He suspected neither Churls nor Berun would accept an apology or fail to see through his justification.

An explanation, then. If he could make them understand the nature of his order, the specific reasons for his joining, they might help reorient him to his original purpose.

He had no intention of broaching the issue of intimacy with Churls—the thought of doing so horrified him—but he wondered if they might be able to reset their relationship, return it to its beginning. Dreaming of a physical encounter, ludicrous though the idea was, had distracted him from the memory of Julit Umeda.

Thus resolved to speak of his order, of camaraderie and shared purpose, it came as a surprise when he found himself recounting the events of the morning after the Thirteenth's battle with the Soldiers of the Appropriate Desire. His walk to Querus, Golna's only Tomen neighborhood. The smell of black pepper, cumin, and fennel. The hostile stares of dusky, redheaded men. His own stertorous breath and tightly clenched fists.

"Julit had been cremated at dawn," he said, enunciating with great care, betraying no emotion. "Her father held her skull in his hands while we talked. He pointed to the skulls above the hearth. *Julit's brother*, he told me. *Julit's uncle and grandmother and great grandmother*. He spoke softly, and his wife never made a sound. I wouldn't have known they were crying if the room wasn't so bright. They had placed lit candles on every surface, like they were trying to chase a ghost away.

"They asked me to assist in the funerary rites. According to Abse, spreading ashes is an unclean but necessary ritual in Toma, appropriate for a stranger—or even an enemy—to perform. I fit the definition of both, I suppose. Nonetheless, the request surprised me. I hadn't really expected them to ask. In Knos Ulom, a person's remains are sacred.

"They told me her favorite spot in the city was just under the Physickers' Bridge, on the Quarriton side. I used to go there as a child, too. It felt removed from the city somehow, like someone had set it aside for children. Even the homeless avoided it. The way down was tricky, dangerous for drunk feet."

Berun and Churls stared at the fire. Neither seemed inclined to speak.

Vedas let the silence stretch while he remembered. He had rolled drunks once, a lifetime ago, under the illusion of punishing Adrashi for their false piety. His gang of eleven children, not one above the age of ten, had enjoyed the implicit patronage of the city's Black Suits, who provided information: *This is how you identify an Adrashi*, and the like. The orders had armed the children and informed their rude faith, made them dangerous.

Gave them the confidence to push homeless men from bridges.

Vedas now recognized the evil of this arrangement. He counted among his blessings the fact that Abse had rescued him. Among Golna's orders, only the Thirteenth abstained from supporting the youth gangs. His brothers and sisters conformed to a code of ethics running deeper than mere doctrine. They watched over their recruits, educated and fed them, offered something better than a life on the streets. Even those who still lived at home were allowed to stay in the dormitories—a safe haven for many who would otherwise suffer abuse at the hands of their parents and siblings.

"Faith," Vedas said, angling his eyes to the sky, pressing fingertips to the horns of his hood. The Needle and the moon had risen above the Steps, illuminating the plain with cold light. "Her parents couldn't understand my faith, even though we were both Anadrashi. They had no idea their daughter had become involved with our order. It seemed to disgust them. *We're devout*, the father told me. His wife held her sickle-moon pendant before her, as though she thought it would protect her from me."

Churls cleared her throat. "You took off your suit?"

"No," he said. *No, of course not.* He considered telling her that he had not taken his suit off in over two decades, that he would not do so for something as minor as his visit to Julit Umeda's home.

But it had not been minor, had it? On the route to Nbena, he had replayed the meeting over and over again. Even with the distraction Churls provided, the event continued to haunt his sleep. On one mortifying occasion, he dreamt of Julit Umeda surviving the hellhound attack. Instead of informing her parents of her death, he went to congratulate them on her accomplishment, to welcome her into the order. He had woken from the dream, suffused with warmth, only to have the cold realization seize him again.

"Vedas," Churls said. She leaned forward, one hand raised from her knee as if she wanted to touch him but could not make herself do it. In the glow of the fire, the tattoos seemed to dance on her arm. A bear lunged, spreading its forelegs. A falcon dived, wings pressed tight against its sides. "Did you spread the girl's ashes under the bridge?"

"Yes," Berun said. "Tell us. Did you do it?"

Vedas's mouth was very dry. He moved his tongue around, but no moisture came. "I did," he finally croaked. "I took her ashes to the Physickers' Bridge. I slipped down the hill and located a spot to sit under the bridge—a place I used to go. The tide was low, so I hopped rocks out into the center of the river and smashed the urn. Her parents offered no directions, but that is the ritual among Knosi. We let water or wind carry the ashes away."

"And still you felt nothing?" Churls asked. "No release?"

Vedas breathed deeply into his stomach. He held the air for a moment, and then let it rush out. "No. I don't know what I expected to feel. I've commanded men and women not much older than Julit Umeda. Many times. A few have died. I never felt responsible. I did all that I could to insure their safety. I tried so hard to..."

His head dropped forward. His fingers curled into fists in his lap.

"No, that's a lie. If I tried as hard as I could to insure their safety, they would still be alive. I shouldn't try to convince myself otherwise. Millar Abo, Kelt Abbenajer, Amy Luethr, Somses Xu, Sara and Zeb Jol, Vakim Woril, Samual Honesth, Pylar Romane, Edard Hsui, Julit Umeda—I sent each of them to their deaths. I carry their memories. I can't let them go, even though wisdom says I should."

"Whose wisdom?" Churls asked.

Vedas's features twisted into a scowl. He had expected the question, but the anger it provoked took him by surprise. "Don't," he said. His lips puckered, on the verge of shaping words.

"Don't what?" she said. She held up her hand, silencing any response. "I've tried so hard not to offend you, Vedas, but that's coming to an end, right here: We match honesty with honesty. I see you trying to defend your faith when you and I both know it requires no defending. Adrash exists, and you believe he should be opposed. You believe mankind should dictate its own course. Fine. As far as convictions go, it's not a bad one. But that's not what we're talking about. We're talking about what a man does in the name of his faith."

He started to speak. Again, she stopped him with a gesture.

"Listen, the problem is that you can't separate what you've been told with what you know in your gut to be true. If you believed in your role as wholeheartedly as you want to believe in it, there would be no problem. You wouldn't have to forgive yourself for leading those kids to death because you would have been in the right all along." She chuckled without humor. "I hear you asking a question, but I don't think you're listening to yourself yet."

Berun nodded his great head.

Vedas's fists loosened, and he clasped his shaking hands together. Despite his attempts to hold onto it, the temper that had built while Churls spoke dissolved, settling within his veins, leaving him cold. His head swam as though he had been blindsided by a vicious blow. She had spoken truly: Something did indeed call from within. A question or a revelation. It whispered at the edge of comprehension, awful in its potency.

Instinctually, he fled from it, retreating to a comfortable position.

"I should have protected them," he said.

Churls sighed. From Berun came the odd rustling sound of spheres moving deep within his body. Neither moved, and Vedas admonished himself for a fool. Of course they had nothing to say. How could they put themselves in his position? Had they ever led a team of scared children, or tried to comfort a grieving parent? Certainly, Berun had never done so. And Churls—Churls was traveling to Danoor for personal gain, probably in order to satisfy a debt. Hardly a situation for a responsible person to find herself in.

I would have more luck talking with the ocean, Vedas thought, and rose wearily to his feet.

"Stop," said Churls. "Don't go. You see Berun and me sitting here, listening? If you don't want to ask yourself the question I think you should ask, fine—I'm not going to try to force you. Still, there are other questions. Why did you insist on going to the girl's house in the first place? What did you hope to accomplish? You said this had happened before, so why burden yourself before your journey? It makes no sense."

Vedas swayed where he stood, unwilling to sit back down, unable to walk away. Churls's words passed through him like an arrow through flesh, tearing a new pathway for infection, new doubts to plague his existence.

The sound of spheres moving in Berun's body increased, and then abruptly shut off. "No," he said. "It's not time to answer questions. It's time to listen. Do you know what Nhamed told me about you? He said you're a man of honor. After traveling with you for some time, I know this for a fact." He swiveled his head to stare at the sky. "You're a closed book, Vedas, and more than once I've wanted to knock your head from your shoulders, but that isn't important. You defended Churls when you didn't have to."

His eyes found Vedas again. "Quit lying to yourself. There's only one sure way you could have prevented those children's deaths, and that is by not placing them in danger. If your faith isn't strong enough to withstand the death of a child from time to time, then you will have to stop leading them into battle altogether."

Churls dipped her head in agreement. Her eyes had returned to the fire.

Vedas fought a brief spell of dizziness. His ears rang. His jaw ached.

Before words of denial or acceptance formed in his mind, a scream carried across the Step.

‡

"That's no animal," Churls said. She buckled her sword belt. "A woman or a child, the better part of a mile away. If we were upwind, I doubt we would have heard it." She nodded to Vedas. "We're taking a look, right?"

Vedas said nothing. Another scream sounded.

Berun shrugged.

Churls scowled. "I can't listen to that and just stand here. Can you?"

They ran. Berun jogged beside them, huge feet drumming on the hard ground. Whoever had screamed would certainly hear them coming, if he or she were still alive.

Vedas did not question why he had agreed to go along. He ran, and for a moment forgot his troubles. He had lost weight while traveling, and it seemed like his feet barely touched the ground. Running felt very good, in fact, like punching through an opponent's guard.

"I can see something ahead," Berun said. "Figures, three or four. Not very large, running. They look human."

"Can't be sure of that." Churls drew her sword and held it by the blade, near the hilt for better balance. "Are they moving away from us?"

"No. They're crossing our path, maybe one hundred yards ahead. There's a fourth, definitely, smaller than the others. It's running from them, not far ahead. One of the three following her runs on four legs and is continually jerked back, as if it's on a leash. Sometimes it stands on its hind legs and runs like a man. It howls like a dog."

Vedas concentrated, and caught the sound. "I hear it, too," Churls said.

"Magic or witch-lore," Vedas said. He imagined the fear the pursued child must feel, knowing what followed at his or her heels. "Leave it to me."

Berun's eyes flared. "We haven't decided which side we're on."

"I have a feeling," Vedas said. "I've been on both sides of the hunt. Good men don't draw out the pursuit like this." He pushed his legs harder, propelled forward by a visceral sense of justice. "I'll take all wagers."

Churls grunted. "For once, I'll go with the odds."

Vedas leaned forward into the night, legs as firm as iron underneath him. The hood of his suit tickled over his forehead and cheeks, slid like a lover's caress over his lips. He bared his teeth within the mask. The blood raced in his veins. The smell of his own sweat mingled with the elder-cloth, and it was the smell of home.

‡

They closed the distance. When they were a hundred feet away, the hunters released their howling creature and turned to meet them. Vedas saw that the pursuers were indeed men, squat and strongly thewed. Both carried heavy pickaxes in meaty fists, and waited in ready postures. Vedas looked beyond them as the fourth figure fell under the creature's body, and aimed in this direction. As he passed the two men, light erupted from their bodies. They glowed as if they had been turned to molten metal.

Shit, Vedas thought. He knew enough of magic to recognize it for what it was: alchemical armor. During a battle in Plastertown, a White Suit using a similar spell had fought off seven Black Suits by himself.

"Hold them if you can!" Vedas yelled to Berun and Churls. "I'll take the beast!"

He jumped. His right shoulder hit the creature's upper back and his arms whipped around its chest, carrying the body clear of the child's. He tightened his grip as they slid on the hard-packed soil, allowing the creature no opportunity to regain its feet. It howled, turning its head with blinding speed to snap at his face. The sour rot of its breath struck him like a blow, and its chomping teeth rang an odd metallic sound. It bucked and spasmed under him, but he held fast, pushing its belly into the ground, splaying its arms and legs under his bulk.

In full control now, Vedas put one hand against the back of the creature's head and savagely slammed its face into the ground. He straddled its waist, unmindful of the claws raking along his thighs and buttocks. The suit hardened in defense so that he barely felt the contact, yet the frenzied movements fueled the rage screaming in his limbs. He slid forward, positioning both kneecaps on the creature's upper arms, just below its shoulders. His hips rose into the air, shifting the full weight of his body onto his knees.

The bones gave way with satisfying snaps, and the creature howled. Vedas put both hands on its skull, twisting it back and forth, grinding the creature's face into the unyielding earth.

"Don't. Fucking. Touch her!" he spat through clenched teeth. The blood beat red waves of pressure behind his eyes.

A high-pitched whine reached his ears. He pushed harder to quiet the sound.

"Basuz!" a voice boomed.

"Stop!" another said almost simultaneously—a voice Vedas barely recognized in his fury. A giant hand closed around his torso and lifted him into the air. Iron-hard fingers flowed under his arms and pried them open, forcing him to drop the mewling creature. Somewhere in the back of Vedas's mind, he knew Berun held him, yet he thrashed wildly in the constructed man's grip, roaring like a man possessed.

The single, ragged note held and then fell into silence. He stopped flailing and held his body still, fists clenched, every muscle rigidly defined on his shuddering frame. After a handful of seconds, his chin dropped onto his chest and his body sagged in Berun's gigantic fingers. His jaw throbbed.

"The child?" he said. "She's okay?"

A hand slapped his face lightly, and then lifted his chin. Vedas focused on Churls's face.

"Who are you talking about?" she asked.

"The girl they attacked." Vedas located the two dwarfish men, whose bodies still radiated a warm orange light. He met one's eyes, and the look they returned shocked him. Horror. Fear etched the man's rough features, and he made a warding sign in Vedas's direction, left fist held to forehead and then thrown forward. Adrashi, obviously.

Vedas looked at Churls again. "Where is she?"

She shook her head, eyes locked on his. "Vedas, there is no girl. What we do have are two miners, their slave, and a thief."

‡

Powerful muscle shifted under the slave's hairless skin. He growled menacingly, yet somehow managed to look pathetic. The "creature" Vedas had fought was obviously a man, despite the changes sorcery had wracked upon his body. His lower jaw had been elongated so that it hooked under his nose, cheeks cut so that his mouth could open wider. Saw-edged ridges of metal lined his lipless maw. Limping upright, his broken arms hung uselessly at his sides. He turned on his leash, revealing the scars where his sex had once been.

Now that Vedas saw the man, he pondered how he could have so mistook him for a beast.

It had not been his only blunder.

Indeed, the thief was no girl. Standing a bit above Churls's waistline, the woman's face was a map of wrinkles. Clearly, she did not view Vedas as any kind of savior, for she stood behind her captors as they talked to Berun. She stared at Vedas, expressionless, but he imagined a challenge in the way she held his gaze.

Berun let Vedas down, and told him to unmask himself—to show that he was a man, not a demon. The constructed man explained that, before he and Churls had engaged in the fight, one of the miners had pointed to the fourth and yelled, "Thief!" Berun had understood the Ulomi word immediately, and surmised their identities.

"These are Baleshuuk men," he explained to Vedas. "Corpse miners."

Despite himself, Vedas breathed in sharply.

Churls nodded at his astonishment. "If I wasn't staring at them, I wouldn't have believed it either. No matter who told me." She shook her head and spoke in a softer voice. "I don't know what I was expecting, but somehow they aren't it."

Too stunned to agree or disagree, Vedas simply grunted. His mother had told him tales of the Baleshuuk, the near-mythical suppliers of elder corpses. She described them as impossibly thin like the elders themselves, yet he had heard others describe them as thick or egg-shaped, not men at all. Though few if any of the tale-tellers had ever seen one, the existence of the Baleshuuk could not be denied, as the world continued to receive a steady—though ever more expensive—supply of bonedust and other elder materials. Nos Ulom had become rich by exporting these hard, dwarfish mountain men to Stol and Knos Min, the world's most elder-rich nations.

According to legend, the Baleshuuk extracted elder corpses from solid rock as easily as midwives coaxed newborns from their mothers' wombs. It was said the miners used magic like ordinary men used forks and spoons. Vedas stared at their pickaxes and wondered.

"How can we make this right?" Berun asked.

Vedas struggled to catch the miners' response. They spoke in a thick Ulomi dialect, full of rolled R's and long vowels. Every word Vedas caught—one out of every two or three—seemed a syllable too long. Only superficially similar to Berun's dialect, the Baleshuuk's speech contained numerous alien words that confounded even the constructed man. He shook his immense head, furrowing the shelves of his brows in confusion.

Vedas did not need a translation to read the miners' expressions, however.

"They're very angry," Berun finally confirmed. "They're threatening to return with a full company of their brethren. I've tied to explain our mistake, but they don't seem to understand. *She is a thief*, they keep telling me. It's their right to punish her as they see fit."

"I agree," Churls said. "Can we pay them off?"

The taller of the two miners spoke up.

"'You ruined our slave,'" Berun translated. "'He is worth four ounces.'"

"Shit," Churls said. "We don't have that much to give. Do we have anything else of value?"

A sound came from within Berun's body, as of glass clinking. He reached down and plucked a handful of objects from his thigh. He lumbered forward and bent, presenting them to the miners. Vedas recognized them even from a distance. A collection of spells, the largest of which was a tiny porcelain jar sealed with wax.

"Where did he get those?" Churls whispered.

"A witch attacked us on a pass between the Sawbuck Mesas. I told him not to take her spells, but he did it anyway."

The shorter miner took the spells. He held them up to his ear and recited seven words slowly. Names. He handed six of the spells to his companion, who stored them in a pack hanging from his belt. The stoppered jar remained in the short one's hand. He examined it from every angle before closing his eyes and sniffing its seal.

Suddenly, he grinned. "Yesh," he said. "Yesh. Okee."

The two miners conferred briefly, and then the taller one spoke to Berun. The constructed man's hand engulfed the smiling miner's, a ritual of agreement Vedas recognized from his time at the river docks in Fishertown.

"They've agreed to part ways peacefully," Berun said.

Frowning, Churls said, "They seem happy."

Vedas watched the two miners, faces nearly split with grins. Berun had given away something extremely valuable, apparently.

A tight feeling spread outward from Vedas's chest, observing their cheer. They were still going to kill the thief, he knew. And why should they do otherwise? An old woman with no use? Surely, few would miss her around the cooking fires, the laundry buckets.

Yet he recalled how fast she had run from the howling slave. The way she stared at him even now, unafraid. She had never cursed him with a gesture. He tried to compare her to anyone he had known in his life, and came up empty. A tiny old Baleshuuk woman. Not Churls, nor a little girl with a black sash tied around her arm. Not the drunk he had helped push from the Physickers' Bridge when he was only nine years old.

"We've overpaid them," he told Berun. "Tell them to spare the thief."

BERUN

They made their way northwest toward Lake Ten under the cover of night, avoiding any sign of man. Churls, the least likely member of the party to elicit an aggressive response from the Adrashi men of the Apusht, walked point over the more exposed ground. Berun caused his eyes to revolve around his head, constantly vigilant.

They kept a lookout not only for Adrashi. Raiding parties of Tomen were not uncommon this close to the border. Fiercely independent, the people of the desert nation considered organized religion an abomination, and proselytizing to foreigners a waste of energy. Anadrashi and members of other sects had been known to buy their freedom on occasion, but Berun, Churls and Vedas possessed only enough bonedust to reach Danoor.

During the first night's travel, Vedas kept his eyes fixed westward. "It's hard for me to fully conceive," he said. "I've bought wares in Querus for years. Two of my brothers are expatriated Tomen. I know their reputation, of course. Even in Golna, they cause violence from time to time. Still, Followers of Man—people who should be my brothers- and sisters-in-arms—an entire nation living with such hatred toward its neighbors!"

Churls grunted. "I've never been to Golna, but I know many who have. You know what struck them about the city? During the day, they could walk anywhere without fear. Watchmen were posted to every street, and they didn't appear to be extorting anything from anyone. Don't assume the rest of the world is like home, Vedas. In fact, I recommend you take the worst of what you've heard about other people and assume it's the truth."

"I'd prefer not to form that habit."

"Preference has nothing to do with it. You treat people like they have your best interest in mind, and nine times out of ten you get stabbed." She forced a smile. "Look, I appreciate that you don't like looking at people as suspects, but goodwill only extends so far."

He breathed deeply, visibly suppressing the urge to defend himself, to contradict her words. In the end, he simply nodded.

The act of restraint impressed Berun. Talking about Julit Umeda, the encounter with the Baleshuuk and their slave—the events had changed Vedas in a way the constructed man did not yet understand. The end result, however, was clear: Berun's automatic hostility toward Vedas had dissolved, replaced by a genuine affection for the man's unyielding awkwardness, and Churls no longer carried herself as if she expected a battle.

They pressed on through the hard, folded land. The farther they traveled from the Steps, the harsher the territory became. Winds blew westward through the valleys constantly, striking the hardscrabble earth and whistling through Berun as though he were a dried sponge. The components of his body rasped together shrilly. When he examined his innermost spheres and found them to be caked with layers of dirt, he began cycling them through his body constantly in order to keep clean. When they found water, he washed too.

Anything unrooted to the ground was carried into the dust-streaked sky. It became quite cold, far colder than Casta. Churls suffered the worst. She took a woolen jacket from her pack, removed her skirt, and pulled on tight brown leathers that hugged her hips and buttocks. Vedas took to falling behind so that he could watch her walk. The man fought to hide his attraction, but his eyes gave him away.

For her part, Churls showed no sign of noticing the attention. Doubtlessly, she did. She was, Berun knew, the subtler of the two by far.

The minor drama amused Berun.

He needed amusing. They all did. The Apusht was taking its toll, physically and emotionally.

By the third night, the wind had become more than a nuisance—it had become a frightening adversary. It hid their enemies behind sheets of dust. At times it seemed capable of carrying them into the sky. Around small, smokeless campfires, Vedas and Churls rarely spoke of their goal. They talked as if it had been abandoned. Berun marveled at the human propensity for gloom, which he suspected had infected him as well.

Increasingly, he sensed the presence of his father. Ortur Omali's spirit stalked him across the land, spying, influencing him in ways he could not yet comprehend. The memory of standing over Vedas's sleeping form with Churls's blade in his fist haunted him, causing him to wonder if he would be able to resist Omali's direct command. Though he longed to convince his father of the Black Suit's goodness, he did not desire another confrontation, another demonstration.

Best to avoid it for as long as possible, he reasoned, and muster what strength he could. Every day while his companions slept, he strived to keep his mind from drifting and becoming vulnerable to his father's will. It grew noticeably easier to focus the longer he maintained his manlike form. The more he reigned in his urge to transform, the more rooted he was to the world. As a result, he no longer built structures with his body or split himself in two.

Like a flesh and blood man, he longed for release. The temptation to give in was strong, but he resisted, found ways to distract himself.

The most effective distraction had long since become an obsession. While tracking the travelers' progress across the highest Step on the map he kept superimposed over his vision, he had made a discovery. By concentrating upon a region it would expand and focus, lending him a bird's eye view of the landscape.

During the daylit hours, he found his attention drawn away from the local surroundings to the limits of the known world—to the ocean and its myriad islands. The continent of Knoori held many interesting sights, surely, but he longed to see places unknown to man. In an effort to comprehend the true scope of the world he had only dimly beheld in vision, he pushed at the boundaries of his map. The progress here proved slow, but the effort satisfied him, like a fight well fought but ultimately called a tie.

Beyond the satisfaction exploring the map provided him, four times now he had been able to spot groups of men whose path they would soon cross. It was difficult to locate such individuals under the cover of night, but his skills improved day by day.

Though he could not fathom why, he endeavored to keep his newfound ability a secret. He lied to his companions. *I saw a scout. I heard them approaching.*

Churls was not fooled. For four days she had listened to his explanations without comment, and then: "Tell me what you're seeing right now, Berun."

Caught off guard, he shrugged as though her question confused him.

She smirked. "I'm not an idiot, and you're an awful liar. You couldn't have seen the Tomen raiders yesterday from our position, and this wind makes hearing anything softer than an earthquake impossible. Out with it."

He glowered, searching the darkness at her back. Vedas would return from relieving himself at any moment.

"Berun," she said. "Why keep it a secret?"

"I don't know. What was I supposed to do, allow us to stumble into them?"

"It wasn't just that. I can tell when you're distracted."

His gaze shifted to her face. He examined her features, which had long since ceased to appear typical to him. No, he could not tell if they were beautiful, but such distinctions hardly concerned a constructed man. Of their own accord, the corners of his mouth turned upwards, and a new feeling arose within him, deeper than affection. He had been called out on a lie, and not because the thing had been ripped from his mind, but because another being knew him intimately enough to recognize it.

‡

He did not think overlong about why the thought of telling Vedas filled him with apprehension, for the truth spoke plainly: his father would not have the information in the Black Suit's hands.

Admitting this fact consciously only increased the agitation within Berun. For two days, he waged a silent war of wills against an invisible opponent—a master mage who contorted Berun's mind so thoroughly that it seemed he fought himself. Churls said nothing, but her concern for him was obvious. She kept close by, as though protective of a child.

They set up camp a mere fifteen miles from Bitsan, a small city on the southeastern shore of Lake Ten. He dug a shallow pit for the fire, feeling as though his entire body were close to shuddering apart. As strong as the urge was to remain silent, an equal force compelled him to assert himself. The balance could not last. The slightest tug in either direction would send him careening headlong down a new path.

Ever closer to enslavement, or toward self-determination.

"Vedas..." he said, and the scales tipped. The words flowed from him, accompanied by a sense of release he had not experienced since the night he had held Churls's sword above Vedas's sleeping form. He sat straighter as the great burden of secrecy lifted from his shoulders.

There, he thought when he had finished. *I've told him, Father, and the world hasn't collapsed.*

A deep frown cut furrows alongside Vedas's mouth. He kneaded the flesh of his inner thighs. "How far ahead can you see?" he asked. "Can you see Danoor?"

Aglow with his victory, Berun did not fight the temptation to brag. "I can see the Eleven Sentinels crumbling into the sea north of Grass Min. I have spent hours watching the cloth markets at Levaés. As we speak, sunlight is crossing the first of the Aroonan Mesas. I see all of Knos Min, Vedas. Of course I can see Danoor."

Churls kicked the fire's last glowing coal into sparks, and reclined under the lean-to Berun had constructed. "What does it matter?" she asked. "We won't be there for at least three weeks."

Vedas stared down at his clenched fists, and slowly opened them. "I'm expected in the first week of Royalty." He held a hand up, forestalling her response. "I'm not opening up that old argument or complaining. Still, I won't pretend I like the situation, not knowing what I'll be waking into. If there's a way to be more prepared, I want to take it."

Berun shrugged. "What do you want me to do?"

"I want you to observe the city. At the end of this month, people will start to arrive. Religiously neutral gamblers and fighters from Casta. Adrashi of every denomination and occupation from Stol and Nos Ulom. Fewer are coming from Dareth Hlum, as the trip requires travel through Nos Ulom or Toma. Because it falls on the eve of the half-millennium, Toma has prepared for this tournament for years, and will send thousands of its people northward. The largest group by far will be Knosi, and though they have pledged to keep the celebration peaceful, they will fail."

"How do you know this?" Berun asked.

Vedas sighed. "The tournament has always been followed by small-scale riots. I persisted in believing that this year would be different. I thought the celebration would overwhelm the instinct for violence, even among the Tomen. In other words, I fooled myself. I didn't want to believe the actions of my brothers and sisters could have such consequences." He nodded to Churls. "My eyes have been opened."

Churls met Berun's gaze. "Trust him," she said.

"Hopefully," Vedas continued, "the violence will be restricted to fractious Ulomi and Tomen on the outskirts of the city. If it spreads to the general populace, the whole of Danoor could be in danger. It would be very helpful to know the situation before stepping into the city. In fact, it would be good to know how things progress from the very beginning."

"Why?" Churls asked. "I don't see how that will make a difference."

Berun had been about to say something similar. He stared at Vedas, noting the way the man massaged his hands, how he avoided direct eye contact. Clearly, he would rather not divulge whatever information he possessed. For all the grace and skill Vedas displayed at fighting and hunting, he knew nothing of masking his thoughts. It was odd, Berun thought, that the man's most obvious weakness was also his most endearing quality. Few men made it so far in life without learning to lie.

"I'll win the tournament, or I'll die," Vedas said. "I expect to win. As we've traveled, I've become more confident in my skills." He caught Churls's eye briefly before looking into his lap again. "Our practices have been very helpful. And while it pleases me to think of victory, I now understand its magnitude. Winning the tournament will result in greater changes than I suspected when I left Golna. It's not a mere contest of faith. I thought it was, but it isn't."

Churls cleared her throat, but held her peace. Vedas stiffened, and then relaxed.

Berun considered his companions, the shaky ground between them, and spoke. "If Churls won't say it, then I will. There's no such thing as a mere contest of faith in this world, Vedas. You above all others should know this. To think, even for a moment, that it's possible to wage war against other men without consequence beyond the battlefield is pure idiocy. You're not a fool—don't speak as if you are."

Grimacing, Vedas ran a hand over his face. "Two months ago, I would have taken issue with those words, but you're right: I've been a willfully ignorant fool. Slowly, I'm coming to understand that men of the same order—brothers and sisters who profess the same convictions, curse the same god—can work toward opposing ends. The stated goal of the tournament is to win converts to our faith, to convince people of the power and truth of our vision. Despite my doubts, despite..."

He closed his eyes and exhaled. "Despite Julit Umeda, I still believe in this goal. The world is not Adrash's plaything. Men are not pawns. What I no longer believe in is my right to send an entire city into upheaval."

"How would you accomplish that?" Churls asked.

"Whoever wins the tournament will have enormous influence. Many who hear him speak will act as he commands without thinking." As if he were doing so with great reluctance, Vedas pulled a slim tube from his pack. Its wax seal had clearly been broken. "I opened this just after our encounter with the Baleshuuk. I don't know why I did. I was told not to. It contains a speech written by the master of my order. He has commanded me to read it during the New Year's celebration in the Aresaa Coliseum, which holds one hundred and fifty thousand men. Afterwards, I'm to have the text copied and distributed."

He met Churls's gaze. "I don't think I can do that. Reading it alone may cause a riot. Still, I must read something. They're expecting a speech from the winner." He looked to Berun. "Will you help me? Help me monitor developments in Danoor. Read the speech and tell me I'm crazy, or tell me I'm right to worry. Please."

He held the tube out, offering it to either of his companions.

Churls took it without hesitation.

‡

They arrived in Bitsan an hour before sunrise on the twenty-first day of the month: Qon'as Du'ses, First Day of Learning.

An unexpected blessing for the travelers, it began the Month of Learning for the D'Ari A'draasis, the major Adrashi denomination of Stol's southern lakeside communities. The D'Ari measured the year with a twelve-month calendar, and ended it with thirty-six days of fasting and study. Commerce all but stopped while the sun was in the sky, and tribal hostilities ground to a halt. During the Month of Learning, violence to man or creature was forbidden, a fact all the more remarkable for the legendarily hot-blooded D'Ari.

"I've heard of this kind of luck, but never experienced it," Churls said as she and Berun walked along the city's deserted main thoroughfare. While she had established the city's peaceable nature during her dawn reconnaissance, she had nonetheless advised Vedas to stay at the campsite. "We'd better not push our luck by bringing you into town," she had told him. "It's enough of a risk bringing Berun in."

Berun did not need to ask why she wanted him along. Her look of disgust communicated more than enough. No, she did not like asking for protection, but she was not stupid. Besides warfare, the D'Ari were known for their love of foreign women. Pale-skinned wives commanded a high price from tribal leaders. Even the Month of Learning might not prevent them from laying hands on a freckled Castan.

They found an inn close to the docks. Berun and Churls stepped through the door into humid, candle-lit gloom.

"Try not to attract attention to yourself," Churls said, the hint of a smile on her lips.

For all the alarmed stares their arrival caused, Berun knew few if any of the customers recognized him. The D'Ari had fought for millennia with Nos Ulom over Lake Ten's trade routes, and by every account disdained all things Ulomi. When a tribal leader took an Ulomi woman as his wife, he removed her tongue so that she could not talk of her homeland. Conceivably, if the men in the inn knew that Berun had killed Patr Macassel, they would welcome him as a hero.

Though he would not voice it to Churls, he found himself wishing for the exact opposite. A vexing wrath blossomed within him, spreading rapidly outward from his central components, causing his body to vibrate from head to toe. He pictured himself knocking the inn's customers aside as if they were ragdolls, pulping skulls between his palms.

The spheres of his knuckles spun, and a new sensation struck him:

Pounding. Fists beating on an immense door within himself. Ortur Omali, struggling to be free, to assert his will once more—to disprove Berun's recent victory over him. The reverberations shook Berun, rattling him to the core. For several seconds he feared he might fly apart, and then two voices spoke at once:

Berun, his father said, speaking with the sound of a thousand trees being ripped from the earth, tugging his creation away from the real world. Black spots—shadow moths, flakes of ash—swam before his eyes, obscuring his vision.

"Berun," Churls said, tugging in the opposite direction. Away from madness. She spoke his name a second time.

It was enough, barely, another near-defeat. The hex dissolved inside him, and the smoky interior of the inn snapped into focus around him. His joints sagged. He gripped the back of a chair to steady himself, and the wood shattered in his fingers.

Sound ceased in the room. The man at the table before Berun showed teeth, put a hand to the hilt of the dagger strapped horizontally on his stomach. His companion's fist tightened around the handle of a heavy mug.

The bartender ducked behind his counter briefly, and rose with two cocked crossbows. Instead of arrowheads, both bolts were tipped with ampoules: magic enough to hurt a constructed man, perhaps.

"Sorry," Berun said, brass voice loud in the crowded room. He straightened slowly, careful not to bump his head on the low ceiling. Talk started up again. The drummer and tambourine player resumed their soft rhythm, and the bartender put his weapons away.

Churls clapped a hand to Berun's broad back. "Congratulations on not attracting attention to yourself." She spoke loudly enough for him alone to hear. "And so much for a month of peace. What the hell happened there?"

Berun navigated the tables and chairs slowly, glad for a moment to think. He had not told Churls of his father's appearances, of course—but now that Vedas was out of earshot, he seriously considered doing so. He searched for resistance, and found none. Perhaps Omali could not rouse the energy after another failure.

What could be the harm? Churls might have something to say.

A server, clothed in a single fold of carmine cloth clasped at the neck, waited for them at a free table in the back corner. She swayed in time to the hypnotic beat, alternately exposing and covering her nakedness. Berun peered around and realized that, but for the servers, Churls was the only woman present. The men stared at her hungrily, causing the anger to flare inside him again. He clamped down on the emotion, suspecting now that his father could use it as a doorway.

He pulled a chair out and knelt on the floor. Still, he loomed over the table.

"Coffee and hash," Churls said to the server, who sashayed away.

Anticipating her question again, Berun held his hands up, palms forward. "I don't know." He reconsidered the lie. He trusted Churls. "That's not true. My father speaks to me in dreams. Sometimes, I'm fully awake. I think he wants me to kill Vedas, but I don't know if he's sure about this. He spoke to me, just a moment ago."

Her eyebrows rose fractionally. "Isn't Omali dead? No, that's not important. Are you going to kill Vedas?"

He admired the way she asked the question, as though she were asking about a cut of meat, no tiptoeing around the issue. "No," he answered. "I'm not going to kill him. I like him. Since his decision to rewrite the speech, I like him even more. The world already has enough killing in the name of

Adrash. Besides, a riot would delay the real tournament."

The corners of Churls's mouth turned down. Not for the first time, Berun wondered if they would end up fighting in the same bracket. Would she drop out if this were the case? He hoped so, for he could not imagine taking her life.

"You like him, too?" he asked.

"Shit." She groaned and leaned onto her forearms. "What the hell's wrong with him? What the hell's wrong with me? I'd like to chalk it up to old age, but I don't feel that old. Sure, I like him. I have goddamn dreams about him. The kind I haven't had for two decades. And what do I get for my obsession? Next to nothing. He ignores me and I'm nervous as a fucking newborn deer around him."

The way she spoke of herself awed Berun. Despite her uneasy interactions with Vedas, he had not expected it from her. Of all the people he had ever met, she possessed the keenest, most self-assured mind.

Surely, the Black Suit was to blame for the awkwardness between them.

"He looks at you often. You don't see that?"

She grimaced. "Of course I do. So what if he looks at my ass? A man staring at your ass means nothing. He doesn't talk to me like a man talks to a woman. Outside of our sparring sessions, he flinches at the slightest touch. And even if he didn't, how would I respond? He's a religious fanatic sealed in a suit he probably hasn't removed in years. Beyond the logistical problems, that fact means something. I don't like fanatics. My parents were fanatics. My sister's a fanatic."

"And what about the speech? He wants to change it. He asked for help. This means nothing to you?"

"Orrus Dabil Alachum," she swore. "You've thought things through, haven't you, Berun? In truth, I don't know how to account for any of this. Until the night he tussled with the Baleshuuk slave, I thought he was one person. Now I think he might be another. You told me I see something in him, but the truth is I don't know what I see. Most of the time I wish I'd never met him. Then I just wish he'd—"

The server returned, and Churls made her expression blank. She tapped the server's wrist with her index fingertip, and said in a low voice, "There's a gram extra if you can give me some information. We need a boat to Ynon. Doesn't matter what size, but it has to be reputable, and it has to leave soon."

"Reputable?" the server asked slowly. Her green eyes, which had appeared glassy and unfocused a moment before, darted from Churls to Berun. "I do not know what you mean by this word."

"Flags," Churls said. "It must sail under flags. No mongrels."

The server nodded. "How soon is soon?"

"A day, two at most."

Churls's eyes followed the woman through the crowd. She stared at her mug, at the ceiling, anywhere but at Berun. She picked at her food and he kept quiet, respecting her mood, and eventually a man approached the table with an offer.

‡

They exited the inn. Churls squinted into the sun. "I don't want to go back yet."

Berun nodded, and they walked along the shore, away from the docks. He admired the way the sunlight glinted off the waves, the sound of gulls screaming. He imagined what it might be like to smell things. Men always commented upon the smell of water. He considered asking Churls if she would mind if he took a stroll under the glass clear shallows, but rejected the thought. At that moment, she possessed a fragility incomprehensible to him.

She loves Vedas, he thought. Love, too, was unfathomable.

"Even with flags, it's not always safe," she said after some time. "Pirates sail these waters. Maybe our luck will run out on the lake." She squinted into the sun. "Sometimes I think that's what Vedas wants. A big fist to come out of the sky and smash him. A confirmation that fate's aligned against him."

"Maybe." Berun sensed she had more to say, and waited for it.

"I've read the speech," she eventually said.

"I know." He found a flat stone and pitched it hard enough that it was lost to sight long before it stopped skipping. He came upon two large rocks half-submerged in the sand, and picked them up. He turned in a circle, and then laughed his brass laugh. "Look around us, Churls. In an ocean of sand and small stones, these two rocks. Rough around the edges, ready to be turned into weapons." He began spinning them in his hands, grinding them down.

They resumed walking. "What does it say?" he asked.

"It's a call to arms," she answered. "A declaration of war."

CHVRLI CASTA JONS

She had resisted the temptation to masturbate for almost two months. The last time she did so was in Casta, the night Vedas complimented her swordsmanship. With the wind howling over them, she rose to orgasm three times, just thinking of his body so close. She had not known him then, not really: he had been an idealized version of himself, a dream creature.

Now, of course, she held no such delusions. Vedas Tezul was only a man, albeit unlike any in her experience. A confoundingly constant presence in her thoughts, at any moment she could summon him to her mind's eye. Hear his voice as though he stood next to her. Feel his warmth. She could close her eyes and recall every detail of his body.

He had changed a great deal during their journey. As a result of constant walking and lean meals, what little fat he possessed had burned away. His waist and thighs were thinner, not so much that a casual observer would notice, but Churls certainly did. Like a mage studying a book of alchemical diagrams, she catalogued every sinuous line of his physique.

His face, too, had been transformed. During their first days on the Steps, he had lost his razor. A thick, wiry black beard had come in, yet it could not hide the leanness of his cheeks. His hair, just a black shadow clinging to his scalp when she had first met him, grew in as a thick, helmetlike nap sparsely flecked

141

with grey. The wrinkles around his eyes had become pronounced, and the eyes themselves, a deep brown, almost black, seemed somehow more observant.

He had possessed the appearance and bearing of a young man when they left Nbena. He was beautiful then, definitely. He was gorgeous now—a singular creature that moved with the grace of a stag, unrushed and fluid. He held himself with a natural poise, as though the world fit him perfectly, conforming to his will as surely as his suit conformed to his body.

She pictured this man, an older and perhaps wiser man, as she touched herself under stained sailcloth blankets. Her hammock swayed to the violent listing of the ship, but she was determined, matching strokes of her labia with the violent movement, now and then pushing a fingertip deeper, brushing her clitoris lightly. She flexed her buttocks in time, imagining Vedas turning her sideways in the hammock, fingers prying her legs apart, an obsessive fantasy of being exposed by him again and again.

His beard rough against her inner thighs, ticklish against her anus as he lapped at her.

Probing her fingertip deeper, she pressed against her clitoris, rotating over the small, firm organ with increasing vigor. Imagining a tongue, a mouth. The occasional rasp of teeth, shocking and almost painful.

Sailors called to one another on the deck above, sounds muted by wood and rain pounding on wood. The brass bell of Berun's voice, calling encouragement. The constructed man loved being aboard the ship.

She sensed that Vedas was awake too, listening. Sailing did not agree with him. He worried about pirates and sinking, and his body had yet to acclimate to the motions of water. He fought every wave, attempting to right himself instead of moving with the motion. Time would undoubtedly prove his facility with this mode of travel, but in her fantasy he already moved with the confidence of a man born on the lake.

After finishing with his tongue, he wrapped hard arms around her lower back and pulled her from the fishnet—tightly hugging her so that she could not fall any lower, could not kiss his mouth or neck. She gripped his scalp, running nails through his short, thick hair. She tried to link her feet together behind his back, but it was too broad. His fingertips tightened into her skin, and he crushed her stomach into his face.

She breathed faster in the hammock, fingertip moving in rapid circles over her clitoris.

He held her down against the rough floor, hands tight around her wrists.

They kissed roughly, tongues flicking, teeth occasionally clicking together. His mouth tasted like almonds, and she swallowed his saliva. She thrust her pelvis upward, trying for contact, but he held his body above her, hips high off the floor.

"Please," she said, and he knew what the request meant. He lowered himself slowly until his weight rested fully on her. He let go of her wrist, and both of their hands descended. She pulled her skirt high around her waist, and he formed an opening in the suit material, allowing his rigid cock to spring free.

She reached for it. He batted her hand away.

The ship rocked from side to side. The sailors' voices grew louder overhead. Churls bit her lip until it hurt, a sharp counterpoint to the waves of pleasure radiating into her stomach and legs.

He slid his length into her slowly, and she tightened immediately around him, willing him deeper. The smooth, slightly cold material of his suit slid along her thighs, an alien and unbelievably arousing sensation. As the head of his cock pressed against her cervix, she gasped. He began thrusting, not quickly or slowly, but inexorably. She wrapped her legs around his lower back and rocked into his motions, angling so that his weight fell upon her, forcing his erection to a greater depth.

He gasped. Already, he was close.

In this respect, she suspected her fantasy held truth. She had wondered many times if Vedas was an experienced lover. She thought not. He certainly did not act like one, though he possessed extraordinary control over his body. No doubt, given enough time and attention he would become a very talented lover. But the first time his rise to orgasm would be quick and ungraceful.

Sometimes, she loved quick and ungraceful.

The swells of pleasure crested and broke. Her fantasy faded to nothing as she rode her orgasm through its surges. Her back arched and collapsed in the hammock, and her legs twitched. She bit her forearm, moaning into flesh. Her fingertip twitched on and off the hypersensitive skin of her clitoris as if it were a hot coal. As the spasms wound down, she slid her hand lower and pressed the fingertip against her anus, the merest suggestion of entry.

She pushed a long breath from her lungs, and then grunted as an immense hand slapped the port side of the ship, causing it to list sharply starboard.

Screams overhead, the sound of rushing water, the snap of timber.

The ship righted, fell to port. Her hammock turned over, nearly spilling her out.

Another wave pounded into the ship, but she did not scream. She thrashed in the fabric embrace of the hammock as it spun around a second time, one part of her attention focused on getting free and the other on the deck above.

No sailors' shouts. No feet drumming on wooden planks.

The ever-present thrum of the thaumaturgical engine, a sound that had long since faded into unheard background noise, had ceased.

The ship shuddered again, tilting.

She finally managed to throw the covers from her body. As the hammock swung high, she jumped free, landed awkwardly and rolled into the wall. She shook the impact away, oriented herself, and stood, struggling for balance on the bucking floor. Vedas swung in his hammock along the far wall, apparently unaware of any cause for concern.

She took one step, and the floorboards erupted before her. A jagged ridge of black rock rose up toward the ceiling. Water rushed in through the wound and the ship pitched violently.

Her feet left the floor and the ceiling rushed to meet her.

‡

The lapping of water upon a shore. The call of birds. A dull throb in her head and chest, her heartbeat, slowly spreading to fill her body. She swam through layers of fuzzy sensation into consciousness, into the dim recognition of wrongness. She was hurt, stricken nearly immobile on a beach. Alone, apparently. Minutes passed as she gathered the tatters of her memory and wove them together.

The wind changed direction and the leaves shifted above her. Sunlight tried to force its way in through the shutters of her eyes. She kept it out. The inside of her head felt far too fragile to tamper with. She opened and closed her left fist in the cool sand. This movement alone took a great deal of effort, but she did not stop herself.

Stay awake, she told herself. *Stay here, stay now, stay...*

Her throat was raw and desiccated, as if it had been scoured with dry sand, and her right arm throbbed dully. When she tried to move it, pain flared so violently in her shoulder that she decided never to move it again. At best, it was dislocated. At worst, she was only imagining feelings below the joint, and the limb itself was drifting somewhere in the lake.

As she became more aware, the more her body ached.

Clearly, she was alive. This failed to lift her spirits.

Something approached from the left. She heard the *shuff* of displaced sand as it drew close.

A man.

During her fifteen years of service in the Castan Army, she had spent enough time listening to the oncoming steps of enemy soldiers. Footsteps revealed a man's weight and height, as well as a good deal about his intentions. The man approaching her now was probably over six feet in height, well over two hundred pounds. He was not trying to be quiet. The profile fit Vedas.

Images flashed in her mind: A hammock swinging wildly, the black fabric of Vedas's suit visible through the fishnet. Water sloshing below, rushing in through a tear in the ship's floor, a blade of black stone jutting. A switch of perspective, her stomach rising up into her chest and promptly dropping. Sailing through the air. Out of the corner of her eye, Vedas's hammock overturning. Blackness.

Unlikely, that both of them had made it out alive.

She took a deep breath, though her ribs ached holding it in, and simply waited. Nothing to do but wait. Were she hale, or even only partially inca-pacitated, she would have prepared to defend herself.

Knees dropped onto the sand beside her.

"Churls," Vedas said.

She sighed in relief. The sound wheezed and cracked out of her like air from a dry-rotted bellows, and her fingers tightened convulsively in the sand. Her heart hammered. She did not try to speak or open her eyes, but felt her lips pull into a smile. Even that hurt. Fleetingly, she considered how much the intensity of her reaction would have bothered her if she were not injured so badly. Quite a bit, she reasoned.

"Don't try to talk," he said. "You're fine. I'm going to give you something to drink."

Unable to argue with him about moving an injured neck, she let his hand go under her head. She winced as he lifted it, but the movement did not result in additional pain or the click of broken vertebrae. Something rough and hairy touched her lips, and for a moment she fought to keep her mouth closed. She lost, and a trickle of lukewarm liquid slid down her gullet. It burned as it went, but he was slow and careful pouring. She did not choke. Eventually, she realized it was not water. The sweet taste was familiar.

She must have furrowed her brow.

"It's coconut," he explained. "A fruit that grows on palms. A rare treat. I remembered it from childhood."

"Mm," she said. He laid her head down, and a bit of light peeked in through her eyelids without killing her. She decided speech might be possible. "How?" she croaked.

She heard him sit back. "We ran aground a mile or so from Tan-Ten, and fell on our port side. The storm must have knocked us off course, right into the shallows. Maybe we were running from pirates and ran into the wind to lose them. No way of knowing, because I slept through most of it. The hold was already half full of water when I disentangled myself from my hammock." She heard disgust and embarrassment in his voice. "The oil lamps had spilled, and fire ate at the back wall. The ship lurched against rock. It was clear that we were sinking, but I had no idea how fast. After I'd oriented myself, I noticed you floating near the entranceway. I got you out and swam here."

Churls smiled at his understatement. "You got me out and swam here? How?"

He grunted. "With great difficulty. I can swim, but not well. If my suit didn't provide several minutes of air, I would have drowned. I consider it a minor miracle that we made it without major injury, and I don't generally believe in miracles. Do you feel better?"

Churls concentrated. The pain had increased, yet she did indeed feel better, more in tune with her senses. Experimentally, she turned her head from side to side, wiggled her toes, and lifted her left arm. Each movement was accompanied by its own particular pain, as if she had strained every muscle in her body. She opened her eyes a crack. The blurred outlines of palm trees swayed above her. To her left knelt the black outline of Vedas.

They appeared to be alone. This troubled her, but she could not determine why. Of course, she had more pressing concerns.

"Yes," she assured him. "A little better. Not much. What's wrong with my shoulder?"

He shifted. Slowly, she was able to focus on his face. He would not meet her eyes.

"What?" she asked, and lifted her head to see. Pain flared in her ribs and she dropped her head back down. "Orrus fucking Alachum! What the hell's wrong with me?"

The weight of his hand fell on her upper chest. "Please," he said. "Your shoulder is dislocated."

"How did that happen?"

"I don't know. You must have gotten knocked around before I found you." Softly, he swore—a first, in her experience. "Never mind. I'm not being honest with you. I know why your shoulder is dislocated."

She opened her eyes and found his. He met the stare for a second only, and then looked away. Being forced to press for an explanation would normally have bothered her, if not for the obvious fact that he was so troubled.

"Why?" she asked.

He leaned forward, cupping his chin and mouth with his right hand. His words were muted as a result, and she had to strain to hear them. "I swam as far as I could, Churls, but I still couldn't make it. The waves were too high. I lost my direction and went under, hitting submerged rocks. I tried to grab onto a few that rose above the water, but I couldn't get a grip. I still had air, but I couldn't swim anymore. Too tired. The next time waves threw me against the rocks, I tried to lift your body onto them. I think it worked, because I started to sink. Alone."

He massaged his jaw as if it pained him. He nodded, an almost imperceptible movement. "I knew I was going to die, and I didn't care. I gave up, but you saved me."

For a moment, she thought she had misheard. "I did what?"

He leaned forward and slipped his arm under her shoulder blades. In one smooth movement, unmindful of her protests, he lifted her into a sitting position. She had been prepared to scream, yet it never came. The pain faded so quickly she barely registered it, and he supported her in the new position while her spasming muscles calmed and the inside of her head stopped revolving.

"You pulled me from the lake," he said softly. Warm breath on her ear. "With one arm. You grabbed my wrist and dragged me onto solid ground. You looked like you were standing on the water, but I soon realized that I had dropped you onto a flat shelf of cobbled stones. An ancient dock, worn down by the waves. I could barely see it even when I sat on it.

"My legs collapsed under me when I tried to stand, and so you dragged me behind you, all the way to shore. Your right arm flopped uselessly at your side, a result of lifting me. I kept calling to you, but I don't think you heard over the storm and the waves."

Churls lifted her head. It weighed too much, so she let it fall against his. "What happened after that?" she whispered.

She felt him shake his head. "It's insane, ridiculous, but it happened. Once we were past the waves, you dropped my wrist. When I turned to you, your eyes were closed. I spoke your name, and you wouldn't respond. Your body glowed from the inside. White, like the moon. It peeked out from under your eyelids. I touched your hand, the glow faded, and you crumpled onto the sand. I know it sounds crazy. I've tried to reason it out, but I can't."

Churls closed her eyes, listening to the swift beat of her heart. Vedas's hands pressed against her chest and back, cool and firm—and suddenly, she recalled her fantasy. With his body so close, the invention became more real in her mind than any story he could have told her. Pulling a two hundred and fifty pound man from the ocean? Glowing like the moon? She did not want to think about such things. Focusing too intensely made her head ache. Drifting felt so much nicer.

Yet something nagged at her. A piece of the puzzle was missing. She tried to stop thinking about it, but knew it would come now that she had admitted its existence.

"There is one other possibility," Vedas said before she could ask the question. "You could be a witch."

She did not dignify this with a response. Her heart was not prepared for jokes.

"Do you think you can stand?" he asked.

"I don't know." She exhaled slowly, evenly, preparing herself for movement. "Why?"

While still supporting her, he rose from his knees into a crouch. "I'd like to reduce your dislocation now, if possible. It's a common injury while training. I've done it before. It will heal faster the sooner I get to it."

"What do I have to do?"

He lifted her easily. She gasped when her arm fell, and he told her to let it hang, which hurt slightly less. Standing on her own was difficult and painful. Her legs shook and she doubted they would hold her weight. Thankfully, he supported her every movement, and finally leaned her against a tree trunk. Her eyes fluttered with the strain. She registered her surroundings as a collection of vertical shadows and harsh light.

"Something else," she whispered. "Vedas..."

He said nothing in response. Perhaps he had not heard.

She breathed shallowly as he lifted her arm and placed his shoulder under her armpit. She wished he had given her something to bite.

"This is going to hurt," he said.

"I know," she managed through gritted teeth. "Just get to it." She took a

deep breath, and in this moment it came: the question that had been nag-
ging at her demanded a voice.

"Berun?" she asked.

Vedas paused, and she knew the answer.

"Sorry," he said, and rose from his crouch, levering her humerus downward against his chest, forcing the ball back into its socket with a loud pop.

She screamed, and then the lights went out.

‡

He wove a sling for her shoulder out of palm leaves and a larger one to hold
her body, and then set out across the island. He stopped to feed her coconut
flesh, urged her to drink. She rocked in his arms like a newborn, drifting
in and out of dream-troubled sleep. Each time she woke, the visions had
already faded, leaving her with only a vague sense of loss.

The waking world was little more than a dream itself, a series of confusing tableaus. The sun progressed in jerks above her. The ground rose and
fell so that the view upon waking was always different. A shimmering lake
with Vedas's reflection in it, her own face peering over the side of the sling.
Flashes of light, the sun through tree trunks. A squat, ugly animal standing before them, grunting, stamping hooves into the black earth. A wall of
hieroglyphed stone.

Vedas stood upon the gnarled, red-black spine of the island, which extended northward to a distant shore. She sat up to take in the view and
promptly fell back, exhausted by the minor exertion. There was a city on
the western shore of Tan-Ten, she knew. Its name eluded her. *A gambler's
paradise*, someone had once called it.

She licked cracked lips. "How far?" She could barely hear herself speak.

"Four miles, give or take."

"What's it called?" she managed, but fell asleep before hearing the answer.

Upon waking, trees surrounded them again and the name had come to her.

"Oasena?" she asked.

"Yes. Only a couple miles to go, but the sun is going down. We'll have to
stop soon."

She drifted away yet again. The next time she woke, night had fallen. She
lifted her head and peered around. A fire smoldered before her, casting weak
light over the small glade Vedas had chosen for camp. He slept on the bare
ground at her side, sprawled as though he had collapsed there. She reclined

on a bed made of palm leaves, angled so that she sat upright, cushioned so as not to roll to the side and injure her arm.

Her bladder ached. The makeshift bed rustled loudly as she struggled to rise, but Vedas did not so much as twitch. Probably exhausted, she reasoned, guilt constricting her chest with astounding force. Her mind had cleared and the weakness in her limbs was gone. She walked on stiff legs into the black forest to relieve herself.

As she stood from her crouch, a single white light appeared in the distance. Every time she blinked, the ghost of her daughter drew closer.

"Hello, Fyra," Churls said.

She allowed the girl to take her hand. Once again, she felt nothing at the contact.

The forest slowly grew in detail around her. She stared at the stars through the broad leaves, and eventually found the moon. A neat half circle, it nearly touched the black line of distant treetops. Almost morning. She had slept one whole day, and almost through the night.

All at once, she understood what had happened after the wreck. The obvious conclusion.

She had glowed white like the moon.

Vedas had saved her life, and in exchange Fyra had saved his—the girl liked him, after all. What shocked Churls most was not that the thing had happened, but that she accepted it so readily. It brought no joy to know she was safe, that Vedas was her hero, and that the dead could exert control over the living. At no point had she been offered a choice. She wondered if she had ever been in control. If she ever would be.

She removed the sling, rotated her shoulders, and held her right arm horizontal without pain.

"Did you do this?" she asked.

Yes, Fyra answered. *Do you like it?*

"I'm not sure."

The long pause made Churls look down. Fyra had screwed her face up tight, just like she had done as an infant. The expression that always preceded a fit.

"Stop it," Churls said. "You're not a little girl anymore."

Fyra frowned. *You don't like it? I can do other things. I've been practicing.*

Ice formed in Churls's chest. "What other things, Fyra? What else have you done?"

I'm not alone, Fyra said. She let go of Churls's hand and faced her mother. *There are others here. They're everywhere. Some of them teach me things, like the trick I used to save Vedas. Don't tell me I shouldn't have done* it. *He would have died, Mother. You would have missed him.*

The child was smart, Churls gave her that. She kneeled, and though it pained her to do so, she stared her daughter directly in the eye. "That's not what I asked, Fyra, and you know it. Don't brag about what you can do, and then tell me nothing."

Fyra reached out. Churls flinched, but resisted backing away. The child's hand passed into her chest, but all Churls felt was the steady thrum of her heart. Fyra's head cocked slightly to the side, and her eyelids fluttered closed.

I can see it, Fyra said. *Your heart. I can see through you, like you're made of ice. I met a dead man, and he showed me how to read what's inside people. He taught me to fix things that have gone wrong. There was something wrong with your heart, Mama. I fixed it. I fixed other things, too. Clogs in your veins. Scars in your womb. When Vedas pulled your shoulder into place, he damaged your nerves. He didn't mean to, just like I didn't mean to hurt you when I used your body to save him. I fixed everything, and now everything is better. Me, I did. I'm not a little girl anymore.*

Churls breathed long and deep through her mouth, pushed her fear to the side, and said the exact opposite of what she truly felt.

"I'm proud of you."

Fyra's eyes opened, flaring bright enough that Churls had to shield her own. *Really, Mama? The dead people don't tell me that. They tell me not to meddle. The world is for the living, they tell me, even when they teach me things. Don't meddle, they say. They're very angry that Vedas saw me, but I think they're wrong about everything. It's good what I'm doing, right?*

"Right," Churls said, throwing good sense to the wind. Considering how quickly her life had been hurled into disarray, how swiftly the revelations were coming, perhaps the best course of action was to embrace change. Never one for improvisation, always one for planning, she wondered how long she could sustain this philosophy before it drove her mad.

I have to go, Fyra said. *It's almost sunrise and they're yelling at me to stop, but there's one more thing I have to tell you. About the metal man with the blue eyes.*

"Berun?" Churls's heart leapt in her chest. "You saw him?"

Fyra beamed. *He saw me. At the bottom of the lake. That made the other dead people really angry, but I didn't care. I showed the metal man where to walk. I think he might have heard me, too.* She turned away, staring into the distance. She bared her teeth, flickered like a guttering candle. *Leave me alone!* she yelled, and faced Churls again. *I have to go. I hate them. Wait for the metal man. He'll be here soon, even if they don't let me show him the way. He'll find you. You'll wait for him, won't you?*

"I will," Churls promised.

‡

She encouraged Vedas to keep sleeping, but the man would not rest.

"We need to reach the city as soon as possible," he said. "Who knows how often boats leave for Knos Min? We can't afford to be delayed any longer."

Despite these words, he stopped often to listen. He looked over his shoulder, as though expecting a visitor at any moment. She read the pain on his face, and kept her mouth shut. In turn, he suppressed his curiosity about her impossibly rapid recovery.

She did not volunteer the information—did not even think about what Fyra had done. Finding a way to stay on the island long enough for Berun to reach them preoccupied her completely. She had no desire to deceive Vedas, but she would in order to allow the constructed man time to find them. A day at least.

She need not have worried.

The diffuse light of dawn revealed Oasena to be little more than a township. Nothing larger than a fishing boat floated in her shallow bay—certainly naught capable of crossing a hundred-mile stretch of open water. Vedas enquired in a bakery and discovered that a thaumatrig, a vessel most likely similar to the drowned *Atavest*, arrived from Ynon once a week. It docked for half a day and then returned.

"Tomorrow," Vedas said. "And it won't leave dock until the evening."

The muscles in his jaw twitched as they walked to the inn the baker had recommended. Churls resisted the urge to ask about the fare. He would give the details when he was ready. In the meantime, she took in the town's thatched single-floor houses, the somber flat-featured countenances of the townsfolk. The women walked bare-breasted, flat dugs hanging over short dresses woven from palm fibers. They rustled as they walked. The men looked much like the women, though their garments were of brown cloth.

Churls noted their corded arms and thick thighs, how their bodies moved and their eyes tracked, and surmised they would be formidable opponents.

An odd mood drifted through her. Not joy, no, yet it was a close cousin. Despite Vedas's dour air, she drank the sunlight as if it were an elixir. The corners of her mouth turned upward without her willing them. Somehow, she knew Berun would arrive before the ship left. They would arrive in Ynon safely. She considered the possibility that Fyra had rearranged her mind, but dismissed it. Pointless, to conjecture.

After a lifetime of useless and obsessive conjecture, this thought shocked her.

They reached the inn, and sat at one of its four small tables. A woman came from the kitchen, nodded, and went to fetch their food.

"Only the one option, apparently," Churls said.

Vedas glowered. "We won't reach Ynon until late on the first."

Calculating quickly, Churls's good mood faded. From Ynon it was perhaps seven hundred miles to Danoor. By all accounts, the trail to Danoor was well trod, but thirty miles a day for twenty-four days, during the darkest month of the year? It could be done, but she and Vedas would be exhausted by the time they reached the tournament. Undoubtedly, he had already made the calculation.

"The fare?" she asked.

"Six grams," he growled. "They can extort because so few boats come to Tan-Ten."

She smiled weakly. "But we have enough, Vedas. Barely. It can be done."

Neither of them had lost any money. Anyone smart enough to buckle her sandals carried her dust close to the body in waterproofed fabric. It was too easy to spill liquid and lose it all. Churls and Vedas had discussed their funds as they walked that morning, with one important omission. Before leaving Nbena, she had sewn a new pocket on the inside of her vest to hold the dust Gorum had given her. So far, she had not needed to touch it.

Between the three of them, there should have been enough—she should have been able to keep her stash a secret. But who knew what had happened to Berun's dust? Saying they could make it on what remained was a lie, and Vedas knew it.

Shit, she thought. *There goes my gambling fund.*

She reached inside her vest and removed the wallet. It lay on the table between them, an indictment. Proof she had kept it from him. Vedas stared at it, expressionless.

"It can be done," she said. "We'll make it to Sent in nineteen days, and rent horses for the stretch to Danoor. That's forty, maybe fifty miles a day. We'll be at the tournament by the twenty-fourth."

The innkeeper came out of the kitchen. Churls palmed the wallet, and they proceeded to eat fried trout and grilled asparagus in silence. Vedas could not sustain his glowering completely, however. Now and then he looked up, an expression she had never seen written on his face. Wonder, perhaps, or astonishment.

"What?" she eventually asked.

He jumped slightly, as though he had been far away in his mind. "Something just occurred to me," he said. "My decision has been made for me. Abse's speech went down with the *Atavest*. I now have no option but to rewrite it."

‡

In her dream, she walked down a long hall with doors on each side. Endless doors. She chose one at random, and inside sat Fyra. The child opened her mouth to speak, but another voice spoke instead. A voice from the waking world, calling her back.

She woke, and lay very still, eyes open, concentrating. It had not been just a dream. Someone had called to her. Someone had called her name, and then Vedas's name.

There! *Chuuurrlls. Veeedaas.*

She threw the covers to the side. Vedas jumped up from the floor, ready, but Churls silenced him with a gesture. She tapped her ear, and he listened.

His eyes widened.

They raced down the stairs and out the front door.

"Chuuurrlss! Veeedaas!" the voice called—closer, from out of the depths of black forest before them. A voice like a bell, deep and resounding in the pit of one's gut. Hearing it, Churls's heart pumped harder, strong and healthy and alive. She had not known how much the voice meant to her—how greatly she had come to rely upon the constructed man's presence as she walked, as she slept.

Again he called their names. Loudly enough to wake dogs and set them barking.

And then, a low rumble came to her ears. A steady drumming. Huge, heavy feet pounding the earth. Closer and closer.

Voices rose in Oasena, and the dogs began to howl.

Churls grinned, and stepped forward to meet Berun.

EBN BON MARI

For a month, the same routine before breakfast: With the assistance of a recall spell, Ebn watched the disastrous encounter with Adrash—over and over again methodically, like a composer playing an identical refrain to resolve an irksome melody. The spell made her forehead throb as it pushed against the confining walls of her skull, yet she persevered. She had missed something. Some detail that would help her to interpret the events that had transpired.

Adrash gestured at the statue.

Stop, Ebn commanded, stilling the image in her mind's eye. As always, and despite the pain of holding the memory still, Ebn lingered on the god's perfection. The graceful, sculpted proportions of his body. The lines of tension that defined the muscle and sinew of his back and extended arm. More than any other feature, she admired the flawless pearl complexion of the divine armor, an artifact she knew felt like the finest elder-cloth. Cold, infinitely smoother than skin. Her tongues stirred in her palms at the thought.

Her desire nearly overcame her every time. The memory wavered as though she viewed the scene through fire, and then lust gave way to sadness.

She would never possess such beauty. She had been a fool to think she could.

Enough, she told herself. *Enough foolishness.*

She resumed the memory at quarter-speed. Adrash shattered the statue

155

with a gesture, sending a thousand sharp-edged fragments of marble toward the mages. His eyes blazed brighter than the sun.

Stop, right before the first impacts. At the time, Ebn had been focused on Adrash, but in her recall it became possible to examine the other mages, who extended in a glittering arc just slightly out of focus in her peripheral vision. Sunlight reflected on the polished black skins of their suits. Qon's feet were only just visible above her. Pol floated directly opposite her. Ebn focused on his face, but read nothing new in his expression.

She moved forward in time slowly, by now familiar with the grim details. She had erected a shield with plenty of time to spare, perhaps because she had subconsciously expected the attack. Silver veins flickered on the surface of Pol's suit, signaling that he too had erected a protective spell. Eighteen others, mostly talented young mages, acted quickly to defend themselves, using spells both ordinary and exotic.

Three—Qon included—cast a fraction too slowly, deflecting only some of the stone fragments.

They did not die immediately.

The remaining seventeen mages were cut to shreds near-instantaneously. Ebn watched them die. She made herself do it, though the section she suspected of holding a clue came afterwards. Replaying the entirety of the disaster was her penance.

Gota fi Junnun, only sixteen years old but a promising student, face flayed as his helmet burst, torso pocked with innumerable small holes, bloomed an aura of blood that vaporized instantly around him. Hamen i Loren, Ebn's one-time lover, a man of immaculate taste and speech, was cut nearly in two by a large flake of marble. Intestines bubbled and burst from both halves of his body. Zi-Te bon Ueses, martial arts master and gambling enthusiast, was sliced from clavicle to groin but stayed conscious for several seconds, screaming a fine red mist.

Ebn watched each fatal blow, reversing the spell repeatedly so that all of her officers could be accounted for. Her stomach did not turn as it had the first few times—proof a person could grow used to anything.

In the midst of the chaos, Adrash disappeared. Ebn reversed and slowed her memory to a crawl. No fade, no wavering around the god's body, no sign at all that he would vanish. Clearly, nothing could be gleaned from this portion of memory, yet Ebn lingered on it every time. The god stood, fixed as stone. Then he did not, and it was as though he had never existed in that place. The raw power needed to enact such magic boggled her mind, horrified her in a way the deaths of the mages did not.

And here, in the vacuum Adrash had created: An anomalous event that had eluded her for the first two weeks of her search through the recalled memory. She chastened herself for taking so long to spot it, but knew how lucky she had been to notice it at all. Certainly, she could not be blamed for missing such a slight gesture during the disaster. Qon's hemorrhaging had occupied all of her attention.

The sequence lasted only four seconds. Immediately following Adrash's disappearance, Pol swiveled his head toward the moon, eyes clearly tracking a moving object. He ripped his gloves off and made a gesture, as if he were turning a globe in his hands. A heartbeat later, his eyes widened and his mouth fell open. It was this expression—so odd on Pol's typically controlled features—that had first alerted her to the moment's significance.

Stop. Ebn returned to the beginning and replayed the sequence slowly. By its nature, a recalled memory wanted to move at normal speed, and her head ached with the strain of holding it back.

There. Between these two seconds, she told herself. Something out of place.

Again. Again. Her temples pounded.

Nothing new revealed itself, yet she knew in her womb that Pol had done something highly irregular. After years of traveling in orbit, she had learned to trust her intuition. The obvious conclusion was that he had seen Adrash leaving and cast a spell in response, but Ebn could not make herself believe this. Pol's magical faculties had not progressed beyond hers. His lore was not so esoteric that she could not recognize it.

Frustrated, she moved forward to the second event of note. She watched herself fumble to hold the flaps of Qon's suit closed, willing them to mend while her friend hemorrhaged, coughing clouds of blood that frosted on Ebn's helmet. She pulled Qon to her chest and attempted to extend her spell of protection around them both. Tired from casting her own disastrous spell of influence at Adrash, the minor charm proved beyond her abilities.

In the final seconds of her life, Qon pointed in the direction of the Needle. Her expression alone had caused Ebn to turn, yet the view did not impress anything upon her. Despite repeated and painstaking examination, the spheres appeared unaltered.

Of course, she had not trusted her eyes alone. Queries over the last month had confirmed her suspicion: since the disaster, the telescopists had not observed a major change in the Needle's alignment.

Nonetheless, Qon and Pol had seen something. Had they actually followed the god's flight?

Or had they seen something else entirely?

‡

The recall spell faded. It exited through the sutures of her skull, easing the pressure within.

Why, she asked herself, *have I allowed this to happen?*

She could not pretend ignorance. She had angered Adrash by attempting to sway him with magic, an aggressive act to which he had responded in kind. Perhaps if she had stuck to her own plan and merely projected good-will it would have worked, but she had been unable to keep her own desire from coloring the spell. Just as she had feared.

Undoubtedly, Adrash had recognized her. Sixty years was no time at all for the god.

Had she truly expected a second attempt at seduction to meet with favorable results? Certainly, she had known the risks. Perhaps she simply had not cared about risk. Qon's life, the lives of her officers? They meant nothing in the face of her overwhelming desire to possess Adrash. This had been the true reason for approaching the god, not good will.

No. Ebn rejected the idea that she had lost her moral bearing completely. True, she had let her desire cloud her judgment again, but the ultimate goal remained the same. Adrash must be convinced of the world's worth.

She sighed, massaging a kink in her neck. She rose from her couch and walked naked onto the balcony, where the air was cool and smelled strongly of leaf rot. The chill of fall had seeped into everything, but she lay on the flagstones anyway. For a few minutes she shivered, waiting for the stone to warm beneath her. The morning sun soaked into her eggplant-colored skin, feeding her nutrients essential to the functioning of her body.

Slowly, the details of the encounter with Adrash drifted from her mind. Though she would never admit it aloud, in a way the disaster had freed her. She could sink no lower. Soon, she would receive a summons from the king. He would question her judgment, and she would defend herself. Defending herself, she would finally understand the how and why of her actions. It had always been this way, testing and retesting in response to the expectations of others.

She would triumph, and renew her purpose.

Someone knocked on the door. Ebn heard the whisper of slippered feet as her servant jogged to the entry, and then the girl's high, fluting greeting. The response, however, could not be understood. The voice was too low, the rhythm of speech oddly clipped.

The short exchange over, soft feet whispered toward Ebn.

"What?" she asked. She did not open her eyes.

"There is a man here to see you, magess. Shavrim Coranid."

"I do not know a Shavrim Coranid, girl. You have a list of my acquaintances. Unless he is on official business, send him on his way."

"He is not on official business," a deep voice sounded.

Ebn's eyes snapped open and she rolled to the left. She had not yet drunk her daily alchemicals, but enough magic remained in her veins from the previous day to cast one or two spells.

Binding the intruder seemed best. She rose to her feet and thrust her hands forward in one fluid motion. The spell moved visibly along her arms, like waves cresting and breaking under her skin. Thin lips pulled back from small, sharp teeth.

She paused. The man whose bulk filled her doorway held no weapon. His hands were crossed on the immense drum of his belly.

Two stubby horns sprouted from his temples.

"I have information about one of your mages," he said. "For the right price, I will tell you interesting things about a young mage named Pol Tanz et Som."

‡

Per his suggestion, they sat on the balcony. He did not want to ruin her delicate wrought-iron furniture. "I weigh four hundred and sixty-seven pounds," he explained.

Ebn could not place the man's accent, but his lineage was clear enough. Though surgery and magic could produce a hybrid in appearance, she knew this was not the case in regard to Shavrim Coranid. Very likely, he had worn tight-fitting clothing so that his nature would be obvious to her. His every muscular twitch fascinated her, yet she fought the urge to stare.

She recognized him, of course. How had she not noticed his uniqueness the night he had called a dragon from the sky?

By surprising her, the man had gained the high ground.

He would not be allowed to keep it.

She remained naked. The man had already seen her unclothed, so there could be no advantage in dressing now. Such an action would only reveal her discomfort. Best to affect an air of amused disdain, talk as if she were accustomed to unannounced visitors and their implied threats. She would not ask how he had reached her apartment without identification, how he had convinced her servant to let him in, or how he had lived anywhere near the city without the academy discovering him.

This last proved hardest to resist. At her core, Ebn was a scholar. To her knowledge, no quarterstock of Shavrim's obviously robust mental and physical health had ever been discovered. She resolved to cast a tracking spell upon him as he left, so that she might observe him remotely before taking further action.

The servant returned with tea and poppicut pastries, and then retreated.

"How much?" Ebn eventually asked. Her expression did not change, nor did her tone. They had been discussing fall, the myriad colors of dying leaves.

The corners of Shavrim's eyes crinkled. "One pound."

Ebn smiled openly but did not laugh. "Ridiculous. I do not know what kind of information you have. I will give you an eighth of a pound, and you will tell me something of value. We will proceed from there."

"You misunderstand me." The man leaned forward slightly. "I know the worth of my information, and by all accounts you are a trustworthy woman. I do not need to see the dust right now. If you agree to pay me afterward on the condition of the information's value, it will be sufficient. You are a sorceress. I am a wyrm tamer. If you wish to detain or punish me, I cannot hope to resist. Trust, then, will bind us."

Ebn considered, then nodded agreement. "Out with it," she said, all pretense of gaiety extinguished.

Shavrim held three thick fingers up. "Pol is dissatisfied with your leadership and he intends your downfall. I do not yet know where or how he plans to do this, but he intends to do it soon. Do not underestimate his power. Despite your attempts to keep alchemical resources from him, he has acquired the materials he needs."

Two fingers. "He has somehow managed to knock one of the Needle's spheres out of alignment. Very minutely. Most likely, your scholars did not recognize it. Adrash changes their direction often enough that it probably seemed like another of his minor whims, yet if you examine your logs you will see that a slight adjustment was made on the seventh sphere from the moon at the exact moment of the god's attack. "

One finger. "Prior to or just after your encounter with Adrash, Pol began to modify his body in some way. His reactions are quicker—unnaturally so. His spell-casting is improving by leaps and bounds. As I am sure you have noticed, he has taken to wearing black, close-fitting garments, designed so that only his face and hands show. He will not undress completely in my presence."

‡

Her fingernails bit into her palms. The tongues pushed back.

"You and Pol are lovers," she said.

His amber gaze did not waver. "Yes."

Her hearts shuddered in her chest, restarted off-kilter. A pressure built in her throat, as if she were being strangled. She had known it. Of course she had. The boy had always been so self-assured. He carried himself like someone who enjoyed fucking. She could see it, clearly. She was no fool, and she had her jar of sex spells to prove it.

Get off it, she told herself. *That is the least important fact you have learned.*

"Thank you," she said, and stood. She snapped her fingers and her servant appeared in the doorway. "Retrieve one pound, four ounces of dust for this man." She looked down at Shavrim. "You did not lie. That was certainly worth the money."

The quarterstock furrowed his brows. "Please sit down, Magess bon Mari."

She met his stare, shrugged, and sat. She did not doubt the man's intentions even slightly. Now that she knew the truth about Pol, the whole world felt bright and clear, her path through it obvious. Not a comforting truth, no, but knowing it was better than believing a lie.

She would crush Pol. She would force him to love her and then watch him die.

"I will take the extra dust," Shavrim said. "But you deserve something for it."

"You have more?" she asked. "He must have told you that I love him. Surely he has seen it. He has known me for too long." Her voice dropped an octave, became a warning. "I do not want to hear any more about his disdain for me. Clearly I mean nothing to him. If you have ever loved, you know this kind of pain."

He smiled without humor. "I have been betrayed before, and have no desire to increase that particular pain. Instead, I will offer you a small boon: Garrus

Eamon. He works at White Ministry, in the morgue. Recently, he was caught filtering alchemical materials from corpses. He and Pol are lovers."

She filed the name. The quarterstock had given her more than he needed to.

He stood, and offered his hand. She took it, the first time she had touched another person without her gloves on in over three decades. He did not flinch when her tongue tasted his palm.

As she walked him to the door, she marveled at the way her life had been overturned. It had happened so quickly, so cleanly, an entire limb cut from her body without pain. A few exchanged words with a stranger, and she was a new person.

She had also figured out the anomaly in her memory. When Pol removed his gloves, for a split second he revealed a small patch of lustrous black on his wrist. Ebn visualized it clearly.

A tattoo. She would not even need to use the recall spell to confirm it.

Had he really been stupid enough to use alchemical paint on his own skin? On the other hand, if it worked...

At the door, she faced Shavrim. It shocked her to find that he stood a few inches shorter than her. "Why did you do this?" she asked.

"I need the money."

"Enough to betray a lover?"

He shrugged his immense shoulders. "My work as a tamer does not pay well, and Tansot is a poor place to be a fighter. Still, I am a fighter, and Danoor is fast approaching."

POL TANZ ET SOM

Pol had spent much of his adolescence along the docks of Ravos, Pusta's capitol city. There he watched the fishermen pull their catches from the teeming sea, corded arms and calloused fingers quick with the rusty latches and mechanisms of their enormous trap baskets. Naked, they scampered with odd grace over the monumental wire and steel structures suspended between the docks, dodging the man-sized pincers and jagged jaws snapping at them from below.

Their dexterity astonished and thrilled him, as did their scars and missing limbs, which rarely impeded them in their tasks. Such devotion to work had made Ravos the most successful exporter of seafood in all of Knoori. The fishermen were beautiful and dangerous and proud of their craft, and they shared their bodies as freely as they shared labor. They did not look down on an elderman boy, especially one so eager to learn.

Had Pol's mother known the way he spent his evenings, spreading his legs for men of low caste, working, drinking and carousing with laborers, she would have locked him in a cell. Had he been dimmer or less intellectually inclined, she certainly would have found him out.

Despite the time he spent with fishermen and dockhands, he did not echo their concerns or beliefs. They were a fascinating people in their own right, but hardly examples for an elderman boy. He used them, first for pleasure and then for their unique perspectives.

Few noble-born men cared to know what laborers thought of the world. Unbeknownst to the aristocracy, labor guildsmen communicated across national borders, irrespective of the restrictions placed upon them by government. They exchanged information on trade and common magical practices, and maintained extended family ties.

In Pol's opinion, these comprised the least significant percentage of exchanged information. The majority of laborers in Knos Min, Nos Ulom, Stol and Casta practiced a highly fluid form of oral storytelling called adrasses, which recounted moments in Adrash's life upon the earth. An adrass—the events of which often began thirty millennia or more before the present age, far beyond the scope of recorded history—never referred to the god's ascension into the sky. It never referred to the Needle, or the obvious threat its existence posed to the world.

Such tales transcended the rude boundaries of Adrashi and Anadrashi, for while no sane man could deny the god's existence, he could interpret events as he saw fit—a fact that contributed to the continual development of adrasses. Even Orrust and Bashest sects, a small minority in most nations, took part in the telling, incorporating the legendary events of Adrash's life into the traditional stories of their own deities.

The fishermen of Knoori's coasts shared a particularly rich canon of adrasses, compiling the numerous tales of Adrash's life as a sailor. Of course, the people of Jeroun generally agreed the god had exiled himself to the ocean for a period of time prior to his ascension into the sky, yet only the most conservative Adrashi claimed to know his reason for doing so. Largely uninterested in his motivation, fishermen of all varieties celebrated Adrash's incredible feat of navigating the ocean with tales of superhuman strength and daring.

According to the fishermen of Ravos, the god had set sail from their very docks. They claimed he saw their bravery, their clean sweat, and was so inspired that he decided to embark upon his own adventure. He formed a ship out of steel and glass without the assistance of tools, fusing the materials together with the light from his eyes. Once finished, he pushed the vehicle out to sea alone, battling beasts along the way.

Convictions were split on the ship's name. Some swore it was *Aberrast*, others *The Oabess*. Its prow was a knife blade, fine enough that creatures learned to steer clear of it lest they be cut in two. He piloted the sixty-foot vessel alone with a crank drive and propeller of his own design. Many adrasses differed in this account, insisting that the ship was powered by sail or by thaumaturgical engine, but the fishermen of Ravos loved nothing more than a display of muscle.

They downplayed the role of the divine armor in Adrash's life. In their accounts he only grew to rely upon its power later—during the unspoken period after he left Jeroun's surface. They saw the god as a being of superhuman sinew and bone, relying upon his strength, wits, and nautical skill. Some went so far as to claim he found the armor itself while at sea, that it was a gift from the Ocean Mother, no greater than his whalebone sword Amedur, his shark-toothed club Xollet, or his narcroc-ivory spear.

Oftentimes, the armor, swords, whips and spears came second to Adrash's most treasured possession: The sentient dagger Sroma, which he had carved from the rib of a giant elder corpse he found floating around Iswee, the floating island on the other side of the world. He carried the dagger onto the sodden land and battled the reanimated elders who defended it from man. He used it to carve the wooden skyboat *Dam Tilles*, which astronomists claim sits atop Mount Pouen, under the crystal dome that covers the island of Osa.

Adrash slept with Sroma, never let it leave his side. The Ystuhi, a religious sect of crab-catchers who inhabited the south Pustan coast, still carved blackwood statues of the god with elaborate whorls cut into his skin and the outline of the dagger between his shoulder blades. They believed Adrash had loved the weapon enough to embed it in his flesh.

A Pustan fisherman's version of Adrash would be unrecognizable, unbearably offensive, to the conservative Adrashi nobles of Stol or Nos Ulom, who revered the god as all-powerful and immutable, as distant from man as scrub grass was to sentinel oak. In this regard, Pol stood somewhere on the fringe of both groups. In the days of youthful revolt, he had been much influenced by the fishermen. In truth, he still considered Adrash a vengeful, even capricious lord. But in accordance with conservative Adrashi ideals, he believed Adrash had always possessed the armor. His other weapons were the stuff of myth.

No god would debase himself with such crude tools. Only man and elderman relied upon the strength of bone and steel.

‡

Mid-afternoon, Pol walked to the docks to buy a set of knives. Not any knives, either. He required a very specific design for his purpose. Garrus had recommended a bladesmith in Vanset, but Pol did not trust Ulomi and decided on a shop Shav recommended in Little Demn. He admired Tomen for their serious, frequently violent practicality. If anyone could make a knife suitable for an assassin's hand, a desert man could.

He met every stare in the street, unafraid. The unsheathed blade of his liisau caught the sun, announcing his presence from several blocks away. For someone like Pol, Little Demn was just as dangerous during the day as the night. Men could easily see him for what he was: not only an Adrashi, but one who actively sought peace with the devil.

It was an important distinction, for just as many types of Anadrashi zealot existed as Adrashi. Roughly equal in number but generally less organized than their god-worshipping brethren, one basic belief bound them: Adrash should not be worshipped. The reasons for this numbered in the thousands, but roughly boiled down to two philosophical stances—the canonical and the personal.

The Black Suit orders, for instance, taught that Adrash actively sought the destruction of the world, and could only be kept at bay by displaying one's faith in mankind, by cursing the god at every opportunity, and by physically besting those who worshipped Adrash. Though they acted in the community, they primarily expressed their faith through planned, bloody encounters with similarly outfitted Adrashi orders. Their faith was a thing of rigid order, tradition, and—though they would not admit it—a certain measure of symbiosis.

This expression contrasted sharply with that of the Rinka, a fraternal organization of former Adrashi in Northeastern Casta. Bound by the shared experience of family abuse, the members expressed their ecstatic faith in city squares and markets. Crying and screaming were encouraged as part of the proselytizing. Members often renounced drinking and gambling, and preached nonviolent opposition to Adrash through meditation and fasting.

Tomen rejected both the canonical and personal stances. They considered the existence of Adrash—whom they considered to be a demon of great power—to be a practical affront to humanity, and reacted in kind. Reasoning that Adrash drew strength from his worshippers, the men of the desert took every opportunity to take the lives of Adrashi, as well as weak-wristed Anadrashi. They valued freedom and self-sufficiency above all else, wrote no creeds, proselytized not at all, and committed no violence upon their brothers. Some claimed that within Toma existed the most peaceful society on the continent.

Along its borders, however, more men died in combat than anywhere else on the continent—a situation mirrored in their expatriate communities. But for the presence of the city watches, places like Little Demn were for all practical purposes border towns at war.

Pol interpreted the looks he received correctly. They would gladly gut him if given the opportunity.

A month ago, he might still have chosen to travel alone, but he would have seriously considered the consequences. This morning, however, he had not given it a second thought. Cool fire moved along his nerves, twitched the muscles in his fingers, urged him to move, to strike.

Do it, his stare mocked. *Attack.* He knew with every ounce of his being that an entire army could not stand against him.

He had moved the Needle.

Every day since Ebn's disastrous mission, he had awakened to the same nervous sensations, the same memory of knocking one of Adrash's spheres out of alignment. He recalled the pain of the sigils awakening upon his body—the mounting, rapturous pressure of the unknown spell straining for release—the vaguely disappointing knowledge that he had acted too late to save his brethren—and then the near-instinctive unloading of his pent magic upon the first target that came to mind. He tried to summon the exact feelings to him again, lingering on each detail as one might linger on a lover's touch.

It had been a gift from the void. A call to action, proof he could no longer sit by and let events continue unchecked. He would answer the call and make himself a leader of men, but to do so he knew he must prepare carefully.

For a brief period after the disastrous encounter with Adrash, he worried he had become too addled to continue painting sigils on his skin. But, despite all of the energy coursing through his system, his hands were sure with each stroke. He even found himself painting his back, as though his fingers had eyes of their own. Sometimes it seemed the sigils were painting themselves. The marks became more complex, esoteric, and dangerous. He became a collection of alchemical lore. A weapon.

His power would soon eclipse Ebn's. Possibly, it already had.

Odd now that I must search for knives, he thought. Such crude implements, yet he did not want to rely solely upon spells and sigils. He would not underestimate Ebn, a craftsman of magic with few equals, a mage who responded to attacks with cunning and raw power. She had even swayed Adrash, if only for a moment. Undoubtedly, she had examined her memory of the failed mission. Perhaps she had discovered what Pol had done, knew his power for the threat it was.

During the final confrontation, she would not allow sentimentality to cloud her judgment.

In this, they were bound. He prepared himself, and thought up novel ways to kill a master mage in orbit.

‡

Shav weighed the knife, flipped it a few times to test the balance. Ten heavy inches of steel, a straight handle accounted for half its length. The teardrop blade, edge ground to razor sharpness, accounted for the other half. Per Pol's request, the bladesmith had bound a fine layer of charcoal to its surface so that it would not reflect light. It was a simple, elegant weapon, a tool clearly intended for killing.

"I told you he was good," Shav said. "When will the others be ready?"

"Week's end, he said."

"You must have been robbed."

Pol smiled. "Yes, I was, and he took some convincing. He told me that if he accepted my business, he would be dead by week's end."

"Nonsense." Shav stood and threw the knife overhanded into the target Pol had fixed to the wall. His next throw hit flat and clanged to the floor. "Why is this shaped so?" he asked, running his finger over the chisel-shaped tip of the handle.

"I have designed the knife carefully," Pol said. "Once thrown, it has two tasks. First, it must shatter Ebn's helmet. Second, its weight must carry the blade forward into her skull. In many ways the handle is more important than the blade."

Pol gave this information without hesitation. He had long since ceased keeping secrets from Shav. He no longer hid his sigils. Though he had not yet discovered a use for the quarterstock, his idiosyncratic presence was oddly comforting. Furthermore, he was an excellent lover. Even his smell, which seemed to always carry the salt and rot of the sea, had an odd charm. It amused Pol to think he had once been intimidated by the quarterstock.

Shav turned his hand. The knife disappeared into his sleeve. He thrust his hand forward, and the knife appeared in it. He grunted in surprise at the blood welling up from his calloused thumb. "Why is the blade so sharp? You can practice with a dull knife, can't you?"

"No." Pol took the weapon from him. He hefted it and then flicked it underhanded into the target. "I will not chance it. The weight of the practice knives needs to be exactly the same as the killing blade itself." He pulled the knife free and repeated the throw. He moved back a pace and hit the target handle first, but got it the next time, and the next.

Shav watched, brows raised. "You've thrown knives of this design before?"

Pol shrugged. "No."

"Maybe you shouldn't get used to this, then. Handling the knife, yes, but maybe not the throwing. No doubt, it will fly differently in the void." Shav sat at the table and tore a piece of rouce bread, dipped it in green olive relish. He gestured for Pol to do likewise. "Maybe you should practice in orbit."

They sat in silence and ate. Shav's intelligence never ceased to arouse Pol's interest. Curious as to his strange companion's education, he had made subtle enquiries at the academy but discovered little. Of course, Shav claimed to have done many things. He had been all over Knoori, claimed to have fought in a dozen wars, many of which were happening simultaneously. He had sailed the ocean and planted his feet on foreign soil. For many years he had kept his identity hidden, staining his skin with a semi-permanent black ink.

Pol dismissed much of the history out of hand. The quarterstock was mad, a charming and startlingly keen liar. At times he had seemed almost prescient, but now Pol suspected he was merely a skilled observer. A man could appear to do miracles if he watched others closely enough.

"That is my intention, yes," Pol finally answered. "Unfortunately, I believe I am being observed constantly now. This morning, I breakfasted with Ebn. All scheduled solo ascensions—and thus all independent projects of study in the void—have been placed on hold. She wants the mages to maintain a constant presence above Jeroun from now on. Comprised of eighteen half-day shifts, the watch will operate as an early warning system of sorts, possibly even the first line of defense against Adrash. A ridiculous concept, of course, but Ebn is insistent.

"I have been assigned the twice-weekly task of ascending to orbit and relieving the first and fifth shifts. As you may have guessed, I will not be alone in this task. Loas, the most senior mage next to Ebn now that Qon is gone, will accompany me. He is highly skilled in the lore and unquestionably loyal to Ebn. I must find a way of silencing him so that my target practice is not revealed."

"Won't it be revealed the moment you take on another partner?"

"No. Ebn's resources are stretched too thin. It will be weeks before she can find a replacement for Loas. For a time, at least, I will be left to my own devices. Even if I am wrong, it should not be too difficult to arrange yet another accident in the void. Many of the voidsuits were damaged when

Adrash attacked."

Shav shook his head. "This is far too complicated. Why not simply replace this Loas with someone you can convince to keep your secret? Someone you can buy?"

Pol had already considered this and rejected it. "Beyond the fact that Ebn would find my request for a replacement highly suspicious, I would not attempt to bribe another mage. Only someone in a weak position would accept such an offer, and sooner or later he would realize how much more there is to gain by turning me in. No, I must convince Loas to help me lift the helmets and targets into the void. I will tell him it is a last minute request from Ebn. And then, once we have reached orbit, I will kill him."

"Your plan hinges on one act of deception? What if he doesn't believe you? He will not ascend with you, but go immediately to Ebn."

Pol ground his teeth together. "I have no other options, Shav. I have so few resources at my disposal, no friends conveniently placed in positions of..."

He paused, struck dumb as the answer suddenly revealed itself.

He had finally found a use for the quarterstock.

"But perhaps I have been looking in the wrong places," he said. "It occurs to me that you may be of some assistance."

Shav chewed thoughtfully for a moment. "You want to use my dragon as a pack animal."

"Yes," Pol said, impressed once more with the quarterstock's acumen. "I want it to carry the helmets and targets so that Loas's curiosity is not aroused and my hands are free to attack. I can manage the weight of the helmets and targets from that point on."

"Sapes and I can only travel so high, which means you must strike your enemy well before reaching orbit. Gravity won't be on your side, so you'll have to act very fast. Are you sure it wouldn't be wiser to kill him at your convenience and allow me to transport your materials later?"

"I am sure. Time is of the essence."

"His death must look like an accident, Pol."

Pol closed his eyes, picturing the spell he would cast. His fingers twitched on the tabletop, and his tattooed skin puckered with gooseflesh. The sigils seemed to assert themselves more and more every day, whispering possibilities, temptations. "I can do it. Can I rely on you?"

Shav stood and stretched. An erection pressed against the fabric of his pants. He wrapped his fist around Pol's bicep.

"Of course you can. You..."

His eyes rolled up into his head and he shuddered, fingers tightening on Pol's arm. Pol waited, mildly amused by the display.

"The elderman," Shav said once the seizures had ceased. His voice was deeper than Pol had ever heard. Almost painfully hoarse, it quavered as though the quarterstock were in agony. "The elderman's name is Orrus. He is my father. He has won his first battle and will soon leave for his second. He is frightened, as he should be. He knows a wiser man would hoist sails for the outer isles, leaving the world behind. Instead, he contemplates taking from the Lord of the world his most prized possession. He is a fool."

The quarterstock knelt. His right index fingertip traced the lines of the flight sigil tattooed on Pol's shoulder. "Before he leaves, my father tells me to contemplate death. He tells me to feel my mortality in the creak of my bones and the soreness of my muscles. *With every heartbeat, you are closer to death*, he says. He forces me to smell the stench of his underarms—the smell of the body birthing and decaying life at the same moment. He tells me to know, intimately, every sign of weakness in my body, and then reject each in turn.

"He breaks my arm with one blow, kicks me as I writhe on the ground. *Remember this lesson above all others*, he says. *The body heals. It responds to trauma, to pain—not with fear, but with purpose. So must you. You need not die, my son, but in order to continue living—*"

Shav stared into Pol's eyes.

"*—you must suffer.*"

PART FOUR

VEDAS TEZUL

The Locborder Wall extended three hundred and fifty miles along the western shore of Lake Ten, from the foothills of the Aspa Mountains in Nos Ulom to the screwcrab warrens of Toma. Begun in the twenty-third century and finally completed in the thirtieth, its length documented Knos Min's former glory, before Nos Ulom and Toma applied pressure west and northwards on the larger nation's borders, reducing its area by half.

Once, an army had slept atop the wall, guarding its hundred gates and the various villages clinging like barnacles to its lakeward side, but the increasingly aggressive gestures of Nos Ulom and Toma forced Knos Min to fill many of the gates. By the midway point of the one hundred and twenty-fourth century only the three largest remained: Ioa, Ynon, and Defu. The villages had been abandoned long before and were crumbling slowly into the lake.

Adrash chose this moment to send his two smallest weapons to earth. They struck the ocean to either side of Knoori, sending tidal waves to the coasts, water vapor and dust into the sky. Thus began the Cataclysm—a tragedy of such monumental proportions that, one thousand years after it occurred, few referred to it at all. When the clouds finally parted, ending the decade-long winter, the population had been reduced by fifty percent.

175

Nothing lived along the shores of Lake Ten, which did not thaw completely for twenty years after the Cataclysm.

As the continent grew warmer, men gradually returned to the lake, and it was not long before they discovered something extraordinary. Previously unknown species of fish had survived the great freeze, breeding in vast numbers under the thick ice. Large and oily-fleshed, the animals represented not only survival, but prosperity. Generations could grow strong on food such as that. Nations whose borders had not shifted perceptibly during the famine decade now found themselves fighting to keep their waterfront property.

The race to repopulate had begun.

Without a doubt, the nation of Knos Min came out ahead. It owned two hundred and seventy miles of Locborder and its most strategic docks. A vast infrastructure for repopulating cities, fortifying armies, and communicating over vast distances still existed. The old capitol, Danoor, the new capitol, Grass Min, and the sprawling equatorial metropolis Levas sent their best engineers, fishermen and soldiers to the three cities of the lake—Ioa, Defu, and what would come to be the most important, Ynon.

Instead of waging a war of territorial conquest, however, the administrators of the three cities simply fortified the two borders abutting the shore and concentrated on hauling everything they could from the great lake. Dried and fresh fish went to all corners of Knos Min. They traded none of their catch, no matter how high the demand grew throughout the rest of the continent. All resources went to feeding, to growing. Immigrants pored in from across the continent and Knos Min welcomed them, demanding nothing but labor and loyalty of arms.

The first thing many new citizens learned about was the history of Locborder Wall, which had grown as a symbol to encompass the hopes of an entire nation.

As a child, Vedas had learned this narrative. All Knosi children did, no matter how far they had strayed from their homeland. The residents of Golna's affluent Tannerton had even erected a miniature replica wall alongside their tiny manmade lake, Tenia. Its placement confused the neighboring boroughs because it blocked the view of the water. Few understood how large Locborder loomed in the Knosi consciousness.

In Golna, Men of the Republic were considered arrogant by many of their neighbors, yet this was an unjust prejudice. Tomen were not proud of their deserts? Castans did not admire their own enterprising natures? Arrogance defined Knosi no more or less than the other peoples of Knoori. Anyone who sought to know them would come to the same conclusion.

At least, this is what Vedas had heard. He steered clear of his fellow expatriated Knosi instinctively, like a man avoiding estranged relatives. Abse had once encouraged him to spend more time in Tannerton and Foxridge, but he balked the moment his foot stepped into either neighborhood. The people were too uniform, too like Vedas. Their high cheekbones and wet soil complexions, their broad shoulders and straight backs—all of these things made them more alien than familiar.

An irrational reaction, surely, but Vedas could not control it. He had aligned himself with the Thirteenth Order of Black Suits, and by so doing had left his people behind.

‡

The entry guard looked him up and down, took his name, and waved him through.

As simple as that, Vedas returned home. Yet instead of passing into the city he stood alone under the immense, arcing gate, feeling its thousand tons of basalt pressing down upon him.

Stepping out of the shadows should not be such a challenge, he reasoned.

Surely, the air smelled no different in Ynon than it had in Bitsan. In the early morning light even the architecture looked the same: Two- and three-story buildings of sun-bleached sycamore planks. Every fourth or fifth one had been painted, as if the owner could not stand the regularity. Locals glanced at his suit in mild curiosity as they walked by, yet their eyes passed over his features without a second glance.

He folded his arms and leaned against the wall, affecting a casual air. His companions would see through it, but he did it just the same.

A mere ten feet away on the other side of the gate, Churls tapped her foot and gave her name, place of birth, and current residence. The guard wrote the information on his form slowly, asked each question slowly. More often than not, her responses seemed to confuse him. He asked her to repeat herself several times. Finally, he stamped a square of cloth, handed it to her, and waved her through. She smirked at Vedas, rolled her eyes.

Berun stepped up, and the process began again. The guard glanced up at the towering constructed man several times—curious, but not overly so. The reaction surprised Vedas. He had expected something more elaborate for

Berun. Backup guards, a robed government mage, possibly even a hellhound or two. But his interview was identical to Churls's, down to the symbol the guard stamped on his cloth."

"Do you think that's odd?" Vedas asked.

Berun pressed the cloth to his chest, absorbing it into his body. "It is, and I'd be surprised if this was the end of it. Nos Ulom considers me a terrorist, as the Republic is no doubt aware. Someone will be watching my progress, and it will be very difficult to identify whom. It could be anyone." He shrugged. "Then again, they say more constructs exist in Knos Min than anywhere else. One more with a bad attitude might make no difference to them."

They entered the city, the streets of which were jammed tight with locals and foreigners on their way to Danoor. As the sun rose above the rooftops, ever more travelers poured from the doorways of hostels and inns and began making their way toward the western edge of the city. They waited in long lines to buy overpriced jerky and dried fruit, canteens, and sleeping packs. Vedas tried to suppress a growing sense of urgency. They would get through the city exactly as fast as everyone else.

Churls bought a change of light clothing, a new sleeping roll and blanket, and eventually located a bladesman's. She selected a corroded vazhe the owner strongly discouraged her from purchasing. He suggested a Tomen rekurv instead, a Fazees cuass, even an Ulomi dueling rapier.

"That will not even slice bread!" he called from the door as they walked away.

Churls ran her hand over the rusty blade. She popped a reddened fingertip in her mouth and smiled. "Castan steel. No substitute."

They waited in more lines. Vedas and Berun stood back a pace as Churls argued over this price, this item's quality, this vendor's attitude. Finally, finished with their shopping, they moved toward the outskirts of the city. Churls maintained a vocal presence in the crowd, striking up conversations, directing slow walkers to step aside.

Vedas watched her, amazed that anyone could be so confident in a foreign land.

He existed in a state of agitation, constantly on his guard. Curious strangers brushed their fingertips over his suit, tried again and again to strike up conversation. Men with features that mirrored his own stood in doorways and peered down from balconies, smoking joss and drinking wine. This was their city, their country. They stared at him through their long, meticulously matted locks, demanding an explanation.

Who are you? Where have you been, and why have you returned?

The answers eluded him. He struggled to feel a sense of brotherhood and failed.

No, Vedas could not call his return to Knos Min a return home.

Berun gawked at the constructs around him. Mostly small creations in the shapes of dogs and cats, there were only a few of more intricate design and obvious intelligence. A giant wrought-iron centipede with the head of a dragon. A centaur of constantly shifting gold plates. They hailed each other with waves of their appendages.

One in particular, whose form was an intricate silver and black elder, struck up a long, convoluted dialogue with Berun as they entered the ragged line of travelers striking upon Grass Trail, the eight-hundred-mile path leading from Ynon to the capitol of Grass Min. Its voice was deep but lacked resonance, grating like the magically recorded lectures Abse played to the Thirteenth's youngest students. Its tall, finely articulated body clicked metallically as it moved, jerking from position to position. An awful composition of sounds and colors, it was one of the ugliest things Vedas had ever encountered.

"Name is Tou," it finally got around to announcing. "Remember you."

"Oh, yes?" Berun rumbled, face turned away from the other construct. "I don't think we've met."

"Haven't. Heard about you." Tou craned over Berun to peer down at Vedas and Churls. Mechanisms whirred behind its thin, severe face. Four multicolored gems twitched in its eye sockets. "Haven't heard about you," it said.

Churls looked up at the hideous face. "Go away."

"Thank you," Berun said after the creature had left. "All of these constructs unnerve me. I don't know how to react."

"Any time," Churls said. "Better to not have him around anyway. Seems like the type to spread rumors, not that anyone would understand him."

Berun chuckled. "At least he's never heard of you two."

"Yeah." Churls poured a pinch of dust into her palm, spit on it, and began polishing her new sword as they walked. "First bit of good news in a long while."

‡

Grass Trail rose and fell gently on Hasde Fall, the wooded hills west of Ynon. Sugar maples and sycamores dropped their dying leaves on the stone-paved roadway, creating a multicolored blanket that rustled under the travelers' thousand feet. Sturdy wooden bridges crossed the occasional brook or small river, where fish were plentiful and easily caught. Despite the travelers' disparate backgrounds and religious perspectives, a congenial atmosphere prevailed. Were the weather not so nice, the surroundings not so beautiful, it might well have been a different story.

For all of the land's natural appeal, no one veered far off the road. The Republic owned and maintained the land, barracked its soldiers on it, and looked unkindly on those who trespassed. No signs were posted—none were required. Knos Min, for all of its legendary restraint and religious neutrality, maintained the continent's largest army and jealously guarded its supply of elder corpses. Even in the present age where men feared an end to this supply, The Republic's magical resources were legendary, as evidenced by the number of constructs owned by ordinary citizens.

Rumor spoke that a bare handful of miles from Grass Trail, Baleshuuk had not only discovered a near limitless vein of elder corpses, but were tunneling to the center of the world. Shielded under megatonnage of rock, mages of all kinds developed powerful new alchemies. Outbound mages trained in rooms where the effects of gravity had been canceled. Armies of constructs and hybrids enacted the great wars of history over and over again, in preparation for a great, continent-spanning war.

Vedas saw no reason to distrust or believe these rumors. Stol possessed outbound mages and Baleshuuk—surely Knos Min, with its obviously vast magical capability, had developed programs to maintain its position. The specifics hardly mattered to ordinary men.

Yet the second night out, such speculation dominated conversation around the campfire. Nboles, an elderman bowyer traveling to Danoor to sell his wares, sat cross-legged on his wheeled construct-trunk and spoke of the Osseterat, a hybrid ape of immense intelligence. "They live in this forest," he claimed. "The more they observe men, the more they become like men. They are stronger and faster, however. When and if the white god destroys the world, the elite of the Republic will enter the earth through tunnels only they know about. Like the Baleshuuk, they plan on surviving. The Osseterat will be their servants."

His voice became hushed and he cast glances into the forest on either side. "But what if they cannot control their new beasts? Maybe the apes won't want to be servants. Maybe they're planning, even now."

Churls laughed out loud. "A bowyer, huh? You missed your calling. But telling tall-tales doesn't pay as well as selling bows, I suppose."

The elderman managed to look offended without shifting a muscle.

Vedas observed the curious interplay between journeying strangers, intimidated and bemused by their easy discourse. He thought wistfully of the day that had passed. He and his companion's swift progress had made conversation impossible.

Of course, Churls did not mind the conditions. She enjoyed the hearty exchanges, the playful insults and rumoring. Her eyes fairly glittered in the firelight. Unabashedly loud, her voice echoed into the forest. She told a joke, then told it again. Vedas kept his eyes on her more often than not, both compelled by her manner and convinced that if he only focused hard enough on her no one would feel drawn to engage him.

He knew the placement of each Knosi around the campfire. Two women, traveling together. Two men, traveling alone. He sensed their gazes upon him, and wondered what they read in his features. Did he fit the mold of their race, or had time away from Knos Min left a mark upon him? Perhaps he had ceased being a son of the Republic long ago.

And if I've relinquished my birthright, he thought, *what difference does it make? I am Vedas Tezul, of the Thirteenth Order of Black Suits. That is enough.*

He repeated these words, as if they might eventually ring true.

Now and then, he ventured a glance at Berun, whose attention could not be wrested from the three constructs closest to him. Concentration formed deep furrows between his brows. Occasionally, spheres rang together deep inside his body, startling those nearby. Vedas felt an intense communion with the constructed man. Surrounded by his own kin, he too struggled to place himself in context.

A voice interrupted Vedas's pondering: "May I sit?"

Vedas looked up at a thin, dark face. White teeth, though not really a smile. The man wore dun-colored robes and two weapons hung from his belt sash: a short, curved blade and a short horseman's pick. Rust-colored and painstakingly matted, his long hair wound around his head like a starched strip of cloth.

A Tomen, the first Vedas had seen on the road.

"Of course," Vedas said, and scooted closer to Churls to make room. The woman to his left, a Castan gladiator built like a bull, rose smoothly and walked away from the fire.

The Tomen ignored this. Slowly, so as not to cause alarm, he removed his sash and placed his weapons on the ground before sitting. The smell of fennel and mejuan, a mild hallucinogen, rose from his robes.

"*Feda Adraas*," he said, bowing his head.

"*Adraas Esoa*," Vedas said, surprised to find he remembered the formal greeting: *I curse Adrash—Adrash hears you*. Tomen spoke a distinctive dialect of the common tongue of Knoori as well as several ritual languages, some of the most common phrases of which Vedas had learned in the abbey.

"Thank you," the man said. "I have had bad luck, finding a place to sit. Fesuy Amendja is my name. Opas is my home."

"I am Vedas Tezul. Golna is my home."

Fesuy nodded. Something moved under the skin of his cheek, and he made a loud sucking noise. Though the Tomen only spoke to Vedas, the other travelers had lapsed into silence, watching. Of all the peoples of Knoori, Tomen very likely suffered the most intense prejudice. They were not even liked by most other Anadrashi, and for good reason. Tomen respected Tomen and no one else.

Vedas did not care about this. He merely wanted to be left alone.

"Golna, yes," Fesuy said. "I recognize it, your accent. I am well traveled. Still, it is a surprise. There are not so many far easterners in these parts. Are there Knosi in Golna?"

"Yes, two communities exist. I don't visit them often."

Fesuy spit a mejuan pod into the fire. He reached into the folds of his robes, brought forth a leather bag, and popped another pod into his mouth. He offered a second to Vedas.

Vedas stared at the proffered drug as if it were a live coal. "No, thank you."

"Not for you," Fesuy said. He tipped his head to stare at Churls.

Churls shrugged, reached across Vedas's chest, and took the gift. She bit the stem off and spit it into the fire. Fesuy followed, and they toasted before putting the pods in their mouths.

Berun's glowing eyes shifted from one to the other, obviously curious. The ritual seemed to satisfy the rest of the travelers, as wine bottles were suddenly uncorked and passed around. The elderman bowyer lit two long pipes and passed them in opposite directions. Conversation renewed.

With attention now shifted away from him, Vedas relaxed.

"I know your faith," Fesuy said. "No drugs, correct?"

"Yes," Vedas answered. "And alcohol only during celebrations. In my order, even that is discouraged."

"This is a shame. Traveling through life without release." Fesuy leaned back, and Vedas followed his gaze. They cursed Adrash together, one set of fingertips touching horns, one palm blocking out the Needle. The Tomen sighed. "I have seen only one other blackskin on the road. People say the rest came through weeks ago, from all over the continent. You are late for the revelry, yes?"

"Yes," Vedas admitted. "Though I hope to be there in time to fight."

Fesuy looked him up and down appraisingly. "Out of all Golna, you were chosen?" He smiled. "I am indeed honored to sit with you. Perhaps my worries about reaching Danoor in time are unfounded, for this is an auspicious sign—one that I will mark in the morning with an invocation. If you allow it, of course. Will you accept this small gesture in your honor?"

Berun shifted next to Churls, who raised an eyebrow when Vedas looked at her.

"Sure," Vedas told the Tomen.

‡

Pressure built in Vedas's chest, staring at the dead woman.

She was built like a bull. Her bulk lay on the paving stones, and her skirt was pulled up around her hips. Her neck had been expertly cut, deeply enough to sever the spinal cord without severing the flesh at the back of the neck. After death, her head had been tipped to the side so that the gaping wounds were exposed. Then her killer had shat on her face. Flies buzzed around the mess. A line of ants crawled through the blood to reach her.

Vedas refused to look at the horrible thing the killer had done to her womanhood, but an Ulomi man named Spofeth had no such inhibitions. He knelt at the woman's feet and stared. He claimed to have once acted as a policeman in the Pontiff of Dolin's Army, but he spoke too finely to convince Vedas of this. His wife had found the body before most of the others woke.

"Easy answer, here," Spofeth said. "We all saw her walk away when the Tomen sat down. Clearly, he didn't like that."

As much as he disliked the man's tone, Vedas could not but agree. The cut was too fine to have been done with a straight sword. And they had all seen the gladiator insult Fesuy. It was enough for the travelers to condemn the man. It was enough for Vedas. The Tomen had seemed pleasant enough in the short time they had conversed, but that was immaterial.

Will you accept this small gesture in your honor? the man had asked.

Sure, Vedas had told him, not knowing what it meant. How could he have known?

A Knosi man stepped forward. Vedas recognized him from the fireside. His white cassock marked him as an Adrashi priest, though Vedas did not know the variety. The man had seemed kind enough the previous night, had even smiled at Vedas and offered him wine which Vedas refused. A scar ran from the corner of his left eye to his jaw. It twitched as he looked at the dead woman. His mouth worked at words before they came out.

"We will bury her, and I will perform rites."

Spofeth pointed to the tattoos of serpents winding around the gladiator's heavy thighs. "She was an Usterti, Father. Witches don't believe in Adrash."

"That is irrelevant," the priest answered, iron in his voice. "Whether she believed in Adrash or not, Adrash knew of her existence. Did anyone here know her? No?" He turned to Vedas. "You knew her killer. You talked to him. Now you will carry his victim's body." He cut Vedas's reply off with a gesture. "I am not placing blame. Adrash has simply put you here now to do this thing."

Vedas thought of several responses and dismissed them all. He looked at Berun. "Will you hold her head?"

Together, they carried the woman a dozen feet off the road, careful not to tear her head from her body. Twice, Vedas nearly vomited at the smell of shit and blood. Berun quickly dug a deep grave in the soft black earth, and then he and Vedas laid the body at its bottom, positioning her as if she were sleeping. A woman Vedas did not recognize tore a length of red material from her skirts. Vedas tied it around the corpse's neck.

Churls offered her hand. Vedas took it, and climbed free. Though the aroma of freshly turned earth filled the air, he could still smell the sour stench of Fesuy's excrement, the iron of the dead woman's juices. The smell would linger, of course. It would follow him for a while until he managed to forget it.

Just as he had forgotten Julit Umeda and all the others?

He caught the priest's eye and felt the first stirrings of resentment. How dare the man tell him to carry the body? How dare the man watch him work, only so that he could spout lies over the woman? She was dead, and the god had no interest in her soul.

People were nothing to Adrash. Adrash would make the whole world a tomb.

Have I forgotten who I am? Vedas asked himself.

Before the holy man could start talking, Vedas signaled to Berun to start filling the grave.

"It is custom to leave it open," the priest began.

"Never mind your custom," Vedas said. "Speak if you must, but speak plainly. Don't insult this woman with your falsehoods. She wasn't a member of your church."

The priest regarded him for a long moment, and then put his right fist to his forehead and extended it to Vedas.

A blessing. A supplication for peace. *Adrash be with you.*

It was the wrong thing to do.

Vedas took a step forward, his fingers curling as resentment bloomed into anger—pure, righteous anger, hammering in his chest, behind his eyes, causing the world to tremble before him. Churls's hand closed around his wrist, but he pulled it away. Another step and another, until he stood before the priest. Every nervous fiber of his being ached to send his fist forward, but he could not make himself do it.

The moment held for a second. Five seconds. Ten. His muscles screamed under the tension.

Will you accept this small gesture in your honor? the man had asked.

Sure, Vedas had told him.

"Vedas," Churls said. "Vedas. What would be the point? The damage is done. She's dead, and she won't give a shit what this priest says." Her voice became gentle. "Let it go."

The tendons in Vedas's neck stood taught. A frown deformed his features.

He spat at the priest's foot and turned away.

Churls and Berun followed him to the road. They retrieved their packs and continued on. No one talked as the sun moved in a shallow arc on the horizon. The travelers they passed neither greeted nor questioned them.

Vedas's hands shook. He washed them in every stream and river. For the first time in his memory, he felt truly unclean, as if his suit were a normal garment that needed to be removed and washed. He fought the urge to scratch, to pull the constricting fabric away from his skin.

‡

Though he was hundreds of miles away, high upon a mesa, he saw it happen.

A massive woman rose from Lake Ten and stepped over Locborder Wall.

Her tattooed thighs were as wide as the city of Ynon, which she crushed under her naked feet as if it were a folded paper toy. Mountains of muscle and fat jumped with each lumbering movement, shaking the water from her body. Droplets as large as lakes fell from her skirt to the earth, crushing hills and mountains, turning fields into mud flats.

Vedas ran from her across the flat top of the mesa, but not fast enough. It would never be fast enough, for she covered leagues with a single step, and his legs were heavy and slow. She would be upon him in no time at all. She roared his name, a bestial sound that threw him to the ground and threatened to rupture his eardrums. He rose and fell again. He started crawling. Over his shoulder he saw her head rise above the edge of the mesa.

So soon! She moved faster than he could ever have imagined.

Her hand reached for him, and it eclipsed the sky.

"Vedas."

The world faded. Flickered.

"Vedas."

He woke. Two glowing blue coals stared down at him from a face composed of brass spheres. A hard hand shook him gently, companionably. A low, brassy chuckle.

"Berun," Vedas said, relieved to be out of the dream. He rose on an elbow to peer past the constructed man's crouched form, and located Churls. She lay close to the smoldering campfire, which was surprisingly far away. "What am I doing over here?"

The constructed man rocked back on his heels with a whisper of metal sliding against metal. "You crawled here. One minute you were sound asleep, the next you tensed. I readied myself, thinking of another cat attack or worse, but when you started crawling I knew that something else was happening. Then you flipped over, and it looked like you were going to start throwing punches. Were you dreaming?"

Vedas lay back. The road was solid beneath him. "Yes. About the dead woman."

A rumbling sound came from Berun's chest: the sound of many spheres shifting position, rearranging themselves. "That Adrashi priest was wrong," the constructed man said. "He made a connection between you and the woman when there was no connection at all. You had nothing to do with her death." The rumbling stopped. "You're a good man, but you're not a whole man. You don't know yourself."

Too tired to protest, Vedas simply nodded.

"The Baleshuuk thief. Why did you save her?"

Vedas thought back, came up empty. "I don't know. I just didn't want her to die."

"And the woman today? Why did her death affect you so?"

The muscles of Vedas's jaw jumped as he bit down on his first response. *It was my fault. If I hadn't agreed to Fesuy's offer, she wouldn't have died.* He wondered for a moment if this was what he truly believed. Could a man be blamed for being in a certain place at a certain time? *Adrash has simply put you here now to do this thing*, the priest had told him.

"I don't know," Vedas said. "It was wrong. Evil."

Berun nodded. "True. A man who does things like that deserves no sympathy. He has become worse than an animal." The constructed man opened and closed his gigantic fists, and his eyes flared brighter. "True, I love fighting. I sometimes enjoy killing. Churls is a fighter, through and through. No doubt, we've both got our share of bloodlust. We've committed sins. But you see the difference, don't you—between us and murderers?"

"Yes," Vedas answered honestly.

"You think we should forgive ourselves our crimes, our mistakes?"

"Yes."

Berun stood, a thousand joints sighing all at once. He stared down at Vedas.

"You should take your own advice."

BERUN

Huge, sluggish fish swam in the stygian depths, their sinuous bodies only partially visible in the weak radiance cast by Berun's eyes. An arm-sized fin waving. A black eyed, blunt-nosed head, needle-toothed maw slowly opening and closing. Dwarfing the constructed man, they swam in close but never touched him. He did not smell right, did not sound right. No beating of a heart, only the steady emanation of heat. Smaller fish darted before his face, attracted by the light and warmth, but these too were merely curious.

He had been here before. During the storm that drowned the *Atavest*, the heaving deck of the ship had catapulted him into the lake, where he immediately sank—for how long, he did not know. In his despair, he forgot to count. All sensation stopped during the fall, which seemed to last forever. And then the silt floor embraced him so gently that for a moment he did not realize the bottom had finally been reached.

Immediately, he had struggled upright in the soft mud and checked his map. Nothing. Knoori did not appear before his eyes. The weight of water prevented him from summoning the map. Lake Ten sunk to a far greater depth than the sea, he had heard, so far that the sun never reached its bottom. If this were true, the likelihood of reaching land any time soon was unlikely, and the island of Tan-Ten nearly impossible. Even if he knew the general direction, how could he walk in a straight line without points of reference?

Of course, such conjecture had been pointless. Long before he reached land, his body would shut down. Like all constructs, Berun's cellular composition was largely elder, and required frequent exposure to sunlight. Unlike the physically weaker but more versatile hybrid animals, a construct possessed no digestive system, and thus could not subsist in the darkness for more than a few days. The full weight of this realization struck him, filled his being with dread so powerful that he no longer felt whole.

Unconnected to his component pieces, a mere collection of marbles, inert.

Unsurprisingly, Berun was not happy to find himself back in this place. How had he arrived here? Where had he last been? He did not know the answer to either question. He watched the sluggish behemoth fish turn around him, recalling the dread, the absolute certainty of death. To be shut off forever: this was the thing Berun most feared. Some men believed in heaven, or at least a type of continuity, and Berun could see why. The body remained warm for a time after it died. It rotted, split apart and offered its contents to the soil, spurning new growth. But a construct was not a man. It went cold, and then became exactly as it was before life touched it.

If souls existed, they resided in flesh.

Berun threw his head back and roared the tone of a great brass cymbal. Dark water muffled the wordless cry, extinguished it only inches from the ringing cavern of his mouth as if it were nothing, had never existed—yet the fish jerked and dropped to the lake bottom around him, stunned or killed by the pressure of his voice. Small and large, they littered the ground at his feet. He took no joy in this. It had not been his desire. He had not acted with intention, only feeling.

The fish lay still, and it was only a short while before others came, curious, and began feeding, turning the water cloudy with blood and scales. Blind, Berun rocked back and forth as the immense, slick-skinned bodies pushed against him. Twice, a mouth closed around his arm, scraping its needle teeth over his spheres before spitting the limb out convulsively.

The feeling of dread increased.

Spheres knocked together in his stomach. A lonely drum roll, echoing into the endless night.

He did not bother to feel hope, for he had no reason to expect salvation a second time. He tried not to conjure the memory of being saved, but it shouldered its way forward: Light blooming in the distance, shifting closer and closer, growing in definition until it became the blazing form of a small girl. White from head to toe, but for eyes the color of light passing through shallow seawater. Her soft voice speaking indiscernible words, her hands urging him forward.

What had he felt? He did not entirely recall. He remembered the slow progress, slogging through knee-deep muck, staring so long at the girl's light that it became his entire world. If he moved too quickly, a cloud of silt rose from his feet, obscuring her from him. Yes, at these moments he panicked, stumbled, fell into the muck. He learned to wait until the cloud cleared, allowing him to find her light again. Only then did he continue on. Eventually, his foot struck rock and the going became even more difficult. He fell into narrow crevices and mired his feet in loose sand, but still he followed the girl. He crawled until his head rose above the water.

It had been madness, yet it could not be rationalized away.

He had reached the island, after all.

Or had he? Doubt took root in his mind. Perhaps he had only dreamed of Tan-Ten, reunion with Churls and Vedas, Ynon and the Grass Trail. Maybe he had not stood on the shore of Uris Bay and looked through the shimmering glass dome at the island of Osa. Those traveling on the trail, even those few who possessed spyglasses and amplification spells, were not able to see that far. They asked him to describe the life that anchored itself to the clear wall. Filled with pride, he had done so. "I see huge vinetrees, crawling toward the sky. I see gigantic multicolored wyrms, perching on the tops of honeycombed nests."

Devastating, to think he had only imagined these wondrous things. Even worse, to know he had never dreamed alone, that he had always been manipulated into sleep, coerced to take part in another's vision.

Have I ever admired something for myself? he wondered. *Am I just a dim reflection of my creator?*

Berun roared again, and this time it was the word *Father*.

‡

The lake bottom shook. Dead fish slipped against one another, shuddering slowly into the muck like earthworms into soil. Berun made his feet large and flat to stay upright. Gradually the tremors subsided, and the bottom of the lake was smooth again, its dead buried.

A light bloomed in the distance before him, like it had when the girl appeared. It jumped closer and closer, moving from one position to another instantaneously. Berun felt the first faint stirring of hope, only for it to be extinguished as the source of light became obvious.

A pair of silver hands.

"Father," Berun said, words now audible. "This is your dream?"

Ortur Omali lifted a hand to his hood and removed it. Instinctively, Berun stepped back, nearly tripping on his oversized feet. The great mage no longer possessed a mouth, just a smooth patch of skin from nose to chin. His skull looked as though it had been crushed and reformed, or pulled like melted wax into the caricature of an elder. His eyes were large, liquid pools of amber in which two doubled irises swam.

This is no dream, Omali's voice resounded in the spheres of Berun's mind. *There never was a dream. This is my place. An extension of my mind. A universe unto itself, folded inside you, enveloping the world. It is both here and not here, alive and not alive.*

"That makes no sense, Father."

Omali's irises spun slowly. *Indeed. But sense is hardly a requisite of existence. Strength and strength alone dictates success. Pure will sets the stars and the planets spinning.*

Berun dismissed this claim as useless. He had no interest in cosmology or philosophy.

"Why have you brought me here?" he asked.

Omali rubbed his fingers together, producing a sound like singing bowls. *You are here because you sought release. When you pleasure yourself, you become susceptible.* He clapped his hands together and they tolled like bells. *You have been bad, Berun. Very bad. You have kept your mind from me.*

"You took control of my body."

Omali's eyes widened. *This was a surprise, that I should treat you this way, my own creation? At what point did you begin to consider yourself an autonomous creature? You are not—nor have you ever been—your own man.*

Indignation pressed Berun's hands into fists. "And yet I've managed to keep you out for some time."

Now the eyes narrowed. *Truly. You have discovered that your physical form and my influence over your mind are related. This is a small inconvenience and a greater disappointment to me. In time I will overcome your resistance, but your character is not so easily mended. When I am animate again, you will submit to some adjustment.*

Berun parsed this language. The possibility that his father existed without a body had never occurred to him, perhaps because he did not want to consider the implications. He had grown in his father's absence, had he not? He had always half-believed himself capable of overcoming his father's dream-specter, but what chance did he stand against the great mage in the flesh? Berun would be defeated, made into little more than a tool. A weapon.

It did not require a vivid imagination to picture the target. Vedas would die, and Churls would very likely die defending him.

The thought of being used to these ends caused a tightening of the spheres in Berun's shoulders and chest—a slight but distinct darkening of his vision, a wavering of the figure before him. Berun raised his right arm, opened his fist, unsure of his intent.

Stop! Omali commanded, and the world snapped back into focus, crystallized on him like ice. *You are not a man. You are my creature.*

Berun resisted the compulsion to lower his arm. It felt as if a great weight had been attached to his wrist. "You have threatened my friends," he said, though opening his mouth and forming words took a massive effort.

I have. Your black-suited friend endangers the balance. Adrash's eyes will soon be upon him. If allowed to live, he may very well throw the world into chaos. You do not see it yet, but you will. He must not fight at Danoor. He must not live.

Omali raised his silvered left hand and touched his index finger to Berun's fist. As the mage lowered his arm, Berun was forced to lower his own. Omali pointed to the lake floor, which began bubbling. A lake of black tar, boiling, from which Vedas's body surfaced.

The puppet—for it could not really be the Black Suit himself—opened its eyes and yellow light poured forth, washing out the scene around Berun.

‡

They stood on the mesa of blooming azure flowers where Berun had first recognized his father. At his feet, once again, a sleeping figure—and this time there could be no doubt as to its identity. Remembering the injury from his previous visit, Berun glanced at his right arm and found it whole.

A prediction that will not come to bear, Omali said. He stood beside Berun, face angled to the sky. *You have disobeyed and disrespected your creator, but you will redeem yourself. You cannot be my sword of justice with a chipped blade.*

"The cost of my freedom is a limb?"

Omali's laughter rang in Berun's mind. *Freedom? Why, the word means nothing to you.*

Berun regarded the body at his feet, its familiar lines. He had tried to see it as Churls did, as a thing of beauty, and failed. Vedas was no more beautiful than Churls, the captain of the *Atavest*, or the Baleshuuk they had encountered on the Steps. Still, his features had become oddly reassuring to Berun.

"I'll resist you," the constructed man said. "I'll win this fight."

Omali turned. He floated up from the ground, orange and red robes flowing around his thin body as though he had been set aflame. Wind blew across the mesa, causing the flowers to undulate like the surface of the ocean.

You will not even try, the great mage said, fingers outstretched toward his creation.

Berun struggled to lift his arm again, and then stopped as realization hit. He would not fight in the world his father had created. He would leave. Prepare himself on his own terms, in his own reality. He allowed his anger to build, let it run through his limbs like molten lead, fusing him in place. Heavy brows came together over bluefire eyes. Brass lips curled back from brass teeth. The expression froze.

He felt the pull his father exerted on every sphere in his body, yet he knew with absolute certainty he could withstand the attack. He had buttressed himself, had become his own man through strength alone. Compressing his component pieces together, he locked himself in place against his father's influence. Deep within his chest, spheres that had always spun stopped their spinning—a fearful but exhilarating sensation.

Indeed, his father had been correct: pure will set the stars and planets in motion. It could also stop them cold.

You will go no further with this, Berun, Omali said. He sent a second, stronger wave of force through Berun's body, trying to bend his creation to his will. *You do not want to force my hand any more than you already have. My compassion extends only so far. If you continue on this path, I will make you suffer. I will scatter you to the eight winds, Berun.*

Berun's strength wavered. He fought the urge to allow himself to expand, to mobilize himself. A voice told him that stopping his spheres would lead to death, but he knew this to be false. He possessed a body just beyond the thin shell of his father's world. He could escape through concentration, through the force of his will.

Omali laughed. *No. I have closed all the doors.*

No, you haven't, another voice countered.

Berun looked down. Instead of Vedas, at Berun's feet lay the girl in white. The girl with blue eyes. Berun's savior.

She stood, and then rose from the ground until her eyes were level with Omali's. The folds of her dress did not flutter in the wind. Unbound hair fell straight over her right shoulder, every pale strand in place. Light blazed from behind her, outlining her small form in fire. She was not a part of Omali's world, yet something of hers seemed to be leaching into his.

Beyond the fact that Berun recognized her from their previous encounter, her features were now vaguely familiar. Her face tickled his subconscious mind, but he had no time to examine it.

She extended her left hand, and the great mage shrank back.

Lavesh atross! he hissed. *So asfelz! Adramass psua!* He weaved graceful charms with his hands, locking long, thin fingers and releasing them explosively, hurling magma-red spells at her. They sizzled through the air, tearing black rents in the dream reality.

The girl smiled, and with a gesture halted the spells in flight, dissolved them. *All wrong. I know all that stuff, and I'm learning new things all the time. You're too old to learn anything new.* She held her right hand out to Berun, but her eyes stayed locked on Omali. *We're leaving. Don't try this again. I know where you live now.*

Who are you? Omali asked. His eyes had become slits of bright amber. His skin had taken on a purplish hue.

The girl shook her head, smile still in place. *Figure it out on your own. We're leaving.*

"Goodbye, Father," Berun said.

He took the girl's hand and they disappeared.

‡

Churls and Vedas woke only moments after Berun. The sun had not yet risen.

He spoke nothing of his encounter, and opted out of accompanying them into Sent to fetch the construct horses. A fellow traveler on the trail had provided the names of a few reliable stablemen, but Berun suspected the affair would take much time and haggling—a prospect he did not relish. Besides, he had much to consider. He watched his companions enter the walled city and then sat down to think.

For the first time in his existence, he noticed a difference between sitting and standing. Resisting Omali had sapped him of energy.

An hour later, the first rays of sunlight found him in a meditative posture, legs crossed, soles upturned on his knees, hands clasped behind his back. One elbow up, one down—this was now the extent of his flexibility. Just as a man understands he cannot turn his neck to look directly behind him,

Berun knew his spheres would no longer rearrange per his command. They were stuck in a matrix, forming one thing only: a bronze man.

The solidification he had effected in Omali's world had crossed over to this one, and stuck. He would no longer form shovels or knives or hammers at the end of his arms. He would no longer carry items within his body. Splitting himself in two and achieving a release, *pleasuring himself* as his creator had termed it, was now impossible.

Though he had gained an advantage over Omali, strengthened his mind against the great mage's attacks, he had crippled himself physically. He could not rotate his spheres or spread himself like a blanket on the earth to take in sunlight. Without this capability, he was doomed to a life of near-starvation. His strength would be a weak thing compared to what it was.

This was not all. He tried to summon his map of the world, and failed.

Devastating losses, undoubtedly—but the suspicion that he had left a stone unturned stayed with him as the morning progressed. Suspicion became dread as certainty lodged within the spheres of his mind.

No, he had not yet discovered the worst consequence of his encounter with Omali.

When the full extent of his vulnerability became clear, it seemed he might tumble into the earth in his despair. He recalled the few times he had been impacted heavily enough that a portion of his body shattered into its component spheres. A sensation beyond pain, it was the awareness of dislocation, the opposite of the release he felt when splitting himself in two. Now that he had lost control of his malleable form, rebuilding himself after such an attack would be impossible. He could very well die. Worse, he could be dismantled as Omali vowed, scattered to the eight winds, forced to live in eternal agony.

Had he been a fool to ally himself with his companions and the wraithly girl with the tantalizingly familiar face? Had he even considered what it meant for him—a constructed man whose mind had never truly been his own—to trust his instinct?

The future was a depthless abyss, a limitless ocean.

And he had leapt into it without a map or compass.

‡

Motionless, he waited most of the morning for Churls and Vedas to return. By the time they wheeled their steel and brass mounts before him, the sun was near its zenith and he had recovered much of his energy—but could he run for four days alongside the construct horses? Forty, fifty miles a day? He did not know, but resolved to test it. Unless it became obvious, neither of his companions would know the full extent of his limitations. He would not burden them with such concerns.

Undoubtedly, they would soon discover he no longer had access to the map. He had been providing Vedas with daily updates on the movements of men in Danoor. The city itself remained peaceable, but several groups of Tomen had gathered in the foothills of Usveet Mesa, west of the city. While Berun and Churls doubted they could rouse the kind of numbers needed to threaten the city, Vedas thought otherwise.

The man would be disappointed, probably angry to discover he could no longer monitor their activity. The knowledge served as a calmative. Perhaps he believed keeping an eye on the situation kept disaster from unfolding.

Having only just won a small measure of freedom, Berun could sympathize with Vedas's frustration. His master had commissioned him with a task he no longer quite believed in. His faith bound him, as did his love for the brothers and sisters of the Thirteenth. He had not spoken of the speech in some time, though Berun had seen him scribbling notes on occasion.

Thankfully, Vedas did not ask for an update upon returning from the city. He and Churls secured their packs quietly, obviously preoccupied. She dropped her pack twice while securing it to her horse, and her angry gaze returned to Vedas again and again. In turn, he kept his back to her, far more attentive to his task than necessary.

To keep from staring at them, Berun examined the constructs, which were beautiful, sleek and seamless and overmuscled. Though not without a certain gaudy grace, the utilitarian touches incorporated into their bodies offended Berun. Saddles had been integrated into their backs, metal luggage loops into their rumps, and in Churls's construct's case, a crossbow holster into the neck. Riderless, they stood perfectly still.

"What's so fascinating?" Vedas asked. As he mounted, his horse twitched its head away from Berun, who had been staring directly into its glass bead eye.

It stamped once, twice, glaring at Berun—more of a reaction than he had expected. The construct probably possessed something of the animal from which it had been modeled: a slice of preserved horse brain or heart. Nothing so exotic as the transferred essence of its creator, of course. In this regard, Berun was unique.

He straightened. "Were they expensive?"

Vedas began turning his head toward Churls, stopped himself. "Yes."

Churls spurred her mount forward. Her face betrayed nothing. "Tell Berun how much, Vedas. Tell him how much we could've had the horses for."

Vedas looked into the sky, shook his head. "Leave it."

"No," Churls said. She nodded to Berun. "Stable owner recognized Vedas's suit. Got stares everywhere we went, in fact. Offers for sex, potions, you name it for the Black Suit. But this stable owner offered two for one. A huge discount, but Vedas here doesn't want it. It's not right, he tells me. *My faith's not for sale.*"

"It isn't right," Vedas said.

Her cheeks bloomed red. "It's my fucking money! We've traveled two thousand goddamn miles together, and your faith's been nothing but a liability. Finally, you get a chance to profit from it, to help out, and you can't do it because it's wrong. I had plans for that money."

Finally, Vedas met her eye. "Oh, yes. I saw the gleam in your eye as we passed the gambling houses."

The muscles in Churls's shoulders and thighs twitched, and Berun stepped forward.

But the woman only spat. "I make my own choices. I take responsibility for myself. I don't let my shit spill over onto others. I doubt you can say the same."

With this, she wheeled her horse around and spurred it northward.

Berun raised his brows.

Vedas sighed. "Maybe I should have done it. Taken the discount. It would have been faster."

"Maybe you should have," Berun agreed. "But I'm not one for convictions, so you can't trust me." Their eyes met. The lines around Vedas's eyes had deepened. He looked years older than when they had left Golna. "Do you have a plan?" Berun asked.

Vedas closed his eyes and nodded. Then he shook his head. "I only know what I'm not going to say. I'm no writer, no philosopher. If I'd known what I was getting into by leaving, I never would have left." He opened his eyes. "And you? Do you have a plan?"

"It hasn't changed," Berun said. "I plan on winning."

"Amen," Vedas said, and kicked his horse's brass flanks.

Berun picked two rocks from the ground and followed, metal soles ringing loudly on the packed earth. Grinding the stones in his hands, he joined the thousand-footed train of travelers following the northwesterly curve of Grass Trail to Danoor.

CHVRLI CASTA JONS

They ran the construct horses from sunup to sundown—a grueling pace, devoid of joy, alleviated by only the briefest moments of rest. At night they collapsed in whatever camp they came upon, sleeping the night through as though drugged.

At noon on the fourth day, the mounts refused to go any further, their contracts at an end. Churls and Vedas immediately dismounted and removed the packs, anxious not to lose their belongings. Churls, who had lived on horseback during her three-year stint in the Castan cavalry, gritted her teeth as she pounded life into her cramped thighs. Vedas, no great horseman, moved about with enviable vigor. Yet another miracle performed by his suit.

Churls's muscles loosened during the fifteen-mile descent out of the scrub hills and into the desert. She shed clothes as the weather grew hot, stripping down to a leather skirt and halter. Before long, even these began to cling and chafe uncomfortably. She considered with some bitterness that in only a few hours it would be cold and windy again, requiring yet another change of clothes. She jealously eyed the loose cotton outfits many of the travelers wore.

From ten miles away, the city of Danoor was nearly lost amid the shifting red dunes that hemmed it on three sides. Usveet Mesa, the largest and most easterly of the Aroonan chain, loomed ridiculously large at the western edge of the city. The mountain's foothills, higher even than those ringing the valley, seemed tiny by comparison.

From five miles away, the mesa's scope became even more daunting. Its nearly vertical wall looked as if it were about to topple over, snuffing out the pathetic signs of civilization lying in its shadow. Churls wondered what it must be like to live in such a place. Did its people grow used to living in darkness for half the day, feeling that weight pressing down?

Perhaps it was not the mountain causing her to think such thoughts, but history itself. According to legend, Danoor had been founded upon the rubble of Hawees, an ancient elder city that had once clung to the mountainside—a city Adrash had razed in celebration of mankind's birth. Precious stones and inexplicable glass mechanisms, proof of the legend's origins, were still being unearthed from underground excavations.

As a youth, Churls had seen a few of these relics on display in Onsa. Her mind nearly buckled as she considered their age—a hundred thousand years, two hundred thousand? Academics insisted the elders had been interred in the ground long before the era of man, the modern and mythic history of which spanned a mere twenty-five millennia. Perhaps Adrash himself did not recall the age of Hawees's beautiful relics.

How, Churls had wondered as she stared at the shattered remnants of an extinct people, could men worship a god who would destroy such precious things? How could men live in a city dedicated to that destruction?

She could think of no worse place to make a home.

On the other hand, she could think of no better place to host a battle between the Followers of Adrash and the Followers of Man.

‡

As they entered the vast tent camp visitors had erected south of the city, the sun disappeared over the mesa, plunging the valley into another degree of darkness. Churls made out the many fires of the Tomen camps Berun had described in the foothills.

"You see them?" she asked Vedas. "Orrus Alachum, they've tripled in size since we last looked! There must be five thousand of them now. What do you think they're waiting for?"

He scratched at his thick, wiry black beard. For once, the weather seemed to bother him as much as it bothered her. His lips were cracked, his eyes red. "The winner, I assume. That will determine which way the riot goes, who they start killing first."

"That's a grim outlook," Berun said. "You think that's their plan—five thousand against an entire city, bloated to twice its normal size by travelers? They've done nothing so far. Maybe they've come to their senses and just decided to enjoy the tournament."

Vedas regarded the constructed man. "You can believe whatever fantasy you like, but I'm done with deceiving myself. We all saw what Fesuy did to that woman on the trail." He squinted into the distance, and then pointed to a pool of firelight below the encamped Tomen. "Another thing—what do you see at the base of the hill?"

"Another group is camped there."

"Notice anything else?"

"No. Yes. The men are wearing uniforms. They're very well organized."

Vedas nodded. "As I suspected. An army battalion, which proves I'm not the only cynical one. The Tomen intend to attack, and the Knosi government knows it."

"They couldn't stop them from entering the city?" Berun asked.

"How?" Vedas spread his arms wide. "The influx of travelers has stretched the resources in Danoor for months now. When you were last able to check your map, that army battalion wasn't here, which means they must have double-timed it from the capitol. All their general can do now is send for more troops and wait for the inevitable. Perhaps they will muster enough to stand against the threat, but I doubt it. We have riots even in civilized Golna. They have a way of spreading."

Churls chuckled at this understatement. She scanned the faces around the campfires, noted the posture of men and women as they walked from tent to tent, trading gossip. They hardly seemed concerned, but only a fool looked to the gathered masses for wisdom.

They reached the first buildings of Danoor proper, which unlike the majority of Knosi cities had never been surrounded by a wall. For millennia its relative isolation had dissuaded conquering peoples, though one could not discount its citizens' legendary fighting skill as an equal factor. Lomen, one of Churls's former lovers and gambling partners, had hailed from a neighboring region, and claimed all children of the mesas were taught to wield the ckomale, a pair of sickles linked together with wire.

Travelers thronged bone-dry streets the color of rust. Everywhere, the color of rust. Except for infrequent splashes of painted wood, the buildings were uniformly and seamlessly constructed of red clay and red sand. They rarely rose above the third floor and seldom existed in anything other than a rectangular shape. The uniformity depressed Churls, but the presence of lavish parks, where broad- and thin-leaved succulents fought for space with thorny, winter-blooming bushes and wiry jocasta trees, compensated for this.

"Not far now," Churls said to no one in particular.

"Yes," Vedas and Berun responded together. Vedas cleared his throat.

Keenly aware of how little time they had left as companions, Churls fought to keep the melancholy from her face. She had failed to determine what Vedas and Berun ultimately meant to her, though she had spent no small amount of time pondering the question.

Perhaps she and Berun could remain friends. He liked her, and might even be swayed to stay with her in the city, even accompany her home—positing, of course, that they did not kill one another in tournament.

But Vedas? She could not be Vedas's friend, even if he wanted such a thing. Her desire would always betray her.

Despite her persistent attempts to reign in her emotions.

Despite the anger this lack of self-control inspired.

The curve of his lips, the timbre of his voice, the way thoughts showed on his face several heartbeats before words ever came out: She had memorized every detail of Vedas Tezul. His presence had long ago become a dilemma, causing her every ounce as much distress as joy.

It ached in her marrow, being so close yet so far.

‡

After nearly two hours of walking, they reached the northern end of the city, which to Churls's eyes was indistinguishable from the southern. The streets were crowded this close to the White and Black Suit camps, filled with the sounds of conversation and trade. Revelers spilled from every inn and restaurant door.

Clearly, lodging near Vedas would be difficult to find. Churls wondered how long it would take for the man to comment on this fact. Undoubtedly, he wondered why his companions had remained with him for so long.

She had no answer. It was foolish to prolong the inevitable, yet she could not help herself. She stole glances at him, found excuses to slow their progress.

It took her a while to understand that such diversions were not only being allowed, but encouraged. Vedas and Berun were dragging their heels. Twice, Vedas complained of soreness in his legs and asked them to stop in a park—an awkward moment, both times, as he massaged his thighs and stretched while she examined plants that held no real interest for her. Berun was no help, standing in place as though he were a statue.

Light spilling into an alleyway marked yet another inn. Unlike the others, it appeared relatively unoccupied.

"We should stop for a drink," Churls ventured. "Say goodbye and all that. Celebrate our arrival and soon-to-be victories." She laughed, and it sounded pitifully hollow.

Berun smiled, nodded. Vedas looked northward, clearly conflicted.

"All right," he said. "Just one."

They entered the dimly lit interior, where the smell of coffee hit Churls like a friendly kiss. Contrasting sharply with the biting cold that descended with nightfall out of doors, the inn was delightfully warm and close. She whistled softly, surprised by the opulence of the room. Voluptuous Knosi women in diaphanous robes reclined on low couches, dipping folds of spongebread into various sauces, sipping from small flutes of wine. The few men, mostly soft-looking Knosi in fine silks, each had two or three women attending to their every need: peeling grapes, massaging feet and shoulders.

Reaching under waistbands.

It was all quite cozy, yet Churls understood immediately why the establishment had attracted so few customers. The influx of travelers into the city must have spurred the opening of dozens of new bordellos, each offering cheap wares. An establishment catering to the wealthy must therefore have seen a drop in business.

Churls had been to more than a few whorehouses in her day, and none of the acts performed within had ever scandalized her. Nonetheless, she could imagine few places less conducive to the kind of goodbye she had hoped for.

On second thought, perhaps it did not matter. Vedas managed to be uncomfortable in any social situation. That he had agreed to a drink at all was a minor miracle.

She sat on a couch and signaled to the bar, at the same time conducting a quick survey of the room. Several of the prostitutes were watching her. Many more had their eyes on Vedas. Churls considered how best to dissuade the women from approaching him, but shelved it as irrelevant. He would not return their attentions.

He sat opposite her. "Interesting choice," he said. "Isn't this out of your price range?"

"A little," Churls allowed. "Where's Berun?"

"He stayed outside." Vedas shrugged. "I looked back, but he just waved me in."

Churls hid a smile behind her hand.

A server arrived—a teenage girl with proportions Churls had once cursed herself for lacking. Now such women looked soft and ungainly to her. Fighting with breasts like that would be almost impossible. How did the girl know who she was without scars, tattoos to prove she had been to this place at this time? Very likely, she had never been anywhere but Danoor, traveled no farther than a nearby quarter to see her parents.

To be the daughter of this man, the wife of this man, etcetera and etcetera. Nothing more.

Churls thought of Fyra. She would be about the server's age if she were alive. What would she have said about her family, her position in the world? Would she have been a warrior, a good lover to a faithful, boring man?

"What is your desire?" the girl asked. She looked only at Vedas and cocked her hip slightly, causing the fabric of her short robe to part, offering him a view of her shaved pudendum. In most whorehouses, this view alone cost money.

The drinks would be expensive, Churls reasoned.

Of course, the girl might have revealed herself on a whim, made a flirtatious gesture for the heroic Black Suit. Vedas had received enough shy looks in the streets, suffered enough awkward greetings. Due to the lack of other suited individuals, Churls gathered brothers and sisters of the Order were not allowed to stray from camp during the tournament. A smart move. Fighters became lax if pussy and cock were free for the taking.

"Tecas," Churls answered. "Two. And glasses of water, iced if you have it."

The server ignored her and lingered for a moment, as if she expected Vedas to speak. He glanced up, eyebrows raised, and then looked away. The girl's exhalation was audible. Churls laughed out loud, breaking some of the tension constricting the muscles in her chest.

"What do you think they'll charge for the water?" she asked.

‡

She watched his hands, which were thickly muscled and large enough to envelope her own. She hated stubby or tapering fingers, but his had grown to the perfect length and thickness. Though somewhat obscured by the fabric of his suit, even the veins on the backs of his hands crossed flesh and bone in graceful arcs.

She had long ago noticed the way he touched himself constantly, compulsively, running his hands over the hard contours of his body—testing the springiness of his ridged abdomen with his fingertips, caressing the inside of his thighs—laying a palm over his heart, rubbing his heavy pectoral muscles as though reassuring himself of his own existence. He did these things, and it did not seem to matter where he was. She assumed the actions were subconscious, automatic, an expression of the sensual he did not otherwise allow himself.

She could not blame him. The things she would do with his body if she inhabited it.

In truth, there was no end to his allure. Sometimes she hated his beauty, considering its existence an affront to her desire. A gross injustice, being subjected to it every day. It had been decades since she had felt so self-conscious about her own looks. Not so much the quality of her appearance, but the differences between her and Vedas.

Walking the streets of Danoor, she had been especially aware of the disparity. Reading judgment in the dark gazes around her was easy. Knosi, after all, were famed for their flawless complexions. Her freckles, a feature she had always been proud of, suddenly seemed like so many imperfections on her sun- and wind-burnt skin.

She ordered a second round, and he did not object or bring up the time.

"A plate of bread, as well," he told the server, for which Churls was grateful. They had not eaten since noon, and the alcohol intensified her hunger.

They continued talking of inconsequential matters, lingering on details of their trip, avoiding any mention of the tournament. His gaze never drifted to the prostitutes, many of whom had situated themselves on couches closer to him. He looked at his drink, his hands. He met Churls's eyes more often as they drank. In order to eat the highly spiced food, they both had to lean toward the table. Twice, they reached for bread at the same time. Once, his hand brushed hers and did not immediately pull away.

An hour stretched to two as business picked up. It became too loud to talk softly, but she did not mind holding her tongue. Apparently, neither did he. She ordered another round, another plate of food. He leaned back and she could not stop her eyes from drifting to the bulge of his genitals outlined by the fabric of his suit.

He folded his hands on his lower belly and sighed. She heard a signal within it, dreaded hearing the words it presaged: *I have to go.*

"I've rewritten the speech."

She blinked, quickly reorganizing her thoughts and suffering a pang of guilt. She had managed to shuffle his speech to the back of her mind, had failed to make her opinion of the document more obvious. It was important. He had asked for her help. But the crash on Tan-Ten had turned her world upside-down. She had spent the last month flinching at every shadow, staying close to campfires for fear of encountering Fyra again.

And the claims the girl had made? Churls avoided thinking of these at all costs. Only the proximity of Danoor had been enough to tear her away from obsessive evasion.

"Oh, yes?" she finally said, hating the tremor in her voice. "You're happy with it?"

He sat up and rested his forearms on his knees. He offered a wan smile. "Happy's not really the word. I'm satisfied with it. I've said what I want to say, instead of what Abse wants me to say. I've..." He gestured vaguely. "I've come to terms with the things I've seen since leaving Golna. I'm not the same man. Abse won't like what I have to say. Many people won't like it. But it's better than the alternative, which is more of the same violence on a larger scale."

She leaned forward. "What about the Tomen?"

He grimaced. "They'll still attack. I don't see a way anyone can stop that. The longer I think about it, though, the more likely it seems that violence will erupt even without the Tomen threat. I can't explain how, but I feel it in the streets, the nervousness. I felt it on the trail, too. Hopefully my message will at least sway the fighting in a different direction, away from innocent people."

He licked his fingers clean, and then frowned. He looked toward the door, making her heart sink. "This talk reminds me, I have to get going. I have a little dust left. Not much, but I should help you pay."

"You don't have to go," she said.

"Yes, I do. The first rounds are tomorrow. You..." He stood, shouldering his pack. His eyes eventually met hers. "You'll be there? For the final fight on the eve?"

Her right hand twitched in her lap. Only a short reach to grab his hand. Only two words: *Don't go.*

"Tell me you will," he insisted.

"Yes," she answered, and watched him leave

‡

Two hours later, she emerged from the whorehouse, drunk and lightened of nearly eight grams of dust. Berun was nowhere to be found, so she bought a packet of sempa resin from a street vendor and smeared it on her gums. After fifteen minutes of searching, she located a normal inn crowded with reveling travelers. She ordered a lager and sat down to survey the crowd. A number of nationalities were represented, though porcelain-skinned Ulomi men comprised the majority, and Tomen were absent altogether.

At a table in the center, a group sat playing kingsmader, a Stoli tile game at which Churls possessed no skill. She knew the rules, but nothing of the nuance.

The inn's banker weighed her dust and counted out four grams in bone chips. All she had left.

She sat down, nodded to her fellow players, and selected her tiles. Across from her sat three young Ulomi men with straight backs and even straighter teeth. The youngest appeared no older than sixteen, and when he moved his arm to raise the bet his robe parted, revealing the white elder-cloth suit he wore underneath.

He caught Churls's stare and smirked. He whispered to the largest of the three, causing this man to wink at her.

She ignored them. It soon became clear that she was not the only one. The couple on Churls's right, a Stoli merchant and his wife by the look of them, frowned at the table every time one of the three men spoke. The cauliflower-eared Castan, a fighter obviously, stared right through them and did not so much as twitch at their bawdy jokes. Only the olive-skinned woman, shaven-headed and ethnically ambiguous, noted their presence with any enthusiasm. She eyed the thinnest of the three, the one with the smattering of light freckles on the bridge of his nose, as if she intended to eat him.

Churls hemorrhaged chips. Before long, she became the butt of the youngest White Suit's jibes.

"You know what they call a woman in the Castan badlands?"

"There are two types of people who can't gamble. One of them is in this room."

"Ever heard of a bluff?"

"What's the difference between an Adrashi whore and an Anadrashi whore?"

She listened and smiled when he or one of his mates announced the punchline. All the while anger stewed in her stomach. Though the boys were young and most likely had not yet mastered the use of their suits, she knew backing away from the table, getting away with a portion of her money, would be the smart thing to do.

Unfortunately, she was not in a smart frame of mind.

The scrape of her chair against the wood floor signaled a situation that would soon get out of hand. A hush fell over the room. The bald woman frowned, picked up all but two of her chips, and left the inn.

"You owe me an apology," Churls said. Her heart boomed so loud she did not hear the words.

The youth rolled his eyes. "I said a lot of things. Which one hurt your feelings?"

Churls leaned forward, knuckles on the table. "Stand up."

The largest called over his shoulder to the bar. "Get her a drink. Maybe then she'll have the courage to ask for a fuck." He looked Churls up and down. "We could fuck you."

A smile touched the corners of Churls's mouth. She switched her grip and overturned the table, sending chips and tiles to the floor. Surprised by her maneuver, the three White Suits tumbled out of their chairs and backed up close to the bar.

She rounded the table and followed with a smile so wide it hurt.

‡

The boy's cheek collapsed under her knuckle, accompanied by the satisfying crack of shattering bone. She followed her fist forward with two quick steps, shoving the boy into his companions. The three fell backward, toppling and tripping over bar stools. Someone screamed and the bartender pulled a crossbow from under the counter. The movement might as well have been in slow motion. Churls hopped forward and slapped the weapon from his hand.

"The fuck you will," she said. "Stay put and shut up."

The boy with the dented face remained down, but the other two regained their feet quickly. The smaller moved away from the counter, putting tables and chairs between himself and Churls. He was not her main concern. He had not been running his mouth. One of those who had was already down, possibly dying, and the other would soon join him.

Blood pounded in Churls's veins violently enough to make her whole body shake. She could not have anticipated how the sempa resin and alcohol would interact in her system, but discovered she liked it.

Fear could not touch her. Vedas was a distant memory.

All that remained was rage, pure and simple.

The big man, barely more than a boy himself, shrugged off his robe and pulled his elder-cloth hood over his head. He smiled and flexed his chest. Like the other two, he was beautiful, broad and sculpted and sheathed in white. His teeth were alabaster tiles, his bone-pale skin shone with health. Unlike his smaller companion, he did not look scared in the least.

"Glad you did that," he said in his thick Ulomi accent. "Been looking for a fight all night. It's too polite, this city."

As he spoke, the material of his suit thickened visibly along his shoulders and forearms. The hood covered his temples, rose over his chin and onto his cheekbones—far slower than Vedas managed with his own suit.

Churls returned his grin. "Pretty boy doesn't want to get his face ruined."

The man gave himself away too easily. The twitch of his right pectoral signaled the punch. As it flew, Churls gripped his forearm in her left hand and twisted inside his guard, pressing her back against the solid wall of his torso. Using his own forward momentum, she bent at the waist, levered down on his arm and threw him. A table split in two under his weight.

To his credit, he rolled clear and stood rapidly, guard up.

She had not moved. "Come on. Clear a way. We'll wrestle."

He kicked the rubble of the table to one side. "Castan fucking bitch. My grandparents have a row of your ancestors' heads mounted above the hearth. You know what grandpa says about them? Know what he says their mouths are good for?"

Churls pushed off from the counter. "I don't care."

The man shrugged. As his shoulders dropped, he slammed both palms into Churls's chest. The graceless, full-bodied attack took her by surprise, forcing the air from her lungs, and she stumbled backwards into the bar counter. He followed with quick jabs, the first two of which grazed her temples.

Buoyed by alcohol and drugs, the light battering amused her. He was not a formidable opponent, despite the speed and strength his suit granted him.

Laughing, she batted the third punch aside, planted both hands on the counter behind her, and thrust her kneecap into his groin. He grunted, unharmed, just as Churls had expected. It was meant as a distraction.

She slammed her forehead into his nose, relishing the crunch of crushed cartilage. He reeled back and tripped on a splinter of wood, crashing to the floor.

She stepped forward and stopped, sword halfway out of its scabbard.

The man was dead.

"Shit," she said. "Shit." She set chair upright and fell into it. "Shit, shit, shit."

She felt eyes upon her and looked up. "Get the fuck out," she told the remaining White Suit. "If your other brother's still alive, take him with you. No. Don't say a fucking word. If you say anything, I'll have to kill you."

Only words. Her anger had expired the moment her backside hit the chair. She watched the man check his dent-faced brother for a pulse—another sign of inexperience. Just a glance at the boy, and she knew he was alive. Take him to a good healer, and he would be as good as new. Being young and resilient had its advantages.

The young man lifted his brother over his shoulder and walked out the door without a word. Undoubtedly, he would return with other members of his order. They would scold him for sneaking out of camp, but they would come nonetheless.

Churls sighed and dropped her chin onto her chest. Anger flared again as her thoughts touched upon Vedas.

In one evening, she had made a mess of everything.

"Barkeep," she called. "You there?"

Nothing. He had probably exited out the back. Very likely, he was now gathering a few reinforcements.

Having been in similar situations more than a few times in her life, Churls considered which would be better: leaving, or pouring herself another drink for the wait.

EBN BON MARI

E bn breathed in the heavily magicked air, the almond-and-blood-scent of elder semen and menstrual fluid mixed with her own juices. "You have been careless," she told Pol.

He lay on his side, tangled in his bed sheets, unconscious. Naked, she sat cross-legged before him, caressing his cheek with the back of one finger, watching the last drop of the spell of compulsion disappear into his ear canal. Her eyes lingered over his form. She outlined the fists on his chest with a clawtip. A tingling moved into her thighs. Warmth spread throughout her torso, rose into her neck and filled her head.

A far more dizzying sensation than she had imagined, being in complete control of him.

This was not the night's only surprise. She had not dared imagine overcoming him would be so easy. Picturing all the ways he might defend himself, she had planned meticulously. Never had a person walked the halls of the academy armed with so many spells. How could she have known a mere act of daring would be sufficient to the task?

Traditionally, a mage did not attack another mage in the confines of her home.

It shocked her to discover Pol had relied upon the force of tradition alone to insure his safety. History notwithstanding, a smart man would have warded his apartment against physical attacks. He would have painted alarm sigils on his bed frame. As it was, Pol's lore had been laughably easy to neutralize. She had walked into his apartment as though it were her own, and ensorcelled him while he slept.

Undoubtedly, she would replay the moment for many years afterward. Finding him asleep, as vulnerable to her as a child. Setting the vitreous sphere of her spell in the center of his perfectly formed ear. Watching it collapse into a puddle and enter him.

Though there was no formal punishment for assaulting Pol in his sanctuary, she would hardly win friends with the action. Of course, she had no intention of anyone discovering it. And even if someone did, who would believe the claim? She had lost some of her clout in the encounter with Adrash, surely, but she was not yet discredited. The foundations sunk over decades of consistent leadership could not be uprooted easily.

No one would suspect anything so disgraceful from the outbound mages' captain.

"You have been careless," she repeated, and flipped the sheet from his hips, revealing the length of his erection. The tongues, which had until now remained in her wrists, emerged from her palms slowly, almost as if the thought of what lay ahead frightened them.

"Wake up," she commanded.

His eyes snapped open, then widened as his doubled pupils focused on her. They lingered on her breasts, her lower stomach. Otherwise, he did not move. Only the muscles controlling eyes and respiration remained under his control. At the same time, her ensorcelment had heightened every sensation, forcing him to the most intense state of physical arousal.

To his credit, he did not panic or struggle against the spell. She could see this much in his gaze, in the controlled manner of his breathing. She knew him very well, indeed.

"You have destroyed your body," she said, idly tracing the sigil tattooed on his shoulder. "And for what? If you had only lingered on your plans a bit longer, you would have seen the error of your thinking. If your mind were not so clouded with arrogance, you might have recognized your inferiority and stayed in your place. Maybe in time you could have become something." She leaned forward and smiled with a mouth full of small, white teeth. "After all, I can only live so long."

She held her hands up, palms forward. The tongues strained toward him.

Now, his eyes showed panic. His breaths came fast and shallow. Prone to mutations, eldermen nonetheless possessed a near-instinctive fear of deformity among their kind. Small deviations from the norm often signaled instability of character. The most extreme mutations revealed hidden talents—the ability to cast terrible, chaotic magic.

Some claimed the proof of such beliefs lay in elderman history. *Here*, some said. *Look at this. We have never been a stable people. We have always been prone to destruction and dementia. Arrogance has always been our greatest sin.*

But Ebn had learned much of human history. She had long ago realized both species held the capacity for good, for evil. Eldermen suffered with the knowledge that they were second best in the world—a sterile, complicated race that looked upon itself as inferior, when in fact the opposite proved true time and again. Even she had all but hidden this understanding from herself. She had held herself back for too long. Mankind and its talented hybrid children needed to change, to prove themselves worthy to Adrash, or Jeroun would be destroyed.

I can bear this message, Ebn told herself. *I can be the leader of this movement. We eldermen must no longer search in the sky for redemption, but amongst ourselves. We must cleanse the world of its waste, beginning with our own household.*

She let her forearms drop leisurely, observing Pol's reaction.

"Does this feel wrong?" she asked as her tongues licked the skin of his shoulder and chest. His skin tasted of alchemical ink, copper and blood. "That I am here in your bed, touching you this way? Are you scared that I will rob you of these symbols that you have painted upon yourself? Are you scared that I will steal your power?" She shook her head. "No. No, I will not do that. They are yours. You will die with them. When your body is burning, they will erupt from your skin like fireworks, signaling to the world that a true sorcerer has died."

She pressed the claws of her right hand into his hip and dug five gouges in his flesh.

Blood flowed. A tremor passed through his lungs. His indrawn breath faltered.

She laughed, and it was an ugly sound.

‡

Her mouth rose and fell on his erection. The head of his cock touched the back of her throat and she gagged, but kept at the task. She let him feel the rasp of her teeth. The tongue of her right palm slipped in and out of his rectum, and her left hand lay under his buttocks. She lifted his hips toward her mouth, simulating the thrusts of sex.

Twice, she thought she heard him moan, but it was only the ragged sound of his breathing. His eyes twitched under their lids. She bit his inner thighs hard enough to draw blood, exciting herself with the small reactions of his body. Fluid dripped from her in viscous strings, hardening into thin crystal spells that cracked under her knees as she maneuvered around the bed, searching for unbitten skin, new angles from which to admire his body.

She longed to have him inside her, but knew doing so prematurely would result in unsatisfactory release and the failure of her plan.

No, she needed to control herself. She had inserted the most important spell, the very same that now dripped from her womanhood, just before breaking into his apartment. A modification of her own spell of compulsion, it was designed to gradually turn her desire into a tool, providing her with the anger to overcome the love she still felt for him.

For despite the damage she inflicted, as yet she could not conceive of murder. Without assistance, she would not do it. She would instead hurt him, humiliate him, possibly even ruin his beautiful body—but she would not strike a killing blow.

Her body did not have more resolve than her mind, yet it needed to.

The smell of the crushed spell rose from the sheets, warmed her lungs and loins. Her labia swelled, pulsed between her legs. She moaned and ground her wetness against his kneecap, smearing a trail of her spell over his thigh. Its surface hardened, cracked, and floated into the air, a fine cloud of diamond dust that settled upon their skins. She imagined with what horror he breathed the magical essence in, uncertain of its exact composition or effect.

It did the same for him as it did for her, filling him with fury sufficient to melt steel. Ultimately, both of their minds would swell with murderous intent—but only she would have the ability to act on it.

Despite the swelling waves of anger, her desire remained. She lifted her head and straddled his hips, positioned so that the head of his cock pressed against her anus. Slowly, carefully, she lowered herself upon his erection. It took much care, for he was larger than she had anticipated, and she did not typically allow a man this access.

"A gift," she whispered, rhythmically tightening her sphincter on the base of his shaft—a surprisingly pleasant sensation. "And a reminder of what you will never experience again." She leaned forward, one hand on his chest and one poised over his face. She pried his left eyelid open with the thumb and middle finger of her right hand, and waited until he met her gaze. "Have you always loved men? Did I mother you too much?" She positioned her index claw over his eye, nearly touching it. "Is that why you never looked at me?"

She paused, and in this moment her spell asserted itself fully, flooding her with surety and purpose. Rage, acidic and deliberate, as inexorable as the revolving of the planets, moved her finger, plunging her claw into the soft tissue of his eye.

The delicate, lashed mouth of his eyelid closed around her finger. The punctured eyeball spasmed. Tears and blood flowed from the wound, pooling in his ear and soaking the sheets under his head. His chest shuddered and heaved under her hand, and his other eyelid fluttered, revealing an amber pool, a madly vibrating hourglass.

Her finger was now buried in his eye up to the first joint. She crooked the digit and tugged, at the same time rising off his erection. After a moment of resistance, the eye came free with a loud *pop* and his penis slid free of her anus. The sharp pain made her gasp, and she inadvertently ripped the optic nerve and blood vessel free from their socket. A mild disappointment, for she had planned to prolong his pain and discomfort.

The breath wheezed from him.

The tongue in her hand flickered back and forth, in a frenzy over its prize. The iron and salt taste of blood came to her, filled her entire.

Two hearts leapt against the confining walls of her ribs as she guided his erection into her. She rocked atop him, searching for the right angle. When she found it, the temptation to begin bucking nearly overcame her.

But she resisted temptation again. Wicked magic flowed within her veins, its temper granting her control over her ferocious libido. She would drag this out, his pain, her pleasure, until she knew for certain she could strike a killing blow. As her hips slowly rose and fell, she crushed his disembodied eye against his chest and smeared the gore over his inked torso.

"Is this your first cunt?" she asked. "It is not so bad, is it? Pol, you fucking fool. If you had but submitted to me every now and then, let your pride falter now and then, you could have fooled me completely. I love you, Pol. I love you." She tightened herself around his cock, hard enough to cause a swift intake of his breath. "But you have known that for some time, have you not? And still you chose to betray me."

She thrust faster, leaned forward to press her torso to his. Turning his head so that only his good eye showed, she whispered into his ear, "Another thought occurs. You intended to betray our faith. You would see everything that I have worked for destroyed, and for what? So that you may influence Adrash to cleanse the world? What inspired such evil thoughts? Certainly it was not me. I would have steered you away from evil."

Her thighs twitched against his hips as waves of pleasure crested and broke throughout her body, and she finally started to buck, slamming her hips into his. Her breaths came fast and shallow. She closed her eyes, moaned his name.

Of their own accord, her fingers crawled up his chest and tightened around his throat.

‡

She had kept the man Jarres in her apartment for two weeks. As the full extent of Pol's betrayal became apparent, the tortures she inflicted upon his lover grew more severe. By the eighteenth day, he was little more than a bloodless husk of flesh, kept mere seconds from death by a collection of preservation spells Ebn had extorted from the Medicines Proctor.

The progression from threats to outright torture had not been rapid, nor had it occurred as a result of the information the man provided. In truth, his account rarely varied. Instead, something within Ebn changed. She listened, and with each repeated word grew to hate the man. He came to symbolize all that had been taken from her by Pol's betrayal.

Her hope, her desire, perverted and made hollow. Her love, turned to hate.

She punished Jarres for reminding her of these facts.

She punished him when her informants revealed that Pol had not called on Jarres's home or inquired at White Ministry hospital, despite the man's nearly two-week absence. This further proof of Pol's callousness enraged her.

Jarres suffered for Pol's sins. He begged, and screamed, and Ebn erected a sound barrier to keep others from hearing.

She listened, and then she stopped listening.

Memories filled her head. Memories of Pol, the shy sixteen-year-old boy who had come into her life. Eating breakfast with him, once every month. Teaching him, watching him grow into an adult. Feeling her lust turn to devotion, knowing she could not control its headlong progression. Love's assumption of her entire life.

Pol's voice came to her on the wind, out of the mouths of strangers, woke her from a dead sleep. Hoping to hear anything new, some sign that he had not actually betrayed her, she lingered on every word and slowly killed Jarres, who only confirmed what she already knew.

The bearded man's voice became ragged. He screamed until he coughed blood. When there was no blood left to thrust up, he wheezed and he cried, and then there were no more tears, no liquid in his body. His eyes stopped tracking and shrunk within his withered face. She anointed him with alchemical salves, spells to keep his pitiful body from failing. Pressing an ear to his chest, she listened to the creak of his lungs, the parched stutter of his heart. Like so many of the sounds she had heard since Shav's visit, these too resolved into words:

You are a relic.

You are a fool.

Finally, she killed the man, silencing his horrendous, dry-rotted voice. But instead of release, the act filled her with new urges, desires that spoke with the rustle of dead leaves and old bird bones, alien cravings that whispered as softly as flakes of rust under one's feet, as quietly as hairs ripped from the scalps of corpses.

She watched the Needle rise every evening, and imagined it descending to the surface. She pictured the fiery gouges the spheres tore in the atmosphere as they fell, the new stars blooming on the horizon, the clouds of molten earth rising into the sky. She felt the world's crust crack beneath her feet. She heard the voices of millions crying to their god for salvation.

Stroking the surface of her voidsuit, she thought of ascending to the heavens—of tempting Adrash to make her vision reality.

Eventually, she found the strength to admit the truth:

Pol's betrayal had infected her soul.

His death was the only cure.

‡

And yet for several seconds she fought her own hands. "Please," she said, unable to halt their tightening on the soft flesh of his neck. Like molten iron freezing in a cast, her fingers hardened into crescent vices. "Please," she begged. "No. Do not do this."

Pol's remaining eye watched her. He breathed evenly, drawing air deep into his stomach.

The muscles of her jaw stood out as she resisted not only the spell, but her own sexual release. Slowly, she ground her hips to a halt. The saliva bubbled on her lips, stretching from her chin to his chest.

"You made me do this," she managed through clenched teeth. "If you had only..."

Her claws bit into the sides of his neck, entered his flesh. His breathing was not impaired, for she had still not allowed the bridge of her palms to collapse onto his windpipe. He closed his eye and a groan built in his throat. It vibrated throughout his body. The moment held—a single note.

She held herself on the verge of giving in, on the edge of climax. He waited for death.

"Wake up!" she commanded. "Wake up and stop this!"

Desperation turned to laughter and the spell thrust her forward, elbows locked so that her full weight fell upon his throat.

It was like falling upon stone. The bones of her hands and forearms rang like bells, accompanied by a pain so severe she toppled sideways from the bed. The agony spread into her shoulders, compressed her ribs and closed her throat. She writhed on the floor as a great light bloomed above her.

The sheets burst into flames, and a figure rose above the fire.

Pol grinned. Pitch smoke billowed from his empty eye socket, as though his insides had caught fire. A wide beam of golden light shot from his right eye. The black ink of his sigil tattoos arced and coiled on his skin, forming the shapes of animals and men—a dragon, soaring across his stomach—an elder, stretching its long limbs into an X. The fists had opened upon his chest, so that two open hands appeared to be pushing from within him, struggling to break free. The wounds she had inflicted upon him closed without scar.

No, she thought. *No. This cannot be.*

The cold light of his eye found her, pinned her to the floor like a specimen on an examination table. Unable to move, a scream welled up from within her but could not escape. She gagged upon it and gagged again, forcing acid into her mouth. It burned as it bubbled up through her sinuses and dripped red from her nostrils. She choked on her own sick.

Suddenly, the light passed from her, and she heaved the contents of her stomach onto the floor. Shaking from the pain, nearly blinded by tears, she managed to say one word:

"How?"

"How?" he mocked, perfectly replicating the strangled tone of her voice. "Through trial and effort. Through pain and devotion. While you plotted revenge, I made myself a conduit for power. A weapon." He descended slowly to the floor. "Commend yourself for taking me by surprise. Your spell was exquisite, and it will not die with you. No, do not try to speak. I will not hear your excuses, your plea. I do not want to hear you say that you love me again."

She regarded him, sigils snaking over his naked form. He was beautiful, and terrible. The aroma of singed meat filled the room. The sound of heavy wings beating.

"You expect anger?" he continued. "Of course you do. You have debased me, torn my eye from my skull. But now you see what I have become, yes? How could you hurt me? In a way, you have actually assisted me. I see now that suffering can be a catalyst, as can fear. Unintentionally, you have hastened a process that I would have labored upon for months, maybe even years. In the space of a heartbeat I have been transformed.

"While your hands moved to finish their task, I learned secrets beyond your wildest dreams, Ebn. In the space of a few heartbeats I saw all of Jeroun, including the land across the ocean, under the clouds, where the elders sleep. I touched the idiot minds of spiders and the labyrinthine minds of wyrms. Over all I felt the mind of Adrash, ticking like an immense thaumaturgical engine. I knew then that he was a man, different from me only in the degree of his power. I saw the worlds he has set foot upon. I saw life, and it is a mystery to me no longer. I know that we are but tourists on this world. Adrash, humankind and the elders—we are all children of the stars."

His gaze focused upon her again, fixed her where she lay, chilled her to the bone. *I have no hope against such power*, she thought.

"No, you do not," he said. "Nor do you have any reason for fear. You will soon be reunited with the stars. There are so many souls to help you on your way." He spread his arms. "Many stay on this world, but never for long. So few things anchor us to earth. The void calls to us, the allure of open roads. All concern slips away, all trace of fear and responsibility. Soon you will forget the petty concerns of life. The acts of gods and men will no longer concern you. I almost envy you your journey."

She wanted to speak, and felt her jaw freed. "Is that what you are now? A god?"

"No," he said. "That will take a bit more time."

She grew colder with each step he took toward her. By the time he reached her feet, she had gone completely numb. All trace of her spell had faded, leaving her resigned. This reaction shocked her for a moment, and then faded. One should not question a blessing, and it felt so good not to worry anymore. Perhaps, she considered, this was what she had longed for all along.

To be overcome. To be bested. *The only true expression of love is submission.*

"Sleep," Pol commanded. "And never wake."

A gentle weight dragged her eyes closed, and true darkness overcame her.

POL TANZ ET SOM

He lifted the blood and the smeared remains of his eye from the mattress particle by particle, leaving the fabric spotless. He walked across the room and opened the window, allowing the globe of congealing liquid to escape. The sound of it hitting flagstones on the pathway five stories below was a muted handclap.

Yesterday, he would not have done this. He had always disposed of blood and other bodily fluids as all smart mages did: by vaporizing them. Material from one's body, most especially blood, could easily be traced back to the owner and used in spells to influence or even control him. The academy possessed no shortage of schemers and usurpers. Cleaning crews also knew how to turn a profit.

He need never worry about such trivial matters again.

"Begone," he commanded. The ash that remained of Ebn's body rose from the person-shaped smudge on the floor behind him and swirled in the air, gathering itself as if it were a spirit risen from the grave. It streamed over his shoulder, spilling into the night to be taken away with the breeze. Turning as the last of it was freed, Pol caught the final scent of her, burnt and sharp yet still possessing the trace of coriander, her favorite scent.

He would miss her, undoubtedly. At times he would be reminded of her, and think of the waste. She had been instrumental in his upbringing, and

219

a great leader in her time. But that was long past. Age and obsession had dulled her edge.

Still, he reminded himself, what a display in her final hour! What stunning brutality and rage! If she had only turned her energy to more worthwhile pursuits. If only she were not so blinded by lust, perhaps she could have been partner to him.

At the same time, had she not defiled him and taken his eye, causing him pain beyond measure, he likely would not have undergone his transition. It might well have been years before he could challenge Adrash...

Challenge Adrash. His lips puckered at this new thought.

Smoke poured from his left eye socket. For a moment, light leaked from the crack of his closed right eyelid. Though one eye was closed and the other absent altogether, he saw his surroundings with perfect clarity. He leaned on the window frame, angling his face to the sky in order to see the leading point of the Needle. Through concentration, he caused the image to bloom, take on detail. His perceptions quickened. The night breeze stilled on his skin, the sounds of the city became a warbling moan, and the three spheres slowed almost to a halt.

All at once they seemed but fragile things. Rickety baskets. Toys.

This new perspective rocked him back on his heels.

Challenge Adrash, he thought again. *Is this truly what I intend?*

He examined this new goal, which had announced itself in his mind fully formed. As if he had been planning it all along. As though it were the only goal.

Searching, he found no other ambitions or enmities—a development as shocking as any he had experienced, for after years of internal dispute amongst his peers he had built up a long list of men and women whose actions had offended him.

As a scholar, he was honor-bound to punish them.

As an ascendant god, however, he felt no such obligation. He no more shared the concerns of the outbound mage than those of the average dock-hand. Even Shav, whose act of betrayal Pol had lifted from Ebn's mind, was not so much forgiven as forgotten.

And when all of his earthly cares had been washed away—when all but one opponent was beneath him? What was he to do then?

He stretched, and the shadow of great wings unfolded from his arms, reaching beyond the walls of his apartment. He sensed he had become a thing of light and smoke, standing on the edge of a great precipice, waiting for the slightest breeze to carry him out over the world.

He opened his right eye and vaporized the wall underneath the open window. Only one step to carry him into the night.

He did not pause to reflect on his life, his accomplishments. He would not mourn the life of one elderman mage, but set his mind to the only appropriate task for a being of his station.

Yes. He would challenge Adrash.

‡

The night held him.

His wings grew hundreds of feet wide, and the black silhouettes of birds and dragons danced upon his naked flesh. A portion of the alchemical ink had gathered at his scalp, covering it like a helm. With a twist of his neck, a thousand fine tendrils erupted and were caught by the wind, whipping around his head before lying in a tapering point between his shoulder blades.

He freed his arms from the shadowstuff of the wings, which continued to beat of their own accord. A simple thought, almost a whim, produced a staff of frozen fire in his hands. Under his fingers its texture was solid, but it weighed nothing. The smallest desire turned it into a gracefully recurved bow, and on his thigh appeared a quiver of golden arrows. He called into being an ax, a longsword, form-fitting armor of glowing plates, each item weightless but diamond-hard.

Laughing, he returned the gleaming items to whence they had come. Mere extensions of his magical will, they would be of no use in orbit. Adrash would not be fooled by toys. Pol had spoken truly to Ebn. He had touched the mind of the god, and it was old beyond comprehension.

An intellect like that would know strength from bluster.

How ridiculous, to think only a short while ago he had plotted to bring knives and a target into orbit. The tools of children, a useless task of revenge. Truly, he had been no better than Ebn. Had Shav not betrayed him by leaving, Pol would still be embroiled in the petty task of killing her. He might never have achieved godhood at all. Surely, the quarterstock deserved as much thanks for his unintended assistance as Ebn, but it was not in the nature of gods to express gratitude to mortals.

Pol rose higher. The wind pulled smoke from his left eye, forming a long streak behind him. Like a fish caught on a line, the golden beam of light from his right pulled him ever upward. His chest inflated slower and slower, drawing increasingly thin air into his lungs. Soon, even the wind stopped. He did not become cold, nor did he fight for breath. He burst from the bubble of Jeroun's atmosphere, shedding his wings in thin streamers of shadow.

It seemed perfectly natural to stop breathing, as he no longer felt the need to draw in air. The void sustained him, warmed him as though he were lying naked in the sun. Having been exposed to the void due to accident several times in his life, knowing the intense burn of its touch, he marveled at his lack of fear.

Could he be so sure of his own power? Might not the effects of his transformation wear off, leaving him to die in orbit?

He let such worries fall away. He would not doubt the evidence of his own senses.

As he pushed himself toward the moon, he instinctively cast a dampening spell to push all thought deep within himself. He closed his mind as if it were a safe, and then turned the key in its lock.

He had entered Adrash's abode. It was only a matter of time before the god found him, no doubt, but Pol would not make it an easy task.

‡

He flew at speeds far beyond the means of an outbound mage, yet the effort took minimal concentration. He was neither taxed nor famished by it, and soon—as though he had woken from a dream—the cratered wall of the moon was before him. A vast ocean of frozen iron, as pale as bone. Lifeless as the void itself.

Pol shuddered when a force passed through him. He shivered as though he had been doused in ice-cold water, and his vision spun. The moon pulled at his body, trying to draw him forward. She whispered to him without words how sweet it would be to give in, to open himself to the void and embrace his fate. A ridiculous proposition, yet he wavered before her immensity, caught in her charisma. How delightful to spiral out of control, let her embrace him as lover. How wonderful to give in to the goddess Noeja.

He nearly let go. He nearly fell. But just before the temptation overcame him, he wondered: *Noeja? How is it that I know this name?*

The force lessened, allowing Pol a moment to gather his wits. The moon still touched him, and for the first time he sensed her personality, frigid beyond the void itself, disdainful of all life. She breathed in and out, expanding and contracting like a glacier in its trough. Relentlessly, she sucked the marrow from Pol's soul. Instead of longing to be closer to her, he now fought the urge to run away. His fear slowly grew, doubled, tripled. He fought to find calm, and came up empty. He too would be empty, a shell, if he stayed any longer.

Fly! he told himself. *Never come back!*

But still he wondered: *Noeja? Who has given me this name?*

The act of questioning was in itself an act of defiance—proof that he would not flee, but instead challenge the force which sought to coerce him—and in response he felt a measure of heat enter his body, easing the cold weight of his fear enough that it could be weathered. He shivered like a bone-chilled man before a fire.

Tell me! he projected into the void. *Who has given me your name?*

It began as a pressure behind his eyelids. It became the drumming of hooves on a baked plain. It became the ocean pounding upon the shore. It became the subterranean rumble of the earth's plates grinding together. Finally, it resolved into words:

Me.

The voice reverberated in the cavern of Pol's skull.

I am the voice of Noeja.

Dust lifted from the moon's surface. The entire planet quavered with the volume of this announcement, as if it had truly issued from deep within the satellite's heart.

Yet it was no goddess who had spoken.

The dread that had pressed upon Pol ceased. In its wake rose the unmistakable air of amusement. Pol was filled with the sense of being humored by a wise superior, of being indulged by a patient guardian.

The voice spoke again: *You are a trespasser here, mage. Prepare to meet your god.*

Pol smiled despite the threat, despite the insult. He had passed the test. He would stand face to face with Adrash. Let the god believe he was a child. Let the god underestimate him.

Pol descended to the moon and stood, the first mage ever to do so. None had dared set foot upon its fractured surface for fear of angering Adrash. He curled his toes into the soft, powdery regolith, soil that had never been touched by air or liquid water. When he lifted his foot, a perfect imprint remained. He walked, he hopped, he leapt forty feet at a bound. He stared up at the first and largest sphere of the Needle, which hung huge in the star-dusted sky, slowly turning.

It was indeed a rickety basket. A toy.

Pol projected his joy and his challenge into the void. He waited for Adrash's arrival, wondering how the god would appear to him now that he could truly see.

‡

Light preceded Adrash's arrival, igniting the moon's edge as though it were a steel blade fresh from the forge. The stars above this curved line dimmed and flickered in response, and to his chagrin Pol found he had raised his right fist to his temple in respect. Much as the voice had nearly bent him to suicide, the light compelled him to awe.

The god rose above the horizon, a second sun. A coruscating yellow-white fire surrounded him, extending miles from his body. For a moment, the shifting corona of flame seemed nothing more than a vain display, but gradually, like snarled paint strokes resolving into an image upon a canvas, its true form became apparent.

Pol's legs quivered beneath him as he took in the bewildering scope of the massive sigil, its lines melting and flowing in a constant state of rearrangement. No, he did not recognize a single configuration—if he spent a lifetime studying the symbol, its meaning would become no clearer. Here was magic on a scale impossible to comprehend.

Fear churned his empty stomach. Lead flowed in his veins, weighing him down, sinking his feet into the sterile ground. He stood transfixed, numbed, waiting for the inevitable: a quick death, befitting a frail, presumptuous mortal...

The inked sigils fell like ashes down his naked form, gathering upon his calves and feet.

Slowly, his knees bent...

No, he told himself. *I will not allow another to do my thinking.*

With great effort, he straightened his legs, swung his frozen limbs, shook the feeling back into his hands. Terror loosened its grip on his hearts, and the blood rushed giddily to his head. Thoughts spun, and then centered. Chastened for falling pray to the god's influence yet again, he reminded himself that he possessed his own set of weapons. Awakened once more, the sigils whirled around his body like leaves in an updraft.

Another flash of amusement.

You do nothing to hide your thoughts, Adrash said. His voice was an avalanche of rocks, the rumbling of a volcano before eruption. *What you have done to yourself is impressive, but you will not last long if you cannot silence that bullhorn of a mind.*

Pol cursed himself. He had allowed himself to be distracted. He reasserted the thought-dampening spell he had let lag and widened his stance. The black forms of halfstags and diamond spiders ran across his torso. A reptilian seabeast slithered up his right leg and a horned snake wound up his left. A thousand wasps roiled in flight on his arms. With a shrug, he unfolded his wings of shadow, spreading them like night's blanket across the surface of the moon. Adrash's light did not pass through.

Better, the god said.

Magic thrummed in Pol's veins, screaming for release. He closed his eyes against the glare and saw his opponent clearly, striding forward, feet above the ground, features serene under the divine armor. He did not appear to rush, but each step brought him miles closer.

I am ready, Pol broadcast.

No, you are not, came the reply. *But you came for a fight...*

Adrash disappeared.

A fist slammed into Pol's stomach, rocketing him backwards. His body cut a deep furrow in the regolith before his foot caught on a submerged rock and sent him tumbling. Dust puffed up around him as his limbs bent and slapped the ground. His lips pulled back from his teeth. His mouth filled with dirt.

Chalked with iron but uninjured, he rose from the ground.

Heavy arms crossed, Adrash stood at the foot of the scar Pol's flying body had created. Waiting.

Pol flung outstretched fingers forward, casting and throwing a bullet of compressed magefire at the god. With heightened awareness Pol watched it move through the void, its boiling blue surface spiderwebbed with black. As it spiraled toward its target, Pol clapped his hands together, cracking the ground at his feet. A crevice opened and shot forward at blinding speed, yet to Pol's eyes it crawled.

The bullet hit Adrash square in the chest and exploded. He did not move as the magefire curled around his torso, writhing upon him as though it were a living thing. Had Adrash been a man, it would have eaten into his skin like an earthmover diving into sand. As it was, the fire failed to adhere and dripped from him in long, liquid strings.

The crevice halted at his feet.

Adrash unfolded his arms. *These are the best of your weapons? You are a fool. Labor at your task another hundred years and maybe you will do more with your powers than nudge one of my spheres. Yes, I know you. You have ambition, but little sense. Still...* He cocked his head slightly. *There is something. Something more than will or talent.* He closed his eyes, and it was as if someone had snuffed out the sun.

There is something, the god said again. *Your voice. I know it. It is as if you wear another's body... We have been at this juncture before, have we not?* He shook his head, and for the first time an expression could be seen under the armor: a slight downturn of his lips, the faintest wrinkle between his brows.

An opportunity. Pol reacted quickly, without forethought, letting the magic speak within him. He would interpret Adrash's words later—if he lived.

The sigils writhed upon his body. They flowed up his legs and torso, gathering together on his arms, turning his skin from mid-bicep to fingertips solid black. Drawing upon the emptiness of the void, moving by sorcerous instinct, he formed an unknown spell between his hands: A dangerous, life-eating thing, a portion of nothingness crystallized, condensed, conforming to the shape of his fingers. Still, the spell was difficult to hold. It wanted to be free. He cupped his hands around it, pressed it into a small sphere. Throbbing in time to Pol's wildly galloping heartbeats, the spell's chill crept up his arms and into his chest. His teeth chattered and then abruptly stopped.

The spit had frozen in his mouth, sealing his jaw shut.

He could not hold the spell any longer. His hands flew apart and the ball of emptiness shot forward—far slower than he had hoped. It expanded in flight, wobbling like a droplet of water, contorting reality as it passed. The stars quavered through its imperfect lens and Adrash bloated into a ridiculous shape.

Pol sagged and ungracefully sat, spent by the casting. If it did not work, he would soon be dead.

Adrash's eyes snapped open just before impact. The spell hit him and instantly collapsed around his body, hungry for warmth. For several seconds the god strained against the constricting envelope, every muscle in rigid definition. He fell to his knees and bent forward at the waist, fists punching into the powdered earth. Pressed on all sides, he curled in upon himself. Just before he stopped moving altogether, the fiery sigil that surrounded him flickered, collapsed, expanded, and collapsed again.

Pol watched, struggling to make his body move. He gathered unsteady legs underneath him and stood. Cautiously, he floated toward Adrash. Though the god had stopped moving, his massive sigil continued to pulse on and off.

Pol faltered at the halfway point, struck dumb by the realization.

His magic is failing him.

Before he could form another thought, his own mysterious talent woke within him again, pounding against the interior of his skull. He threw his head back, but the scream stopped in his throat. Pain lanced through his rigid limbs, gathered in his fingers and toes. The head of his erect penis throbbed as if it were going to explode.

Through the agony, he sensed the casting of a second foreign spell.

Like iron shavings adhering to a lodestone, fragments of voidstuff stuck to his skin, covering him completely, numbing him from the outside in. Trapped, he struggled for control over his body, and lost.

The pain faded to nothing while his mind raged.

The spell moved his limbs. He strode forward, though his feet did not touch the ground. He bent, took Adrash's head in his hands, and lifted the limp body. The god's sigil flickered off every few seconds, reappearing slightly dimmer, slightly smaller each time.

Pol pulled him in close and kissed him at the exact moment the sigil fluttered off.

The moon disappeared. The universe flooded with sunlight—

—and he found himself on a field of blue flowers.

Three figures stood before him. A muscular man clothed in black from head to toe. A warrior-woman covered in freckles. A giant man composed of brass spheres. Adrash's body lay at their feet. The man in black spoke harsh, alien words, and Adrash's divine armor began to smoke, blistering and charring upon his body.

The perspective lurched, and suddenly Pol was flying at great speed over Knoori. Desert. Water. The domed island of Osa in the distance. Land. Pine forests. Finally, the Aspa range. He floated above a mountaintop valley with a lake at its center. Scattered everywhere were ruins, and among the ruins lay thousands upon thousands of elder corpses, naked to the sun. Men gathered around these, hacking them open with stone blades.

The perspective lurched again, and once more he was flying eastward over the continent. His speed increased so that he could not make out the details below. Then he was over water again: Jeru, the Great Ocean. He flew into a wall of cloud and just as quickly was out of it, descending into the alien landscape of a new continent. Glass and steel spires, entire cities of them, rose from the forests, plains and immense lake platforms. Roadways that stretched like ribbons of black silk crisscrossed the ground, and everywhere corpses lay.

No, not corpses. Living elders, glowing with life—merely sleeping. A spear of sunlight shot down upon one, and it lurched to its feet. It turned and stared at Pol with liquid eyes the color of dried blood. A sound built in the space between Pol's ears, rising steadily in volume.

The howl of a wolf.

A hundred thaumaturgical engines churning.

The crumbling of a mountain into the sea.

The elder screamed, and Pol saw no more.

‡

He woke, sprawled on the moon's iron soil. A yellow-white glow faded from his eyes. The spells were still upon his body.

Above him, the Needle was broken, its twenty-seven spheres spread across the sky. One hung stationary only a few thousand miles from the moon's surface. At the limits of unaided vision, another spun so rapidly Pol could not see its rims without quickening his perceptions.

The sight filled him with fear greater than any he had experienced since childhood—the kind of fear he had forgotten he had ever felt. For a thousand years, the Needle had stretched straight and true. Fifty generations of men had stared into Jeroun's sky, reassured or made fearful by the nearly unvarying sight of it. If they did not look too closely or were simply unobservant, they probably believed it did not change at all—that Adrash had no intention of using the spheres as weapons. Pol considered with what horror men would greet the following evening, knowing how wrong they had been.

And you will still be wrong, he thought. *This is not your god's doing.*

He turned his head. Adrash lay on the ground where he had fallen. His chest did not rise or fall. Though whole, the divine armor had taken on a dull, greyish cast.

Pol stood, swaying on unsteady legs but otherwise unharmed. Understanding that a decision must be made, he nonetheless struggled to bring his mind to bear. His thoughts swam in a thick stew, making it difficult to concentrate. He had not killed Adrash—of this he could be sure. That would not be so easily accomplished. Furthermore, why would the armor still cling to the god if no life moved within him?

The best thing would be to flee, Pol reasoned. Too exhausted to cast another spell, he stood no chance against Adrash if he were to wake. Still, Pol did not move. Already, he felt haler than he had when he woke. He resolved to wait a few moments, gather his strength.

A little time, he thought, *and I will be able to cast again.*

He did not have the luxury of rallying his reserves. Adrash twitched, and slowly began to rise. He fell twice, and rose again. Shaking with the effort, he finally lifted his head. He opened his eyes and light spilled forth, growing brighter until it pushed at Pol.

Pol braced his legs and pushed back, but to no avail. The force of the god's gaze buffeted him like a strong wind, and then began relentlessly propelling him backwards.

I would go, the god said. He fell to his knees, but kept his eyes on Pol. *You have done better than I imagined, Pol Tanz, but you have not killed me.*

Pol no longer sensed amusement behind the words, which burned through his mind and constricted the hearts in his chest. He wilted under the force of Adrash's anger. He struggled against the light, all the while knowing he would be a fool to stay.

Run while you can, the god said. *You will not get the opportunity again.*

PART FIVE

VEDAS TEZUL

The dirt floor of the ring had been raked and salted, but the smell of blood and sweat lingered in the huge arena tent. Large, smokeless alchemical lamps hung from oak crossbeams and steel wire far overhead, illuminating the restive mass of attendants.

The light did not reach through the press of bodies to where Vedas sat in the east corner of the tent, however. His black suit and dark features blended with the shadows, and people left him alone. Of course, they knew he was there. They stole glances in his direction, whispered his name. Black Suits of one hundred orders, holding glasses of red wine or yellow lager, sharing joss and eating ostrich rinds from oily bags—the high and the lowborn, master and acolyte, speaking his name, pinning hope upon their champion.

He had killed seven White Suits before dusk. The day before, he had killed eight. Due to the great success of the Black Suits in the tournament, and despite the creative shuffling of the brackets, he had also been forced to kill four of his brothers and two of his sisters. The final bout, after all, could not occur between siblings of the same faith.

It had not pleased him to take any of their lives, but he had done so just the same.

And though it might have been useful to analyze their fighting styles, glean something from his successes, he shied away from these memories. He centered his thoughts, burying the past under a tonnage of mental static as best he

233

could. It was a challenge to sustain this state, despite the practice he had put into it. For two long days, he had not allowed his mind to wander or speculate uselessly. He had not followed the other fights or counseled with anyone about the standings. He had simply fought whoever stood before him.

Grey, his final opponent, was only a name, a faceless rival on the other side of the tent, just as the others had been before dying by Vedas's hand. Undoubtedly, this approach could be seen as dangerously careless.

And yet, only Vedas and one other remained.

Clearly, ignorance had not hampered him overmuch.

His body ached so thoroughly that concentration could not locate a single injury more agonizing than the rest. Lifting a knee, flexing his pectorals, or balling his toes resulted in intense pain. His right shoulder clicked every time he rolled it, and stars flared before his eyes if he tipped his head too far back. His right finger was broken. He suspected his right clavicle and several of his ribs were cracked. The stiffness of his suit alone kept his torso upright and his legs from buckling underneath him.

It had not been so bad, after the first few fights. He had won them handily enough, but this was hardly a surprise during the winnowing stage. The odds fell in a senior fighter's favor. By the eighth round, however, experienced fighters were finally being pitted against one another, and the winners became harder to predict. Men and women who had worn suits for decades traded punches powerful enough to crush elephant skulls, dodged and deflected attacks too fast for the eye to follow, and died suddenly, often before the crowd registered the killing blow.

Victors and dead men were separated by a blink of the eye.

The goal was not to teach a lesson, but to kill efficiently. Retribution or punishment required keeping one's opponent alive—a condition few smart fighters would tolerate. It was too easy to misjudge another combatant's injuries and lose the upper hand. To kill a suited man was not easy, after all. Even mortally wounded, a would-be loser could still strike.

No weapons other than the elder-cloth suits were allowed. None were needed. Sufficiently skilled in the martial arts, fused to his suit to the degree that it seemed indistinguishable from flesh, a man like Vedas became a weapon of awesome power. Only magic posed a significant threat to the brothers and sisters of Black and White orders, but magic too had been outlawed from the tournament.

Aching, struggling to remain upright, Vedas gave up on centering his thoughts and allowed himself to wonder what surprises the man Grey had in store for him. Perhaps he would fight like Ria, the thin elderwoman Vedas had fought in round six—a flurry of deceptively wild punches and knee thrusts, a confusing fusion of techniques. Or maybe he would fight like Osuns, the immense hulk of a man Vedas had fought in the tenth round—a wall of flesh taking punishment without apparent damage, only to launch an offensive so carefully timed it nearly took his opponent's head off.

Or most troubling of all, would Grey fight like Jaffe, the small brother Vedas had nearly lost to in round fourteen? Unable to land a single blow, thrown around the pit like a ragdoll, Vedas had become desperate and thrown sand in the man's eyes. Many in the crowd had booed, but an equal number had cheered when Vedas killed the man.

He carried the guilt of the act with him still. The thought of winning the tournament under similar circumstances filled him with shame, for he knew he would make the same decision again. He had rewritten the speech, and intended to read it.

But who would listen to the words of a coward?

Doubt settled upon his shoulders, weighting his bones so that he sagged even more upon his stool. He might not live to read the speech. His success had never been assured. He could be the lesser man. Had he traveled so far only to die alone? Obviously, this was the case for all but one of the fighters. Why had the thought of being defeated seemed so preposterous? Was he really such a fool as to believe himself invincible, or had he simply pushed his fears to the side for fear of confronting them?

Die alone, he thought.

The two words settled cold and solid in his gut. He clasped his hands together to stop their shaking. Deeper than the exhaustion, heavier than the doubt, the hope he had suppressed welled up within him: a terrible feeling, like standing on the edge of the Steps, waiting for the wind to either tip him back onto land or carry him out over the sea.

He fought the urge to raise his head, and failed. The whites of his eyes reflected the scant light. A brother met his gaze and took it for an invitation to approach. Vedas shook his head, and the man faded back into the crowd.

The frown deepened on Vedas's face as he tried to peer through the bodies. He shifted on his stool like a man in great discomfort. Finally, he stood, craning his neck to see into the shallow bowl of the covered arena. He searched the highest stands, the fringes and the entrances. A persistent person could get into the tent, but could not shoulder into the ranks of white- and black-suited orders, who by right sat close to the action.

He searched for Churls, and came up empty.

‡

"Tell me you will," he had said, and she told him she would.

Leaving her in the whorehouse was not an easy thing to do. He regretted it the moment he walked out the door. She wanted him to stay—this much was clear, even to someone as unused to companionship as Vedas. After months traveling together, he knew her better than he had known any woman, any person, in thirty-four years of life. Still, there was mystery to her, words left unspoken between them. She possessed urges that both scared and compelled him.

He felt crippled by his inexperience. Did she know he had never been with a woman? Likely, she had guessed as much. Did she suspect he had never kissed a woman, never held a woman's hand in romance?

Anyone would laugh at his naivety.

Yet somehow he knew that, if given the opportunity, Churls would not laugh. The woman could be coarse, but she had never been cruel. She listened well when he ventured to tell her about his past. She had not chuckled or rolled her eyes while he talked of Julit Umeda's parents, halting and awkward though his account was. Sometimes, her expression appeared to convey not only sympathy, but a deep understanding.

Of course, sharing on this level occurred with regularity for other people, yet Vedas had rarely experienced it. He wondered, if he had held her gaze in the whorehouse, lingered just a moment more in her company, might she have shown him just how much she empathized?

With every step he took away from her, the more tenuous their connection seemed. It stretched, turning their months together into nothing more than a convenience, a rational arrangement they had arrived upon to keep themselves safe.

The road was lonely, after all. They had grown closer out of boredom. Perhaps he had deceived himself in everything.

Before long, this became his conviction. If she arrived at the tournament, she would be watching out of obligation and nothing more. She would congratulate him, buy him a drink, and say she wanted to see him at her upcoming fights. They would agree to meet up again but attach no importance to the appointment, like all mild friends did in the same situation. Bonds extended only so far.

He reached the Black Suit camp, where his brothers and sisters welcomed him in full companionship. They shared food and space. They introduced themselves and exchanged histories, began songs and dancing. More than a few offered their flesh, but Vedas felt no temptation to accept. Sharez, a lithe northern Castan woman who had caused her suit to grow spiraling horns on her head, made a seam split in her suit, revealing her womanhood. Briefly stricken immobile, he watched as she took his hand and guided it to her.

"Hey," she said when he snatched it away. "Why not enjoy yourself?"

She was beautiful, and he answered honestly: "I don't know."

Though he knew abstinence was not required or even normal in most orders, the sexual abandon of the camp shocked him. He forced himself to interrupt an intimate discussion in order to borrow a razor, shaved his face and head, and then went to bed alone, apparently the only one to do so.

In the White Suit camp, the situation was undoubtedly much the same. Celebrations had a universal nature. For the first time, Vedas understood how odd it was that he had never formed a sexual relationship, never experimented beyond masturbation. Surely, he did not still carry the wounds of youth! He had never looked upon the act of sex with revulsion. Instead, he simply did not consider it an option. But what if he had stayed with Churls? Would she have rented a room, shown him the error of his thinking?

Unable to sleep, he touched himself through his suit. Facing the tent wall, separated from reveling brothers and sisters by a thin sheet of nearly translucent cloth at his back, he knew what he did was ordinary, unremarkable, but as the erection grew under his hand he fought the irrational fear of being observed. Peering over his shoulder, he half expected to find her waiting for him. Smiling so that the gap in her teeth showed. Bending over, peeling leather pants from muscular hips. Running her hands up her backside, lifting her skirt.

Strangely, the paranoia coupled with fantasy produced the most intense orgasm he had experienced in some time. His legs shook and he curled in around the sensation, seeking to hold it in. He gasped unintentionally. A moan escaped his lips.

The sadness thereafter seemed inevitable, an aftereffect of wishing too hard. The cavity he had opened by giving vent to his longing now threatened to consume him. The immensity of the void constricted his chest, stung his eyes. He marveled at all the things he had never experienced, all the things he had never allowed as possibilities.

Traveling with Churls, having her close, had opened the world around him, yet he still struggled to give his desire a voice.

Yes... Yes. Without a doubt he wanted her.

He wanted her for more than sex—more than mere friendship or respect.

Suddenly, the thought of winning the tournament, of returning to his apartment in the abbey and reassuming his routine, seemed an awful fate.

‡

A squat White Suit came out of the crowd. The opposition's official.

"You're due," he said.

Vedas raised his arms and spread his feet for the weapons inspection. He closed his eyes as hard hands flowed over his sculpted body, uncomfortable lest he meet the stares of his brothers and sisters. They would smile, nod encouragement. One or two might spit at the official's feet or say something foul. Vedas needed none of that at the moment. Best he avoid all distraction, go into the fight feeling as little as possible.

Emotion slows reaction, Abse had always said. *Anger just as much as fear.*

Vedas thought of Churls one last time, resigning himself to the woman's absence before banishing her from his mind—a blessedly simple action now that the fight was nearly begun. Familiar sensations flooded his system, focusing his awareness. His pulse expanded to fill his body, drumming a simple beat from head to toe. His suit tightened around him. He did not feel so much as a twinge as his broken finger curled in with the others to make a fist.

The official put his hand between Vedas's legs, ran the tip of a finger along his perineum. He cupped Vedas's genitals, squeezed lightly, and then stood.

"Finished. Let's go."

The crowd parted for them. Vedas looked neither left nor right, and kept his eyes on the floor. He touched no outstretched fingers for luck. His brothers and sisters forgave such things, apparently, for they cheered as he stepped into the packed earth ring:

"Vedas!" "Vedas!" "Vedas!"

The bass throb of a drum underscored the two-syllable chant, though it could easily have been meant for the opposition, who shouted the name of their champion just as loudly. To Vedas, the words lost all clarity and became a simple rhythm.

Opposing factions, shouting with a single voice.

Vedas tipped his head from side to side, loosening his neck. Though no material boundary kept the Black Suits and the Whites from mixing, to either side an arrow-straight line separated them. Once in a while a hand shot out with a rude gesture from one side and someone from the other slapped at it, but this was the extent of their interaction.

Afterwards, however—maybe then someone would push at the border.

And what about the others, the ones who stood behind the gathered orders? Onlookers, gamblers, Adrashi and Anadrashi of a hundred kinds. What would they do if he won, if he lost? And then there were the others waiting outside the tent. The entire population of Danoor, waiting for word of the outcome. The Tomen, encamped in the hills...

Enough, Vedas told himself. *Concentrate on the task at hand.*

He lifted his head and looked at his opponent for the first time. What he saw surprised him, but his features remained blank. Knowing how much even a glance revealed to a smart fighter, he took in details of build and stance without moving his eyes.

She did the same.

For some reason, he had not imagined a woman. Perhaps he had not thought a woman capable of making it all the way to the final bout, but this did not ring true. More likely, he had simply gone with the odds. Sisters comprised less than a quarter of the combatants.

Grey stood an inch or two taller than Vedas, and outweighed him by at least fifty pounds. Her breasts were large, but so flattened by the stiffness of her suit that they looked like immense pectoral muscles. Her gut was a tight drum, her legs barrels of smooth muscle. Her shoulders sloped like a bear's, and her hands were massive. They alone moved, alternating fists opening and closing. Vedas looked last at her face, which was large but not at all unattractive. Together with the build, her unlined olive complexion revealed her as a native of northern Dareth Hlum, a close relative of the Vunni, perhaps.

The head official of the tournament, an impartial representative from the city council, stepped between the two combatants. He reached inside his robes and produced a vial, which he dropped and then broke under the butt of his staff. Vedas's ears popped.

"Silence, please," the official said, voice amplified so that all could hear. "This will be the final bout of this tournament, the final bout of the year. Tonight marks the last day of the half-millennium, and tomorrow the city will begin hosting celebratory games. Whatever the outcome tonight, you will end it peaceably and not sully the merrymaking."

Boos sounded from both sides.

The official frowned. "Battalions are stationed in this camp, at the coliseum, and within the city itself. No leniency will be shown to rioters, regardless of race, class, place of birth, or faith."

"What of the Tomen?" someone shouted.

The official's frown deepened. "A battalion is stationed below them. Another two companies are arriving as we speak. Ample men to quash any violence the Tomen may intend." He bowed to Grey and Vedas. "Good fight."

Vedas's hood flowed to cover his face. Grey did not mask her face completely, but caused her suit to form bars that rose from her chin to the armored bridge of her nose. Shelf-like eyebrow ridges formed and the eldercloth thickened visibly over her ears.

Transformations complete, they bowed to one another.

The fight began.

‡

Vedas was the first to move.

Grey merely widened her stance, turning to follow him as he circled. He kept his distance, watching her smoothly shift weight from foot to foot. She had lowered her center of gravity without bending her back, as if she were squatting over a latrine hole. Though he could not rely upon it as fact, nine times out of ten this posture communicated an unwillingness to reach farther than arm's length for an opponent.

She would wait for him to bridge the gap between them. From there she would try to take him to the floor, counting on her bulk to overcome him. She had probably caused her suit to texture, especially along the forearms and inner thighs, creating a gripping surface to counter the smoothness of her opponent's suit. A conservative strategy, sound but ultimately limiting: Her suit and thick build granted her a great deal of protection against close range attacks, but unless she proved faster than Vedas she would be unable to get a grip on him.

In his experience, the majority of fights ended up on the ground. He knew himself to be a capable grappler, but this time it would not be wise to end up on his back.

Neither would it be wise to rely on one strategy alone.

He limbered up as he circled, purposefully avoiding a fixed stance in order to throw her off. The ragged approach made him uncomfortable, but he thought it wise not to mirror her solid, unchanging posture. He held his fists just below his collarbones in a loose boxer's guard. He spiraled ever nearer to her. She gave nothing away.

Crouching, he swept his right foot at her left calf. She lifted her foot and stamped down, far too slowly to touch him. Otherwise, she had not changed position. Unless she was purposefully holding back, this told him something about her reaction time.

He continued circling. As he shortened the distance between them, her forearms rose. She opened both plate-sized hands and held them out from her body at the height of his biceps. He bobbed up and down and her hands followed exactly.

He shuffled in and jabbed at the right one. Her fingertips brushed the back of his hand, but could not close around his fist.

Quicker that time. Not abnormally agile, but definitely quick.

He continued moving, looking for openings. She continued biding her time, waiting for him to get overanxious and make a mistake. He darted in again and jabbed with his left. She nearly caught it. Her expression never changed.

They watched each other. This could go on for quite some time, he knew.

The crowd made dissatisfied noises. The fighters were silent.

He feinted in, pulling short a right jab. Reaching for his fist and grasping air, she threw her right shoulder forward slightly. He grasped her leading forearm with both hands and pulled diagonally across his chest, trying to throw her off balance. Her weight only shifted slightly, and he backed away before her other hand came into play.

Not fast enough.

Before he was out of range, she darted in for contact. It was a clumsy slap-strike, and the back of her left fist only glanced off his temple. He staggered but recovered his feet, shaking the stars from his eyes. She settled back into her stance. He resumed circling, noting that she now hobbled slightly on her right foot. Though her offensive movement had seemed slight, it had apparently rekindled a previous injury.

He decided to do a foolish thing. Take a calculated risk.

Hoping to catch her off guard, he repeated his last attack exactly. She was not fooled, however. Instead of reaching for his incoming fist, she lifted her right hand above it and closed her fingers in an overhand grip around his wrist. She levered his arm down, slamming her left palm into his elbow—the exact move he had planned for her, only far, far faster than he could have imagined. His right foot came off the ground, followed by the left. His face hit the dirt.

Though his suit hardened around his arm, as she pushed his chest to the ground her weight overcame the resistance.

His elbow snapped, and she pulled his forearm back, twisting it to ruin the joint.

He bit down hard enough to crack teeth.

She ground her left knee into his back, holding a stable position. But as she let go of his useless arm to reach for his head, her weight shifted minutely—just the slightest movement of her knee to the left of his spine, the tiniest slip of fabric against fabric.

It was enough.

Vedas pushed up with his left arm, lifting his chest a few inches, and she overcorrected, trying to keep her knee in place. It slipped clear of his back and he rolled under her pelvis. The entire right side of his body bloomed in agony as his shoulder joint dislocated and his shattered elbow was crushed beneath the weight of two people.

As her hands moved to wrap around his throat, he buried his stiffened middle and index fingers in her right eye socket.

She spasmed and fell forward, dead instantly.

‡

Night had fallen while he and Grey fought, but the Needle had not yet risen.

A group of his brothers carried him from the tent toward Aresaa Coliseum. Jostled atop their shoulders and hands, right arm stiffened against his chest, he demanded to be let down. He needed his speech. He wanted to wash Grey's blood from his body. The sound of the crowd drowned out his voice. He unmasked himself and attempted without success to meet someone's eye. Eventually, nausea and lightheadedness convinced him to stop trying. He closed his eyes and surrendered himself to a rough, two-mile ride into the heart of the city.

A commotion to his left. Shouting. Vedas turned.

Head and shoulders above the tallest man, gigantic hands parting the crowd, Berun swam through a sea of black-suited humanity. He moved in a straight line toward Vedas, unmindful of the blows raining down upon him. Staffs broke upon his head. Blades broke between the spheres of his chest, back, and shoulders.

Someone called Berun's name, and another picked it up.

For a moment, the crowd was split. Brothers and sisters who knew the constructed man's reputation struggled with those who did not, trying to halt the violence.

A line of green magefire arced from a sister's staff and struck the ground at Berun's feet: a warning. The constructed man halted, pointed to Vedas, and bellowed. The noise ate his tolling words. He bellowed again, and this time Vedas heard.

"My friend!"

All at once, it seemed, the rabble cleared a path. They cheered as Berun lifted Vedas from their brothers' shoulders, overjoyed now that the constructed man had declared sides. It did not lessen their violent mania, nor did it stop Adrashi—White Suits, townspeople, and foreigners alike—from continuing to attack the flanks of the crowd. They tried to break the ranks bodily. They stood on vegetable carts and roofs, throwing rocks and refuse.

Despite the official's warning, violence had erupted the moment of Grey's death. The orders had crossed the aisle with fists and staffs raised while Vedas lay trapped under his opponent's body. It could have been no other way, of course. The Black Suits had won, but the Followers of Adrash would not let it rest there. Men would die before the evening was through.

Vedas reached up and pulled Berun's head down. "I don't have it! They wouldn't listen to me. I need to go back to my tent!"

Berun smiled. "I have it, Vedas."

"How?"

"Quick thinking." Berun's eyes burned brighter. "They wouldn't let me in, so I tore the tent down. They showed me where your cot was after that." He shrugged his right shoulder forward, displaying the strap of Vedas's pack. "I checked to make sure it's in here."

Vedas sighed and shut his eyes again. "Thank you."

The river of Black Suits surged forward. Though Berun walked with far more care than the excited brothers had, he could not keep from being knocked about by the movement of the crowd. He could not stop others from bumping into the man he carried, who winced with every jolt and collision. Vedas felt as though his bones had detached from their joints, as though his ligaments and muscles had been pulped to mush. Even with eyes closed, the world spun. He masked himself again to block out the scent of Grey's blood.

Reaching Aresaa took either a hundred years or a few minutes. Once there, a man spoke with Berun. A man who insisted upon introducing Vedas before his speech.

"No," Berun rumbled. "I'll do it. Give me the spell."

A voice amplification spell, Vedas realized.

He felt Berun climbing stairs. He heard the echo of thousands of voices shouting in a great hallway. His name. Berun's name. Then, the roar of an even greater number in open air, louder than the howl of a hellhound, louder than the wildest spring storm. Another set of stairs, much longer than the first, in a closed space that reduced the noise to a dull throb. *DUM-dum. DUM-dum.* A two-syllable word. A name.

Out into the open again. The sound of cheering was a hundred nails driven through Vedas's skull. It went on far too long. "Enough," he finally said to Berun. "Shut them up."

"Yes," Berun said.

Vedas felt the constructed man crush the glass bulb. His ears popped, and the cheering softened. It became a sustained roll of muffled thunder, far more manageable.

"Silence!" Berun roared, and the thunder stilled almost completely. He lowered his friend to the ground.

Vedas stood without aid, unmasked his face, and opened his eyes.

Tiers upon tiers of people—one hundred and fifty thousand of them—had gathered to hear him speak. Anadrashi of every stripe, from every corner of the continent. More souls than a person could take in at once. Vedas turned a complete circle, staggered by the dimensions of the coliseum. Though he and Berun stood on a four-story wooden platform erected in the middle of the arena, they were not quite level with the lowest stand. Perhaps the stories his father had told him as a child were not so preposterous, after all. *Once, when the river Koosas flowed strong and wild, Adrash would fill Aresaa with her water and float great warships upon it...*

Berun's hand came into view at Vedas's shoulder. In it was a folded piece of paper.

‡

"Shit," Vedas said. *Shit*: The first unintended word of his address, echoing off the distant stone walls of the coliseum.

He unfolded the speech. The words swam on the paper for several seconds before organizing themselves in a recognizable fashion. He had written a full page in his small, tight handwriting. Four paragraphs, including an introduction wherein he thanked the city of Danoor and its representatives, everyone in the coliseum, the brothers and sisters of the Thirteenth, and Abse for sending him to the tournament.

Suddenly, the words of gratitude seemed unnecessary, even ridiculous. He skipped them and began with the second paragraph. Afraid to miss or mangle a single word, he read slowly, methodically.

"Respect for my abbey master notwithstanding, I cannot deliver the speech he instructed me to read. It encourages violence on a massive scale, violence that will result in the deaths of hundreds, if not thousands, of Adrashi and Anadrashi alike. It is the kind of message the Tomen are waiting for, but we cannot side with them any more than we can side with Nos Ulom or Stol. I do not wish to start a war, and yet I believe this is what I am being encouraged to do. I am no one's puppet."

Vedas paused his monotone reading. The stands were quiet, waiting for him to continue. He skimmed more lines, more words that only repeated his point. Unneeded clarifications. Entreaties for reason, for compassion. He skipped the entire third paragraph.

"Brothers and sisters, we are here tonight for the wrong reason. We are here because we have been told it is important to wage war upon those who disagree with us. We have been told that by winning the war Adrash is kept at bay, yet we have no proof of this. We gain the advantage over our enemies for a time and then lose it. The Adrashi do likewise. Despite the changes in fortune, Adrash still threatens us with destruction. Mankind is still held captive."

He lifted his hand, but stopped before rubbing his eyes. The smell of blood had alerted him. He became aware of a noise—the buzzing of a beehive, water cascading over rocks—and wondered if the sound arose within his own mind.

"While children are trained to kill, trained to hate, the white god waits. He waits for proof that mankind is worthy of destruction. How, I ask you, is our war supposed to convince him? How is it supposed to hurt him? I look around and it is clear that we are only hurting ourselves."

Pausing, he squinted to make out the blurred lines.

The Followers of Man need to stand...

Join with our Adrashi cousins...

He had written more—more entreaties and encouragements, words meant to ease the impact of his words. An open hand instead of a fist. Nonetheless, he let the speech fall between his fingers. He would not talk to his brothers and sisters as if they were children, or draw their conclusions for them.

The words that came next had not been written. They had been carved into the soft tissue of his brain over the course of the last three months. They had lain in wait for this moment.

"Our fellow man is not the enemy. Adrash is the enemy."

He looked up. What he had only half-heard before was the sound of one hundred and fifty thousand people in an uproar. The stands heaved like the surface of the ocean. Items arced through the air, littering the arena floor. An arrow fell just short of the platform. Magefire ignited from a thousand staffs, forming constellations in the tiers. As Vedas watched, a man fell from the lowest stand. Four stories. He did not get up. It would only be a matter of time before chaos reigned. Soon, more people would not fall from the stands. They would be pushed.

Vedas turned to Berun. "I did this?" he whispered.

"Not you alone," the constructed man said. He did not look down. Instead, he pointed to the eastern wall of the coliseum.

It took Vedas a moment to understand what he was seeing. When he did, panic gripped his throat with icy fingers.

The first two spheres of the Needle had risen into view, but they were not at all where they ought to be. They lay side by side, nearly touching. As he watched, a third came above the coliseum wall—a much larger sphere than it should have been.

Adrash had broken the Needle, and it would not take long for people to place blame.

"Time to go," Berun said.

BERUN

A dog lay in the flood gutter outside the boarded-up inn, wheezing into a puddle of its own blood. Its left forelimb was a flattened mess, as though a huge-rimmed wheel had rolled over it. Its chest was caved in and four great claw wounds had spilled the steaming contents of its bowels onto the ground.

The girl in white stooped to look at it. She reached into the animal's chest, a frown of intense concentration on her unlined face.

Sometimes they can be fixed, she said.

The dog twitched. Its chest inflated, accompanied by a high-pitched whine. Broken ribs straightened under its short-haired skin and its intestines slithered back into its belly. Slowly, even its leg started to puff up from the ground. It howled, and then abruptly stopped breathing.

The girl stood. *Sometimes they can't.*

She looked up at the small, two-story building, which had been barricaded from within, splintered wooden boards nailed across its two broken windows. Whoever was inside had undoubtedly blocked the front and back doors with furniture.

She's in there, the girl said.

Berun saw no reason to doubt her. Not long ago, she had led him to the foot of the hills that rose from the salt flats northwest of the city. She told

him of the monastery that lay nestled in the valley between them, where
Vedas now lay in recovery. She touched his leg, infusing him with energy as
though he had lain in the sun for hours. Then she had led him back through
the chaotic streets of Danoor, always a move ahead of the roving bands of
rioters and Tomen, to this small inn on a side street that looked like every
other side street in the city.

The owner tried to throw her out, she continued, *but she paid him more
money to stay. She couldn't walk, and for a long time I couldn't find her. She can
keep me away if she really wants to, but I don't think she really knows that. She
just does it.*

He did not ask the girl for more—*How do you know her? Why do you
care?*—for there could be no doubt any longer. She was Churls's daughter.
Unable to speculate upon how she existed and what her nature might be, he
nonetheless saw the bloodline clearly. How had he not noticed it before? The
bone structure, the eyes, the almost invisible smattering of freckles across
her nose—they were her mother's, almost exactly.

Of course, Churls had never mentioned a child, but he had seen the woman
naked on the morning of the cat attack. Though she moved to hide it while
she bathed, he nonetheless saw the scar on her lower belly. Undoubtedly, she
had reasons for not volunteering this information.

And he would never ask. Nor would he ask her daughter to tell him the
story.

This did not mean he intended to say nothing. He had suppressed his
displeasure during their headlong rush to the city, but now he gave it voice.
"If you can give me energy and almost heal a dying dog," he asked, "why
didn't you treat Vedas?"

The girl appeared next to him. She took his hand, though he felt no pressure at her touch. *I was scared. I don't want him to know about me. Hurry!*

His craggy brows met over his nose. "He was asleep the entire time, girl.
I only woke him before I left for the city." His fingers curled into fists. "You
had more than enough time."

She stamped her foot, but it made no sound. *I was scared!*

"You'll do it later, then? When you've got your courage back?"

I'll think about it. She disappeared, and reappeared a moment later. *The
man inside heard you talking. He's waiting with a weapon behind the bar. A big
gun with two barrels. There's a table turned over in front of the door, and a lot
of chairs piled behind it.*

Berun's anger did not fade. The girl spoke too flippantly about Vedas's health for his comfort. He briefly considered threatening her, telling her he would not retrieve Churls unless she agreed to make Vedas well, but could not make himself do it. Most likely, Vedas would not die from his wounds. Churls very well might come to harm if she remained in the city any longer.

He positioned himself before the door. "Where is she?" he asked.

Upstairs, third door on the left. She's asleep and probably won't wake up soon. She's recovering. The girl stared at her feet. *She made some bad choices and nearly died, but I made her better—mostly better. That was before I helped you find the monastery. I hope she likes what I did. I want her to not be angry at me anymore.*

He could not say why, but these words stilled his remaining anger. He found himself fighting the urge to praise the girl for helping Churls. He wanted to make her smile. She reminded him so much of her mother, damaged in ways beyond his comprehension. Perhaps this was not unusual. Maybe all men were fractured in the same sense, and only he had been blind to it. Still, he thought not. He liked Churls, more than he had ever liked anyone. He liked Vedas. He shared their concerns, though by all rights he should not.

The thought lingered, troubling: He should not? Who was to say what he should and should not do? His father no longer controlled him—how dare his mind act as though it were not his own? He was free to align himself with any person or philosophy he chose.

Resentment moved through him like lightning through sky.

He kicked the door, which splintered down the center but did not otherwise budge. Its edge cleared the frame as his foot struck again. Furniture crashed to the floor inside. Wooden legs snapped as the table fell over. A third kick knocked the door off of its hinges, sent it spinning into the dark interior.

In the silence that followed, he heard the distinct *click* of someone cocking a hammer. He identified the weapon from this sound alone: an alchemical cannon, a handheld weapon capable of hurling an iron ball at great speed.

"Hold it!" he bellowed into the room. "I know you have a cannon. Don't waste your shot on me, it won't do any good. I'm just here for one of your guests. Once I have her, I'll leave, and you can board up again."

A flash of light. The bullet stuck his forehead, rocking him backwards. He did not even hear the discharge, so loud was the tone that reverberated throughout his body. He hummed like a struck tuning fork.

Pain. One or two of his spheres had been knocked loose by the blow.

"I've got another coming!" a voice called. "Don't come any further!"

In four heavy bounds Berun had the innkeeper by the collar. He slapped the weapon from the man's hand and lifted him from behind the bar.

The temptation to hurl him into the street nearly overcame Berun, yet he resisted. Hurting a blameless man would not ease his temper. He hungered for a fight. Once he got Churls back to the monastery, he would return to find a contender. Rioters or Tomen, Adrashi or Anadrashi—it would not matter as long as they stood a small chance against him.

"Stay put," he said, blue eyes flaring brightly enough to illuminate the room. "Don't try to stop me. Don't call for help. Don't send anyone else to do these things for you." He put the man down and turned toward the stairs.

On second thought, he turned back.

"The Castan woman is my friend. If you helped her, then you've got my thanks."

‡

On the night of their arrival in Danoor, he had left Churls and Vedas at the door to the brothel. He did not want to intrude while they said goodbye. Hopefully, they would speak plainly and honestly with one another, but he did not think this likely. It had been one way with them for too long, and Vedas could not afford to be distracted now.

After a long day of running, Berun felt on the verge of toppling over in the street. He rounded a corner and sat against a wall next to a refuse pit. He did not drift into dream or lose consciousness. Nonetheless, time progressed without him. Only when he caught himself tracking shadows along the ground did he realize morning had come. Of course, Churls was long gone, and the man who tended bar in the brothel offered no clues as to her whereabouts.

With no leads, Berun made his way to the tournament grounds. He attended the first day of fights, most of which were held in open-aired arenas, little more than shallow bowls dug out of the hard earth. Careful not to be seen, he watched Vedas from a distance. He had no desire to distract the man. Moreover, he did not want Vedas to know that Churls was not in attendance.

He need not have worried. Vedas had eyes only for his opponents. Brothers and sisters clapped him on the back as he made his way from bout to bout, and he stared straight ahead. Now and then a White Suit spat at his feet while he rested for a moment between bouts. He did not appear to notice. He did not even pause to look at the chalked bracket diagrams that had been posted at each arena.

Berun attracted attention from others, however. Men who knew his reputation conversed with him, posed for alchemical image-castings next to him. Surprisingly, as many Adrashi approached as Anadrashi. Only Ulomi avoided him altogether.

"Word has it you came here with the Black Suit, Vedas," a fat Stoli merchant said. "He won't make it through the day, I reckon. There are bigger and faster men than him."

"You've seen him fight?" Berun asked.

The merchant pulled on his mustaches. "Well, no. But I've heard others talk about him."

"Are you a betting man?"

The merchant looked like he had been asked if he breathed air. "Of course! Last year twenty percent of my income came from fight winnings. My wife has been asking for a badlander maid for years, and I was finally able to afford one."

Berun clapped the man's shoulder hard enough to make him wince. "When it comes to the final bout, if I were you I'd bet black. Your wife will thank you."

Ten rounds occurred the first day. Vedas fought eight White Suits and two of his own brethren. He won each handily except for the day's final, which occurred after nightfall in the immense covered arena. At eight feet tall, the huge Tomen from Bolas towered a foot and a half above Vedas, outweighed him by two hundred pounds. His strategy, taking punishment until an opportunity opened for an offensive, was simple but effective. Vedas worked every angle without apparent damage, and was caught twice by bone-crushing punches.

But finally, inevitably, the Tomen made a mistake. He caught Vedas with a powerful left hook and—instead of falling upon his opponent as wisdom dictated—attempted to stomp down on Vedas's head. Vedas caught the foot and toppled the man forward. From a crouch Vedas jumped six feet into the air and landed knee-first on the man's lower back, where the suit material was thinnest.

Spine pulverized, legs jerking uncontrollably, the Tomen did not beg for his life. Nor would it have been granted to him, for the rules were clear. Perhaps he appreciated falling to a brother rather than an enemy.

Vedas straddled the man's shoulders and broke his neck.

Afterwards, Berun followed his friend discreetly from the arena to his tent. At its front entrance, Vedas turned to the raucous group of brothers and sisters that had followed him home.

"Get the fuck away from me," he said.

A silver-haired woman stepped forward, hip cocked playfully. "I watch you all day, Vedas Tezul. You need a relax, brother. I can give."

"Yes!" one of the men called. "Go for him!" another said.

Vedas's features twisted. He scratched at the neckline of his suit, as though the material irritated him. Berun had never seen the gesture before.

"I've had a long day," Vedas said. "Longer than yours by far. I want a meal and I want to sleep. If you interrupt either of these things I'll kill you."

Undoubtedly, this was an empty threat, but the woman did not know it. She and her friends sulked off, and Berun remained near the tent's entrance for a time, quietly turning away anyone other than tired fighters—anyone who might keep Vedas from his rest. He then returned to the city and searched unsuccessfully for Churls. When morning came he walked back to the tournament grounds and lay in the sun before the bouts began at noon.

‡

He did not enjoy the second day of fighting. Without adequate time to re- cover from their recent beatings, even the strongest fighters became sloppy. Men lunged gracelessly for the quick kill, taking chances no competent fighter should. They went into bouts with broken shoulders, arms, and legs. On one occasion, a woman pulled herself into the ring with a shattered pelvis. After eight years of brawling, Berun had never seen anything like it. A tournament was not supposed to be a battlefield where men were broken, but a place where skill reigned.

Pathetic, how much joy the suited spectators took in watching their most proficient fighters gutter out like candle flames. How the orders roared when two men on quivering legs eventually fell into one another, clumsily reach- ing for the other's throat. Few shined as brightly as Vedas, yet as exhaustion set in everyone resorted to dirty tactics.

Yes—even the best of them. Berun left the arenas when Vedas threw sand in his opponent's eyes in the fourteenth round, and did not come back until the final. He knew Vedas would make it there.

Both of the final fighters accounted well for themselves. They proved calm and deliberate in their strategies, but Berun saw the underlying weakness in the set of their shoulders and the imprecision of their footwork. So far gone with fatigue and injury, neither would have stood a chance against a healthy opponent.

When the end came, it was mercifully quick.

Subsequently, Vedas lacked even the strength to push Grey's body off him. Several brothers hoisted Vedas on their shoulders, and did not listen to him when he demanded to be put down in order to retrieve his speech. The crowd had become violent, and the Black Suits wanted to get their champion to Aresaa.

Berun wondered if they had anticipated the content of Abse's speech. Probably they had—most likely they looked forward to a violent message, an excuse to turn their newfound power against their enemies.

As Berun ran to the Black Suit camp to retrieve the speech, he considered how vastly his opinion of Vedas had shifted over time. Once, the man had seemed self-centered and haughty, shockingly ignorant of the world beyond Golna. Only on rare occasions had he shown potential. Certainly, he had saved Churls's life. As a result, Berun's affection for the man grew.

Ultimately, however, Vedas had only won Berun's respect by choosing to rewrite the speech. This decision changed everything. It proved Vedas cared more about people than faith. If he had not mentioned the speech, or worse yet believed its message wholeheartedly, Berun would have turned his back upon him with little regret upon reaching Danoor.

Aresaa affirmed Vedas's commitment once and for all. He stood before one hundred and fifty thousand people and declared war against God. He spoke nothing of faith, manipulated no myth to support his argument. Had he congratulated the gathered Anadrashi on their good works, told them to continue praying and fighting for the destruction of their enemies, they would have showered him with wealth enough to sustain him for the rest of his life.

Instead, he marked himself for death. He spoke words to spark revolution.

The spheres of Berun's body shivered with pride to hear Vedas's voice echo off the walls of the coliseum, to see the effect it had upon the assembled people. They were already rising from their seats. Some spat angry words, red-faced with indignation. This was not the message they had come to hear.

A growing minority held their fists aloft, shouting words of encouragement. They had waited for this message, even if they had never admitted it aloud.

Nonetheless, these few would not stop the majority from tearing Vedas apart.

And then the broken tip of the Needle rose above the coliseum, sending a wave of dread through the restive crowd. Soon, thousands of Tomen would flow down the hillsides and flood the city, carving its citizens from crown to sacrum with their recurved swords. For a time, even men who had been inspired by the speech would blame Vedas. Looking to the sky, counting the dead, they would say, *You have angered God!*

Berun knew then with absolute certainty that he must carry Vedas to safety. When men regained their courage, he must be alive to inspire them again.

‡

Berun crossed the northwestern border of Danoor, entering the salt flats of Neuaa at a run. At his back large portions of the city burned. Its light sent his shadow into the darkness, toward the hills and their hidden sanctuary. Before him the broken spheres of the Needle spread over the horizon in disarray. In another two hours, the sun would rise and they would be safe.

Churls shuddered in his arms. Her eyes snapped open. "Berun? What are you doing? Where..." She moved her shoulders, raised a hand to her face and groaned. "Make the world stop moving. Stop. Stop right now."

"No," he said, and kept running.

"Fine," she said, and threw up all over his chest and herself.

He stopped and let her down. Unable to stand on her own, she leaned against him. He helped her remove her leather halter and shook the clear fluid from it. There had been no food in her stomach. Shivering, she turned and pressed her body against his.

"You're warm," she said. "I never noticed that before."

He smiled. "You're probably the first to notice it."

"Do you have my pack?"

"Yes." He removed it and helped her get a heavier shirt on.

The edges of her wet halter gripped between two fingers, he lifted her again and resumed running. She curled in his arms and closed her eyes, though he knew she did not sleep. Every now and then she raised her head to stare forward, and he wondered what she expected to see. The salt flats extended for miles in all directions, and the hills where Vedas rested could not yet be seen. She did not comment on the Needle's new arrangement.

"How did you find me?" she asked when they were but a handful of miles from their destination.

"The map returned to me for a while," he lied. "You and Vedas both appeared on it."

She peered up at him, clearly skeptical. "Right."

As he began ascending the ancient switchbacked path up the grassy hill-side, she asked, "What about Omali? I thought you lost the map when you threw him out of your head. Does this mean he has power over you again?"

He grunted. In truth, he had tried not to think of his father. "No, I don't think so."

He halted atop the rise above the small valley. He knew where to look, and still it was difficult to locate the door of the monastery or its many-slitted windows. The single-room building had been built into the hillside without disturbing the lines of the slope. As a result, it was almost completely hidden from view.

Churls peered over his arms and then slumped back against his chest. Perhaps she had been expecting a fire, or some other sign of the valley's habitation.

"Vedas did it," he said.

She did not move. Did not breathe.

"He won the tournament and gave the speech, Churls. He told his brothers and sisters not to fight the White Suits anymore. He told them to fight Adrash. This was enough to upset people. And then the Needle rose, of course. When the crowd saw it, they blamed him. They would have killed him."

She inhaled sharply. "He's alive, then?"

"Yes, Churls. He's alive. Injured, but alive. He passed out soon after the speech. I carried him from the coliseum to here. He only woke up right before I left."

He paused. He had always known he would tell her, yet he had never found the right expression.

It was too late to worry about such things now.

"Your name was the first word out of his mouth."

The breath came out of her in one long sigh, and he began the descent into the valley.

CHVRLI CASTA JONS

THE 2ND AND 3RD OF THE MONTH OF ASCETICS, 12500 MD
THE NEVAA SALT FLATS, THE REPUBLIC OF KNOS MIN

They stood together on the hilltop. Usveet Mesa was a black wall on their right, stretching over the horizon at their backs. The cracked-tile floor of the ancient lake Neuaa lay before them, glowing orange in the fading light of dusk. Directly across the twenty-mile expanse, the city of Danoor still smoldered. Without any breeze to speak of, a hundred thin pillars of black and grey smoke rose straight into the sky, connecting earth and heaven.

"We're stuck here, then?" Berun asked.

Churls nodded. "They're looking for Vedas, and they know you helped him escape. I didn't get wind of it, but someone's probably still looking for me, too. I didn't hole up in that hotel for nothing." She kicked a rock, sent it tumbling down the slope. Visiting the city had not put her in a good mood. "I'm sure the guard doesn't give two shits about me, but the Ulomi White Suits? I bet even in the midst of chaos they're angry about the murder of one of their champions."

Berun grunted, and she wondered what he thought of her, now that he knew what had occurred after they split up the first night. Even then, he did not know everything. She had not told him about stealing the bar's chip money, or how she found another group of White Suits the next morning and got herself in even more trouble. They broke her left femur and cracked her pelvis. They did not rape her, but that was hardly the only way to humiliate a person.

And of course, she had not mentioned being healed by Fyra while she

256

slept—this, despite the fact that she suspected the girl had led Berun to the city to find her. She was not ready to discuss her daughter's ghost with anyone.

"Most of the Tomen have retreated into the hills," she said. "Some say they're waiting for Vedas to return, but I don't think that's very likely."

"Why do you say that?" he asked.

She shrugged, and wiped a strand of hair from her eye. "Why would they listen to Vedas? I can't imagine people who love fighting more than Tomen. You think they'll quit killing their enemies and start working with everyone else toward the nearly impossible goal of killing Adrash? That's ridiculous."

His thousand joints whispered as he crossed his arms. "Perhaps they've been waiting for the right message. You didn't hear him, Churls."

I didn't, she thought, and felt the familiar stab of guilt. *I let him down.*

She did not doubt Vedas's message had been powerful, yet it did not change her opinion of Tomen. The rest of the world might rally around a far-fetched dream—perhaps even Nos Ulom would one day see the threat of destruction for what it was and attack Adrash—but Toma would not. She had seen what Fesuy Amendja did to the Castan gladiator. She had made herself look.

"Will Vedas be a leader, Berun? Can you see him rallying Knosi and Stoli mages alike to battle? Sending them into orbit to die? Inspiring farmers and bartenders and fishwives to take up arms against Adrash?"

He turned to regard her. "You could ask him."

She spat. True, she could ask him. Lying within touching distance as he slept most of the previous day away in the monastery, masked and healing from injuries she could not see, she had resolved to do that very thing. She would ask him about everything once he woke.

Yet she had not done it. They had spoken less than a handful of sentences since he rose with morning's first light. Now it was as if a great gulf lay between them. They had become strangers again.

"I don't think he wants that," Berun eventually said. "He doesn't see himself as a leader."

"The good ones rarely do," she replied, surprising herself. She had not meant to say it. It sounded too much like an endorsement. At the same time, her dissatisfaction made little sense. Had she not been the one who challenged his faith in the first place? She had read the original speech, after all, and knew it for what it was.

By all rights, she had more reason than anyone to be happy with his transformation.

But obviously, she reminded herself, *I didn't help him when he asked. I kept my true opinion to myself—and why? Because I feared his reaction. I didn't want to burn a bridge.*

She exhaled loudly. "He would be a good leader, I think."

"Yes," Berun said. "You should tell him."

"He needs to tell himself," she said, thus skirting the issue. "He needs to take responsibility for his words. By leaving the city, he has left a vacuum someone will soon fill. I was in the city for less than two hours, and in that time I heard rumors of half a dozen men acting in Vedas's name. Calling men to them. Forming armies. One in particular—a quarterbreed gladiator, some are claiming—is rallying men in the Old Quarter. He has a wyrm at his command, they say."

Berun angled his face to the sky. "Perhaps this man means to help us."

She laughed. "Whether or not it's his intention, chances are he'll want to keep his power once he's got it. A man who leads others quickly gets used to calling the shots. He rarely likes it when his general comes back, quoting the regulations."

Berun looked back at the city. She chewed her lip and hoped he would say no more. Darkness was nearly upon them. Shivering as the first of night's breezes caressed her, she thought how awful it was that she did not want to be outside or inside. She did not want to be in Knos Min at all. To be home, where everything smelled of mildew and salt, where she did not have to always think of Vedas!

"Is your father still alive?" Berun asked.

"I don't know," she lied—an automatic response. Her mother had never allowed her to speak of the man, though when she was small he stopped by every now and then. He wanted to see her, but only when he drank. She had always imagined he felt remorse for leaving her, somewhere deep down where his sober mind could not find it. Yes, she knew where he lived, and a few other things about him. He probably would not recognize her if they passed one another on the street, but she would know if he died. "Why do you ask?"

"I wonder what it would be like to know for certain that Omali is dead. I fear my father will return. I fear..." He rocked from foot to foot, as though the ground were burning underneath him. "I fear father is the wrong word, but I'm used to it. I'm not a man."

She wrapped her arms around herself. "Is that a bad thing?"

He nodded. "It is if you want to understand yourself. You have examples everywhere. There's a person. There's a person. Where do I look? I can only look inside. There are times when I feel anger building within me, violence I don't think I can control. I wonder if it's me or that bit of my father that I'll never lose. If it's not me, then I have no purpose of my own. It would mean that I am now, and always will be, someone's puppet."

All of a sudden he stopped moving. His eyes dimmed in a way she had never seen. She reached out automatically, afraid he would fade and never reawaken.

"Are you my friend?" he asked.

"Yes," she said truthfully. "Whether or not you're a puppet."

‡

Bars of moonlight glided slowly around the interior of the monastery. For the better part of an hour, she watched one move slowly over her foot. She observed another crawl across the rough-hewn face of Adrash carved into the middle of the stone floor. No light touched Vedas where he lay on the other side of the room, but she watched two bars come within inches of his outstretched left hand.

It was perfectly comfortable in the small oval room, neither stuffy nor drafty. The temperature was just right. Shallow depressions spaced regularly along the wall fit a body well, smoothed as they had been by the backs of sleeping monks. The stone held the warmth of the day, or perhaps the memory of the generations that had rested upon it.

She could not sleep. It took all of her attention to keep the thoughts circling around the inside of her skull—and she knew they must keep moving, otherwise something out of the whirlwind might grab her, latch on, and open itself for examination.

Only, one would not be corralled. A white spark moved against the flow, shouldering its way through the other thoughts, demanding attention. Churls beat it back, sent it tumbling into the maelstrom.

But it returned, again and again.

Fyra.

Without a voice, the girl called to her mother. Churls felt it in her bones, the near-physical pull of her daughter's need. She knew the feeling well, despite years trying to forget it. She remembered returning home from whatever campaign in whichever province, picking up Fyra from her grandmother's. She remembered how she and the girl occupied Churls's small seaside house, little more than strangers. The way Fyra hid behind furniture, staring with wide eyes as though she thought her mother was some sort of monster.

All the while Churls had known, had felt as solidly as a punch to the gut, the intense ache of a child who wants something she has never known.

Because Churls had wanted it too, long ago.

Cursing Berun for putting the thought of family in her mind, she finally gave up, resigning herself to the meeting. She stood, briefly considering whether or not to buckle on her sword. It seemed pointless now. If the girl could heal a broken leg and a cracked pelvis, not to mention a hundred small bruises, she could surely take care of anything that chose to attack Churls from out of the night.

Vedas did not stir as she left. She located Berun atop the hill, keeping watch, motionless as a statue, and kept her eyes upon him as she walked quietly beside the long, thin pond that stretched like a scar down the center of the valley. The water narrowed to a point at the valley's northern end, inserting itself into a crevice, a twisted crack in the hills wide enough for a single person to walk. She felt drawn to enter here, and did not fight the urge.

A small stream of cold water flowed under her boots as she walked forward, and it occurred to her how odd this was. The verdant hills housing the valley rose from ground that saw rain less than a handful of times every year. Koosas, the only river within a hundred miles, had been redirected into Danoor many eons ago, sucking the surrounding earth of moisture.

Where did the valley's water come from?

As if in answer, she followed a turn and came to the crevice's end. She stepped out of the earthy shelter of the hills onto the baked crust of the salt flats. Suddenly, it was cold, dry enough to shrivel her lips against her teeth. She looked back and saw the juncture where the flats stopped and the hill territory began. It was a perfectly smooth line, as if the two regions had never been joined. She stepped back onto the black soil and stone, crouched, and put her hand to the earth. It was moist. She took another couple steps back and did the same. Between two rocks a small trickle of water ran. Cold, almost sweet on her tongue. Not a trace of salt.

Somehow she knew it would be as cold during the heat of summer as it was now.

Mama, Fyra called. *I can't go in there.*

Churls sighed and walked back. Fyra stood on the salt flats, the tips of her slippered toes at the dividing line. Churls leaned against the crevice wall and raised her eyebrows.

"Why is that?"

There are some places the dead can't go. Too much magic keeps us out. She lifted her heel and grimaced, as if she were pushing at the boundary with the tip of her foot. *I don't like being kept out.*

"Then how did you know about the monastery? How did you lead Berun here?"

A grin. *I knew you'd figure it out. You're so smart, Mama. I heard about this place from a dead man named Ulest, and then I told Berun how to find it. He was so tired from running, and I helped him with that, too. I made it so he won't be so tired all the time.*

Churls digested this. The act seemed markedly more impressive than healing a person, but perhaps it was just a matter of her own ignorance. Still, Fyra's knowledge was undeniably growing—and with it, presumably, her power. If the girl became angry, all the magic in the world might not be able to hold her back.

"Does he know who you are?" she asked.

Fyra shrugged. *Maybe. He's not as smart as you. He's like a little boy.* She looked up until Churls met her stare. *You don't want him to tell Vedas about me, but I don't think he will. He hasn't even told you about me, and he tells you everything. I think I'm his one secret. Everybody's got at least one—except Vedas, maybe. He can't keep a secret. You've got lots, though. Isn't it funny, how everybody shares except you?*

A muscle jumped in Churls's jaw. "Is this why you wanted to talk, to tell me I don't share?"

Yes. But there's more. I want to help. Some of the others do, too.

"Others?" Gooseflesh rose on Churls's arms and neck. "You mean the dead."

I only said some. Fyra shook her head sadly. *Some of them are angry about Vedas's speech, but most of them don't care. They say it doesn't matter what happens to the living now. They tell me to shut up. But the ones who still have people they care about don't think like that. They don't want to see the world destroyed. It's good to have a home, even if you leave someday and never come back.*

"You would fight Adrash? What can you do?"

Fyra managed to look insulted. *We can make people stronger, like I did for you and Berun. We can see inside anything and make it better. I'm good at it. I can show others.*

"Won't Adrash see? What if that's the thing that sets him off?"

That's why some people tell me to shut up. They think I'll attract too much at-tention and get everybody in trouble. Fyra curled her lip. *They're cowards. What can Adrash do to us? He never even noticed us. And we'll do it in secret. We'll make everybody stronger, but we won't make it a show. Still, we can't do anything if you won't let us.*

Churls almost laughed, but the horror of this statement stopped her cold. It all depended on her say-so? A war against Adrash, the awakening of an army of the dead, up to her alone? She could not make that decision now. She might never be able to make that decision.

She struggled to form an adequate response. She did not want Fyra to misinterpret her intentions. To her surprise, she also found she did not want to hurt her daughter's feelings—or close off the possibility of help entirely.

"I'm not even sure I want to fight, Fyra. I'm not sure I believe in this war. Give me some time to think."

You're lying. Fyra's expression conveyed what she thought of liars. *You'll follow Vedas wherever he goes because you love him.*

Churls did not bother to deny this. Love did not solve the problem. It never had.

"I can't tell the dead what to do, Fyra. You'll have to decide for yourselves."

You have to do it. The others aren't special like me. They won't break the rules like I do. They want a living person to tell them. They picked you. You just have to talk to Vedas first. He will help you. Promise me you'll talk to him, and don't lie to me like you did before.

Too tired to argue anymore, Churls nodded. She would not pretend there was any other way. Events had proceeded far beyond the realm of her understanding. Vedas needed to know. Not because he possessed any more intelligence or knowledge than she, but because she needed someone to share the burden with her.

"Is that all?" she asked.

One more thing. Fyra held out her hand.

Churls took it. It was no more substantial than air, of course, but she could no longer claim to feel nothing at Fyra's touch. Warmth flowed upward from her wrist, suffusing her body like smoke filling a room.

She stepped onto the flats, and the wind did not bite or suck the moisture from her skin.

I want you to look at the stars with me, Fyra said.

They lay on the parched earth, connected at the hands.

Tell me about her. The way you did when I was little.

Churls recalled with perfect clarity. She had buried the memories, but had never truly forgotten. On clear summer nights, sometimes she and Fyra had slept on the roof of Churls's house. Listening to the sound of waves crashing against the rocks below, she made up stories for her daughter's amusement— stories of gods and goddesses waging war across the void, giant ships sailing the oceans of other worlds, and kingdoms spreading their fingers toward the ends of creation.

Now and then, she told the story of a little girl who jumped from star to star, trying to find her way home. Aryf. It took Fyra years to realize the girl's name was her own spelled backwards.

Do you remember, Mama? Fyra asked.

"Yes," Churls answered. "Yes, sweetie, I do."

She blinked, and the tears spilled over. She had not expected them to come, but they came nonetheless.

‡

Vedas stood in the center of the room, staring down at the graven image of Adrash. He had removed his hood, and held his left fist at the base of his neck. Slowly, he inserted a finger between suit and skin and tugged, stretching the elder-cloth ever so slightly. He did not look up when she walked in, though he could not have failed to see her.

Exhaustion loosened her tongue. "How long has it been, Vedas?"

He opened his mouth, took a deep breath and exhaled before speaking. "Twenty years. More than half my life." His eyes roved around the room, landing everywhere but on her before returning to the floor. "It's odd, but I never used to think of it as odd. I haven't felt sun or water on my skin for two decades. I haven't touched anything or anyone in that time."

This was an exaggeration, Churls thought—surely. Someone, an instructor or a friend, had run their naked fingers through his hair or patted his cheek, offering comfort. Someone had kissed him, an innocent overture between adolescents. He had not abstained from sex completely. He had taken lovers before suffering whatever wound crippled him.

She would be a fool to take his words literally, yet the images failed to resolve in her mind. She could not imagine him receiving or giving affection to anyone.

The man she had grown to love did not dissolve where he stood. He was still the same man. Rather, she realized how greatly her desire blinded her to the reality Fyra had known all along: Vedas spoke the truth. He had not touched another soul in twenty years. He had kept the world at bay with a thin fabric shield.

And yet, surely the suit was inconsequential. With or without it, he would not know how to comfort a crying child or hold the hand of a sick friend. He did not know how to kiss or make love.

Churls considered this, and her desire remained.

"I want to touch you," she said.

He did not move except to tighten his fist around the fabric at his neck.

Heart pounding at her foolishness, she took two steps toward him. The room was not large. If she took six or seven more steps, she would be standing before him.

"I want to touch you, Vedas. Will you let me?"

Slowly, he unclenched his fist and spread the open hand upon his chest. He still did not look at her, and when he spoke he did so clearly, forming each word carefully, as though he did not want her to misunderstand.

"I have pictured touching you, Churls. I have pictured taking off my suit and making love to you, but you should know that I cannot do it all at once. It won't..." He shook his head. "It will not be like it is in my head."

She smiled and took another two steps. "I know that, Vedas."

He swallowed, and ventured a glance at her face. She noticed for the first time how deep the wrinkles around his eyes had become, how sharp his cheekbones. His lips trembled in the pauses between sentences.

"It is not just my inexperience that makes this difficult. It is the fear of changing into someone I do not know. Perhaps I have already gone too far by disobeying Abse. Maybe I am no longer a Black Suit already. If I love someone outside the order, reason says that I cannot remain in the order. If I choose to do this now, I will be a man without a home."

His eyes found hers and finally lingered. His hand strayed near the collar of his suit again.

"Churls. You have to understand this above all else. There is no return from this decision."

"No return," she agreed, crossing the space between them. "I understand that."

EPILOGUE

The battle with the outbound mage had left Adrash physically drained, a state he had not experienced in many millennia. He needed time to recover before gathering the spheres.

Secrets had been stolen from his mind. A new god had announced himself. The corners of Adrash's mouth curved upward. He closed his eyes, but despite his exhaustion could not still his thoughts. A renewed lucidity had come upon him, as though the encounter with Pol Tanz et Som had lifted a veil from before his eyes. He floated above the surface of the moon and let his mind drift through thirty thousand years of being Jeroun's god, alighting here and there on an event, examining it for its potential. Memories that had become indistinct over the centuries now opened for him, unfolding in his mind with such dizzying, ecstatic clarity that ghosts breathed, extinct species lumbered across plains, and crumbled cities rose from the ocean.

He longed for the heat and chaos of battle, and then he longed for sensual delights. He caused his vision to become a combination of both, displacing events so that they flowed seamlessly into one another. The culminating moments of the Battle of Keyowas led to the orgy he had hosted in Knos Min to celebrate his adopted son Iha's coronation. The feast of Nwd'al'Kalah, where he had eaten his first tinpan fruit and battled his first hybrid wyrm, resulted in the destruction of The Seven Cities of Omandeias. With a memory as vast as Adrash's, the permutations were nearly endless. He added flourishes, changing faces, identities, and geographies on a whim. He acted out the parts of hero and villain, or simply observed as events transpired, powerless as any man.

Regardless of these alterations, the exercise soon became mundane, for he could not stop the cycle of history from repeating itself. The names and places changed, but the patterns stayed the same. The rekindling of his memory served only to drive this truth home.

After all, how many variations could be expressed in arrogance, deception, and greed? How many in faith and honor?

He alone could answer these questions, for he had been with mankind from its origin—had witnessed every one of its faltering steps.

In the beginning, he had found the divine armor. Assisted by its strength, he cracked men from their hundred iron eggs. He taught them the use of tools, and then watched from afar as they huddled miserably around cooking fires. Mankind was naive then, unprepared to inherit the earth. Too used to the comforts of their eggs, the reality of survival nearly destroyed them. They adapted, of course, through hardship. They became strong, became worthy of his notice. Yet with time, their concerns shifted from the preservation of their species to the deception of a business partner, the conquest of a neighbor's husband or wife. They returned, ever and ever, to the source of ease, to laziness and avarice and self-destruction. Though all traces of their true nature and history were soon lost, they could not resist becoming what they had once been.

The world was theirs. It always had been.

Men were not evil, Adrash knew. They were simply lazy and opportunistic, courageous and virtuous in very infrequent bursts.

He searched now for those moments of courage and virtue. He delved into his mind and summoned the best of humanity, reliving the moments wherein men had proved their worth. During the siege of Shantnahs, he watched Neaas Wetheron rouse her army to defend the jeweled city. Her voice carried like a bell from atop the mile-high tower she called home. He felt himself swayed by her speech, as indeed he had been twenty-two thousand years ago—but this time he switched sides to turn the battle in Wetheron's favor.

During the destruction of Grass, he watched the valiant efforts of its people to find shelter from the volcano's toxic surge of gas and rock. Not just for themselves, but for their neighbors. As he recalled, he had let the city burn, for its people had turned their backs on him. Now, he placed himself in the path of destruction, turned it away like a man brushing lint from his sleeve. No, it did not satisfy even a little to do this, for the past could not be changed. Nonetheless, he did it, as if to affirm that he would not make the same decision a second time.

Other memories he did not change. Sometimes failure was in itself a form of victory: the act of having tried. He conjured up the original city of Zanzi—a shining ornament of suspended walkways and crystal towers built by magicians only seven generations removed from their egg—and tried to save it once more. His power had just been a small thing in that primordial time, when vast herds of fire dragons still roamed the continent. While he fought one of their number, the people of the Golden City ventured from cellars into the streets, dragging bodies to safety even as the many-legged beast crushed their glass homes and dripped acid onto their bodies. Adrash watched them die. He tried to pull hope from their futile acts of charity.

It was insufficient, and his brittle hope in mankind faltered yet again.

At times his faith had failed completely, and on these occasions he had dredged material from the far side of the moon to build another sphere, another weapon. Try as he might, he could not forgive the men of Jeroun their pettiness, their squabbling, their ridiculous and violent worship.

But he could not condemn them completely. Not yet. There were signs. Still, small thoughts that needed pushing, encouraging. Selfless acts gone unnoticed by the rest of the world.

Sometimes, Adrash imagined he heard the whisper of a familiar voice.

The call of a soul that resounded even in the void. A threat and a temptation. A catalyst.

‡

With the renewed clarity of recollection the battle with the outbound mage had gifted to him, understanding dawned upon Adrash.

He had been a fool to doubt the existence of prophets. He had imagined nothing: No seers had been conjured from the dust of his mind in order to forestall another cataclysm. True, time and isolation had dulled his ears to the sound of the singular voice in which such men and women spoke, but he should not have allowed himself to believe it never existed.

The memory of Eloue, the first to assume the voice of a prophet, bloomed within him.

He had been young, a god for a mere two thousand years. Haughty yet capricious in his hungers, he neither sought nor turned away those who would worship him. He visited Knoori and the thousand island-homes of man that rose out of the shallow sea, besting creatures and performing miracles. Reveling in his power and the thrill of physical conquest, the blood hot in his veins, he found love easily.

After spending a bracingly crisp autumn on Herouca, the lush, sugar maple-covered island that would in time become known as Little Osa, he chartered a yacht cruise around Doec Lake to celebrate the arrival of winter. He discovered the woman alone, leaning far out over the deck railing, staring into the deep luminescent waters, half of which were covered by a shelf of rock—all that remained of an immense cave system the elders had carved into the side of Mount Lepsa, king of the Coriel Range.

He admired her beauty in shadow and light. Soon thereafter he became her lover.

Her name meant "white stone" in a language only Adrash remembered. She lived in the Old Quarter of Tiama, and made her living by way of deception. While a small portion of enchanted blood moved within her, allowing her to read thoughts as easily as normal men read books, healthy minds bored her. Thus, she rarely told her customers the things they needed to hear. Instead, she used her unique skill to obtain power, make money, and amuse herself. She seduced men with her lies and charm, and then took delight in breaking them.

Her eyes were polished amethysts. She rarely smiled. Hairless skin the color of peach-flesh stretched over the muscle and fat of her body in flawless curves. It felt to his lips like orchid petals. When she became excited, a fine sheen of liquid formed on her lower stomach and thighs, and dripped from her womanhood. It tasted to him sometimes like cantaloupe, sometimes like coconut. Though her beauty was clearly a condition brought about through magic, Adrash could not stop himself from worshipping at her altar.

A most alluring pretense arose between them, eventually bound them together. She knew who he was, but treated him as she would any suitor, and he lavished upon her all the appearances of love. They traded lies, and by doing so found what they both needed. She insisted she did not enjoy sex, but he thought otherwise. She told him she coveted his power, and he knew she did not always lie.

"How did you acquire this?" she asked as they lay tangled together on the bower above the Gason-a'Loran street market. Her fingertips brushed across the line on his left wrist where the white material of his armor met black skin. Every now and then he felt her nails, as if she were trying to get under a seam, though she knew full well no seam existed. Many had tried to take the armor—which he frequently wore as a glove when not fully sheathed within it—from him, only to discover it could not be removed by any means.

He groaned, but not without pleasure. He had told her the story on many occasions. It went the same way each time, for the lie was old and worn. The enemies of which he spoke had never existed, nor had the cities and countries he named.

"That evening on Pergossas I led the men in a successful charge, halting the chimera advance line. We lost three hundred men and, weak from blood loss and starving, likely would have lost a great deal more if the enemy had not retreated to the hills outside Nusse, leaving their dead and dying for us. Chimera meat is dreadful, but it is better than dying from hunger."

Playfully, he dug his fingertips into her taut belly. She did not move an inch, and he smiled into her shoulder. Every time they moved even slightly, flowers rustled beneath them. Though winter's chill had not yet left the earth, his ebon skin absorbed the sun's heat and radiated it like a furnace, keeping her warm.

"After dinner, the healthy men went scavenging for weapons and loot. I searched further afield than the rest. I remember that our fires seemed very far away. The moon loomed above me, casting everything in ghostlight. I suppose I was afraid. Then, I saw a flash of white. It stood out because the chimera fought in dark grey armor and blackened their swords. Seeing the glove up close, it felt as if it sang to me out of the night, and I had the inexplicable urge to possess it. It came away easily and pooled in my hand like cool liquid."

"It did not scare you?" she asked on cue, voice low and serious.

"Yes, but I knew immediately that I was meant to possess the glove. I could feel it clinging to the palm of my hand, conforming to me. I took it to my tent and with great reluctance spread it on my desk to examine it. You see, I did not want to let it go. It had only three fingers, a fact I had not considered when I took it from the chimera. Nonetheless, I could not resist the urge to slip it on." He held the gloved hand before her face and split four fingers so that they looked like two. "I cannot properly describe the feeling to you. Have you ever fallen a great distance?"

She shook her head.

"Have you ever killed someone? Or felt close to death? It was very like these things combined."

She shook her head again, and he sighed contentedly. The script still amused him, and not all of it was a lie. The sensations he described were accurate.

"It is just as I thought. It will have to suffice to say that I had never felt such fear and exhilaration. Nor had I ever approached it. I blinked and the glove fit my hand perfectly. I could tell it wanted to be more than just a glove. It wanted my whole body. Some time still passed before I allowed it to cover me completely, to become armor, and this was an experience of another degree of magnitude. Only experience would prove that I could wear it without losing myself to the sensations."

"What about your men? The war with the chimera?"

"As I recall, after finding the glove I abandoned my men on Pergossas. I requisitioned a small keelboat and sailed into the Eenos Ocean."

"Why?" she asked, tearing petals from an unopened rosebud with her fingernails.

He shrugged, chest pulling against her back. "I wanted to be alone."

"What happened to your men?"

He paused. Her question should have been, *Where did you go?* She rarely deviated from the script.

He dismissed it as nothing. "I suppose they died," he answered. "Our brief victory meant little. The chimera had been expecting replacements from Belloja for some time. We had no chance. Why do you ask?"

"You had the glove. With it you could have helped the men."

"No." He disengaged his armored hand from hers and lay back on the bed of flowers. He knew she had no real interest in whether he helped or hurt men. "I did not yet know how to use it, or indeed if it could be turned to violence."

She rose and stared down over her shoulder. She did not look directly at him, instead focusing on a distant point in her mind. "But you," she said. "You know how to use the glove now. There is no limit to your power."

"Hardly," he said. "It only seems that way to you because you have so little power."

He meant the comment as a joke, but her expression showed he had failed. Her brows came together and her lips set in a straight line. Anger, a common enough emotion for her.

Her temper collapsed suddenly, and her eyes became wet.

This, he had never seen. He wanted to be somewhere else, away from a situation he had so clearly misjudged.

"Eloue. What is it?"

Her eyes found his. "Are you ever going to share it with me?"

"No," he said.

‡

On the surface, it was not an occurrence worthy of note. Many people had expected Adrash to share his power, and were disappointed when he did not. Eloue's desire for power did not disappoint him. Rather, her vulnerability did. He had not expected it, and his response shocked him. He recoiled from her and left Herouca with a feeling uncomfortably close to fear.

He had not felt fear in a long time, indeed.

Her voice lingered in his mind—her touch and smell and taste, but mostly her voice. On regular occasions he woke from deep sleep, sure he had heard her calling to him. He began to suspect more than her vulnerability had driven him away. He examined his memories of her with the perfect recollection of a young god, and in examining heard what a normal man could not hear: Layers of sound, dense and sharp, pulsating like the stars at the limit of his vision. Eloue's true voice was bliss and terror—the twitch of muscles in a man's leg before coitus and the sound of the void freezing his lungs. It both invited and repelled.

No, he had not loved her. He came to realize affection had never drawn them together. No cute lie or routine bound them. Instead, a force beyond reason had compelled Eloue to him, and he to her. After several years away from Herouca, he could not deny this fact any more than he could deny his armor's overwhelming need to be worn. Perhaps, instead of running he should have stayed and bested his fear. Had he turned his back on a great gift, an arcane magic?

More troubling still, he wondered if he had left a great weapon in the hands of an enemy.

He grew tired of thinking about it, tired of being intimidated by the unknown.

When he returned, Eloue was already dead, her home a slag-pile. Powerful magic had been brought to bear by a competitor or jealous suitor. Adrash had no interest in retribution, for her death freed him of his burden of thought. He bestowed his blessings upon the people who worshipped him and moved on. He visited the Royal Courts in Knos Min, from which his descendants, or those who pretended to be his descendants, ruled.

But the whole affair troubled him vaguely, as if something had soured in his stomach. He vowed never to set foot on Herouca again. It was only one island, and being there reminded him of his idiot fancy and miscalculation. He had squandered a possibility.

With effort, he managed to forget Eloue's voice. He traveled his realm and found lovers to replace her—women and men who had never heard of Herouca, some of whom had never heard of Adrash. Far from the epicenter of his influence, on islands unlinked to Knoori, where the men had long ago forgotten the magics needed to cross the ocean, he begat children and raised dynasties. When a place ceased to inspire him, he left.

‡

Four millennia after men spilled forth onto the world's surface, even the most advanced peoples of Jeroun had lost the ability to navigate the shallow sea and defend themselves from its creatures. The islanders disappeared due to disaster and famine, but Knoori's population continued to grow, flourishing under the stern eye of Adrash.

He made Zanzi his home. Situated at the center of what would one day be called the Aroonan Mesa, his villa overlooked the million homes of The Golden City, the largest and most beautiful metropolis in Jeroun's history. From there he traveled the continent, vanquished the last of the fire dragons, brought low the mage-kings who had installed themselves in various locales, and monitored the use and trade of elder corpses.

He reasoned his strength was not so great that another might not rival it. Though they lived in a state of suspension, the elders of the Clouded Continent were powerful enough to keep men from seeing their land, and Adrash from setting foot upon it. If the near-dead could do so much, perhaps a man might one day do more. And if the elders one day woke, who knew what powers they could bring to bear?

Of course, time would prove these fears ungrounded. Over the next two millennia he tested the limits of the divine armor, growing stronger and stronger until even the elder magic could not restrain him. He walked the Clouded Continent, grew to know its slumbering people through their beautiful artifacts. Cities that spun slowly like leaves on water. Crystal windmills half a mile high. A stadium seated for millions with a lake at its center.

A field of glass war machines whose angular surfaces glittered in the sun.

Fearing the elders were the source of Eloue's true voice, he took one of their number to a secluded island and allowed the sun to revive it.

They battled like old enemies. The elder's aggression surprised Adrash, as did its expression, which so closely mimicked a man's. Perhaps the creature had sensed Adrash's intentions all along, knew it could not match him, and so spent its final energy on hate. This pride suited the creators of such breathtaking monuments.

Yet for all of its vitriol, the creature was easily overcome.

At no point did Adrash hear anything other than the sound of its breathing. It was not an enchanted being—merely a strong one. The realization was little comfort, for he had come no closer to understanding the nature of Eloue's magic.

And then, three thousand years after her death, he heard the voice again, calling from the bottom of the world.

‡

He came to the largest of the southern islands curious. He remembered cracking an iron egg on its cold, weathered rock surface, sure the men who spilled forth would perish in the harsh land. To find its people not only surviving, but thriving, after five thousand years heartened him. After all, the ocean was no friend to man, nor were its inhabitants. Oft-times, the world itself seemed inimical to man, especially those who lived on the islands. Air currents sent locusts, dry weather, and disease. Volcanoes and earthquakes returned the islands to the sea.

Eighteen-year-old Tsema had never heard of such things. If the people of his land had ever suffered, he did not care. He heard music in his dreams and on the wind, and re-created it. Not for money or fame did he play. He played because it hurt not to.

A creature born of the island's exotic magics, the smooth, long lines of his body revealed a peculiar heritage. Eyes flashed orange to match the short fur covering his whip-thin body. His fine-boned face looked more animal than man depending on the angle. His hands were large and calloused. The seven triple-jointed toes of his feet helped him adjust the innumerable gears and cogs of his musical instrument, a four-story building of driftwood and stone, thin slabs of transparent crystal and glass. He called this machine The Element. He carried two wrenches curled in his tail, and from his belt swung a collection of lesser-used tools of odd design.

It took one hundred men to haul the creaking instrument at a snail's pace across the stepped rock surface of the island, and another fifteen men to feed them. People claimed the boy's closest attendants lived on his music alone, but any fool could have smelled the mythmaking in this. For all of the magic virtuosity the boy displayed, Tsema was no miracle worker. He had no interest in redemption, yet the people read much in his tales. He became a prophet. Even the island's king listened to his cryptic lyrics with a keen ear.

When Adrash heard the boy's voice for the first time, the world ignited and blackened in the corners of his eyes. Underneath the rich tenor and the clanging cacophony of The Element, the boy's true voice shrieked at a stone-shattering pitch. He was not as strong as Eloue had been, but in time he surely would be. Adrash had become sensitive to the voice after so much reflection.

Other things he had always seen. The auras of most men radiated tones of grey and barely rose from their bodies even when excited, but the boy's flared violet and orange, coruscating in wild arcs from his body when he sang.

Just as with Eloue, Adrash could not fight his attraction.

They lived together in the top floor of The Element, where the boy proved an excellent lover. He clearly did not live only for music, yet he sang often during their lovemaking. The otherworldly timbre of his voice aroused Adrash's libido, focusing his awareness of pleasure as it had never been focused. The boy's confident touch reminded Adrash of Eloue. His body responded as hers had. The armor—which Adrash still wore as a glove—fascinated him, though he knew nothing of its reputation.

"What does it do?" he asked.

"Does it have to do something?"

The boy spread Adrash's armored hand palm down on his thin, furred thigh. "Can't feel where it ends, where skin begins." He turned the hand palm up. "Can see no lines under it. No heart line, no love line. No age line! Man can hide that, powerful doing."

Adrash shook his head and moved his hand up the boy's thigh. The boy had not seen him covered by the armor completely, and Adrash did not intend to show him. "I acquired it in Loreacte," he lied, referring to the half-mythical land he had claimed was his home. "A clothier had it under the counter, and I saw it. He would not let me try it on, but I convinced him.

I knew immediately that I'd made a mistake, but in the end it is harmless. I have even grown to admire it."

"Love it." The boy covered Adrash's hand with his own. "Want one just like it."

The subject came up again and again. Adrash recognized the boy's desire to possess the armor and fed it, though he could not say what compelled him to do so.

He woke one night to find the boy rubbing oil on his wrist, where the armor fused with his skin. It burned slightly, but not enough to have woken him. Instead, he focused on a low sound that came from inside the boy. It reminded him vaguely of the crash of surf on rocks, wind rustling the leaves of a tree. He had never heard it before.

"What are you doing?" he asked.

The boy's head jerked upwards. His eyes were solid yellow-white. A growl began low in his throat, rumbling down through the register, into the depths of the earth below them. Before the command had been given, the armor tickled on Adrash's wrist, began rising up his forearm. He placed his palm upon the boy's chest, tried to push him down, and found that he could not. The boy gripped his forearm in steel fingers, as if trying to stop the armor's advance.

"Want it," the boy said. "Off. Now."

White rose above the boy's fingers, and Adrash felt a surge of strength flow through his limbs. Cold purpose flooded his mind. He took hold of the boy's free arm and threw him from the bed. The furred body crumpled like a stuffed toy as it hit the sharp teeth of the giant gear projecting into their room. Vertebrae snapped audibly as his head ricocheted off the metal.

Adrash stood and regarded the body. For several seconds, it seemed to him that the world was mute, that all sound had been cancelled.

He had listened to the boy's voice for so long he had ceased to hear it.

He vowed never to let this happen again.

‡

He encountered the voice of the prophet many times after Tsema. A thousand years passed between occurrences, two thousand—never more than three. Adrash heard it more clearly each time, but grew no closer to understanding its nature. For twenty millennia, the voice announced itself across the face of Jeroun, inhabiting the bodies of young and old, male and female and elderman. Its avatars were heroes and sometimes villains, but they were never ordinary.

Each attracted and repelled Adrash. As he grew ever more powerful, testing the ultimate capabilities of the divine armor, the fiercer those who spoke with the voice pursued it.

Sleum Edylnara, who wielded the crescent aszhuri blade with a dancer's grace and made love like an animal, tried to decapitate Adrash during one of their practice sessions. Adrash caught the blade in his hand, broke it, and strangled the woman. She did not beg for her life or try to tear Adrash's fingers from her neck. Instead, her eyes had slowly turned to golden fire as her true voice singed the inside of Adrash's skull.

Kengon Asperis Dafes, the Necromancer of Bridgtul, fed Adrash a potion that paralyzed him for several minutes. While Dafes's back was turned, the armor covered Adrash's body and began filtering the poison from his system. Adrash watched as the necromancer attacked with magefire, enchanted blades, and corrosive liquids. He felt nothing, cocooned safely inside the impenetrable white material. When he finally could move, he moved swiftly, crushing Dafes's skull between his palm and a marble autopsy table. The rumbling voice warbled and died, but its echoes resounded in his head for weeks thereafter.

Open Water, Full Chieftain of The Whal, Lord of Spearhandle, pushed an enchanted whalebone dagger through Adrash's left kidney during an orgy the two hosted. By this time, nearly twelve thousand years after Adrash had first heard the voice, the armor had fused with his system to such a degree that he barely felt the wound—the kidney itself healed in the blink of an eye. He twisted, pulling the dagger from Open Water's hands, and with the light from his eyes vaporized the chieftain before his closest allies and lovers. Those gathered fell to the floor and worshipped Adrash.

As time went on, the avatars of the voice ceased to be a challenge. Their acts became ever more aggressive, but depressed Adrash with their predictability. As his own power grew, he forgot his original goal, which had been to understand the voice. Like the elders, it too had proved a weak enemy.

But he wondered if the voice might one day be heard on a grand scale. What if it woke the elders and urged them to take up their glass war machines, if it persuaded mankind to gather its forces in alliance? Perhaps then he might be threatened.

Adrash discovered he desired this. Not entirely. Not yet.

Nonetheless, he could no longer bear to live in the world. With no enemies to fight and little inclination to continue policing mankind, he ascended to heaven. Weariness rooted deep in his bones. The cords linking him to mankind frayed and nearly severed.

He knew an illness had taken hold of him, but felt powerless to stop it.

He built weapons of destruction, and extracted frail promise from the minds of men.

He waited for the voice to return. Surely, it had noticed his absence. He imagined it, waiting in hibernation, gathering its power for a final confrontation. Eventually, it would announce itself. This time, he would leave it alone. Let it come to him.

He waited, and grew impatient. Impatience eventually led to weariness, weariness to forgetfulness.

‡

After three days of resting, reflecting upon the past, Adrash opened his eyes.

The light of realization spilled forth.

The cratered surface of the moon sped by beneath him, bright as sun-bleached bone. Adrash smiled within the divine armor's embrace, and turned to regard Jeroun.

Four voices rose in concert from its surface with a clarity that made his bones shiver.

How he had not heard them before was a great mystery. That such souls had been hidden from him seemed nearly impossible, especially considering his first encounter with Pol. Alone, the elderman had moved one of the spheres. The act should have aroused Adrash's curiosity, yet he had written it off as an unusually powerful spell, similar to the one the elderwoman had used to bewitch him. Certainly, the outbound mages had progressed a great deal.

As, apparently, had the voice.

Voices, Adrash corrected himself. Perhaps there had always been more than one, and his ears were simply too unrefined to notice.

Regardless of the number, whatever produced the phenomenon had evolved beyond his capacity to recognize. While he waited for a sign from below—or merely for his indulgence of mankind to end—his enigmatic opponent had altered itself to fool him.

Of course, the strategy had worked. His deafness had left him vulnerable to the elderman's second attack.

Yes, the new god had stolen things from Adrash's mind, had taken them as easily as a man takes a toy from a child. Pol now knew the secret of the Clouded Continent, the location of the nameless valley that contained thousands of elder corpses, and something of the nature of Adrash himself. He knew with sufficient power any man might be a god. Perhaps he had even discovered the other voices, well before Adrash.

Adrash's cock stirred at the memory of the encounter. Such a beautiful creature, Pol Tanz et Som, composed of nothing but muscle and bone and anger. Such a vicious, self-serving mind, the fire of it leaking out of his left eye like smoke from a fumarole, the searing heat of it focusing like a spear point from his right. He would gather power to him and use it, turn good and evil to his own devices. But he was not yet ready, and so his voice roared in frustration from Jeroun's surface. Clearly, his allegiance had shifted. He meant to unseat Adrash.

What he intended beyond this, Adrash did not know.

Turning his attention elsewhere, Adrash closed his eyes again, listening.

The second voice:

Brassy thunder, the ringing of a hundred bells, the rolling of a thousand metal spheres. The sound gained strength slowly, inexorably, like a mountain shuddering into the sea. Adrash plucked memories from Berun's labyrinthine mind, marveling at the course of the creature's development. Solidification had changed the constructed man, making him frailer physically but stronger mentally. How handily he had defeated the mage Omali! Adrash could not piece together how this was accomplished, which only added to his fascination. He felt an odd kinship with Berun, whose mind could be cold and uncaring to so many, warm and sympathetic to but a few. A mass of contradictions, not unlike Adrash himself.

One thing was clear: Berun would stand behind his friends.

The third and fourth:

Churli Casta Jons. Vedas Tezul. Looking upon them now, he experienced the tug of shared pleasure, the slip and tangle of two souls entwining. He let the harmony of their voices fill him until he felt on the edge of some great precipice, as if his own personality might be overcome, and then backed away. He did not revel in the sensations of their lovemaking, though he easily could have. To do so seemed almost sacrilegious.

Despite their physical weakness in comparison to Pol and Berun, Adrash sensed these two posed the biggest threat to his existence.

For all the secrets that lay buried within her, Churls saw the world with startling clarity. She considered Adrashi and Anadrashi to be the same useless creature. Experience had shown her that worship blinded men to the truths: *Adrash is no redeemer. Adrash will destroy the world.* As she thought of the faithful, her true voice rang like steel against steel. She would not flinch from the war her lover proposed. She would look straight ahead, because only ghosts stood at her back.

Vedas, on the other hand, had only recently found his conviction. He had not yet discovered the strength of his own will. He loved Churls. Oh, yes, he loved her, as strongly as he hated the hand that had molded the world—a place where young boys were defiled and then turned into killers. Even as he and Churls embraced, he thought of killing. He rehearsed the words he would say to the people of Jeroun. Words meant to incite deicide.

The man possessed abilities he had never dreamed of. He would become a leader of men, inspiring them to take up arms against Adrash. His words would thunder across the skies, waking the elders from their slumber.

As a result, there would be a war.

Adrash considered the prospect of his own death.

He knew he could extinguish this possibility, here and now. He could send his weapons down. It was what the elders wanted, certainly. They longed to see dust covering the earth, cleansing the world of man, assured that they alone would wake from the cataclysm. Even the Baleshuuk could not survive without the sun.

The elders' entreaty was faint but never-ending, and Adrash had long ago pushed it out of his mind. He knew he could not choose the long-limbed folk over his own people—at least not yet. If he chose to blanket the world in dust, it would not be due to any outside pressure. It would not be his blessing upon the elders, but a result of mankind's choices.

How much time would it take for the war to reach him? It might be a great while before the four voices rallied enough support to truly challenge him.

Months, maybe years of anticipation.

He wondered if he could wait that long.

A GLOSSARY OF TERMS

Academy of Applied Magics—The Kingdom of Stol's most well-respected academy for the study of magic, and also the only known center for the study of outbound magics.

Adrash—The god of Jeroun, wearer of the divine armor. Thirty thousand years ago, beyond the memory of man, he cracked mankind from iron eggs and helped them populate Jeroun. He is rumored by some to have once been a man. The divine armor—an artifact of unknown origin, superficially similar in some ways to elder skin/elder-cloth artifacts—affords him powers beyond any man or elderman, to the point that he can survive in the void and create the planetoid-sized spheres of the Needle from the raw substance of the moon.

Adrashi—One who believes in Adrash's benevolence and his intention to redeem the people of Jeroun. In general, Adrashi are more organized than Anadrashi. In Nos Ulom and the Kingdom of Stol, Adrashism is the state religion.

Alchemical (Solution)—A broad term for all solutions composed of materials harvested from elder corpses. Alchemical solutions are the base for every spell. Alchemical ink is a particularly regulated—and highly expensive—form, as it is quite dangerous to the uninitiated mage.

Anadrashi—One who believes in Adrash's malevolence and his intention to destroy Jeroun. Anadrashi also believe in mankind's fitness to rule Jeroun on its own. In general, Anadrashi are less organized than Adrashi. In Toma, Anadrashism is the state religion.

Baleshuuk—The highly secretive corpse miners of Nos Ulom. A dwarfish race of men, Baleshuuk have for thousands of years used their magics to extract elder corpses from the ground. Primarily stationed in Knos Min and Stol, where the largest mines exist, their existence even in these places is largely unknown to the general populace.

Bash—A goddess, whose worshippers form a very small minority in Dareth Hlum, Casta, Stol, and Knos Min. Bashest sects worship her as the mother of Adrash. They believe that she will ultimately convince Adrash not to destroy Jeroun.

Black Suits—A martial order of Anadrashi found in all nations of Knoori except Nos Ulom. Marked by their black elder-cloth suits and the distinctive horns they cause to form on the hoods of these suits, their primary goal as an institution is to fight White Suits and win converts to the Anadrashi faith. By doing so, Black Suits believe they strike a blow against Adrash, keeping him from attacking Jeroun. Black Suits orders are relatively uncommon and secretive outside Dareth Hlum and Knos Min.

Bonedust / "Dust"—Pulverized elder bone used for various purposes, including currency. Rubbed on almost any surface, it acts as a protective, shielding the material from damage as well as extremes of temperature. It is also a base material for many alchemical solutions. When ingested, it hydrates the body. In many areas, bonedust is contaminated—sometimes purposefully cut—with other substances. Like every other elder artifact, bonedust is subject to periodic inflation due to supply issues.

Casta—Newest of Knoori's nations, a democracy having no official state religion. The capitol of Onsa, located on the northern coast, is its second largest city after Denn. Unless locally enacted, in Casta there are no laws prohibiting gambling, prostitution, or drug usage, but there are strict laws prohibiting sectarian violence. Castans of the north are generally light skinned, often freckled, while those of the interior and south are generally darker, shading into slate colors in the badlands. Geographically, Casta is split between the fertile rolling hills of the north and the semi-desert and desert badlands of the south.

The Cataclysm—The decade-long winter caused by Adrash sending the two smallest spheres of the Needle into the ocean to the east and west of Knoori approximately one thousand years ago.

Construct—A magically created intelligence, housed in a variety of different body types. The body and mind are typically composed of bonedust, metal, and a collection of more esoteric materials, the exact "formula" of which is the construct-maker's closely guarded secret. Casta and Toma are the sole nations that do not regulate the creation of constructs. They are most common in Knos Min.

Dalan Fele—Dareth Hlum's five-hundred-mile-long defensive wall, which forms the nation's western border with Casta. Seventeen gates allow access to and from the interior of Dareth Hlum.

Danoor—The oldest inhabited city on Jeroun, and the third largest by population in Knos Min. It is situated on the plains just east of the Usveet Mesa, and has for hundreds of generations hosted the Tournament of Danoor.

Dareth Hlum—One of Knoori's nations, a democracy having no official state religion. The capitol of Golna, located on the eastern coast, is its largest city. Generally, Dareth Hlum allows public, organized fights between Adrashi and Anadrashi sects as long as no onlookers are harmed. Citizens vary widely in appearance, but skin hues are generally darker than the people of northern Casta, Nos Ulom, or Stol. The most geographically diverse region of Knoori, the various mountain chains that cross the nation contribute to many different types of climate and terrain.

Elders—The extinct race that preceded man's birth on Jeroun, whose artifacts and landworks are of a scale beyond the means of mankind's magic to reproduce. Little is known of their culture, but many uses have been found for their buried corpses. Primarily, they are used to create alchemical substances. Their eggs and sperm—next to skin the most prized of all elder substances—can be used to inseminate any living animal and produce a hybrid creature. Extrapolating from the nature of hybrids and manufactured elder artifacts, scholars note that elders must have been extremely long-lived and hardy, as well as photosynthetic. Due to their continual harvesting for thousands of years and the increasing depth which miners are forced to go to acquire them, elder corpses are ever more expensive. Some fear the supply will soon run out.

Elder-cloth—Any material containing thread made from the skin of an elder. Far stronger than normal fabrics, over time elder-cloth binds itself to the wearer, assisting in limited biological functions. If close-fitting and of a high grade, elder-cloth makes the wearer stronger, faster, and less subject to physical harm. Like all elder artifacts, cloth of this kind must be exposed to sunlight often in order to continue functioning. Elder-cloth can be dyed any color.

Elder Skin—Skin harvested from elder corpses. The second most prized and thus expensive of all elder materials, elder skin is used almost exclusively for the production of clothing, being used as thread to make elder-cloth and as a leather item itself. When worn as leather, it grants its wearer increased strength, speed, and protection from injury. Though not as malleable in nature as elder-cloth, leather of this kind forms a bond with its wearer to such a degree that it can be commanded to move remotely. Because of the damage it causes to the brain, ingestion of elder skin is illegal throughout Knoori.

Elderman / Elderwoman—A hybrid of man and elder. Exhibiting great intelligence, physical stamina, and speed, without age-nullifying spells their average lifespan is somewhat less than forty years. On average, their magical talent far outstrips that of humans.

Hasde Fall—The wooded hills west of Ynon in Knos Min. Rumors say that the Knosi government possesses magical facilities and training grounds underneath the earth in these hills.

High Pontiff of Dolin—A man or woman elected by his or her peers to head the Orthodox Church of Nos Ulom. In many ways the most powerful of Knoori's religious heads, his or her position is neither hereditary nor guaranteed for any length of time; he or she may be elected out of office at any moment. Due to the nature of conservative Adrashism and its role as the official state religion, the Pontiff exerts a great deal of secular control in Nos Ulom.

Hybrid—The product of an insemination of elder sperm or egg and another animal's sperm or egg through artificial means. The resulting creature generally exhibits greater intelligence and physical stamina than its non-elder parent, but also diminished lifespan and deformities. A large percentage are stillborn.

Iswee—Home of the hibernating elders, located on the other side of Jeroun. Hypothesized about by the outbound mages of Stol who have seen the constant cloud cover, its existence is unknown to others.

Jeroun—The home of man and elder, a highly habitable planet with one moon.

Knoori—The largest continent of Jeroun and the sole home of man, composed of the nations of Dareth Hlum, Casta, Nos Ulom, the Kingdom of Stol, the Kingdom of Toma, and the Republic of Knos Ulom. Though several large islands lay off of its coast, none are currently inhabited.

Knos Min—Knoori's oldest nation, a republic having no official state religion. The capitol of Grass Min, located on the northern coast, is the third largest city next to Levas. A haven for intellectuals and expatriate professionals, Knos Min is the most magically advanced nation of Knoori, possessing roughly half the continent's elder corpse reserves. Long rumored to have a corps of outbound mages and other martial mages, the strength of the nation's military is rivaled only by the Kingdom of Stol's. Knosi are only marginally less uniform in appearance than the Ulomi, displaying dark brown skin tones and wiry black hair. Generally flat and arid, the nation nonetheless possesses several great mesa ranges, atop which the ground is quite fertile. Old-growth forests grow in the southeastern lake region.

Lake Ten—Knoori's largest lake, from whose fresh waters Knos Min, Toma, Stol, and Nos Ulom take a great deal of their sustenance. Officially, its waters are not the property of any one nation. Its shorelines are, however. Its sources are the Thril Rivers, which begin in the Aspa Mountains in Nos Ulom. Its sole outlet is the Unnamed River of Toma.

Locborder Wall—A defensive wall that extends three hundred and fifty miles along the western shore of Lake Ten, from the foothills of the Aspa Mountains in Nos Ulom to the screwcrab warrens of Toma. Its length defines the greatest border along Lake Ten that Knos Min ever achieved. The vast majority of its length still belongs to Knos Min.

Lore—The combined skills, practices, and traditions of a particular mage or mage group.

Mage—A human or elderman whose education grants them a great deal of knowledge about spell creation and casting. Mages are both self-taught and formally trained, though certain nations and regions discourage the independent practice of magic. The most specialized of all mages—the outbound mages—can perform feats of almost incalculable power, lifting themselves from the surface of Jeroun and surviving in the void of space.

Magics—The creation and casting of spells. The word is nearly synonymous with Lore.

Medicines—The branch of magics that deals with the physical form of the body. Often considered the least demanding of all magics due to the great efficacy of elder alchemicals on the body, medicines is one of the most common and necessary of all magical disciplines.

The Needle—Twenty-seven iron spheres Adrash created from the material of the moon, held in orbit as a visible threat to the people on Jeroun. Though they have maintained a stable arrangement for a thousand years, for the first five hundred years of their existence the spheres were arranged in a number of ways.

Nos Ulom—One of Knoori's nations, an oligarchy having Adrashism as its official state religion. The capitol of Dolin, located in the central valleys just north of the Aspa Mountain chain, is a relatively small city of less than fifty thousand souls. Of all the nations of Knoori, Nos Ulom is the most repressive, its government the most autocratic. Ulomi are the continent's most uniform people in appearance, displaying unblemished, cream-colored skin and generally curly, straw-colored hair. Geographically, the nation is mountainous in the south and composed of high, fertile tableland and pine forest in the north.

The Ocean—Variously known as the Sea, Jeru, or Deathshallow, the ocean is shallow and laps upon the shores of many islands. It harbors a startling variety of marine life, much of which is quite dangerous to man. Due to this danger, it has not been navigated by man for many thousands of years.

Orrus Dabil Alachum—A god, whose worshippers form a very small minority in rural areas of Dareth Hlum and Casta, especially in the badlands region of the latter. Myth tells that he is the son of Adrash. Orrust people believe that it is not Adrash moving the spheres of the Needle, but Orrus—and that by destroying Jeroun, he will give birth to a new paradise.

Osseterat—Hybrid apes of near-human intelligence that are rumored to live in Hasde Fall.

Outbound Mage—A mage trained specifically to achieve orbit and travel in the void. Stol alone openly uses this type of mage, though rumors suggest that Knos Min also possesses outbound mages. Though a few outbound mages have been human, the overwhelming majority of them are eldermen, who exhibit a greater potential for magic and greater stamina. Each mage wears a vacuum suit—composed of leather made from elder skin—on which he or she paints sigils. The mage also wears a dustglass (bonedust-reinforced glass) helmet. The suit and helmet protect the mage from vacuum for a brief period of time should his or her spells fail. The purpose of the outbound mages is to monitor Adrash, though much knowledge of Jeroun has been gained by the activities of the corps as well.

Osa—A large, circular island in Uris Bay. It is covered by an artifact of high elder magic, an immense glass-like dome upon which a variety of life clings. Wyrms and other large creatures, most not seen on the mainland, live near the dome walls. With intense magnification, abandoned cities can be seen on the slopes of Mount Pouen, the island's largest peak. No openings appear to exist in the dome.

Pusta—An exclave of Stol. The capitol is Ravos, located on the northern coast. Differing from Stol in many respects, the culture of Pusta inherits much from its multiethnic fisheries, which are the most technologically advanced in Knoori and extend along the entire coastline.

Quarterstock—The extremely rare offspring of a hybrid. The majority of hybrids are sterile, and the vast majority of their offspring never come to term. Even if they do, a very small percentage live. Of those that live, an even smaller percentage are unaffected by mental or physical retardation. No comprehensive study of a healthy individual—human or animal in origin—has yet been conducted.

Sigil—A particular type of spell that is painted on a surface using alchemical ink. It is usually "activated" by the recitation—verbally or, if the mage is sufficiently powerful, mentally—of a specific set of words.

Sorcerer—A mage.

Spell—An alchemical solution that—when activated by thought, incantation, or physical action—produces a magical effect. Hundreds of thousands of such spells, each varying according to the particular mixture of elder components, are produced and cast every day for a variety of tasks. The easiest spells to produce and cast affect inorganic materials: moving the elements, creating a current, etc. The most difficult spells to produce and cast affect living substances: changing one's structure, extending one's life, creating constructs, etc. The efficacy of a spell decreases the farther away the mage is, a fact which makes influencing an object over long distances—as in the sending of a message—difficult.

The Steps of Stol—An earthwork monument created by high elder magic. It begins in the fertile southern plains of Stol, extending some eighty miles to the coast and more than four hundred along it. Ascending to a height of twelve thousand feet in seventeen evenly spaced, gently sloping rises, the Steps stop abruptly at the ocean. Most of Stol's elder corpse reserves are buried within it.

Stol—One of Knoori's nations, a kingdom having Adrashism as its official state religion. The capitol of Tansot, located on the eastern shore of Lake Ten, is its largest city. Moderate Adrashism is the general rule and all Anadrashi sects are allowed to live peaceably within the kingdom's borders, though they suffer persecution in the central valleys. After Knos Min, Stol is the most magically advanced nation of Knoori, possessing roughly forty percent of the continent's elder corpse reserves. The only state with a known outbound mage program, the strength of the military relies much upon magical developments from the Academy of Applied Magics. Stoli people vary widely in appearance, but are generally light skinned. Geographically,

Stol is generally hilly in the north, descending into fertile valleys in the central region, and rising to great heights on the Steps of Stol in the south.

Tamer—A mage who specializes in taming and controlling large, exotic, and hybrid animals. Their lore is far more esoteric and difficult to master than the many readily available spells used to help control draft animals, entertainment animals, and pets. In rare cases, the tamer achieves a type of telepathic bond with his or her animal. In Casta and Stol, the most daring and specialized type of tamer exists: the hybrid wyrm tamer.

Tan-Ten—The island at the center of Lake Ten. Oasena is its only city. The people of Tan-Ten have never shown interest in power or political maneuvering, but have on many occasions successfully defended their island from invaders.

Thaumaturgical Engine—A construct used to create kinetic force. Unlike constructs that mimic biological creatures, an engine is rarely imbued with more than the most basic intelligence needed to follow simple directions. Due to the expense of creating and maintaining engines, those produced are most often used in barges or other large transport vehicles.

Toma—One of Knoori's nations, a kingdom having Anadrashism as its official state religion. The capitol of Demn, located on the southern coast, is its largest city. Possibly the most religiously militant of all the people of Knoori, Tomen nonetheless value the personal, non-dogmatic expression of Anadrashism more than any other. The people vary considerably in build, but are generally dusky skinned and rust-haired. Toma is the most arid nation of Knoori and, but for the Wie Desert in the southwest, the hilliest.

The Tournament of Danoor—The decennial tournament between Knoori's White Suit and Black Suit orders, which occurs on the last day of every decade. A fighter is chosen from every town numbering more than 2000 souls. He or she then travels to Danoor and is allowed to fight in the tournament. In the end, one Black and one White remain. Accordingly, along the way fighters will inevitably have to fight brothers and sisters of their own faith. The New Year celebration starts after the tournament champion's speech, wherein he or she typically extols listeners to convert to the winning faith.

Usually, secular fighting tournaments begin the next day.

Ustert—A goddess whose worshippers form a relatively large minority in Casta and Knos Min. A loosely organized sororal community of mages and apothecaries (often referred to as witches, though this term is widely used even in Adrashi and Anadrashi contexts), Usterti profess a variety of beliefs, bound only by the understanding that the goddess governs all existence. Due to this ambiguity, a great deal of mystery surrounds the community.

The Void—Near-Jeroun orbit and outer space.

White Suits—A martial order of Adrashi prevalent in all nations of Knoori except Toma. Marked by their white elder-cloth suits, their primary goal as an institution is to fight Black Suits and win converts to the Adrashi faith. By doing so, White Suits believe they encourage Adrash to redeem Jeroun sooner. Orders are relatively uncommon and secretive outside southern Nos Ulom, Dareth Hlum, and Knos Min.

Wyrm—A dragon of immense size. Highly intelligent and extremely temperamental, they do not come into contact with men often. This is due mostly to the fact that most food is taken from the open ocean. Only a small minority of dragons hunt large prey on the continent. Hybrid wyrms are not common, but do exist in Stol and Casta.

ACKNOWLEDGEMENTS

This list used to be much longer, but I realized at three pages that including everyone I feel grateful for just isn't practical, especially since I've forgotten some of their names. So, if you're not specifically listed but you did indeed talk with me about my writing—on the internet, during a van ride from Sedona to Phoenix, at a convention, etc.—please know that I appreciate your interest and advice.

As to the people I can't possibly *not* name...

Thank you, Amy Martin. I wouldn't have completed this book without your support. I know that sounds trite, but it's true and it's important you know how much it means to me. Because of you, I've achieved a dream that for years I was scared of even admitting.

Thank you, Winter Martin, for being the muse for the little ghost I never intended to write.

Thank you, Mom. I love you—more. I hope you realize that any courage I've displayed in life (and this includes writing a book, I think) is due to your example.

Thank you, Dad. I'm more like you every year, but still not enough.

Thank you, Josh Jernigan, Amy Jernigan, and—of course—Benjamin Calvin Jernigan. If everyone proves a quarter as enthusiastic about my book as you guys are, I'll sell a billion copies.

Thank you, Ashly Jernigan, for taking chances. You may not know this, but when you moved to New York by yourself it inspired me to start taking some of my own chances.

Thank you, Brennan Jernigan. *No Return* is, at least in part, a story about a man learning to do the right thing. You, more than anyone else, are responsible for this emphasis on morality.

Thank you, Elizabeth Hand. I wish you could be my first reader every time.

Thank you, David Anthony Durham. I appreciate your advice, your advocacy, and especially your friendship. There are scenes in this book I didn't want to write, but I wrote them because you put the worm of doubt in my mind. The work is better for it, I think.

Thank you, James Patrick Kelly, for pushing me when I needed some pushing. I revise things now, which should make you happy.

Thank you, J. M. McDermott. Not only did you recommend this novel to Night Shade, you've continued to be one of my most vocal advocates.

Thank you, Benjamin Turner, Keith Potempa, Allister Timms, Adam Mills, and Scott Wolven. I'm indebted to you all for reading large portions of *No Return* and offering comments.

Thank you, Whiskey Swim Club: Paul Kirsch, C. Liddle (Caspian Gray), Asher Ellis, and Ben Burgis. I don't really like any of you under normal circumstances—and I certainly don't respect you—but there's nobody in the world I like being drunk in a pool with more.

Thank you, Justin Tribble, Brett Wilson, Angela Still, Will Ludwigsen, Tarver Nova, Catherynne Valente, Ian Withrow, Michael Kimball, Jenn Brissett, Taylor Preston, Nancy Holder, Robert Stutts, Evan Dicken, Dina Milum, Ashley Bernard, Marty Halpern, Richard Cambridge, Desiree Ducharme, Angi Zollinger Christiansen, assorted cousins and aunts and uncles, and the cast and crew of the Stonecoast MFA program. Your counsel and encouragement have been invaluable.

Thank you, Ross E. Lockhart, for reading my manuscript, convincing everyone at Night Shade that it should be bought, and helping me turn it into a better book.

Thank you, Jason Williams, Jeremy Lassen, Amy Popovich, Dave Palumbo, Tomra Palmer, Liz Upson, and all the other folks at Night Shade Books.

Thank you, Robbie Trevino. I hope the story I wrote is pretty good, but even if it isn't you created something awesome out of it.

Lastly and most importantly:

Thank you, reader, from the bottom of my heart. I'm delighted and humbled that you've bought, borrowed, or stolen this book. Know that I wrote it as a means of communication between the two of us. I hope you'll reach out and begin a conversation by email or—even better—in person at a convention.